VALHALLA'S FURY

BOOK 4 OF THE CHARLEMAGNE'S CROSS SERIES

DONOVAN COOK

Boldwood

First published in Great Britain in 2024 by Boldwood Books Ltd.

Cover Design by Head Design

Cover Photography: Shutterstock and iStock

A CIP catalogue record for this book is available from the British Library.

Paperback ISBN 978-1-80483-839-6

Large Print ISBN 978-1-80483-840-2

Hardback ISBN 978-1-80483-841-9

Ebook ISBN 978-1-80483-837-2

Kindle ISBN 978-1-80483-838-9

Audio CD ISBN 978-1-80483-846-4

MP3 CD ISBN 978-1-80483-845-7

Digital audio download ISBN 978-1-80483-844-0

Boldwood Books Ltd
23 Bowerdean Street
London SW6 3TN
www.boldwoodbooks.com

To Elizabeth,
who never lets us sleep.

CHARACTERS

FRANKS

Charles – son of Torkel and grandson of Sven the Boar

Hildegard – mother of Charles and abbess of Fraumünster

Duke Liudolf – duke of Saxony

Roul – spy for King Charles of West Francia

Father Leofdag – priest from Hedeby

Gerold – former slave and spy for Duke Liudolf

King Louis – king of East Francia

Bero – King Charles's spymaster

DANES

Sven the Boar – former jarl of Ribe, grandfather of Charles

Thora – former shield maiden

Rollo – son of Arnbjorg

Alvar – hirdman of Sven's

Ingvild – Thora's aunt

Audhild – Thora's cousin

Jorlaug – daughter of Thora's cousin

Sigmund – son of Rollo
Halstein – leader of Danes raiding along the Loire River
Gudrod – son of Harald Klak
Torgny – friend of Rollo

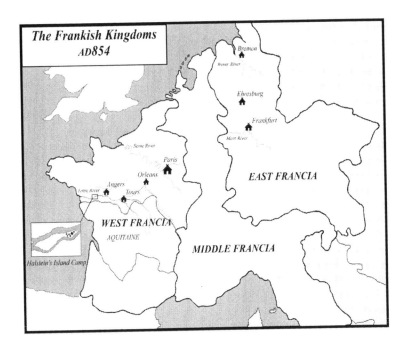

The Frankish Kingdoms
AD854

Bremen
Weser River
Ehresburg
Frankfurt
Main River
Seine River
Paris
Orleans
Angers
Loire River
Tours
WEST FRANCIA
AQUITAINE
EAST FRANCIA
MIDDLE FRANCIA
Halstein's Island Camp

1

BREMEN, LATE SUMMER AD 854

Abbess Hildegard closed her eyes and saw the flames chewing through the thatch roof of the great hall in Ribe. She shuddered as the terrified screams of women and children rang in her ears and felt the smoke which filled the hall burning her nose and throat as she struggled to breathe. Mothers huddled over children to protect them from the burning bits of straw which floated down as the flames consumed the roof and made their way down the timber walls; all the while a small red-headed girl with a button nose glared at her, unafraid of the surrounding flames. *This is hell*, Hildegard thought. This is hell and they are all going to burn for their sins. The Danes for believing in false gods and she for abandoning her son.

'The king is on his way.' The words of the servant broke Hildegard from her nightmare and she opened her eyes to find that she was not in the burning hall any more, but that she was safe in Bremen. Duke Liudolf's men had snuck into the hall while the Danes were distracted by the fire the duke's men had started and freed her and Duke Liudolf, but the only reason she was standing here in the room of King Louis of East Francia, her father, was because Sven the Boar, a man she had hated and feared her entire life, had allowed her to escape. All because of a deal her father had made with Sven and one she knew he had no intention of keeping.

Hildegard thanked the servant and crinkled her nose as the smell of the burning hall still filled her nostrils. She had bathed more than once. She had washed her hair thoroughly and had replaced her dirty clothes with a new habit so that she looked like who she was: an abbess of the church and a servant of God. But the stench of the burning hall was still on her, no matter how many times she bathed or changed. After she had bathed, Hildegard had gone to the church and had prayed for the men who had lost their lives in Ribe and, more importantly, for the soul of Bishop Bernard, who had been killed by the Danish priest, a man so vile she refused to picture him in her mind. Not that he needed her invitation, as he seemed to enjoy violating her thoughts when she least expected it.

Hildegard took a deep breath and walked to the window of the room she was in, peering outside while she waited for her father. Hildegard had decided it was best to see him in private because she knew the conversation they needed to have was not for the ears of others. So she had not gone to the hall in Bremen, but had instead gone to his room. It was the largest room in the house, which belonged to one of the king's cousins, and had a bed much bigger than her father needed it to be, but he was the king. Large windows lit the room up and added some warmth, while the walls were decorated with colourful paintings and even one of her father. On the far side of the room stood a small table with a bowl filled with clean water and a beaker of wine with two cups, although Hildegard was sure she would not be offered any wine.

Lost in her thoughts, Hildegard watched a group of boys running around outside in the streets, their laughter reaching her ears and making her think of her own son, Charles. She thought back to meeting him for the first time earlier that day and knowing that he was in the same house as she was made her heart beat faster. Charles was smaller than she had thought he would be, his red hair badly cut and his face dirty, but the boy's blue eyes were sharp and she sensed an inner strength that he could only have got from his father. Hildegard's heart had beaten so hard, she had worried it might stop as she stared at the face that reminded her so much of Torkel, the Danish warrior whom she had fallen in love with when she was still too young to understand that there were consequences for every action.

And Charles was not the only consequence of that love affair. As soon as Charles had been born, her father had chased Torkel and the newborn baby out of Frankfurt, his capital, and sent her to a nunnery. In her anger, she had made another mistake, one which was far worse than the birth of Charles. She had stolen the Cross of Charlemagne and given it to Torkel. The cross was sacred, and she knew her father and his brothers, the other kings of Francia, believed that whoever possessed the cross would be the next emperor of a combined Francia. But Hildegard had never believed in that. She only knew that the cross was more important to her father than anything he owned and that was why she had her maid steal it and give it to Torkel. She had hoped that when Charles was old enough, he would bring it to her and she would know that he was her son. Their meeting had been too short, though, and Hildegard wondered if she would be able to see Charles again. That was why she was here, in her father's room.

The floor creaked behind Abbess Hildegard, startling her as the image of the heathen priest came to her mind. She gripped the large golden cross she wore and turned to see her father standing in the doorway, with an eyebrow raised and a curl in his lip. King Louis of East Francia was a large man – much larger than Torkel or his father,

Sven – with dark hair and a thick beard. Her father had been a warrior in his younger years, and still had the bearing of one, and though Hildegard had never feared him, she had to admit she was nervous of the way he scrutinised her. She let go of the large golden cross and straightened as she tried to fight the butterflies in her stomach.

'Father.'

'Hildegard.' The king walked to a table on the far side of the room and rinsed his face before he filled a cup with wine from the beaker the servant had brought in not that long ago. 'You've been to see him?'

Hildegard nodded, knowing her father was talking about Charles. Duke Liudolf had told Hildegard how Ivor Guttromson, the man who had taken Charles from Sven, had brought her son to him while she was in Ribe looking for Charles. Ivor had wanted to make a deal with King Louis: Charles for her father's support to become the new king of Denmark, but Ivor was now dead and Charles was her father's prisoner. 'He looks just like Torkel.'

King Louis grunted, but said nothing as he stared at his wine and Hildegard knew he had seen it as well. She was one of the few who really knew her father and who could read him. That was why she had been his best adviser for many years.

'Duke Liudolf told me of the deal you made with Jarl Sven.'

King Louis emptied his cup and filled it again as he ignored the drops of wine on his tunic. 'To trade you for the boy. Hardly seems like there is a point to it now, doesn't it? You have been returned and from what Duke Liudolf tells me, the last time you saw Sven the Boar, his hall was burning and he was fighting for his life. God willing, the bastard is already dead and we never have to say his name again.'

Hildegard gripped the cross around her neck again. 'We believed he was dead before, only for him to return to life. And besides, the only reason Sven let me go was because he hoped that you would keep your word. Otherwise I might have died in Ribe.' King Louis grunted again as Hildegard took a deep breath to calm her anger. 'What will you do with Charles?'

Her father lowered his cup and stared at her, his face darkening, and Hildegard almost regretted asking the question. For a while, King Louis stared at her, his finger tapping the rim of his cup, before he said, 'I don't know yet.'

'I want to take him back to Fraumünster with me. Find him a place there where he can study to become a priest.'

'No.'

Even though Hildegard had expected that, the word still felt like a kick to the chest. She steeled herself and said the words she knew her father would hate to hear. 'He is my son. I want him near me.'

King Louis glared at her. 'That boy is never leaving my sight, not while he still breathes.'

'He is my son!' Hildegard clenched her fists as she felt her anger engulf her.

'He is a sin! He is a blight on our family and a reminder of how I was shamed and humiliated because you had to open your legs to a fucking Dane!' King Louis's face turned red and, for the first time in her life, Hildegard understood how fearsome her father must have been on the battlefield.

'You loved that Dane,' Hildegard said, only to remind her father how he had treated Torkel as a son. How he had doted on the boy and taught him how to fight with a sword and spear.

'And look what that got me! A bastard grandson and a daughter good for nothing other than being sent to a nunnery!'

Hildegard tried to ignore the pain in her chest caused by her father's words as she refused to back down. 'You benefited from my position more than you would have done if you had married me off to some old man for a political alliance and you know it.'

King Louis stared at her, his mouth a tight line in his beard. 'Some good had to come out of that. But, by God, I swear you will never see that boy again. I forbid you from talking to him or even saying his name in my presence. And if I find out that you are talking to him behind my back, then I will strip you of your position and marry you off to one of the sons of Jarl Torgeir of Hedeby!'

Hildegard's breath caught in her throat and she took a step backwards, as if she had been struck by her father's fist. 'You cannot—'

'I am the king and your father! I can do as I please and you will obey me!'

Hildegard glared at her father as he stared her down, almost willing her to fight back, but then she took a deep breath to calm her nerves before she said or did something which would anger her father even more. Not because she feared what he might do to her, but because of what he might do to Charles. Hildegard was beginning to wonder if Torkel had not done the right thing by sending Charles to Denmark. 'As you wish, Father,' she said in the end, but already Hildegard was trying to think of a way to get Charles away from here. She wished Gerold was still by her side. The young man would have known of a way to sneak Charles out of Bremen, but Hildegard didn't know if he still lived or if Sven had killed him. The last she had seen of the dark-haired man was when the godi had walked into the house Sven had kept them captive in and pointed his sharp knife at Bishop Bernard. Gerold had attacked him, but somehow the old godi had avoided Gerold's attack and had knocked him out with the handle of his knife. That was when the godi's young servant had walked into the house and grabbed her, while the godi ordered Bernard to strip. The old bishop had been so afraid and so confused that he had done what the godi had asked and had followed him while the godi's servant had tied her hands and dragged her out of the house. Hildegard shuddered when she remembered the fear in Bishop Bernard's eyes as the godi told him to drop to his knees. His pleading eyes staring at her. Hildegard had never felt so useless in her life. She had always been the one in control, the one with the upper hand, but that night she could do nothing but watch as the godi's knife opened the bishop's throat and spilled his blood for the false gods of the Danes.

'Hildegard, are you listening?'

Hildegard blinked the memories away and realised that her father had spoken to her.

The king frowned at her and then repeated the question. 'How did Sven get hold of my grandfather's cross?'

'Because of me.'

Her father scowled as his knuckles whitened around his cup. 'Because of you?'

She nodded and then told her father how she had the maid steal the cross from his room and how she had given it to Torkel.

'You gave the Cross of Charlemagne, the most important thing in all of Francia, to the Dane so he could give it to your bastard son?'

Hildegard tried to ignore the large vein that throbbed in her father's temple and worried that it might burst as she nodded. 'I was angry at you, Father, and wanted to hurt you.'

'It was you then who started the rumours that it was stolen by someone sent by one of my brothers?'

Hildegard nodded again. 'I didn't want you to chase after Torkel or my son.'

'Instead, I wasted years and money sending people to my brothers' kingdoms to search for the cross which had been in my kingdom the entire time.' His hands trembled and Hildegard wondered if she should tell him that Sven no longer had the cross. That it had been stolen by a man most likely sent by her uncle, the king of West Francia. Before she could get a chance, though, her father said, 'Well, it looks like I still have some use for your son then.'

Hildegard's breath caught in her throat as she realised what her father meant. 'You cannot.'

King Louis took a step towards his daughter, his face dark and his nostrils flared. 'That cross is more valuable than the life of your bastard son. You better run back to your church and pray that Sven survived the attack on his town, because the only way your boy lives is if Sven gives me the Cross of Charlemagne.'

2

A FEW DAYS LATER, OFF THE COAST OF SAXONY

Sven closed his eyes and took a deep breath of the salty air, savouring it as seabirds soaring above the sail of his ship screamed. He gripped the rudder tighter as the hull struck a wave, the vibration of it awakening long-dormant instincts and making him alter the course ever so slightly as wind filled the large sail. Seawater sprayed over him as another wave crashed into the side of his ship and Sven licked his lips, smiling as he fought the waves and wind, his ship filled with warriors who lounged around, sharpening weapons and telling stories. But then he opened his eyes and thought about his destination. His brow furrowed and his jaw muscles tensed.

Sven eyed the sail, made of wool and greased with horse fat to strengthen it, bulging as it caught the wind. The sail was not new. It would have taken too long to make, and Sven didn't have enough gold to buy one either. Instead, they had taken one of the old sails and patched it up as best they could with the women of Ribe working day and night to make sure it was ready in time. Sven had paid them as well as he could, but he needed most of his gold for the warriors who had decided to follow him. Not that there were many of them. Apart from Thora – the shield maiden who was the daughter of one of Sven's dearest friends – and Rollo and Alvar, his two giant champions, there were barely enough men to fill half the ship. More warriors had wanted to join him, but fathers and wives had forbidden it, insisting that Ribe needed men to protect her walls and to rebuild the hall that had been burnt down when Ivor and Hallr had attacked. But they were not the ones who had burnt the hall down. That was the Franks. Men of Duke Liudolf of Saxony, who had been sent by the king of East Francia to demand that Sven release his daughter, the mother of Sven's grandson. And the worst of all was that Sven had helped them to escape after some of Ribe's warriors had turned against him. His side bore the fresh scar from that betrayal.

The people of Ribe had all gathered on the wharves when Sven had left the town that had belonged to his father and his father before him. He was the last of his line who would be jarl of Ribe but he was glad to leave the town which had caused him nothing but misery. The people of Ribe were glad to see him leave as well. They had not wanted him as jarl, not after all he had done and the lives that were lost because of him. No one had cheered as his men rowed the ship down the river. There was no sacrifice to the gods, asking them to ensure that Sven and his men return safely. Neither was there a farewell song. All there had been was silence. Silence and grim stares.

A squealing laugh made Sven look at the small red-headed girl who was leaning over the gunwale, her legs kicking wildly as one of the men held on to her so she could see the dolphins that played in the surf just ahead of the ship.

'She knows no fear. I don't know if that is a good thing or a bad thing.' Thora leaned on the side of the ship next to Sven and squinted at the water as her hair lifted in the sea breeze. Thora wore the brynja Sven had given her after the battle in Ribe, her sword at her side, and a smile on her face. Her light-coloured hair was braided so that the wind wouldn't blow on to her face. She wasn't unattractive, with her wide hips, and Sven knew that some even thought she was beautiful, but Thora cared for none of that. She was a warrior. Her broad shoulders and the scar above her left eye showed that. As did her ability with a sword and shield. Thora was taller than Sven, but then so were most people, because Sven was almost short enough to be called a dwarf. In fact, many did when they wanted to taunt him, but it had been a long time since that had annoyed him. Now, he embraced it and used it.

Sven grunted and turned his attention to what was left of Thora's family as they sat near the girl. Her aunt, Ingvild, her cousin, Audhild, and Audhild's daughter, Jorlaug: the red-headed girl who seemed like she was trying to catch the dolphins with her bare hands. 'She's too young to understand that Midgard is a frightening place.'

'No, that's not true.' Thora smiled as she watched her niece. 'Her father was murdered and she saw what Odinson had done to the Christian priest. She just thinks that when she is old enough, she can defeat all those who wish to harm her and her family.'

Again, Sven grunted as he remembered feeling the same once. 'Then I pray to the gods that she never learns the truth about life.'

Thora scrutinised Sven before she asked, 'You really think the king of the East Franks will be there?'

There was the beach where Sven had first met Louis, the king of East Francia. But he had just been a young prince then and Sven had been an arrogant jarl who believed he could not be defeated. Prince Louis had proven Sven wrong and had taken his only son as hostage to make sure that Sven never raided his lands again. It was only in the beginning of this summer that Sven had learnt that his own brother had conspired with the Franks and King Horik of Denmark, who had died during the battle at Jelling,

to make sure that Sven raided that area and that he brought
Torkel, his son, with him. His brother was dead, killed by Sven the
same night he learnt the truth, but now Sven had to go back to
that beach. He could only pray that King Louis would keep his
word and that he would be there with Charles. Because that was
the deal they had made. A swap. Hildegard, who had been his
prisoner, for Charles. But Sven no longer had Charles's mother.
His eyes fell on Gerold, the young spy who worked for Hildegard
and who had betrayed Charles earlier that summer. The Frank
glared at him as he sat tied up by the mast, his face bruised from
his fight with Thora. Sven was still annoyed that she had not killed
the bastard like he had told her to, but there was nothing he could
do about that now.

'The gods must be amused that we are going back to the place
that caused the demise of the mighty Sven the Boar.' Thora read
his mind and Sven could do nothing but tighten his grip on the
rudder. She was right, though. Sven had tried to rescue his son,
but the gods had seen to it that it never happened. After that, he
drank too much to cope with the pain of losing Torkel to the
Christian god and when he had accidentally killed his wife, Sven
had fled. He had run off into the night with nothing but a stained
tunic and his trousers. For the next eighteen winters, Sven had
wandered the length and breadth of Denmark, trying to find
enough ale to drown the memories and to kill himself. But Odin
had made sure that Sven survived it all. The cold winters, the wild
beasts and the bandits.

'The gods can go fuck themselves,' Sven muttered, wishing
there was ale on the ship.

Thora gripped the Mjöllnir around her neck and Sven knew
he shouldn't be cursing the gods, not while they were at the mercy
of Njörd, the god of the seas, and Rán, a giant and the mother of
the waves. Sven rubbed the faded raven tattoo on his shaved head

and wondered if the All-Father was watching him. Did Odin really care about where he was going or why?

'So what is the plan?' Thora asked. Sven glanced at the pouch she was wearing on her belt and thought about the large golden cross inside, with the large ruby in its centre and its edges rimmed with different coloured gems. Just below the large ruby was the sign of the man the cross had once belonged to, and on its back was a mark of something he had added to it. The Cross of Charlemagne. The cross that had got his son killed and his grandson taken from him. The cross the kings of Francia believed would make them emperors, but that had only cursed his family more than it had already been cursed by Sven's arrogance. 'Do we tell King Louis that we still have the cross?'

Sven raised an eyebrow at Thora as the ship rode another wave. 'You really think Charles's mother will tell King Louis that the cross was stolen?'

Thora shrugged. 'I think we should assume she did.'

Sven rubbed his bushy beard, which had more grey hair than the red it had been once. 'Aye.' He followed the path of one seabird, but then ignored it and wondered why he still searched for signs from the gods. 'Let's keep that to ourselves for now. If the gods smile on us, then King Louis will give us Charles and we can go somewhere else and live in peace.'

'And if not? He has his daughter back, after all.'

Sven glanced at the seabirds again. 'I don't know.'

They were distracted by Audhild scolding Jorlaug for almost falling overboard as she overreached to touch a dolphin. If it hadn't been for the warrior holding on to her, then she would have been gone, but luckily for them, the man was paying attention.

'Land!' came the call from the young warrior at the prow of the ship, who had been tasked with watching for dangers ahead of them. Sven wondered if he should mount the prow beast which was still safely stored under the deck of the ship as he adjusted course to avoid a large wave, but then decided against it. He had not come to raid, so there was no need for the beast to scare the spirits of the land away.

Sven's hands trembled as he stared at the beach in the distance, even though his old eyes could barely see it. But then he didn't need to. Sven doubted he would ever forget the sight of that beach as Rollo walked over to him, the giant warrior already in his brynja.

'So we expect a warm welcome?'

Sven's brow creased as he tried to see the beach near the river Elbe. To the south was another large river which led to Bremen, a trading town that Sven had attacked when he was still a young warrior, but he had not led that attack. Guttrom had. The beach was flat and muddy, and when the tide was high, the water would almost reach the small dunes further inland. When the tide was out, then it felt like you had to walk all day to reach the dunes from the water's edge. It was not the best place to raid from as you had to rely on the tide to be high to escape an attack, but that was the reason Sven had gone there in the first place so long ago. Because he knew no one would expect it. Now he wished he had never set foot on that cursed beach.

'It could be a trap. King Louis might have an army there waiting to kill you as soon as you get off the ship,' Thora said and Rollo nodded.

Again, Sven glanced at the seabirds and resisted the urge to rub the large ivory Mjöllnir he wore around his neck. 'Aye, so he might. Rollo, make sure the men are ready for whatever the gods have planned for us.'

Rollo nodded and walked towards the prow, barking orders as he went. He went to his own war chest, where his wife and son, Sigmund, were sitting. Rollo was another who had brought his family with him, having decided, just like Sven and Thora, to cut his ties with Ribe. Sigmund, a winter younger than Charles but already taller, leaned over the side as the beach got closer.

Sven pulled on the rudder and aimed the ship for the same spot where he had beached his ships the last time he had been here, his heart beating faster than it had done in many winters, and his back already slick with sweat. He felt Thora's eyes on him and was glad that she stayed quiet.

Warriors rushed around, putting armour on and grabbing their shields from the side of the ship. Some rubbed their Mjöll-nirs or the other pendants they wore as they prayed to the gods. Knuckles turned white as they gripped spears, swords or axes. Rollo and Alvar stood by the prow of the ship, the two giant warriors dressed in brynjas and wearing their helmets. They both had Dane axes in their hands and would be the first off the ship as soon as she came to a stop on the beach. Sven should have been there with them. His feet should be the first to touch the Frankish sand, but he was too old and too tired. This summer had taken most of his strength, and Sven just wanted to rest. He also knew that if he jumped off the ship, his left leg would only cause him to collapse into a heap on the beach and that would not look good in front of the young warriors who had followed him. So Rollo and Alvar would be the first ones to meet whatever enemy awaited them.

'It seems quiet,' Thora said as they got close enough to see the beach properly.

Sven agreed with her. The few children on board, along with Jorlaug and Sigmund, had been herded to the mast by their mothers so they would not impede the warriors, but Sven noticed how Jorlaug wanted to join the men as the girl, not caring that she was only six, fought against her mother's grip.

Looking back towards the beach, Sven thanked Njörd that the

tide was high as he guided the ship by memory to the spot where he had last seen his son. It meant that they did not need to sit here and wait for the water levels to rise. That would only have made it worse for Sven, as it meant he'd have to sit here and stare at the cursed beach. If he closed his eyes, he could still see Torkel, only nine winters old and surrounded by Frankish warriors, staring at Sven as he sailed away with what had been left of his forces. Sven had arrived that day with three ships full of men and had left with barely enough men to crew one ship. Thora's father had been one of the few who had survived. Rollo's father had not, and neither had the fathers of many of the warriors on the ship. Sven wondered if they knew this was where his arrogance had got their fathers killed. He glanced at the land behind the beach and remembered the forest that had stood behind the small rise. That was where Louis had hidden the cavalry force that had defeated his warriors, and Sven couldn't help but wonder if King Louis would do the same again. Just like he couldn't help but wonder how many of the few warriors he had with him would survive this beach.

'Furl the sail!' Rollo shouted from over his shoulder and warriors rushed so they could untie the ropes and pull the sail in. Sven grunted in satisfaction at how efficient the men were.

The ship slowed down as the sail was tied up and Sven looked past the two giant warriors by the prow at the beach, more concerned by the lack of Frankish warriors than he would have been if there was an army waiting for him. He felt Gerold's eyes on him and wanted to stab the bastard's eyes out, but then took a deep breath and tried to ignore the young Frank.

'Brace!' Rollo called out moments before Sven felt the vibration under his feet as the keel of the longship struck the sand. The warriors were all prepared and stayed on their feet, but some children fell over, much to the amusement of Jorlaug.

Before the ship even came to a stop, Rollo and Alvar jumped overboard and a group of men followed them, as Sven gripped the rudder and growled as he fought to keep the ship straight. Rollo and Alvar ran a few paces, the others behind them, until they were out of the surf and formed a shield wall to defend them from any who dared to attack. But the only noise they heard were the seabirds, whose calls sounded like mocking laughter to Sven. He waited a few more heartbeats, Thora standing beside him with her hand on the hilt of her sword, and scrutinised the beach and the land beyond it.

'There's no one here!' Rollo yelled, and Sven grunted as he let go of the rudder and walked towards the prow. His hand went to the Mjöllnir around his neck as, even after all this time, he could hear the sounds of the battle he had fought against Prince Louis. He could still hear the swords striking shields and the men calling to their gods. Sven shuddered as the sounds of the cavalry tearing through his men came to him and was unaware of Thora behind him.

'Sven?'

'Huh?' He blinked to clear his mind of the memory and then realised they were all waiting for his orders. 'Send scouts, let's find out if anyone is waiting for us.'

'And what do we do if King Louis is not here?' Alvar raised an eyebrow.

'We wait.' Sven turned and walked to the middle of the ship, where someone had put a boarding plank for the women and the children. Although all the children had already jumped onto the beach as soon as they realised it was safe. He glanced at the sky and tried to gauge the flow of the wind. The tide would be going out soon and they would be trapped here until it returned. 'Prepare a camp. There is a forest not far from here where we can find some wood for a wall.'

It didn't take the men long to build the camp. Trees were chopped down from the forest and brought back to the ship where they were cleaned and used to make a fence around the ship and the few tents which had been put up where the land was still dry. They left a small opening in the fence, which was guarded by two warriors and a log, which was placed in front there so that if anyone thought of attacking them, they would have to either move the log or climb over it. As soon as a large fire was started, the women started preparing fish stew from fish some of the warriors had caught during the day while the children explored the beach.

'The men want to go inland. They want to raid,' Rollo said as he sat down beside Sven. A few of the warriors within earshot glanced at Sven to see how he would respond.

Sven shook his head. 'No raiding. We are here for my grandson. As soon as we have Charles, then we can go somewhere where the raiding is better.'

'And how long do you reckon we have to wait?' one warrior asked, his face showing his disappointment at not being allowed to raid.

'Until that bastard Louis shows up with my grandson.'

'And if he doesn't?' Rollo frowned at Sven.

Sven glared at the flames as they leapt to the sky. 'Then I will burn his kingdom to the ground.'

3

BREMEN

Charles sighed as he stared at the blurred words on the pages of the Bible in front of him as he sat on the floor. He glanced at the door of the small room he was still kept a prisoner in, with the thin straw mattress for him to sleep on and the bucket in the corner, when he heard footsteps outside, his heart racing until he realised it was the warrior who guarded his room moving around. It had been three days since he met his mother for the first time and he had not seen her since. She had told him they would speak again, but she had not returned that day or the day after, no matter how long he had sat there, staring at the door and jumping to his feet every time it opened. Only Father Leofdag came to him, to bring him food and make him read the Bible and pray. He looked at the priest as he sat on the only stool in the room and waited for Charles to read the next lines to him.

'Charles. You are not reading.'

Sighing again, Charles looked at the old Bible in front of him. He squinted as he tried to focus on the words, words that had once filled him with joy and meaning, but now felt empty. He opened his mouth to read, but then pushed the Bible away.

'Why is she not visiting me?' He looked towards the door again, almost willing his mother to walk in. But nothing happened.

Father Leofdag frowned, and then shrugged. 'I wish I knew, Charles. But even I have not seen her since they returned from Denmark, but...'

'But what?' Charles jumped to his feet as he sensed there was something Father Leofdag wanted to say, but couldn't.

Father Leofdag rubbed his bent nose, which had been broken after he had been punched by Jorlaug's drunken father earlier in the summer. 'I sense that something is happening, but I'm not sure what. Every time I see Abbess Hildegard in the church, she seems distracted. Like she is struggling with something.'

Charles had told Father Leofdag that Abbess Hildegard was his mother the day after they had returned. He had been told not to tell anyone, but he couldn't keep it to himself and he felt like he could trust the priest. Father Leofdag was a thin man and even at the age of nine, Charles could tell that he had never lifted a weapon in his life. But Father Leofdag had stayed with Charles since he had been abducted by men who had pretended to be his grandfather's friends. Even when it had put his own life at risk, which had surprised Charles because he had believed that Father Leofdag was a coward. 'You see my mother in the church? Have you spoken to her?'

Father Leofdag shook his head. 'I can't just approach the daughter of the king of East Francia.'

Charles jumped to his feet. 'But you have to.'

'And what would I say to her?' Father Leofdag paled, as if the thought of talking to Charles's mother was so frightening. Charles had been told that she was one of the most important people in East Francia, but he didn't understand why that would make people scared of her. She was an abbess of the church and it was her duty to care for the people of East Francia.

'Ask her why she hasn't been to visit me. Ask her why I have to stay in this room.' Charles tried to think of more questions and one popped into his head. A question he had been struggling with since he had found out who his mother was. 'Ask her why she had left us and why I was told she was dead.'

Father Leofdag lowered his eyes and took a deep breath. 'Charles, those are questions you need to ask her yourself.'

Charles turned and kicked the Bible across the room as his hands balled up into fists. Pages flew as the Bible struck the wall, something that would have terrified Charles not so long ago, but now he barely even noticed it. 'But I can't! I can't because she doesn't want to see me!' He dropped to the floor, crossing his arms as he glared at the Bible.

Father Leofdag reached out to put a hand on his shoulder, but hesitated. Instead, he walked to the Bible, which he picked up with the loose pages, before closing it and dusting its cover with his hand. 'I don't believe that she doesn't want to see you.'

'Then why hasn't she? It's been three days!' Charles pouted.

'I don't know, Charles. Just like I don't know why you were told that she was dead. But if I had to guess at the reason, I would say it was to protect you.'

Charles's eyes widened. 'To protect me? How would that protect me?'

Father Leofdag shrugged. 'I'm just a simple man, Charles. I was born on a small farm to poor parents who couldn't feed me. So they gave me to the church so that I had at least a chance to survive.'

Charles frowned at the priest. He had never wondered about where he had come from or why he had joined the church. It was something Charles had wanted to do himself before his father was killed and he had fled to Denmark to find his grandfather. But now, he was wondering if that life was really for him.

'I don't understand the politics of kings and lords, only what the Bible tells me. But your mother is not only an abbess, she is also the daughter of the king. That puts you in a very dangerous position, Charles, and it does help to explain a lot of what you have been through this summer. I think your parents believed you would be safer if nobody knew who you were and who your mother is.'

Charles felt the anger build up in him as he listened to Father Leofdag. Safe. That was the last thing he had been this summer. Before his father was killed, Charles had believed his life was horrible. Boys in Hügelburg picked on him because he was too small for his age and because his father was a Dane. But now, after everything that had happened, Charles wished he could go back to that life. At least then his father would still be alive and Charles would still understand his place. But now? 'But I'm not safe! My father died, my grandfather was attacked! Thora, Alfhild and Oda. All of them hurt or killed because of me!'

Father Leofdag looked at the Bible in his hands. 'No, Charles. Not because of you. None of this is your fault, and I know you think this, but God is not punishing you.'

'Then why is this happening if it is not because I'm being punished by God?' Tears started running down his cheeks, but Charles did not care as he wiped the snot from his nose with the back of his hand. 'God is angry at me and so is my mother! That is why she doesn't want to see me!'

Father Leofdag's head jerked back, his eyes wide. 'Charles, why would she be mad at you?'

'Because… because I told the king that my grandfather has the cross.'

Father Leofdag shook his head. 'No, Charles. I don't think she is mad at you. And none of this is your fault.'

'Then whose fault is it?'

Father Leofdag shrugged. 'This might be no one's fault. The world is a cruel place, Charles. That is why we pray to God and His Son for their guidance and protection.'

Charles turned away from the priest. 'God doesn't care about me any more.'

'I do not believe that, Charles. God has a plan for you, and even though you can't see it yet, one day you will understand.'

Charles clenched his fists. 'The Danes believe the same about the Norns. That the Norns have already decided their fates. Thora told me that.' Charles had not liked that idea. He did not like that his life was not his to control. He had also thought that the Norns were cruel for what they had done to his grandfather. And now he was starting to think that God was as cruel as the Norns. If this was really part of God's plan for him, then why did he have to suffer so much? Why did everyone around him have to die? 'What if God is just as cruel as the gods my grandfather believes in?'

Father Leofdag did not respond and when Charles turned around, he saw the young priest just staring at the Bible in his hands. After a while, Father Leofdag looked up, his eyes red. 'I will talk to your mother, Charles. And I will pray for you.' With that, the priest left the room, leaving Charles more confused than angry.

Charles walked to the straw mattress on the floor and lay down, hugging himself. He thought of his father, and then his grandfather. He thought of the boys who had always picked on him, especially Pepin, who had been his only friend once, but then sided with his bullies. Alfhild, the young slave, and Oda, Rollo's mother, both dead because of him. *How could all this be part of God's plan?*

4

'We've got company,' Alvar said, shielding his eyes from the morning sun as he stared at the approaching group.

'You think it's King Louis?' Rollo asked, following Alvar's gaze.

Sven stood and stretched his old back as he scrutinised the small force gathering near the beach. It was the day after they had arrived, and Sven was ready to leave. He had spent the night tossing and turning in his tent because every time he closed his eyes, he relived the battle he had fought against the young Prince Louis, and relived the sight of his son on the beach as he sailed away. Even now, if he closed his eyes, he could hear his men screaming as the Frankish cavalry tore through them. Sven had woken up this morning with a pounding headache and feeling like the gods had used him as target practice. On top of that, his back hurt, his left leg hurt and his neck was stiff. And he couldn't even drown the pain away with ale because they only had so much of the stuff and so he was limited to only one cup in the morning. And Sven doubted the Franks would provide them with some. So he was desperate for that bastard Frankish king to arrive so he could get his grandson and leave this cursed beach. But as he frowned at the small force in the distance, he doubted that that was the king of East Francia.

Thora saw the same. 'No, King Louis would arrive with a larger army to show his strength. And they have no flag to identify themselves.'

'A local leader?' Rollo, now also standing, scratched his neck. All around them, the men had noticed their visitors and were glancing towards Sven and Rollo. Some men gathered their weapons, and a few even started putting their jerkins or brynjas on. Women looked up from the cooking pots to see what was happening and as soon as they spotted the Franks, called the children to them. Some complained, especially Jorlaug who wanted to fight the Franks, but they were soon herded towards the ship. Not that it would do them much good. The tide was out, which meant the ship was just sitting in the mud, like a sleeping beast.

'Make sure the men don't do anything dumb,' Sven said as the Frankish force made its way towards them. Stretching his neck, Sven studied the man leading them on a horse, but he couldn't make out the Frank's features. The way the Frank carried himself told Sven the bastard would be arrogant and already he didn't like the man. Not that he liked many Franks or Christians. Sven glanced at the forest in the distance as he walked towards the Franks, doing his best not to limp as Alvar went around the men, telling them all to be ready, while Rollo and Thora flanked him. His fingers twitched as they longed to grip his Dane axe, but it was still on the ship. Rollo, though, had his Dane axe with him, and Sven wondered if the giant warrior slept with the axe by his side.

'What do you think they want?' Rollo asked.

Sven shrugged. 'Probably to ask us the same thing.'

They stopped by the large log that protected the entrance to their encampment and waited for the Franks to come closer. Sven's warriors were gathering behind him and, when he glanced over his shoulder, he was surprised to see that some had their shields. He then saw the boys, led by Sigmund, Rollo's son, running back to the ship to get the rest. Jorlaug, Thora's niece, had to be pulled back by her mother, the red-faced girl straining like an attack dog.

'She's got the making of a vicious warrior.' Alvar smiled.

'Aye, Frigg knows that's what worries me,' Thora said.

Sven ignored them as he looked at the Frank on the horse again, his face stern as he led his men. His hands were trembling, though, which made Sven nervous. The only thing more dangerous than an arrogant man was an arrogant man who was afraid. It made him unpredictable and reckless. Sven raised an eyebrow when he realised the Frankish leader was younger than he had expected, and he wondered about the older man rushing to keep up with the young Frank.

Seabirds screamed from the clouds above them as the Frank stopped his horse more than ten paces away from them and glared at Sven. 'Who are you and what are you doing on my father's land?' the young Frank asked in the Frankish tongue, his hand on the hilt of his fine-looking sword.

Sven didn't respond. Instead, he studied the man, with his dark hair which was cropped around his ears and neatly trimmed beard. The Frank wore a fine leather jerkin, its surface gleaming and with not a single scratch on it, while his fur-rimmed cloak barely lifted in the breeze. None of the Frank's men had any brynjas and only the few hardened warriors around him had leather jerkins and weapons of note. The rest of the men, which numbered about the same as Sven's, only wore thick woollen tunics and carried spears. And they all looked nervous as they stared at the Danish warriors behind Sven. Sven glanced at the sky, scratching his beard as he searched the few clouds and the seabirds flying amongst them. 'It might rain later.'

Thora looked at the sky above them and shrugged. 'If you say so.'

'Answer my question, you heathen scum!' The young man's face went red. 'In the name of our Lord and King Louis of East Francia, I demand to know who you are and what you are doing on my father's land!'

Sven gripped the hilt of his sword and took a step forward. He smiled as a few Franks stepped backwards and tried to remember whom this land belonged to. But he didn't know. All he knew was that they were in Saxony, which meant Duke Liudolf controlled these lands. He wondered if the man on the horse was the duke's son, but doubted it. The young bastard looked nothing like the duke. 'I am here to see your king,' Sven said in Frankish. 'So turn your little horse around and go fetch him for me.'

The Franks gasped but Sven didn't know if it was because he spoke their tongue or because of what he had said. Not that he cared.

The young Frank's nostrils flared. 'How dare you speak to me like that, you heathen scum? Don't you know who I am?'

Sven tilted his head as he looked up at the Frank on his horse. He doubted the man was one of King Louis's sons, so he must have been the son of some local town leader. No one important and not someone who would have known about his agreement with King Louis. And only Odin knew if that agreement still stood. 'Boy, I don't care who you are, and call me scum one more time and I will send you to meet your god.' The Frank's warriors bristled at that, but Sven ignored them. 'I am here to meet King Louis of East Francia, as we had agreed.'

The young Frank clenched his fists around the reins of his horse. 'I know nothing of this agreement.'

'Because you are not important enough to know about it. So I tell you again. Turn your horse around and go fetch your king.'

'Tell me what to do one more time, Dane, and I will kill all of you. My men outnumber yours.'

Sven glanced at the nervous-looking men behind the Frank and smiled. Even the few warriors amongst the Frank's men looked uncertain. 'Your men might outnumber mine, but my men are all warriors. Can you say the same about yours?'

The old man who had been struggling to keep up with the young Frank stepped forward and spoke to the young man. 'Let's not be rash, Reinhold. Your father would not want you to kill his men in an unnecessary battle. Perhaps it would be wise to send a messenger to Bremen. We know that King Louis is there.'

Reinhold glared at the old man, who had the sense to step back so that he was out of reach.

'You better do as the old man says, boy.' Sven was losing his patience with the young bastard who was trying to make a name for himself. He had killed a few young men like that in Denmark this summer already and did not want to do the same in Francia. Not until he at least had his grandson back.

'My father gave me command of these men,' Reinhold told the old man, who shook his head, and Sven knew what was coming.

'He did that so you could find out who these men are and what they want, not to fight them.'

Reinhold glared at the old man and then at Sven. His hand went to his sword. 'I'm only going to tell you once more, heathen. Get back on your ship and leave these shores or my men will kill you all.'

Again, Sven tilted his head at the arrogant Frank. He wondered why young men had to be so foolish, but then remembered he had been the same. Worse even, because he had killed his father and his brothers so that he could be the jarl of Ribe. Something the gods had been punishing him for ever since. 'Your men? And what will you do? Sit on your pretty horse and then run away as they die? Don't be a fool, boy, and do as the old man says. Send word to your king and tell him Sven the Boar waits for him and wants his grandson back.'

Reinhold's eyes widened as the old man paled. 'Sven the Boar? *The* Sven the Boar?'

Sven had not wanted to use his name, because he was concerned about the reaction he might get. Charles had told him that many still spoke his name in fear, but he had hoped that it would frighten the young Frank. Loki, the god of mischief, had other ideas though, as Reinhold's eyes glinted in the sun. Sven had seen it many times before and took a step back before the words even came out of Reinhold's mouth. 'Kill them! Kill the Danes!'

'Shield wall!' Sven bellowed as Thora handed him his shield and his men stepped forward, locking their shields together.

'Reinhold, no!' The old man's words were drowned out as the few Frankish warriors roared to get their courage up. The rest of the Franks hesitated, but then joined the attack. The young Frank spurned his horse forward, and the animal leapt over the log while the rest of his men slowed down to get over it. Reinhold drew his sword as he neared the shield wall, but then his horse shied away as the man behind Sven jabbed his spear at its face. The young Frank was not prepared for that and lost his balance as the horse turned, but then Sven lost sight of him as the first of the Frankish warriors reached the shield wall. They were not trained to fight like the Danes and didn't slow down, so the rest of the Frankish men could catch up. Perhaps they believed their god would aid them and kill Sven and his Danes for them. But their god must have blinked at that moment because the first warrior died before he could even strike a blow. Rollo had opened up his shield and had chopped down with his Dane axe, its heavy blade cleaving through the Frankish warrior's chest and spraying Rollo with blood.

'Odin!' the giant warrior roared and the rest of the Danes joined him.

Sven lifted his shield to block a one-handed axe before stabbing its wielder in the leg from under his shield. As the Frank dropped to his knee, Sven punched out with his shield and knocked him out, wondering why he always had to fight to solve his problems. Because Sven was tired of fighting. He was tired of shedding blood, even though he knew that was the only thing he was good at. Beside him, Thora dispatched another of the warriors, cutting his throat open with her sword and drenching them both in the bastard's blood, before forcing another to duck behind his shield as she stabbed at him.

'Kill the heathens!' Reinhold shouted over the sounds of his men dying on the beach. He was standing away from the fighting, his horse nowhere to be seen, as he waved his sword in the air. Sven gritted his teeth as his anger at the coward took hold of him.

He blocked another strike, and Rollo killed the man. A farmer, by the looks of him, and then Sven stabbed the next one in the stomach. The man wore no armour, and Sven's sword easily tore through his muscle and his insides. The dying Frank grunted and his eyes filled with fear as Sven pulled his sword free and pushed him to one side. He was about to take a step forward when Rollo shouted, 'Hold!'

Sven stopped, his breathing ragged, even though it had just been a brief fight. With his blood still pumping in his ears, Sven wanted to be annoyed at Rollo for shouting the command, but then he saw why the giant warrior had called for the men to hold. The Franks had broken and were running for their lives. Sven hawked and spat as he watched them flee. Those who could, anyway. The beach in front of him was littered with dead and injured Franks, and Sven glanced over his shoulder and was glad to see that all his warriors had survived.

'Sven.'

He glanced at Thora and saw where she was pointing and smiled. Reinhold, the arrogant young Frank, was trying to limp away. He must have injured his leg when he had fallen off his horse and none of his men, apart from the old Frank, had stayed behind to protect him. 'Bring them to me.' Thora nodded and took three men with her to collect the two Franks. 'Alvar, clear the dead from here. Otherwise those bastards' – he pointed at the seabirds already forming a thick cloud above them – 'won't give us any peace.'

Alvar smiled and gathered enough men and started dragging the dead Franks away. Those still alive were killed, while a few of the younger warriors stripped the Frankish warriors of their armour. Sven left them to it as he walked back to his tent, his hands shaking from the battle. He hadn't gone far when he heard a scream behind him and turned in time to see the young Frank launch himself at Thora. The warriors with her stood back as she stepped out of the way of the Frank's sword swing and kicked him to the ground. She kicked him again before two of the men with her grabbed the Frank and pulled him to his feet. Thora collected his sword, which he had dropped, and pointed it at the old man, who shook his head and followed them back to the camp.

Sven sighed as he reached his tent and grimaced as he knelt down to reach the bucket of water outside his tent. He washed the blood off his hands before he wiped his face clean and was about to call for some ale when there was a commotion behind him.

'Get your filthy hands off me, you heathen bitch!'

Sven turned around and saw Thora throw Reinhold to the ground to the amusement of Sven's warriors. He glared at the Frank, his sword trembling in his hand as he took a deep breath so the sea air could calm his anger. 'I'd be careful what you call her,'

Sven said in Frankish. 'She'll cut your tongue out and make you eat it, before she does the same to other parts.'

The Frank paled as his eyes darted to Thora. 'L... let me g... go. I beg you. I'll give you everything you want. Gold, jewels. Enough to fill your ship with. Just let me go back to my father and I swear on my soul, I'll make sure you get it all.'

Sven took a step forward and grabbed Reinhold by his hair. 'Let you go? And how do I know you won't just run off and come back with a bigger army?' Sven doubted the young bastard could muster more men, but he still wasn't going to let him go.

'As God is my witness. I won't do that.'

'I don't trust your god.'

Reinhold gulped, his wide eyes darting all over the place. 'Then take Hartwig. You can keep him hostage until I return with your payment.'

The old Frank hissed at that and Sven clenched his fist in the young man's hair, causing Reinhold to cry out. 'I have a better plan,' Sven said through clenched teeth. He looked at the old man. 'Who is his father? Is he important?'

The old Frank glared at Reinhold. 'His father is Lord Theodard. He answers only to Duke Liudolf and King Louis.'

Sven nodded. 'Then take a message to this Lord Theodard. Tell him that Sven the Boar has his son and that if he wants to see him alive, then he needs to make sure that King Louis is here by sunrise tomorrow with my grandson. And if your king isn't here by then, then I'll tie large stones to this bastard's feet, row him out to sea and send him to Rán's hall. She likes them young and alive.'

Reinhold paled and tried to turn his head to Hartwig, but Sven held on to his hair and wouldn't let him. 'Hartwig, please, I beg you. Do what the man says.'

Hartwig gave Reinhold a look of contempt and, for a moment, Sven worried the old man might just tell him to kill the bastard.

But then, he said, 'As you wish.' With one last glance at Reinhold, the old Frank turned and walked away as Sven explained to everyone what had been said.

'You sure he will do it?' Rollo raised an eyebrow at him.

Sven glared at Reinhold as the seabirds screamed and started their feast. 'This bastard better pray he does. Otherwise, we sacrifice him to the gods.'

5

Charles glared at the warrior sitting with him on the cart as it rocked along the uneven road, but the man was too busy joking with his companions to notice. Clouds blocked the sun and Charles hoped it wouldn't rain because he didn't have a cloak with him, but the birds flying around and singing from nearby hedges made him think it wouldn't. Not that he would know, anyway. Charles understood little of nature, despite his father trying to teach him. He often wished he had paid more attention because then at least he would have fond memories of his father instead of the ones where his father tried to teach him to be a warrior.

That morning, a warrior had barged into his room while Father Leofdag was there and had dragged Charles out of the house and into a busy courtyard. Father Leofdag had rushed after them, demanding to know what was going on, but another warrior had silenced him by gripping the hilt of his sword. Charles had been stunned when he saw the courtyard filled with many warriors, all of them checking armour and weapons while Duke Liudolf walked around barking orders as others followed him. Horses whined and somewhere a man shouted as a horse kicked at him. That was when Charles saw the cart he was being led to and panicked when the warrior told him to get on it. Father Leofdag tried to find out what was happening and where they were taking him, but the warriors only ignored the priest. Charles then saw his mother climb into a carriage ahead of him. He wanted to call out to her, but his voice got caught in his throat when he saw King Louis glaring at him. Father Leofdag wanted to go with them and was about to climb onto the cart after Charles when one of the warriors pushed him to the ground while the others laughed, leaving Charles confused as to why Christian warriors would treat a man of God like that. He resented the warriors for treating Father Leofdag badly. The priest had been with him ever since Hedeby, when he had tried to help Charles escape Ivor's men, while Rollo was fighting them. That was the last Charles had seen of Rollo, and he had often wondered what had happened to the giant warrior, especially after Ivor had recaptured Charles.

Charles sighed and looked ahead of them to the carriage that was heavily guarded by the warriors on horseback as he tried to ignore the warriors' voices and creaking of the cartwheels. Unlike the warriors who guarded Charles, those men wore chain-mail vests, and all of them had spears and swords. The man in the cart with Charles only had a spear and a knife, and his leather jerkin looked like it might have been older than him. Charles's attention went back to the carriage at the front as a crow cried out from somewhere. He knew his mother was in that carriage, along with her father, King Louis. Duke Liudolf, his face still bruised from the battle in Ribe Charles had been told about, was somewhere ahead of them as well, leading the column as they travelled along the pockmarked road to a destination that Charles was unsure of. He guessed they were travelling north because of the way the sun had moved during the day, but he couldn't understand why. Charles had assumed they were going to Frankfurt, the capital of King Louis, but that was to the south. Not north.

They stopped at an inn along the road as the sun sat low on the horizon, but Charles soon realised that he would not get a nice bed to sleep on as he was sent to the stables with the cart. Two warriors watched him through the night so that he couldn't run away, but Charles didn't know where they were, so even if he had wanted to, he wouldn't know where to go. Charles struggled to sleep as the heat of the day vanished under the moonlight, and he spent most of the night shivering on the cart, until one of the warriors gave him his cloak. The man gave him a sympathetic smile which left Charles confused, but he was glad for the cloak as it warmed him up enough to eventually fall asleep. And for once in a long time, he did not have to worry about the dreams that usually plagued him. The following morning, the same man gave him some thin porridge to eat and told Charles he could keep the cloak. The other warriors made fun of him, but the man didn't seem to care. Charles didn't have much time to eat his porridge though, as soon the signal came for them to leave again. He caught another glimpse of his mother, but just like the day before, she never looked his way and Charles was surprised at the anger he felt as he wondered why she was ignoring him.

'Why are we stopping now?' one warrior asked as the column came to a halt later that day. The sun was at its peak and many of the warriors seemed grateful for the break when Duke Liudolf called for them to halt from the front of the column. Charles tried to see where they were as one of the horses attached to the cart lifted its tail and relieved itself, but the surrounding landscape looked the same here as it had everywhere else along the road. Farms and small towns were dotted between fields and forests, with livestock roaming around and grazing on the grass. Charles noticed there were more seabirds flying amongst the clouds, although the only reason he knew that was because one almost shat on him.

'A midday break?' the warrior in the cart asked, his voice sounding hopeful.

The other warrior, an older man with a limp which reminded Charles of his grandfather, shook his head and scowled as he tried to see what was happening at the head of the column. 'Something else is going on.'

'Perhaps we reached our destination?' someone else asked and Charles stretched his neck to see what was happening at the front of the column. He was also hoping to catch another glimpse of his mother.

'Where are we going anyway?' the warrior in the cart asked, surprising Charles. He had thought these men knew about their destination.

'Where the duke tells us to go,' the older warrior said. 'Stay here. I'll find out what is going on.' The others nodded as the man walked to the front of the column and Charles distracted himself, just like his grandfather often did, by following the birds as they flew above him. Although, Charles knew that the reason his grandfather did that was because he was looking for signs from his gods.

'So?' one man asked as the old warrior returned with a smile a short while later.

'We're not there yet, but we are close.'

'So why did we stop?'

The warrior scratched his chin. 'A group from a nearby town approached. One of them, the lord of the town. It seems the man's son decided to confront a group of Danes who landed on the beach a few days ago' – the warrior glanced at Charles, whose heart was racing as he wondered if it was his grandfather – 'and the idiot got himself taken captive.'

One of the warriors raised an eyebrow. 'Been a long time since we had Danes in this area. They usually prefer to go upriver and attack the towns.'

'Aye. Perhaps this group just wanted to rest. Doesn't matter. God knows they'll be dead before the sun sets.' The warriors laughed at this as Charles gritted his teeth.

'It's my grandfather, Sven the Boar,' Charles said, glaring at the warriors. 'And he has come for me.' Charles's heart raced as he wanted to believe those words. King Louis had mentioned a meeting on the beach, and Charles could smell the salt in the air and see the seabirds, which meant they were near the coastline.

'Aye, well, if it is, then I doubt the old bastard will leave the beach alive. Not with the small army we've brought with us,' one warrior boasted.

The older warrior frowned at Charles. 'You think the king knew about this? Why else would he bring so many men with him?'

But before anyone could answer, the signal came from the front for the column to move and the warriors fell back into place. The man in the cart chewed on his lip as he stared at Charles.

'You really think it is Sven the Boar? Your grandfather?'

Charles stared at the man, trying to make himself believe it was, despite what he had said before. 'She told me he would find me.'

'She?' The warrior raised an eyebrow as he gripped the cross around his neck.

'Thora.' Charles gripped the small wooden cross around his neck as he wondered if she was there as well and then frowned when he thought about seeing his grandfather again. The last time Charles had seen him was in Guttrom's tent when Sven was fighting the man who had claimed to be his friend. Would he be happy to see his grandfather or would he be angry at him for abandoning him to fight the king of Denmark?

They moved in silence, the warriors all scanning the surrounding area with their hands near their weapons as if they expected an attack while the cart rocked as the horse struggled on the uneven path, forcing Charles and the warrior to grip the sides. After a while, the column stopped and Duke Liudolf came towards them. He stared at Charles with his brow furrowed, which made Charles think that Duke Liudolf was worried about something.

'Bring the boy. But do not harm him.'

The men frowned at each other and a few of them shrugged as Charles jumped off the cart, glad to be able to stretch his legs. But his relief was short-lived as one of the warriors grabbed him by the shoulder as if to stop him from running away, and flanked by two other warriors, they followed Duke Liudolf towards the dunes Charles could see ahead of them. His mother was already there, as well as King Louis, and Charles saw both of them staring at something on the beach. Once he reached the top of the dunes, Charles gasped when he saw the small camp. A few tents were dotted on the edge of the beach and were surrounded by a wooden fence. Just behind the camp, lying on the sand, was a ship that had been beached, its flat bottom keeping it upright. Charles's eyes widened as a group gathered by the opening in the fence, behind a large log, and he spotted two men who were much larger than everyone else. Charles smiled when he realised Rollo had survived whatever had happened in Hedeby and had returned to Ribe. And then his heart thudded in his chest when he saw the light-haired woman, wearing a chain-mail vest and with a sword on her hip, standing there as well. If it wasn't for the warrior still gripping his shoulder, Charles would have run towards her and hugged her. The last time Charles had seen Thora, Ivor had stabbed her in the stomach and Charles had believed she was dead until his mother had told him she still lived. And beside Thora stood a short, fat man, his head shaved, and even though Charles could not see it, he knew there was a faded tattoo of a raven on his grandfather's head. Charles's hands trembled as he stared at his grandfather and felt the old man's eyes on him. The seabirds had gone quiet as they stared at each other and for the first time since they had left Bremen, Charles feared for his grandfather's life as he glanced at the smiling King Louis.

'Looks like the bastard survived the battle you told me about,' King Louis said, 'although he doesn't have many warriors with him.' Some of the warriors laughed at this and Charles realised the king was right. His grandfather had very few men with him, far less than the king of East Francia. 'Duke Liudolf, make sure the men are ready. And no one attacks until I give the word.'

Charles stared at King Louis, his mouth open in shock. He looked at his mother, hoping she would say something. This time, she gave him a quick glance and shook her head, although Charles didn't know what that meant. He wanted to run to his grandfather, to warn him of what King Louis was planning, but then the warrior behind him tightened his grip on Charles's shoulder, making him wince.

'My son!' someone shouted and Charles saw an old man he had not noticed before. 'I can't see him.'

'Your son will be fine, Lord Theodard. If the heathens even think of killing him, they'll all be slaughtered,' King Louis said.

'But how can you trust the heathens won't kill him?'

King Louis glanced at Charles and smiled. 'Because we have something they want.'

6

'That's a lot of them.' Rollo frowned, but Sven detected no fear in his voice. He doubted the giant warrior understood what that felt like. The few warriors that Sven had all got to their feet and stared at the large force that appeared in the distance and, as before, the women ushered the children towards the ship as seabirds cried out above them. To Sven, it sounded like the birds were mocking him for thinking that it was a good idea to come here with such a small force. But at least this time the tide was on its way in, so if they had to, they would be able to escape. Sven just prayed it would be with Charles by his side.

He hawked and spat as he glared at the Frankish army on the dunes. At the centre of the army stood the dreaded cavalry which had decimated his warriors the last time he had been here, while foot warriors spread out on either side, their spears glinting in the late afternoon sun. And just ahead of the Frankish army stood a group of people. Sven recognised Hildegard and Duke Liudolf, but as he scanned them, he saw no sign of Charles. He did see the man he thought was King Louis though, and felt his anger grow in the pit of his stomach.

It had been four days since they had been attacked by the son of the local lord and despite Sven threatening to kill the young Frankish bastard, he still lived, but only because Sven knew King Louis would make him wait. It was his way of showing that he was in control and, as much as Sven hated that idea, he knew the Frankish king was. Sven was in King Louis's domain, outnumbered and with his grandson a hostage of the Frankish king.

'Probably here to kill us,' Torgny, an experienced warrior and close friend of Rollo, said.

'Aye, Odin knows they can try. These Franks are no match for our Danish steel,' Rollo said, and the men cheered.

Sven grunted. He knew Rollo was keeping the men's spirits up, but he also knew that if the Franks did attack, then they would all die that day. He still remembered the last time he had faced King Louis on this beach. Sven had also believed that the All-Father would guide him to victory. He had believed that right until the Frankish cavalry had come charging out of the forest not far from the beach. Sven could still hear his men scream as they were torn apart by spears and trampled on by the horses. He rubbed the ivory Mjöllnir he wore around his neck and prayed that the same would not happen today. 'Rollo, you stay and command the men. Make sure they are ready, but stay in the camp.' Rollo nodded, but said nothing as Sven eyed the small cavalry force on the dunes. He would not be surprised by them again. As long as his men stayed behind the wooden fence they had built, then the cavalry could not get to them. They still would not win if there was a battle, but at least the fence would slow the cavalry down and allow most of his warriors and the families to escape.

Sven glanced over his shoulder and saw that all his warriors had their armour on and their weapons ready. He grunted in approval and did his best not to limp as he made his way to meet the man that had helped to ruin his life. Sven also had his brynja on, but wore no helmet. His head had been shaved that morning so that the raven tattoo on his scalp was visible, and his beard combed and braided. Sven wore two golden arm rings on both his wrists and had his Dane axe strapped to his back. He prayed he would not need to use it, but was determined to look like the warlord he had once been. First impressions could win battles for you, which was why most warriors did their best to look as intimidating as possible before a battle. If you could make your enemy doubt himself, then the battle was already won. But Sven knew King Louis would not be intimidated by him. He had won the only battle the two of them had fought against each other.

After taking a deep breath of the sea air and glancing at the sky, Sven spread his arms wide to show that he wanted to talk. Thora and Alvar flanked him, and a handful of chosen warriors followed behind. Men chosen for their experience because Sven wanted calm heads around him. Thora wore no helmet, because she didn't have one and because Sven had wanted it that way. He wanted the Franks to be confronted by a shield maiden because he knew she would make them feel uncomfortable. The Christians hated the idea of women fighting battles and killing men. It threatened their idea of themselves and Sven wanted to play on that. But he could not take credit for all of this. Many nights had been spent discussing how they would greet the Franks, with Thora and Rollo coming up with most of the plans.

Sven grimaced as he stepped over the log with his left leg and carried on for a few more paces before he stopped. They were far enough away from his camp to make King Louis feel comfortable to talk, but close enough to retreat to safety if the Frankish cavalry attacked them. He scrutinised the Frankish army as a group broke away and made their way to the beach. He guessed there were about a hundred warriors, many more than his twenty or so, but then he forgot about that when he caught sight of the small boy standing on the dunes, wearing a cloak that was too large for him and surrounded by Frankish warriors. His heart thudded in his chest as a similar image from many winters ago came to him and Sven clenched his fists as he tried to stay calm.

'They're keeping Charles back,' Alvar said, seeing the same thing.

'Aye, a smart move,' Thora said. 'If they brought him with, then what is to stop us from just attacking them and taking Charles?'

Turning his attention to the approaching group, Sven felt the vein throb on the side of his head as he glared at the man who had taken his son from him. The man who had ruined his reputation. King Louis of East Francia walked with his back straight and his head held high. He looked like a man who had the upper hand. A man who could have them all killed with the nod of his head. And the seabirds above Sven laughed because that was all true. King Louis wore a simple crown on his head and had a sword on his waist, with his right hand resting on the pommel. Sven wondered if that was the same sword King Louis had fought him with the last time they had met, but doubted it. Swords didn't last that long, unless you never used them in battle. Like the strongest warriors, they eventually broke or became too dull to ever be used again, no matter how many times you ran a whetstone along its edge.

'He's younger than I thought.' Thora raised an eyebrow.

Sven grunted. 'He was barely a man the last time we met. Yet he still defeated me and took my son.'

'Are you sure we shouldn't give him the cross?' Thora asked. 'It might be our best chance of getting Charles back, especially now that we don't have Hildegard any more.'

Sven grunted again as he eyed the Frankish cavalry on the dunes. None of them had dismounted and that made him nervous as he saw a few of the horses pawing at the sand. 'You really think he will let us leave here alive if we give him the cross? The moment he has it in his hands, his cavalry will charge and kill us all. Even the women and children.'

'How can you be so sure?' Thora frowned at him, but he saw in her eyes that she had the same concern.

'Because that is what I would have done. He wants that cross and if it is really as dangerous as Odinson believes it is, then it's better not to give it back to the Franks. Denmark is still weak after the death of the old King Horik and I doubt the new wearer of Denmark's crown can hold the Franks back.' Especially if he relied on the support of snakes like Jarl Torgeir of Hedeby, the man Sven believed was responsible for the attack on Ribe. But there was nothing he could do about that, so Sven had given Torgeir his victory and left Denmark. 'If the gods are with us, then the bastard will honour his deal and give us my grandson back.'

'And if they're not?' Alvar asked.

Sven glanced at the giant warrior and saw his narrowed eyes. 'Then it won't matter. We'll all be dead before the sun sets.'

Alvar nodded, but did not seem affected by Sven's words. 'Why don't we trade Gerold and our new captive for Charles?'

Sven thought of Gerold and Reinhold, both tied up and guarded in the camp. 'King Louis won't even blink if we kill either of them now. They're not important enough.'

Thora glanced at him, but she said nothing as the Franks stopped a few paces away.

No one spoke as Sven and King Louis glared at each other. Even the seabirds, which had been crying above them only moments ago, had gone silent, as had the wind. It was like the entire Midgard was holding its breath. Or perhaps it was just that Sven could hear nothing other than the blood rushing in his ears as he pictured himself launching at the king of East Francia and beating him to death. Sven ground his teeth as King Louis smiled at him.

'Sven the Boar. By God, I could not believe it when I was told you were still alive. And here you stand, with that same anger in your eyes. Shorter than last time we met, though, or perhaps that's just my memory playing tricks on me.' The handful of warriors behind King Louis laughed, but Sven ignored them.

'What's he saying?' Alvar asked because King Louis had spoken in Frankish. Thora shushed him. King Louis glanced at her and raised an eyebrow, as most Franks did when they saw a woman dressed like a warrior.

'Give me my grandson.' The words struggled to come out of Sven as he fought to contain his fury. He clenched his fists to stop himself from grabbing the hilt of his sword, because he knew that might cause the Frankish warriors to attack and then he would lose Charles forever.

'Why would I do that?' King Louis asked, his face bored.

'We had a deal.' Sven glanced at Duke Liudolf, who wouldn't meet his eyes.

King Louis sighed. 'The deal was an exchange between us. My daughter for your runt. But I have my daughter. Duke Liudolf brought her to me, so I have no reason to give you your grandson.'

Sven had expected King Louis to say something like that, but the words still angered him. 'The only reason Duke Liudolf could bring your daughter to you was because I let them go.'

'But you didn't really have a choice, did you, Jarl Sven? Your town was under attack and your hall was burning. And judging by how few men you have, I'd say that you lost your town.'

Sven glanced at Hildegard, but her face was like the stone in the mountains of Norway. Hard and uncaring. Sven wondered if she had spoken to Charles and what she had said to him. Had she turned the boy against him? He focused his attention back to King Louis. 'I defeated those who attacked Ribe. Killed their leaders and chased them out of the town. But Ribe is no longer my concern. I just want my grandson back and be left in peace.'

King Louis laughed. 'Men like you will never know peace. Even after I told you to never come back to my shores, you still assembled more men and tried to come back, knowing what I would do to your son.' Sven's eyes widened which only caused the king of East Francia to laugh again. 'Yes, Sven. I knew you tried to come back. The only reason I didn't kill Torkel was because you had failed. God had sent a storm that crushed your fleet and sent you running back to your cave.'

Sven growled, remembering the storm that had come out of nowhere and sunk two of his three ships. Men he had paid a lot of gold were sent to Rán's hall under the waves and no one wanted to sail with him after that because they believed he had been cursed. The Christian god did not have the power to send a storm like that. It had been Njörd and Odin. Sven had always believed that. They had punished him for losing his son to the enemy.

Again, King Louis laughed at Sven's silence. 'Ah, Sven the Boar. How history repeats itself. Here we stand again on the same beach where I defeated you. You on the losing side and me with your grandson in my possession. And just like with your son, you will sail away and leave him with me.'

Sven's knuckles turned white as he clenched his fists, his mind racing as he tried to think of a way to get his grandson back. But there was only one other option, one that Sven knew would cause his death, but if he couldn't leave here with Charles, then did it really matter?

'But there is a way you might get your grandson back. Although God knows I wish you had more men.'

Sven frowned. He was about to tell King Louis about the cross, but the Frank's words made him keep his mouth shut.

King Louis sighed. 'My daughter convinced me there is a way

you can be useful to me, and if you succeed, then you can have your grandson.'

Sven noticed how Hildegard glared at her father and wondered what this deal was. 'What do you want?'

'I'm sure you've heard about the problems in West Francia.' Sven hadn't, but he kept quiet. 'My son is on his way with a size-able force to claim Aquitaine, but he is not as determined as I need him to be.'

'And?'

King Louis smiled. 'And I want you to make sure he succeeds in claiming the throne of Aquitaine before my brother, the king of West Francia, can bring her to heel.'

Sven raised his eyebrow. 'How do you expect me to do that?'

King Louis shrugged. 'You are Sven the Boar. The Danish jarl who gave my father's empire nightmares. I'm sure you'll find a way. Raid the coasts if you have to. Burn some churches, I don't really care. Just make sure my brother is too busy dealing with you so that he forgets about my son.'

Sven scratched his beard as he thought about what the king of East Francia had just told him and tried to work out if it was a trick. Thora stepped forward and leaned towards him.

'What's he saying?'

Sven explained what King Louis had said and saw Thora frown before she shook her head.

'Why not just—'

'No,' Sven interrupted her, not wanting Thora to mention the Cross of Charlemagne. He knew Hildegard and Duke Liudolf spoke their tongue and was certain King Louis did as well. 'This might be better.'

Thora raised an eyebrow at him, but Sven ignored her as he glanced towards where Charles was standing.

'So, I help your son take Aquitaine and you give me my grandson back?'

King Louis nodded, but Sven still felt uncertain. Everyone that had come to him with a deal, an offer to help or with a trade proposal had betrayed him, but Sven could see no other option than to accept King Louis's demand. And that angered him even more. He glanced at the seabirds flying above him and thought he saw something that looked like an eagle or a hawk, but wasn't sure, and so dismissed it.

'Give me my grandson now and I'll do what you ask. I swear this by Odin and the sacred tree.'

King Louis laughed. 'You really expect me to trust the word of a heathen?'

'You expect me to trust the word of a Christian?'

'But you, Jarl Sven, have no choice. I have your grandson, just like I had your son once.'

Sven gritted his teeth as he resisted the urge to launch himself at King Louis. He even wondered if he would be able to kill the bastard before his men could protect him, but then dismissed the idea. When he had been younger, he might have, but not now. Not with his left leg and his back constantly hurting. Sven searched his mind, trying to find another option, but could not, so he took a deep breath. 'Fine. At least let me speak to the boy before we leave.'

King Louis thought about it and Sven saw that Hildegard did not like that idea, but she kept quiet. In fact, Sven was surprised she had not said a single thing during the entire meeting. The king of East Francia turned and gave a signal to the men on the dunes and one warrior brought Charles towards them. 'I'll give you a few moments, but mark my words, Sven the Boar. Fail me in this and you will never see your grandson again.'

Sven nodded as King Louis and his entourage took a few steps back. Thora and Alvar came forward and Thora asked in a soft voice so the Franks could not hear her. 'Sven, why not just tell them we have the cross? We can't go raiding West Francia.'

'She's right,' Alvar said. 'We don't have enough men for that.'

Sven knew they were right. 'The gods know that if we give them the cross, then we die on this beach today. And most likely Charles dies as well. His men outnumber us and his cavalry have all stayed on their horses, most likely waiting for the signal.'

'You really think his mother will allow that to happen?' Thora asked.

'She couldn't stop him from taking Charles away from her the first time. He is the king. I don't think there is anything she can do to stop him if he decides Charles needs to die.' Sven's heart raced as he saw Charles approach. The boy hesitated as he walked past his mother and glanced at her, but she seemed to ignore him. 'Also, Denmark is weak. We give him the cross, he kills us and then marches his army into Denmark. Wipes out our gods and forces everyone to bow to his god.' Sven hawked and spat. 'No, we keep the cross and we go raid West Francia for him. At least that way, we live and so does Charles.'

'And what is to stop him from killing Charles anyway?' Alvar asked.

Sven chewed on the inside of his cheek. It was something he feared as well. 'All we can do is hope that he doesn't, as long as things go his way.'

'You sure we can trust him?' Thora asked.

Sven glanced at her and then at Charles as he stopped a few paces away. 'I'd rather trust the ice giants of Jötunheimr before I trust any of them.'

7

Charles's knees trembled as he stood in front of his grandfather and Thora. His mouth was dry and his heart raced so fast he was afraid it would run away. He had watched his two grandfathers from a distance and wondered what they were talking about, but he could see that Sven was angry. He had learnt to read the signs of when his grandfather saw red, so Charles knew things were going against him. That was why he had been surprised when King Louis had turned and raised his hand. At first Charles had thought that it was a signal to attack, and he wanted to scream, to warn his grandfather and Thora, but then the warrior behind Charles grabbed him by the shoulder.

'Come.' He had dragged Charles down the dunes.

Charles had almost tripped a few times as he struggled to get his feet to move and as they had approached the group with his mother, he had paused and tried to get her attention. But as before, she never looked his way. Charles still didn't understand why, and if he hadn't been so nervous, he would have been angry. But the warrior dragged him past her and, before he knew it, he was standing in front of his grandfather and Thora.

Thora took a step forward and knelt down in front of him as his grandfather glared at the warrior holding on to him, his fingers digging into Charles's shoulders, but Charles ignored the pain.

'That's what you look like without a bruise on your face.'

Charles smiled. There had barely been a day this summer when he wasn't bruised, but no one had smacked him recently, so all his bruises had healed. 'I thought you were dead.'

Thora rubbed his hair. 'It'll take more than a weakling like Ivor to kill me.'

'Where is Ivor?' Charles thought of the man who had kidnapped him. 'He gave me to Duke Liudolf.'

Thora nodded. 'We know. Ivor is dead. I killed him.'

Charles was glad Thora had killed Ivor, even though he knew it was a sin, but he didn't care as he frowned at his grandfather. For many weeks now, he wasn't sure how he would feel if he saw Sven again. His grandfather had lied to him and had decided to go fight a battle instead of staying in Ribe with him. But now, staring at the old man, his eyes more tired and the lines on his face deeper than before, he wanted nothing more than to get on his ship and sail away. The anger he saw in his grandfather's face, though, made him realise that was not going to happen. 'I have to stay, don't I?'

Thora nodded. 'But we'll come back for you, I promise.'

Just like my grandfather promised my father, Charles thought, but did not say.

'I'll let you talk to your grandfather,' Thora said and stood up.

Charles's mouth was dry as his grandfather limped towards him and winced as he knelt down. 'Charles.'

'Grandfather.' Charles's hands trembled, so he hid them behind his back.

They said nothing as they stared at each other in silence after that. Charles's hands still trembled while his grandfather's eyes looked over his shoulder at the people behind Charles, before they glanced at the birds flying above them.

'Did you know that my mother was still alive?' Charles asked.

His grandfather closed his eyes and took a deep breath. 'Aye. I found out after our first night in Ribe. From the Frank you had stabbed.'

Charles's eyes widened. He had believed that he had killed the man and had been consumed by the guilt of that. 'H... he was still alive? B... but you told me I killed him.'

Sven sighed and glanced at his feet. 'I did. I believed it would make you stronger, but I was wrong.' He looked at Charles again, his old eyes red with tears. 'I tried to make you be who I wanted you to be, instead of learning who you are.'

Charles's eyes widened at his grandfather's words, and then he frowned when he thought about it. Sven had wanted him to be stronger. Something Charles never believed he could be. Yet, over the last few weeks, he had survived everything God had thrown at him. He felt less fear than what he had before. But there was still one thing he needed to know. 'Why didn't you tell me about my mother?'

Again, Sven glared at the people standing behind Charles. 'Because I was afraid that if I told you, then you would want to go to her.' His grandfather's honesty caught Charles by surprise, as well as the pain he saw in the old man's eyes. 'For longer than I can remember, Charles, I was lost. All I wanted was to die, to end my existence on Midgard. But then you came along and gave me a reason to live again. When I found out your mother still lived, I was afraid of losing you again. So I kept that from you. Made you believe she was dead.' Charles felt the tears build up in his eyes and he tried to say something, but the words would not come to him. He did not know how to respond, so instead he remained silent. His grandfather put a heavy hand on his shoulder. 'Charles,

I hope that one day you can forgive me. I should have listened to you. I should have been a better grandfather instead of riding off to battle. I wanted to be a better grandfather than I was a father, and I failed in that. Just like I failed you.' Again, Sven glanced over Charles's shoulder. 'If you want to stay here with her, I will understand. I will take my men and leave you in peace. So you can be a Christian priest, just like you wanted.'

'No!' Charles's response surprised both of them and he had to look at his feet as his grandfather frowned at him. 'She doesn't love me. She doesn't even look at me.'

Sven sighed. 'Charles, she travelled to Ribe, into a land where people hate Christians, to find you. I don't know much about her, but I'm sure she wouldn't have done that if she didn't care for you.' Charles frowned at his grandfather. 'But she is the daughter of a king and you were born out of wedlock. The Christians don't like that, so as much as she wants to, she can never be a real mother to you.'

Charles nodded as if he understood, but he didn't. He looked at Thora, who had been more of a mother to him than his own, and then at the camp behind them where Rollo stood, leaning on his large axe as he watched them. He thought of going with them, but then remembered what life had been like in Ribe. His grandfather waited as Charles glanced over his shoulder at his mother. He wanted to get to know her and to spend time with her, even if his grandfather had told him he never would be able to. Charles took a deep breath and said, 'I don't know what I want.'

'You don't need to know what you want. Not yet anyway.'

Charles nodded again, but still didn't understand. He looked at his grandfather and tried to swallow back the tears. 'I guess I can't go with you.'

Sven shook his head. 'King Louis wants us to help his son take Aquitaine. If we do that, then he says he will let you come with us.'

'Where is Aquitaine?'

Sven shrugged. 'Somewhere in West Francia.'

'Do you believe him?'

Sven glanced over Charles's shoulder again. 'No.' He sighed and then looked at Charles, his eyes suddenly hard. 'Charles, you need to be very careful. As long as you are in East Francia, you are not safe. So be aware of those around you.'

'You don't think my mother will protect me?'

'I don't think she can, even if she wants to. But I swear on your father's memory that I will come for you, and if you want to, we can go far from here, far from anyone who wants to harm us.'

'That's long enough,' King Louis called out from behind Charles, whose heart raced at the sudden thought that this might be the last time he ever saw his grandfather again.

After glaring at King Louis, Sven took the large pendant from his neck and gave it to Charles. 'Take this, keep it safe and it will do the same for you.'

Charles looked at the large Mjöllnir in his trembling hands. It was the size of his thumb and made from ivory of the tusked seal from the north, although Charles had never seen these animals, and was beautifully carved with swirls and patterns. 'You gave this to my father.' The first time Charles had seen his grandfather's Mjöllnir was after his father had died. It had been in a pouch his father had told him to give to his grandfather, as was the Cross of Charlemagne.

'Aye, on this very beach.'

Charles gripped the Mjöllnir pendant in his hand and felt it dig into his palm before he took the small wooden cross from his neck and held it out for his grandfather. 'And this will keep you safe.'

Sven stared at the cross and smiled as he took it and hung it around his neck. 'May your god protect you, Charles, and keep you safe until I can come back for you.'

Charles stared at his grandfather and he struggled to stand up. 'And may your gods protect you, grandfather.' Sven nodded and stroked his hair, as a tear rolled down his cheek and into his beard, before the Frankish warrior dragged Charles back towards King Louis.

King Louis glanced at the sun, which was already making its descent. 'You have until sunset tomorrow to leave my kingdom. If you are still here after that or if your men attack any of the nearby towns or farms, then my cavalry will kill every one of you and your grandson will never become a man.' Charles noticed how King Louis didn't acknowledge him as his grandson and knew he would never be accepted in East Francia.

Sven's faced hardened as he bared his teeth at the king of East Francia. 'We'll do what you want, but if you harm my grandson, then I'll burn your kingdom to the ground.'

Charles shuddered at the anger he sensed in his grandfather's voice, but took comfort in his words. Because Charles knew they were true.

* * *

Sven stayed where he was and watched as Charles was taken back to the dunes.

'What of my son?' an old man standing behind King Louis asked, his lips trembling and his eyes pleading.

King Louis glanced at the old man and then at Sven. 'Return Lord Theodard's son to him, unharmed.'

Sven hawked and spat. 'We will return his son when we leave. That way, I can make sure we don't get attacked until then.'

'How do I know my son still lives?' Lord Theodard asked.

Sven raised his hand and waited as the young Frank was brought forward. Lord Theodard gasped at his son's bruised face, courtesy of some of Sven's men. 'He fell off his horse,' Sven said when he saw the raised eyebrow of King Louis, who then grunted.

'Make sure he doesn't fall off any more horses.' King Louis turned and walked away, his entourage following him. Lord Theodard looked at his son and then glared at Sven.

'If you harm my son...' The words ended there as Sven smiled at the old fool. He knew Lord Theodard couldn't do anything. He had already lost enough men against Sven's small force. 'Heathen bastard,' Lord Theodard muttered and then rushed after the king.

Hildegard stared at him for a few moments, her face unreadable, before she turned and followed her father to the dunes and beyond. Sven was beginning to wonder if he had made the right choice in letting her go that night in Ribe. He had hoped that King Louis had been a better man and would honour his word of the trade, but in the end, he was just like every other Christian Sven had ever met. Deceitful.

Only Duke Liudolf stayed on the dunes, and Sven guessed he was tasked with the duty of watching Sven and making sure he left. Sven glared at the duke for a short while before he turned and made his way back to his camp. He needed some ale to calm his rage, but knew that wouldn't happen, so instead he just clenched his fists and pictured beating King Louis to death in his mind.

'What happened?' Rollo asked when they walked past him.

'King Louis is using Charles to turn us into his mercenaries,' Thora said, and Rollo frowned. 'He wants us to raid West Francia to distract her king so that his son can take Aquitaine.'

'Where's Aquitaine?' one man asked.

Thora shrugged. 'Somewhere in West Francia.'

Sven stopped in front of his tent and closed his eyes as he took deep breaths, but that did not stop the anger from coursing through him. 'Fucking bastard!' He kicked his stool, which almost hit one of the warriors. Everyone stopped what they were doing and stared at him.

'Sven?' Thora put a hand on his shoulder.

Sven glared at her. 'He wants to use my grandson, just like he used my son against me.'

'So what do we do?' Alvar asked.

Sven took a deep breath and sighed. He looked for his stool so he could sit down, and then remembered he had just kicked it away. So he turned around and glared at the dunes where Duke Liudolf still stood with the Frankish cavalry. 'We go to West Francia and do what Danes do best. We raid, we burn and we plunder. And we pray to the gods that it is enough to get my grandson back.' The younger warriors in Sven's army smiled, and Sven couldn't blame them. For him, it was all about getting his grandson back. For them, it was following Sven the Boar and filling their war chests with plunder, as well as growing their own reputations. But Rollo and the older warriors all frowned.

'We don't have enough men to go raiding West Francia.'

Sven glanced at the giant warrior. 'I don't need men. I just need my Dane axe and my anger.' Even though some of the warriors cheered, Sven knew Rollo was right. He barely had twenty men with him, nowhere near enough to cause enough problems for the king of West Francia.

'I know where we can get more men,' Alvar said, and Sven raised an eyebrow at him. 'My cousin, Ebbe.'

'Thought he was dead,' one of the men said and a few grunted as they agreed.

Alvar shook his head. 'No, Ebbe still lives. I think.'

Some laughed at this as Thora asked, 'And how can Ebbe help us?'

'He sails with Jarl Halstein. Last I heard, they were raiding West Francia.'

Thora looked at Sven as Rollo nodded. 'Odin knows we need more men and someone who knows West Francia. Might be a good idea.'

Sven rubbed the faded raven tattoo on his scalp, feeling the few spots where he had cut himself as he thought about it. It had been many winters since he raided that part of Midgard and his memory only seemed to be good at remembering his failures. 'Where are they camped?'

Alvar smiled. 'Last I heard from a trader, they were camped somewhere along the Loire River.'

Sven frowned and then looked at the dunes again. 'Get everyone ready. We leave as soon as the tide comes in.'

'Sven, we have until tomorrow. Why leave in the middle of the night when the tide comes in? We don't know the waters,' Thora said.

'Because I'm leaving on my terms. Not his. And besides, I know these waters better than even the Franks.' Everyone around them nodded and smiled at Sven's words, apart from Thora who frowned. 'What?'

Thora glanced at the men around her who were all staring at her and, after a deep breath, said, 'Sven, do you really think we can trust that King Louis won't just kill Charles as soon as we leave?'

Sven scowled. He had the same fear eating away at him, but there was nothing else he could think of doing. 'I don't know, Thora. We can only pray to the gods that his mother will make sure that doesn't happen.'

'Do you really think she has that much influence over her father? Especially now.'

'Thora is right,' Rollo said and Sven sighed. 'Charles's mother might be an important woman, but her father is still the king. I doubt she would be able to stop him from killing Charles if that was what he wants to do.'

Sven looked at the small wooden cross Charles had given him. His grandson had told him that Torkel had made it. 'What other choice do we have? At least if we do this, then there is a chance of getting Charles back. If we stay here, then he definitely dies.'

'If you stay here, he dies,' Thora said. Sven raised an eyebrow at her, not sure what she meant by that. 'You have to go to West Francia and raid. But that doesn't mean that someone can't stay behind and follow them. The gods might even smile on that person and they can find a way to rescue Charles and bring him to you.'

Sven gaped at Thora, and so did those around them. He was sure he knew who that someone was, but he still asked the question. 'Who is that someone?'

'Me.'

'No,' Rollo said before Sven could even respond. 'It will be too dangerous. If they capture you, then you're dead.'

Thora smiled at Rollo. 'If they capture me. I'm a woman. In a dress, most of them won't even pay any attention to me. I might even get close enough to Charles to grab him and escape.'

'No,' Rollo said again and looked at Sven for support. 'Sven?'

But Sven did not respond. Instead, he stared at Thora as he played with the wooden cross in his fingers.

'Sven, let me do this,' Thora said. 'I failed to protect Charles from Ivor. It is my fault that he is in the hands of King Louis. Let me make amends to you and him.'

'We all failed him, Thora. Me more than most.' Sven looked at the cross in his hand again.

But Thora shook her head. 'No, you entrusted his safety to me and I let you down.'

Sven sighed and then looked at the sky, hoping that this time the gods would give him a sign, but apart from the seabirds in the sky, he saw nothing.

'I think she is right,' Alvar said, surprising everyone. 'We can't trust the Franks and of all of us, Thora is the best person to do this.'

'Aye,' Sven said. 'You are right, Alvar. And that is what concerns me.' He looked at Thora. 'But how are you planning on getting close to him? You don't speak the Frankish tongue.'

Thora shrugged. 'We still have Gerold. I'll take him with me.'

'No!' Rollo said again. 'That snake can't be trusted. We're better cutting off his head.'

'He owes me his life. I could have killed him, should have that night in Ribe. But I didn't. And besides, I can deal with him.'

Everyone fell silent as they stared at Sven, waiting for his decision. Sven rubbed his eyes as he longed for the days when he had no responsibilities. But those days had disappeared the day Charles had come into his life and Sven knew he needed to do what was right for the boy. 'Best wait until nightfall before you set off. They'll have people watching us. And Thora, if Gerold causes you any problems, then you kill him.'

Thora nodded. 'I won't let you down, Sven.'

'I know.'

'If Aunt Thora is staying, then so am I!' Jorlaug screamed as she ran towards her aunt from behind Sven's tent.

'Jorlaug, come back here!' her mother shouted, but Jorlaug ignored her as she stood beside Thora with her arms crossed and chin lifted. The men laughed as Sven frowned at the girl.

'No, Jorlaug, you must stay,' Thora knelt down and said to her niece.

Jorlaug's lips pouted at her. 'But, Aunt Thora, I want to help you.'

Thora smiled at her. 'You can help me by helping Sven protect your mother and grandmother.'

'But...' Jorlaug looked around her and then at Sven, who nodded at her. 'Fine.' She lowered her head and walked towards her mother, the men still laughing at her.

While Thora was convincing her niece to stay, Sven dug around in his war chest until he found what he was looking for. He took out the sax-knife, the one he had given to Charles, and stared at it as he remembered how Charles had hated the weapon. Sven had found it amongst the rubble of the burnt hall and had been surprised that it had not been damaged. He turned and handed it to Thora. 'Give this to Charles.'

Thora took the sax-knife and frowned at him. 'Are you sure that it is necessary?'

Sven wondered the same, but hoped that if Charles had the knife, then he might be able to protect himself if Thora wasn't there. 'Aye.'

Thora nodded, but her frown told Sven she did not agree with him. Sven, though, could only hope that he was doing the right thing.

'And what about the Frank?' Alvar pointed to Reinhold, who was looking at them, his eyes filled with fear.

Sven glanced at the setting sun and knew they didn't have long before the tide started coming in. 'Strip him of everything and leave him on the beach.' The men cheered and Reinhold screamed when some of the warriors grabbed him.

Frigg, mother of gods. Watch over my grandson and Thora. Make sure they come to no harm. Odin, lend me your strength so I can bring chaos to the Franks.

8

PARIS, WEST FRANCIA

Roul walked along the corridor towards the hall of King Charles, the king of West Francia. The spy had to resist the urge to clutch the large golden cross that was in a pouch under his cloak, but his fingers still remembered the feel of it as he had barely let it go since he had left Hedeby on a trader's ship more than a week ago. The trader was one of Roul's informants, a Dane who had kept him informed of what was happening in Denmark so that he could protect his king. The journey had taken longer than Roul would have liked because they had to sail around Denmark, avoiding raiders and bad weather. But God had been kind and neither of those had been a problem for them.

Along the way, Roul had learnt of the attack on Ribe, the town he had been in not that long ago and where he had stolen the cross from, and wondered what that meant. Was it retribution from God because they had dared to touch something as sacred as the Cross of Charlemagne? He didn't know and still struggled to make sense of what he had been told. Ivor Guttromson had allied with another jarl and had attacked the town. Roul knew Ivor wanted Sven the Boar dead for the death of his father, but he never believed he would attack the old bastard in his own town. Neither did he believe other jarls would support him after his father's failure to take the throne of Denmark. Roul had spent the entire journey home trying to make sense of that, and also trying to work out if the claimant to the Danish throne, a young man also named Horik, had anything to do with it. He had learnt that Horik had allied himself with Jarl Torgeir of Hedeby, and that Horik's chief adviser, Jarl Hovi, was Horik's brother-in-law. Roul had spent many sleepless nights trying to find a way to use that information to his advantage. And Roul needed every advantage he could find, because although he had the Cross of Charlemagne, he did not have the other thing his king had sent him to get. The illegitimate grandson of King Louis of East Francia. Roul had had the boy in his grasp, but he then had made the only mistake of his career as one of King Charles's top spies. He had trusted Ivor, a greedy Dane, to watch over the boy while he travelled to Ribe to retrieve the cross. He had been arrogant and believed that he could still control the Dane, even after telling him he would not support his attempt to become the king of Denmark. Unsurprisingly, Ivor had betrayed him and now the boy was most likely in the hands of King Louis. Roul had been unable to get confirmation of this and prayed that King Charles had not learnt of this. He also prayed that his luck would hold and he could convince King Charles that the boy had died in some unfortunate accident. Children died all the time, so it wasn't too unbelievable.

As Roul walked along the corridor, he sensed movement in the shadows, but kept his hand away from the knife he kept in his belt. He knew that no one would kill him in the hall of King Charles. But that did not stop the grimace on his face when he saw who stepped out of the shadows. Bero, the king's spymaster and Roul's superior. Bero was also the one who had killed the man who had taken Roul off the streets and taught him everything he knew. Like

Roul, Bero had a forgettable face and his hair was the same as everyone else's. The only difference between the two spies was that Bero had more lines on his face and more grey in his hair. But that did not fool Roul. He knew Bero was still as dangerous as always, more even because he knew Roul wanted to take his place as the king's spymaster.

'You finally return to us, Roul.' Bero glanced behind Roul. 'Alone, again.'

Roul gritted his teeth and then took a calming breath. 'And where are you sneaking off to, Bero? Off to fuck one of your dirty whores?'

'Like the one you have been paying to get information on me?' Bero smiled as Roul barely raised an eyebrow. 'Yes, I know about her. Have known for a while. I wonder what she's been telling you.'

Roul resisted the urge to plunge his knife in the rat's gut, only because he knew the king would have him executed for killing his spymaster in his hall. 'Enjoy your moment, Bero. I might stand here alone, but I do not come empty-handed.'

The smile never left Bero's face. 'So you say. Well, I hope that whatever you bring is enough to calm the king. It would be a pity for you to lose your head because you trusted the heathens.' Bero walked away before Roul could respond, and his mind raced as he tried to get the meaning of Bero's words. Did he know about Ivor, or was he talking about the Danish trader?

Roul's instinct told him to turn and to run. To get away from Paris and West Francia as fast as he could, but Roul forced himself to ignore the warning voices in his head. Bero was only bluffing. And even if he knew about Ivor's treachery, he did not know that Roul had the Cross of Charlemagne. No one knew that. So he took a deep breath and fixed his cloak, before he made his way to King Charles's hall.

After the usual formalities with the warriors who guarded

the entrance, the usual comments about him being a rat and taking his weapons from him, Roul found himself facing his king. The hall, made of wood but with its walls painted white and decorated with bright tapestries and the banners of King Charles, was filled with petitioners vying for the king's attention, so Roul had to wait. Through the large windows, he could tell it was only midday and hoped he would not have to wait for too long as he turned his attention back to his king. King Charles was thirty-one years old, but his face was already lined with stress and the constant pressure of being a king. But it was not just the usual pressure that was ageing King Charles early. It was the constant raids by the Danes and the Norse on his kingdom, the rebellions by those loyal to his nephew, Pepin, and now the threat of a war with his older brother, King Louis of East Francia.

King Charles looked up from what he was doing and his face darkened when he saw Roul, who realised that he should have listened to his instincts. The king signalled for everyone to leave his hall, which they promptly did as the warriors who guarded the king gave them no choice. Many of the people raised eyebrows at him as if they wondered why he was so important that they had to be chased out of the hall. Only the old bishop and Ignomer, the old warrior who never left the king's side, remained. There were even rumours that Ignomer stayed in the room as King Charles fucked his wife or one of his many mistresses.

'Roul, you finally return. We were worried that you got caught in the troubles in Denmark.' King Charles smiled at Roul, but there was no warmth in his voice.

'My lord king.' Roul bowed. 'Things were more complicated than expected in Denmark.'

'Nothing complicated about it,' Ignomer said, his voice gruff. 'Your plan failed. The man you had sent to Denmark is dead, his rebellion failed, and King Louis's son is still on his way to Aquitaine.'

Roul glared at the old warrior. 'Guttrom might have failed in his rebellion, but we still have what we need. And even the failed rebellion could benefit us.'

King Charles's eye lit up as he leaned forward on his throne while Ignomer frowned at Roul. 'You have the boy and the cross?' the king asked.

Roul sent a silent prayer to God that his plan worked before he responded. 'The boy is dead. He died as Guttrom's son tried to take him in Ribe.' Roul worried about the king's raised eyebrow as he delivered that news, but he continued with what he hoped would keep his head on his shoulders. 'And as for the cross.' Roul took the pouch from under his cloak and handed it to his king.

King Charles held the pouch in his hands, his eyes fixed on it as his breathing had stopped. It was almost like King Charles was too afraid to open the pouch and look inside. But eventually, he took a deep breath and opened it. Both the old bishop and Ignomer watched with wide eyes and bated breath as King Charles pulled out the large golden cross, its edges rimmed with different coloured gems. Roul watched with satisfaction as King Charles turned the cross over in his hands and studied it, but then he frowned as the king's brows furrowed.

'Bishop, hand me the manuscript from your library.'

The old bishop nodded and gave the king an old manuscript, while Roul's instincts were screaming at him to run. He stopped breathing as King Charles's eyes ran over the lines in the manuscript and then flicked to the cross and him. After a while, King Charles lowered the manuscript and stared at Roul, his face dark.

'Roul, where did you find this cross?'

Roul frowned, wondering what the king had seen in the

manuscript. 'I took it from a chest in the sleeping quarters of Sven the Boar. Barely made it out of the room when the bastard stumbled in.'

King Charles nodded, his eyes on the cross again, while he tapped the manuscript on his leg. 'And you say the boy is dead?'

'God knows I wish it wasn't so, my lord king.'

King Charles glanced at Ignomer and Roul sensed that something was wrong. In his mind, he ran over the events of the day when he had found the cross. His fight with Sven and the other warriors as they barged into the room. How he had hidden in an empty house and waited for dark before he slipped out of the town, not before killing the drunk who had told him where Sven's grandson had been staying. His heart raced in his chest and already his mind was trying to work out how to escape from the hall, but Roul fought to calm his nerves.

'I see,' King Charles said, and then threw the manuscript at Roul, who resisted the urge to flinch as the manuscript struck his chest. 'Read it!' the king demanded, and Roul picked up the manuscript with its frayed edges, his eyes skimming over the text until he came to a paragraph that described the Cross of Charlemagne. His heart raced even more when he realised that the cross he had just given to his king was not the right one. Again, his mind went over the events of that day, but there was nothing to tell him that Sven had fooled him. The old bastard had fought for the cross like his life depended on it. His mind spun as his vision blurred.

'My king, I...' Roul stammered, trying to make sense of what was going on. For the first time in a long time, he was lost for words. Roul had believed that the cross he had was the real cross. He had no reason not to believe that. He had found the cross in Sven's sleeping quarters, in a chest full of the boy's clothing. Sven had fought him for the cross. His warriors had spent the entire day searching for him.

'One more thing, Roul,' King Charles said to him, his knuckles white as he gripped the armrests of his chair. 'If the son of Hildegard is dead, then why did we hear about a small red-headed boy in the custody of the Duke of Saxony? A man we know is a close friend of my niece.'

The hall spun, and Roul had to fight not to collapse. He knew then he should have listened to his instincts before he entered the hall. He also knew that Bero meeting him outside the hall was no coincidence. The bastard had known about this and wanted to taunt him. Roul stared at King Charles, a man he had faithfully served his entire life. A man he had killed for and the man who was about to order his death. He dropped to his knees before the words could come out of King Charles's mouth. 'My king, please forgive me. I swear by God that I believed the cross was the real one.'

'And what about the boy?' the king asked, his voice filled with anger.

'I... I... had the boy, but was betrayed by the heathen Danes. They took the boy to your brother instead.'

'So, King Louis has the bastard son of his oldest daughter?' King Charles asked, his mouth almost frothing.

'God knows the boy is probably already dead,' Ignomer said, and the bishop scowled at him.

'Yes, I can't see my brother letting the illegitimate son of his daughter live. Especially not after all the trouble he caused.' King Charles glared at Roul. 'So, Roul. Where is the real cross? How do we know my brother doesn't also possess it?'

Roul opened his mouth to respond, but then realised he didn't know. He didn't know where the cross was or if King Louis of East Francia had it.

'I see,' King Charles said when Roul didn't respond. 'Then you are of no use to me any more. A pity, I had such high hopes for you, Roul.'

Roul's eyes widened when he saw Ignomer give a signal to the warriors who guarded the door behind him. But he could not let himself be captured. Bero would convince the king that he had important information and would use that excuse to torture him until the end of days. His mind still racing, Roul jumped to his feet, causing the old bishop to cry out in shock, and turned to face the warriors behind him. The warriors barely hesitated as they rushed at him. Roul dodged the first, pulling the hidden knife from his belt, and then stabbed the other under the arm as he tried to grab him.

'Kill him!' Ignomer roared, and the remaining warriors pulled their swords from their scabbards and came at Roul. Roul's eyes darted around the hall, trying to find a way out as one warrior stabbed at him. He twisted out of the way and just avoided the sword swing from the second warrior. Someone screamed behind him as he dropped to the floor before the first warrior who had attacked him could stab him in the back. Rolling to his feet, he dodged a fist aimed at his face and then found himself facing the entrance to the hall with the three remaining warriors behind him. Without a look back, he raced for the door, already plotting how he was going to get his revenge as King Charles shouted, 'Don't let him escape! Get back here, Roul!'

9

BREMEN

'You're going to get us both killed!' Gerold complained as they stared at the large house where King Louis and Hildegard were staying. The house was guarded by the king's elite warriors and even the nearby streets were filled with armed men, glaring at anyone who went near the house. Thora tried to ignore Gerold as she fidgeted in her dress, which was too small for her, and wondered if Charles was also in the house. She had brought none of her dresses with her as she had come to Francia to fight and had to take one from one of the other women who had travelled with them from Ribe. But her shoulders were broader than the other women and so even the largest dress they had was still too small for her. Before she had left, Thora had given Charlemagne's cross to Sven, who hesitated as if he was afraid of the cross before he took it, but they both knew she could not keep it with her while she followed Charles. If she was caught and the Franks found the cross, then Charles would almost certainly be killed. Thora also didn't feel comfortable keeping the cross with her while she travelled with Gerold. All he would need was to get a glimpse of it, and her life would be over.

Thora had never been in a Frankish town before, but was amazed at how similar it was to both Hedeby and Ribe. The houses were different, though. The ones in Bremen had holes in the walls and were all painted white, whereas the houses in Denmark had no windows and only a hole in the roof to let the smoke from the hearth fire out and to let fresh air in. Thora preferred the houses in Francia, even if they were too close together. She imagined they smelt a lot fresher and had more natural light unlike the houses she had lived in. The people were similar to what she was used to, apart from the fact that she didn't see any women trading or running a business. But she knew that, unlike in Denmark, where women could trade and run businesses, Christian women couldn't. The women she saw here were either chasing after their children or preparing meals and spinning yarn. Their dresses were also different to hers, which caused some people to stare at her, although she knew that would happen. The dresses the women wore in Bremen looked more like long tunics with a belt around the waist, unlike the strap dress she wore over a smock. Some women also had their heads covered, which Thora had found strange, but knew it had something to do with their faith. She also doubted that Frankish women carried swords wrapped up in clothes to hide them and had a sax-knife hidden under their dresses. Everything else was the same. The stale stink of too many people living close together and the constant noise that made her ears ring, especially after spending some time on a ship in the stillness of the seas. Unfortunately, the noise was not enough to drown out Gerold's whining.

Her eyes stung from tiredness as she had not slept for two days, not trusting Gerold to kill her or run away, even though he had promised he would help her get to Charles in exchange for his freedom. But the fact that he had only done that with Rollo's knife at his throat made it hard for her to really trust him. It was late in the day when they reached the town, and neither Thora nor Gerold believed that King Louis would leave that day, because the day after was the day that all Christians went to their churches. But that suited her because Thora hoped she could then get close to Charles, and perhaps even free him. Then all she had to do was find a way to get to West Francia and to this Loire River she had never heard of. Thora resisted the urge to rub the Mjöllnir hidden under her dress as she prayed to Frigg. Thor was the god most prayed to for protection, and Thora hoped that the thunder god was watching over Charles, but she also felt that she needed the motherly protection from Frigg. And not just that, Frigg was also the goddess of magic, and Thora was sure they'd need a lot of that to pull this off.

'Where do you think he's going when he leaves Bremen?' Thora asked as she watched the warriors around the house.

'How in God's name should I know?' Gerold responded, his face dark and his arms crossed. Thora clenched her fists as she tried to resist the urge to stick her knife in his throat. She was already regretting bringing Gerold with her, but she knew she had no other option. Thora did not speak the Frankish tongue, apart from a few words she had learnt in Hedeby, and a Danish woman travelling on her own would draw too much attention. 'He could be going anywhere in East Francia. It's a large kingdom.'

Thora had stopped listening to him when she spotted Hildegard leaving the house. She remembered the look on Hildegard's face when her father spoke to Sven and knew that Charles's mother was not pleased about using her son as leverage to get Sven to raid West Francia. But there was something else Thora had seen in Hildegard's eyes. Something she thought she could use, especially as Thora wasn't sure how long Gerold would help her. Her heart raced when she made a decision that she could only hope was the right one and turned to Gerold, who was glaring at

Hildegard. 'We need to talk to her,' she said, and followed Hildegard without waiting for a response from Gerold.

'You're going to get us both killed,' he growled behind her, but
then followed anyway.

They followed Hildegard towards the church, and Thora
knew she shouldn't be surprised that Charles's mother went
there.

'You can't go in there!' Gerold hissed behind her.

'Why not?' Thora knew what the spy was going to say, but
asked anyway.

'Because that is a house of God and you are a heathen.'

Thora shrugged, even as she resisted the urge to grip the
Mjöllnir pendant around her neck. 'I've been in the church in
Hedeby many times and nothing happened to me.' She paused as
Hildegard went to the altar and, while Charles's mother stood
there, Thora glanced around the stone building, which only had a
few people inside. It was much larger than the church in Hedeby,
and Thora raised her eyebrows as she scrutinised the stone
columns supporting the roof and the many benches. Pictures
showing people who Thora guessed were important to the Christians were painted on the walls and she frowned when she saw
women with wings hovering over a woman holding a child. Thora
knew they were not Valkyries, but was still surprised at how much
they looked like Odin's women warriors who decided which of the
dead went to Valhalla.

A noise from the front of the church drew Thora's attention,
and she saw Gerold sneaking towards Hildegard and wondered
about the way he clenched his fists. 'Bastard,' she muttered as she
thought the young Frank was trying to escape and she rushed to
catch up with him.

Hildegard turned just as Thora grabbed Gerold's shoulder and
her hand went to her mouth as her eyes widened at them. But

then she dropped her hand and straightened her back as she glared at them.

'What are you doing here?' Hildegard said in the Danish tongue. 'Do you want to get Charles killed?'

Thora glanced around the church and saw that no one was paying any attention to them. The one priest who had been there had disappeared and the other people were too busy finding other things to be interested in. 'I am here to make sure your father doesn't do that.'

Hildegard's eyes widened. 'You are putting my son in more danger by being here, especially if you are going to attack people in a church.'

Thora raised an eyebrow when Hildegard did not deny that her father might decide to have Charles killed. But then, she was sure it would not be the first or the last time a king killed a child to protect his throne. 'I'm not attacking anyone.'

'Then why are you sneaking up on me?' Hildegard looked at Gerold, her brow furrowed as her shoulders seemed to tense. 'Gerold, I am glad to see that you still live. I feared for you that night in Ribe.'

Gerold's jaw muscles clenched and then his eyes went to the large cross hanging on the wall behind the altar. 'God ensured I lived, my lady.'

Hildegard's hand went to the cross around her neck and Thora thought she saw regret in her eyes before she blinked it away and looked at her. 'Why are you here? You risk my son's life.'

'That is exactly why I am here. Sven doesn't trust your father and Odin knows neither do I.'

Gerold hissed at her using the All-Father's name in the church, but Thora did not care.

Hildegard glanced at Gerold as she fidgeted with the cross around her neck. 'Gerold, wait here.' Gerold looked like he was about to argue with Hildegard, but then he nodded as she took Thora's arm and led her to where they could not be seen from the door.

'You don't seem pleased to see Gerold,' Thora said, and couldn't blame Charles's mother.

Hildegard sighed. 'Because, and God forgive me for saying this, I'm not. I've come to realise he is not what I thought he would be. Even I wonder if I can really trust him. And you are right. I also fear that my father might decide Charles is too much of a threat and there is nothing I can do to help him if that happens.'

'I thought you have influence over your father.'

'I did, but after what has happened, my father doesn't trust me any more. I am as much of a prisoner as Charles is. The only difference is my father cannot lock me away like he has my son. But he can stop me from returning to my abbey.' Hildegard stared at Thora, and Thora frowned at the look in her eyes. 'So you came to kidnap my son?'

'Kidnap?' Thora felt the spark of anger in her gut. 'I am here to make sure Charles grows to be a man and if it means rescuing him and taking him to Denmark, then that is what I will do.'

'I will not let you take my son away from me.' Hildegard glared at Thora, who wondered if she had shown the same anger to her father when he had taken Charles from her.

'Charles is not safe in Francia. Even you must see that.' Thora sighed. 'By the gods, I am not here to fight with you. We both want to protect Charles, and I thought we could help each other.'

Hildegard seemed to study her before her eyes went to where Gerold stood glaring at them. 'You are right. We must put our differences to one side for Charles. I'll keep your presence a secret. If my father finds out that one of Sven's warriors is here, then only God knows what he will do. And in return, you can watch over

Charles for me. And if the time comes when he is in danger, then you can...'

Hildegard could not say the words, but she didn't need to. Thora knew what she meant, so she nodded. 'I'll need new clothes. This dress is dirty and draws too much attention. And a way to get close to him.'

Hildegard raised an eyebrow at Thora. 'I didn't think you wore dresses. Only trousers and leather jerkins.'

Thora smiled. 'Sometimes trousers and armour have their place and other times dresses have theirs.'

Hildegard nodded. 'I'll see what I can do.'

Thora glanced at Gerold. 'I'll keep him with me for now.'

Again, Hildegard nodded, but Thora noticed she was gripping the golden cross around her neck. 'Thora, be careful. For your sake and my son's.'

Thora looked at the cross behind her. 'Don't worry. I'll make sure nothing happens to Charles. Even if I have to kill your father to keep him safe.'

10

FRANKFURT, A FEW WEEKS LATER

Charles pushed the Bible away, his frustration making it hard for him to read the words on the page. The candle on the table fluttered, casting strange shadows on the walls of the room they were in. Charles's new prison. But he had to admit that this one was better than the servant's room he had stayed in in Bremen. The room was larger and had a proper bed with a thick straw mattress and a table with a chair. There was a small crucifix on the table, which Charles hated looking at, and a Bible which Father Leofdag made him read every day. The chamber pot was cleaned out every day and, along with the small window, the room smelt better than the last one he had been kept in. Charles was also given better food than what he had been fed in Bremen, although he had to sit at the table in the mess with the other priests and listen to their boring conversations. Charles would rather have stayed in his room, but at least he was allowed to leave this room, if only to eat and to visit the lavatory, always accompanied by Father Leofdag, though. But despite all that, this was the last place Charles wanted to be. Before his father had been killed, Charles had dreamt of living in a monastery with a large church and reading the Bible every day, but now it all felt like a lie to him.

'Charles?' Father Leofdag glanced at him. 'We haven't finished reading the page yet.'

Charles glared at the priest who had been with him all the way from Denmark. 'Why can't I see her?' It had been three weeks since they had met his grandfather on the beach in Saxony, and Charles had not seen his mother since. He knew she was in Frankfurt. Father Leofdag had told him that, but still she had not come to see him and every time he had asked about her, Father Leofdag had given him the same response.

'You know it's not possible, Charles.' That same response again and Charles was getting angry at always being told that.

'Why not?' He slammed his fist on the table. 'Why is it not possible?'

Father Leofdag raised an eyebrow at his outburst. 'I really think you should stop wearing that heathen symbol around your neck. You're starting to behave like them.'

Charles glared at Father Leofdag as he gripped the Mjöllnir his grandfather had given him on the beach. His throat tightened when he remembered what his grandfather had said to him and stared at the Bible. It was not new, its leather cover was scuffed, and the pages looked like they had been touched by too many hands. Charles had spent his life wanting to have a mother, just like all the other children he had known, but now, even though she was still alive, he still did not feel like he had one. 'My grandfather said she could never be a real mother to me, even if she wanted to.'

Father Leofdag frowned. 'I sometimes forget how wise your grandfather can be.'

'Because you think all heathens are dumb,' Charles said

without thinking, startling Father Leofdag, who blinked rapidly as he struggled to come up with a response.

'You are right, Charles. Perhaps I let my religion get in the way of how I see the Danes. And perhaps your grandfather is right about Abbess Hildegard.'

'But why? Why can't she be my mother? Why can't I live with her and not in this room?' Charles crossed his arms as he puffed his cheeks out.

Father Leofdag glanced around the room with a raised eyebrow, as if he believed someone was listening to them. 'Because of who your mother is, Charles. An abbess of the church cannot have children, you know that. And besides, she feels you are safer here.'

Charles felt himself getting angry again, even though this was not the first time he and Father Leofdag had had this conversation. His grandfather had warned him that he was not safe in East Francia, so had his father before he had died, but Charles struggled to understand why. He was the grandson of the king of East Francia. Why would he be in danger? Charles then thought about the Cross of Charlemagne and frowned. He had no idea where the cross was and guessed that his grandfather had it, even though Father Leofdag had told him he had heard it had been found in West Francia. Many of the traders who travelled between the kingdoms were talking about it and Father Leofdag had overheard them. Charles refused to believe that it was true. His grandfather and Thora would not let anyone take the cross from them. He was sure of that. 'I don't believe you. She is still angry at me and doesn't want to see me.'

'She is not angry at you, Charles.'

'She is, because I told King Louis that my grandfather has the cross.'

Father Leofdag sighed, which only annoyed Charles even

more. 'I really wish you would stop toying with that thing around your neck. I don't understand why you have to wear it.'

Charles looked at his hand and was surprised to see the Mjöllnir was in his fingers again. He had not realised he was rubbing it again. 'My grandfather gave it to me on the beach.'

'I understand, but I don't understand why you have to wear it.'

Charles shrugged. He did not want to tell Father Leofdag that wearing it made him feel safe, because he knew the priest would only dismiss that. And most likely would make him read even more of the Bible. That was all he had done since they had arrived in Frankfurt a few days ago and Charles was fed up with staring at the book that just felt like empty promises.

Father Leofdag moved the Bible so that it was in front of him again. 'Now come, it's almost time for the evening meal and you need to finish the book of Galatians before that.'

Charles sighed. 'Why do I have to read the Bible?'

'Your mother wants you to. She believes it is good for you.'

'How does she know what is good for me if we don't get to see each other?' Father Leofdag did not respond, and Charles fingered the Mjöllnir around his neck again as he thought about his grandfather and Thora. 'Where do you think they are now?'

'Who?' Father Leofdag asked.

'My grandfather and Thora.' Charles stared at his grandfather's Mjöllnir.

Father Leofdag shrugged. 'I don't know. I imagine they must be in West Francia by now, but I have not heard anything.'

'Do you know where the Loire Valley is?'

'I do. I grew up near there.'

Charles's eyes widened as he stared at Father Leofdag. He remembered then that the priest had told him he was from West Francia before he had travelled to Hedeby to preach there. 'Do you still have family there?'

Father Leofdag shrugged again. 'I don't know. I was the youngest and my parents were already quite old when I was born. That was why I was sent to the church. I have not heard anything about my family for a very long time.'

Charles nodded and looked at the Bible, but could not get himself to read the words. 'My grandfather thinks that I'm in danger. He thinks that King Louis might hurt me.'

Father Leofdag said nothing at first, but he rubbed his chin as he stared at Charles. Just when Charles thought he would not respond to that, the priest said, 'God knows I wish it wasn't true, but your grandfather is most likely right.'

'But why?'

'Because you also have the blood of Charlemagne running through your veins. Not only are you a threat to the king and his sons, but you are also an embarrassment to him.'

'An embarrassment?' Charles frowned and remembered what King Louis had said to him before, about how his father had hurt him more than Sven had ever done.

'Your mother is the daughter of the king, Charles. She is not meant to have children out of wedlock.'

Charles scratched his head. 'But then why couldn't my mother and father marry each other?'

Father Leofdag smiled, but not the condescending smile Charles usually got from adults. 'Because the daughters of kings do not marry simple warriors, Charles.'

'But my father was not a simple warrior. He was the son of a jarl.'

'Yes, and I think that is another reason they would not have been allowed to marry each other. Because he was the son of a man feared and hated by the Franks.'

Charles looked at the Bible again as he chewed on his cheek. He still struggled to make sense of any of it, just like he still struggled to understand why his father was killed because of the Cross of Charlemagne and why his grandfather had to attack and kill more innocent people just to keep him safe, or even how that was going to keep him safe. Charles wished he could pray because that had comforted him in the past. But every time he closed his eyes and struggled to find the words, he wondered if God was even listening to him. It felt like He had not done so for many weeks now and Charles still didn't know what he had done to upset the Almighty. He looked at the Mjöllnir around his neck and wondered if he should try to pray to Odin, but then he didn't know how to do that. Thora had told him that the Danes worshipped their gods in a different way to the Christians and Charles was afraid of angering the one-eyed god of the Danes by getting it wrong. With a sigh, Charles took the Bible and forced himself to read the words on the pages, hoping that his grandfather and Thora would come back soon or that his mother would visit so he could get the answers to the many questions he still had.

The church bells rang as the people of Frankfurt made their way to the church. The morning air was crisp and even Charles could tell that summer was ending and that the leaves on the trees would change colour and fall from the branches. Charles had never liked autumn or winter. Not because of the weather, although he always seemed to feel the cold more than others. His father had once told him it was because he was so thin and that once he built the muscles that warriors did, then the cold wouldn't bother him any more. But Charles doubted that he ever would have the thick limbs and broad shoulders of his father. Charles didn't like the autumn or winter because those seasons had made it harder for him to hide in the trees. Charles had always been a good climber and had often hidden from his bullies in the trees that grew behind the church in Hügelburg. But in the winter, the leaves were gone and Charles knew the boys would see him, no matter how high he climbed.

'Come, Charles, we mustn't be late.' Father Leofdag guided Charles to their place in the church, the excitement on his face almost annoying Charles. Earlier that morning, the young priest had come into Charles's room and had told him he had convinced the bishop to allow Charles to attend service that morning. No one knew who Charles really was. As far as they were concerned, he was the grandson of Sven the Boar and hostage of King Louis, just like his father had been. Because of that, most of the priests and servants in the church ignored him. Some even made a point of avoiding him as if he would infect them with heathen magic. But Charles was a Christian, or at least he still thought he was, and he had learnt there was no such thing as heathen magic. Even his grandfather's uncle, the heathen priest, was just a man who liked to trick and scare people. That was what his grandfather had told him, although that didn't explain how the godi knew so much about the cross by just sniffing it. That night in the clearing under the raven tree still haunted Charles as he slept, although he realised it didn't frighten him so much any more. Or perhaps he was too tired to care about the tree and the ravens.

Charles had also been warned not to tell anyone who his mother was, not that anyone would believe him, anyway. Father Leofdag seemed to believe that if Charles got to attend service again, then he might find his way back to the light of God and had told the bishop that it was their duty to help Charles. Charles didn't think it would do anything and, if he was honest, he was not looking forward to the service. He had loved listening to the sermons in the past, but now it all seemed like empty words and false promises. But Charles still felt nervous as they entered the church. His eyes were scanning every person he walked past and every corner of the stone building, hoping that he would get a glimpse of his mother. He didn't know if she would be here and didn't want to ask Father Leofdag because he didn't want to be told that she wouldn't be. He knew Duke Liudolf wouldn't be in the church, because he had been told that the duke had gone back to Ehresburg to deal with other matters. Although Father Leofdag had told him he had really left to avoid the king, who was still angry at him. Charles knew he should have felt guilty, because most of that anger was because he had told King Louis about the cross. But the duke had lied to Charles and had convinced the king to trade him for his mother. So Charles didn't care about whether or not Duke Liudolf was in trouble with King Louis. All he wanted was to see his mother and to talk to her. But as he searched the church, his heart dropped as he saw no sign of her and was beginning to think that she might not be there. Crestfallen, Charles lowered his head and followed Father Leofdag to their place.

As they found their places, Charles felt someone grip his shoulder. At first he thought it was Father Leofdag, but then he realised the priest had hold of his other shoulder, and this second grip was firmer. He turned around to see who it was and gasped when he saw a familiar face smiling at him. Thora. Charles was about to say her name when she put her finger to her lips and, with his heart racing, all Charles could do was nod.

'Charles, pay attention,' Father Leofdag said as the bishop started his service, but Charles was not listening to any of the words that came out of the old man's mouth. Not that he could hear them anyway over the beating of his heart. Thora was here. She was standing behind him. He did not know how that was possible or why she even was here, but she was. As the service went on, he felt Thora tuck something into the back of his trousers, and then she gave him one more squeeze of the shoulder before he felt people move behind him. Charles turned and frowned when he saw an old lady scowling at him.

'What are you looking at?'

'Forgive me,' Charles said and turned forward again. He scratched his head and wondered if he had really seen Thora, or if that was only his imagination. The Danes believed that one of their gods, Loki, liked to play tricks on people and would often make them see things that weren't real. But surely Loki could not affect him here, in a church in Frankfurt. But Charles was certain that he had seen Thora. And then he remembered the object she had put into the back of his trousers. His hand went to his back and he almost cried out in surprise when he felt the handle of a knife. Father Leofdag frowned at Charles, who smiled back, but his heart was racing so fast, Charles was sure the priest could see it beating in his chest. He felt for the knife handle again, just to make sure that was what he had really felt, and when his fingers gripped the familiar handle he knew Thora had been here. Just like he knew what knife that was without needing to see it. It was the sax-knife his grandfather had given him in the forest near Hedeby after they were attacked by a group of warriors. Charles felt his hands tremble as he wondered why Thora had given that to him. He had never wanted the knife and had done his best not to touch it while he had been in Ribe, but now Thora had given it to him and Charles was sure his grandfather had told her to. And then Charles realised he was not upset that Thora had given him the knife. Because it meant that she was really in Frankfurt. His guardian angel was there and Charles knew that no matter what danger everyone insisted he was in, no one would harm him.

Charles smiled at the large crucifix which hung on the wall behind the priest. Not while Thora was there.

11

Thora snuck out of the church while the service was still ongoing, keeping her head low so that she didn't stand out. Something which was easier said than done as Frankish women did not walk like they knew how to kill with sword and spear. Her hands trembled and she could only pray that she had done the right thing. Thora knew Charles hated the knife, but that was before everything had gone wrong and he ended up in Francia. And besides, even before that, she had sensed a change in him. Like he was starting to realise that he would never be a Christian priest, not with the blood of Sven running in his veins. Charles's attack on Rollo's son only proved that even more. The boy was destined to be a warrior, just like his father and his grandfather and their fathers before them. The Norns had already decided that for Charles, whether he accepted it or not.

It had taken them over seven days to reach Frankfurt, and Thora had been stunned by the town built on top of a hill beside a large river. She had always believed that Hedeby was a large town, but it seemed small compared to the many streets of Frankfurt. The town's immense walls seemed taller than Hedeby's and she couldn't help but wonder how many would have to die before they realised they could not take this town. And once through the gates, she had become disorientated by the many people and the noise which was almost deafening, especially after so many days with only birds and rustling leaves to listen to. The houses in Frankfurt were the same as in Bremen, but there were more than Thora had ever thought could fit into a town and she wondered how many people lived behind the town's walls. The smell of so many people almost suffocated her when she had first arrived and she barely had to walk twenty paces before she found a church, some bigger than others. Some, like the one behind her, were made of stone, but many were small wooden churches.

Her first morning in Frankfurt, Thora had thought her heart was going to stop when the church bells rang in the morning, the noise making the walls of her room tremble. Or perhaps that was just her imagination. Hildegard had found her a Frankish dress which fit her better than the dress she had before, although Thora did not know how she had managed that, so she looked less like a Dane and more like a Frankish woman. Thora also had to wear a veil over her hair, something she was not used to, and she found it bothered her more than wearing a helmet. But Christian women did not walk around with their hair uncovered and so she had to do the same to blend in. After that, all Thora had to do was join the many other people who followed the king's column as it slowly made its way south to Frankfurt. Gerold had not been happy about having to stay with her, but Thora thought it might be best. Hildegard had not seemed pleased to see him again and Thora still needed him to translate. But as soon as they had reached Frankfurt, Thora had let him go back to his mistress. It was harder to get through the days and not kill the bastard because of his dark mood and constant insults.

Satisfied that she was not going to see Charles for the rest of the day, Thora returned to the tavern where Hildegard had got her a room near the monastery where they were keeping Charles. She did not like the way the tavern owner looked at her, his eyes filled with suspicion every time she walked past him, but so far Frankish warriors had not barged into her room in the middle of the night. Thora wondered about the young priest who was always by Charles's side as she made her way to the tavern. She couldn't understand why he would stay with Charles all the way from Denmark, and wondered what part he played in all of this. Was he here to protect Charles or to help keep him prisoner? Thora decided that the next time she saw Hildegard, she would ask her about Leofdag. But she didn't know when that would be. She had not seen Hildegard since their meeting in Bremen and had used Gerold to communicate with her as they had travelled to Frankfurt. And this worried her even more as she remembered what Hildegard had told her in Bremen. Was she too locked up in a room somewhere? Thora resisted the urge to rub the Mjöllnir around her neck, especially as it felt like someone was watching her.

Thor, protect me from whatever danger lies ahead, but more importantly, protect Charles. He is in more danger than he really knows.

* * *

Gerold gritted his teeth as he hid in the shadows and watched the heathen bitch return to her room. His heart raced as he pictured piercing her heart with his knife, and it angered him even more that he had failed to do it that night in Ribe. She had beaten him as if he was a young boy and had made the humiliation even worse when she had to remind him of that in front of all the other heathen bastards, especially that fat pig, Sven. He swore to God that one day he would kill them all. But not yet.

As they had sailed to Denmark, Gerold had realised that the only way he would survive and be free again was to play by their rules. So he kept his mouth shut and his eyes diverted. For now, he would do what they asked. He would play the obedient servant, and when the moment came, he would plunge his knife in her chest. And not just hers, he thought as he remembered how he had been left behind in Ribe while the good Abbess Hildegard fled. A growl escaped from his throat. Her time would come as well, but not until he found a way to use it to his advantage.

Gerold had had enough of being a servant to others. It was time he did what he needed to earn his freedom, once and for all. And it would be so much sweeter if Charles and his heathen family died for that to happen.

12

LOIRE VALLEY, WEST FRANCIA

Sven dragged the whetstone along the edge of his Dane axe as he studied the large camp on an island in the middle of the Loire River. That was where they had found Alvar's cousin, Ebbe, and the jarl he sailed with. Halstein. It had surprised Sven at how easy it had been to find their camp. They had sailed for many days around the coast of Francia, attacking small settlements along the way for food and fresh drinking water, and whatever valuables the men could find for themselves. Sven had even found a half-empty barrel of Frankish ale, but that had not lasted long. It was during one of these raids that Sven had learnt the whereabouts of the Loire River. Once they reached the river, it had taken them another day to find the large island with Halstein's camp. The gods had been with them on the journey, even as they passed a large city along the river, its stone walls looming over them, but no one had tried to stop them. The worst they had to deal with was rain and bad winds as they passed the sea between Francia and Britain, a large island Sven had raided in his youth, but his men dealt with the bad weather and Rollo steered the ship through the worst of it.

The camp took up half of the island and was large enough to hold more than a thousand men. Sven had been impressed when he saw the wooden walls that surrounded the camp, as well as the large ditch they had dug in front of the wall. Inside the camp was like every other he had ever been in. Tents were set up wherever they could find space for them and the sun was almost hidden from the smoke from the hundreds of campfires as warriors cooked their own meals or stayed warm during chilly nights. The stench in the camp wasn't as bad as others he had been to, and Sven guessed it was because of the river. The Loire River was wide and provided another source of protection for those in the camp and fresh water for the Danes to bathe in. Wharves had been built for the hundreds of ships docked around the island, and it had taken Sven a while to find a place for his ship when they had arrived. What surprised Sven most, though, was the number of families he saw in the camp. It was not uncommon for wives to travel with their husbands. In fact, a few of his warriors had brought their families with, but he still hadn't expected to see so many women and children here. That, and the smithy that had been set up in the camp as well, told Sven that this camp had been here for several summers. It also told him that Halstein knew what he was doing.

Sven had never heard of the man, but many of his warriors had. Rollo had told him that Halstein had been raiding the West Frankish coast for many seasons and that his name was widely known back in Denmark. Even so, Sven had never heard of him and wondered if they spoke Halstein's name with the same fear as they had his.

Halstein had heard of Sven though, and, like most, was surprised when he learnt Sven was still alive. Rollo had told Halstein that Odin didn't want Sven in Valhalla any more as he was causing too many problems and so had sent him back to Midgard. Sven could only shake his head, as many of the younger warriors had stared at him with wide eyes. He doubted the older ones believed it, but it didn't matter though, because Halstein had welcomed Sven like a brother and the men had cheered and feasted.

'How many warriors do you think they have?' Rollo asked, sitting near Sven and doing nothing. They had been there for a few days already, and Sven had barely left his tent. When he had been a younger jarl, he would have been salivating at the chance of joining this force, but he was old now and his body struggled with sleeping in his tent. Every morning there was a new ache competing with the older ones, and then there was his old wound on his left leg, which did not agree with the climate here, so his limp was more obvious.

'Must be thousands,' one man said and those around them nodded as Rollo moved closer to Sven.

'So what is the plan?'

Sven ran his thumb over the boar head engraved on the head of his Dane axe. 'We need to convince Halstein to increase his attacks. If the gods smile on us, then that should distract King Charles enough so that Louis's son can take Aquitaine.'

'Aye, but we have to be careful,' Rollo said, his voice low so the other warriors couldn't hear him. 'If Halstein finds out why we are really here, then we are in trouble. Doesn't matter if the gods smile on us then. I doubt he would want to work for the king of East Francia.'

Sven raised an eyebrow at this. 'Halstein won't care about that. At most, he might ask for some of whatever payment he believes we are getting. Like Guttrom and Ivor, these men have been taking payments from the Frankish kings for a long time to attack each other. I wouldn't be surprised that the real reason Halstein is here is because one of the other Frankish kings paid him to be here.' Sven felt his heart race as he mentioned Guttrom and his son. When they were both younger, he and Guttrom had taken part in large raids like this, both here in Francia and in Britain. Sven had believed they were friends once, but then Guttrom had betrayed him. All so that he could get his hands on Charles and the Cross of Charlemagne. He glanced at the fresh scars on his knuckles from beating Guttrom to death and wondered if he would meet the bastard in Valhalla. If he did, then Odin would most likely kick him out because Sven would spend the rest of his days until Ragnarök ripping Guttrom apart for that betrayal. Ivor he doubted he would see in Odin's hall of the slain. They had made sure he would never reach Valhalla after Thora had killed him.

'So how do we convince Halstein to do that? His men are still licking their wounds after that defeat.' Rollo scratched his head. Halstein had attacked a town up the river, but somehow the town's forces, led by a priest, or a bishop as they called the senior ones, pushed his men back. That had happened a few days before Sven had arrived and many of the men were still bitter about it.

'We could use that to our advantage.' Sven glanced around him as his warriors were lounging nearby with nothing to do.

'How?' Rollo asked.

'His men will be angry that an army led by a Christian priest defeated them.' Sven thought of the Cross of Charlemagne, which was in the pouch hidden under his tunic. It was not comfortable because the cross was bigger than his hand, but Sven could think of no other place to hide the cross. 'Odin knows I would be. So we use that.'

Rollo nodded, his brows furrowed as he considered Sven's words. 'We can get our men to move around, talk about the attack and anger Halstein's men more. Maybe get them talking about revenge. If his men are already talking about it, and we know Halstein would already be feeling the same, then it would be easy enough to do. We don't even need Loki's talent for deceit to pull this off.'

'But we still need to be careful,' Sven said as he lowered his axe and glared at the group approaching them. In the middle of the group was an old warrior who Sven had not seen for a long time until he had spotted him at the feast that Halstein had thrown for him when he had arrived. Apart from the formal greeting, they had avoided each other, but now the old bastard had decided to irritate him even more.

Sven's warriors stopped what they were doing and watched as the old warrior stood in front of Sven with a cold smile in his grey beard. 'Sven the Boar. By Thor, we must be desperate if we accept you and your' – he raised an eyebrow – 'army.'

Sven bristled and sensed his warriors' anger. They might not have been many, but they had fought many battles over the summer and had proven themselves worthy of Odin's Einherjar. 'Gudrod Haraldsson.' Sven spat the name out. 'With you leading this army, it's no wonder you were beaten by a Christian priest. Hodr would have done a better job of it.'

This time it was Gudrod's time to bristle as Sven's warriors laughed. Hodr was one of the gods of Asgard and he was blind. 'Your father fought for Horik, against my father.' Gudrod's eyes bored into Sven, who glared back at him.

'He did. He also sent your father back to his masters with his tail between his legs.'

Gudrod's mouth twitched, and Sven found some comfort in that. It had been a long time since he had seen the son of Harald Klak, Denmark's former king, who had fought against old Horik when Sven had still been a boy, and he had never liked the bastard. 'I heard you killed your father and your brothers.' There was some muttering from the men, but Sven ignored it. The story of how he had become jarl of Ribe was well known to those old enough. So was the story of his demise only a few winters after. Although, there was one part of that story that only he and Thora knew, and Sven was determined that it stayed that way.

'Aye, I split his skull with my axe and took his town, but that's old news.'

'As old as the gods themselves,' someone said, to the amusement of others. Sven scowled at the warriors surrounding them, trying to find the one who had spoken, but then decided it wasn't important. He was old, there was no hiding from that. So he turned his attention back to Gudrod.

The two men glared at each other before Gudrod nodded. 'Despite our past disagreements, I welcome you to our camp, Sven the Boar. A warrior of your renown will only bring more fear to these Christian cowards.'

Sven said nothing as he struggled to his feet, his face grimacing at the pain in his leg, and took Gudrod's arm in a warrior grip. Gudrod smiled and then left without saying another word.

'Who is he?' one warrior asked.

'And why doesn't he like you?' Rollo added.

Sven sighed as he remembered the days of his youth. 'That bastard is the son of the old king Harald.'

'The one who had shared the throne with Horik, but then fought against him?'

'Aye.'

'And your father fought against him as well?'

'My father and the old King Horik were close friends. Wherever Horik went, my father went as well. It was one of the many things we disagreed on.'

'Will he be a problem?' Rollo asked.

Sven watched Gudrod disappear amongst the many men in the camp and then glanced at the clouds in the sky. It looked like it might rain soon, or at least that was what the pain in his leg was telling him. 'No, Gudrod has lived too long to let the choices of our fathers affect his decisions.'

Rollo shrugged when Alvar arrived with a big grin on his face.

'Where have you been?' Sven asked, even though he knew.

'I've been talking to my cousin, Ebbe.'

'And what's with the grin?' Rollo asked. 'You look like a boy who has stolen his father's mead.'

The comment only made Alvar grin even more. 'Ebbe told me they are going out on a raid tomorrow to get over the defeat at Orléans.' Orléans was the town where Halstein had been defeated, although Sven still did not know where it was, only that it was further upriver.

'And?' Rollo asked but glanced at Sven, no doubt thinking about what they had spoken about not so long ago.

'He invited us to join them.'

'The men could do with a good raid,' Rollo agreed.

Again Sven glanced at the sky. Rollo was right. He was under no illusion that they joined him because they wanted to help him rescue Charles. They wanted to build their reputations and believed that sailing with Sven the Boar would do that for them. But to do that, they needed to raid and fight. His hand went to the Mjöllnir around his neck, but then he found the small wooden cross that Charles had given him. It felt strange wearing it, and that night when he had hung it around his neck, Sven couldn't help but close his eyes as if he expected the Christian god to punish him, either that or Thor would send a flash of lightning to send him to Hel. But none of that happened and Sven had almost forgotten he was wearing it. He wondered where Charles was, whether he was still in Bremen or if he had been taken somewhere else. He also wondered if Hildegard was taking good care of him, but then doubted she would be able to go near him. For King Louis, Charles was a threat, even if the boy was only nine winters old. He was a weapon that could be used against the king of East Francia, but as long as Sven proved to be useful to King Louis, then Charles would be safe. Or so Sven hoped. He then wondered if Thora had been able to get close to Charles, or had Gerold slit her throat in her sleep? When she had first suggested the idea, he had thought it was a good one, but now he was not sure any more. Thora didn't know East Francia or the language, and Gerold couldn't be trusted. She should have killed him when Sven had told her to. But then Sven dismissed that thought. There was no way that Gerold would get the upper hand on Thora. She was one of the best warriors he knew and one of the smartest people. If anyone could find a way to rescue Charles, then it was Thora. Not him. Sven was only good at fighting in shield walls and slaughtering his enemies. Again, he prayed to Frigg and Thor, asking the mother goddess and her adopted son to protect his grandson, before he turned his attention back to those around him. 'Where are they raiding?'

Alvar shrugged. 'A small town near the river. They say there is a church.'

Sven nodded at this. 'Good. Tell your cousin we will join them.' The warriors of Ribe cheered at this as he turned to Rollo. 'Make sure they all know to cause as much chaos as possible. We need to make sure that King Charles knows I'm here.'

'Do you think that's a good idea?' the giant warrior asked.

Sven glanced at his axe again, seeing how the sun glinted off the metal. 'By now, they will know that we still have the real cross. If King Charles finds out we are here, then he will send men after us so he can get his hands on the cross.' Sven thought of the cross again. He was determined not to let it out of his sight, not after what had happened in Ribe. If anyone wanted to take the Cross of Charlemagne from him, then they'd have to kill him first.

'Remember, make as much noise as you can and make sure these Franks know that it's Sven the Boar who is attacking this town,' Sven said to his men as they approached the small town. The church bell was still quiet, but Sven knew it would not be for long. But that didn't concern him. He needed people to know about this attack. He needed word of it to get back to King Charles, and then to King Louis because he was sure the king of East Francia had eyes and ears in the court of King Charles. Sven was leading this attack, the first time he had led a raid since he had lost his son, but Halstein had lent Sven some of his men. Ebbe, Alvar's cousin, was in charge of those men and they would attack the town from the other side. Alvar was with them, with the instructions to make sure they screamed Sven's name as they attacked.

The town wasn't as close to the river as Alvar had led them to believe, but that didn't matter. They had set off as soon as the sun broke the horizon and it was close to midday when Ebbe had signalled for them to beach the ships. The walk wasn't too long and it had given Sven time to get used to the weight of his Dane axe again. He knew there would be no shield walls, so decided the axe would be better, although he still had his sword with him for when the weight of the Dane axe got too much for him.

Sven had decided not to wear a helmet because he wanted the faded raven tattoo to be seen, both by the Franks and the gods. His beard was braided and he had added finger rings to the tip of the braid and wore three arm rings on each arm while his brynja shone brightly in the dim sunlight. He looked like what he had once been. A warlord who struck fear into the hearts of Christians

all over Midgard. But despite that, he still could not get excited
about this attack. Not like his warriors were. All around him, all he
saw were brynjas glinting in the sun and broad smiles. These
young warriors had come to make a name for themselves and they
knew that this attack would be the start of that. But Sven had no
desire to attack people who were just trying to make a living in this
harsh place. It was not that he had gone soft. Sven would not hesi-
tate to slaughter his enemies, but right now he did not see these
Franks as his enemies. His enemies were in East Francia and the
thought he was attacking this town to please them burnt his stomach. With a sigh, he patted the bulge in his brynja, feeling the
weight of Charlemagne's cross against his stomach, and then
nodded to the warrior beside him. The man lifted the horn to his
lips and blew one long blast.

'For Odin! For Sven the Boar!' Rollo, dressed in his finest war
gear, roared as he punched his Dane axe into the air. Less than
twenty warriors stood behind Sven, but they made enough noise
for a hundred men as they attacked the town. Sven heard the
replying horn on the other side and knew that Halstein's men had
started their attack as well. Before long, the bell from the church
tower was ringing, and Sven knew that the townspeople would be
running towards the church for safety. But it would not save them.
They may not have been his enemies, but most of them would still
die this day because of their king and his feud with his brother. *For
Charles*, Sven thought and rushed after his men as fast as his
ageing legs could take him.

By the time he reached the town, the fighting had already
started. The dead littered the ground and Sven wasn't surprised to
see some Frankish warriors amongst them. The Danes and Norse
had been raiding this valley for many summers, so those who
could would have employed warriors to protect their town.

Perhaps that was why this town had been spared the worst of the raiding so far.

Sven gritted his teeth as he gripped his Dane axe in both hands. He stomped towards the fighting and swung his axe into the back of a Frankish warrior fighting one of his men. The Frank arched backwards and his cry died as Sven's man stabbed him in the throat. Sven twisted out of the way of a sword stab and buried his Dane axe in his attacker's stomach. The Frank's leather jerkin offered no resistance and as Sven pulled his axe free, the Frank dropped to the ground, clutching his stomach as his blood and internal organs leaked through his fingers.

'I am Sven the Boar! Fight me!' Sven roared, his battle lust taking over him. He beat his chest with his fist as he screamed out his war cry, but the Franks did not want to take him on. Not when they already had to deal with Rollo cleaving his way through their ranks. Sven watched as the giant warrior used his Dane axe with one hand as if the weapon weighed nothing, and thought about how he reminded him of his father. A man who had been one of Sven's closest friends.

'Die, you heathen pig!' Sven turned and saw the young man stabbing a pitchfork at him, which he batted out of the way with the haft of his Dane axe.

'You think you can kill me, boy?' Sven smiled at the young Frank's shocked expression when he spoke in the Frankish tongue and then opened his arms wide. 'Come on, boy. Kill me. Kill me!' The pitchfork wavered as the young Frank, brave only moments ago, took a step back. 'Kill me!'

The young man hesitated, but then he rushed at Sven. Sven grabbed the pitchfork with one hand and then punched the Frank in the chest with the head of his Dane axe. The Frank fell back, clutching his chest, his face grimacing in pain, as Sven dropped the pitchfork and glared at the man who looked like he had barely seen seventeen summers.

'You really think you can kill me? You, a farmer, kill me when even my own gods cannot?' The young Frank paled as Sven spoke to him. 'Do you know where to find your king?' The boy frowned and then nodded. 'Run to your king, boy. Tell him Sven the Boar has come to punish him for his sins.'

13

Sven's warriors returned to the camp in good spirits, even though there wasn't much plunder to be had in the town they had attacked. The church, aware of the threat of the raiders, had sent most of their treasures away. Those rich enough had fled a long time ago and others must have buried anything of value they owned.

Not that any of that really mattered to Sven. He was not there to make himself rich, so the few trinkets he took from the dead Franks were enough for him. And besides, most of that he had already given to those who had done well during the attack. Young Erik, barely into his beard and on his first raid, had killed a man twice his size, and Sven had given him the gold belt buckle he took from what looked like a wealthy dead man. And then there was Torleif who had killed three men with a pitchfork in his leg.

But what had really made his men, and those of Halstein who had joined them, happy was that they had filled both ships with captives. Women, children and young men who would be sold in markets to the east, although the wealthy ones would be ransomed back to their families. That was where the Danes made most of their money on the raids. Sven knew there was a large market in the kingdoms to the east, lands filled with more sand than water, for young slaves from Francia. Even better if they could read and write. That was another reason priests were always taken, although Sven could never understand why anyone would pay for the miserable bastards who only ever preached about their god and the sins of man.

'We're not going to draw King Charles's eye away from Aquitaine if we only attack small towns.' Rollo stood beside Sven, his Dane axe resting on his shoulder. 'I find it hard to understand why they haven't raided that town before.'

Sven hawked and spat as he watched his men unload their ship of the captives. 'Because apart from the people, there is nothing of value in that town. Halstein's camp has been here for two summers already, so they would have prepared for an attack.'

'Aye, but I still don't understand it.' Rollo eyed up a pretty woman they had captured and Sven could see the hunger in the giant man's eyes. But Rollo had to be careful. Both his wife and son were in the camp, and Sven doubted she would be happy if Rollo was fucking other women. But then, none of that was Sven's concern.

'We never attacked that town because for the last two summers they paid us not to,' Ebbe, Alvar's cousin, said from behind them. Sven scowled at the man, who wasn't as tall as Alvar, but still had broad shoulders and a thick neck. 'But now, they decided they didn't want to pay us any more. Claimed they had nothing left to give us.'

Sven grunted. 'They might have been right. There wasn't much to take from them. You saw yourself.'

'Aye, but Odin knows, we had to make sure they weren't lying to us.'

Ebbe laughed and was about to walk away when Rollo asked,

'What are Halstein and Gudrod's plans? Just keep harassing the local people until there is nothing left to take?'

Ebbe shrugged. 'Only they and the Norns know what their plans are. I just go where they tell me to.'

Sven smiled when he heard Charles's voice in his head. *That means you don't know.* That was what Charles would say when Sven gave him a similar response, and the boy was usually right. It was easier to say the gods had the answers than to admit you did not know. But just like Charles would get frustrated when Sven gave him that response, so Sven was frustrated with Ebbe's response. Sven needed to make sure that word of his presence in West Francia spread far and wide, and that would not happen if he just attacked small villages and farms. Charles would be dead before the winter snows fell. 'Then it's time I have a proper talk with Halstein. Two summers here and he has nothing to show for it. Just a failed attack on some city.' Sven walked towards Halstein's tent and did not see the glare on Ebbe's face. But he did not care about that. He needed Halstein's men to be angry so he could convince Halstein to attack that city again. Or at least attack other places in revenge. That's what Sven would have done if he had been beaten by a priest. He would have burnt every church and monastery he came across. No Christian priest would have been spared, not even to be sold as a thrall. And that was what Sven needed to get Halstein to do. Sven wanted King Charles to have nightmares about what he was doing to the Franks.

Sven ignored Halstein's men as they tried to stop him from entering the tent. He had not even bothered cleaning himself up from the raid and smiled at the grimace on Halstein's face, as well as the other jarls in there, when he stopped in front of him. Gudrod was also there with a cup of ale in his hand, and after a moment's silence, offered Sven one. Sven savoured the taste of the ale as it got rid of his dry throat before he sat on one of Halstein's chairs to take the weight off his tired legs and aching back.

'The raid went well, then?' Halstein had an amused smile on his face.

'Aye.' Sven drank more from his cup. 'A handful of fighting men and farmers. All for barely enough plunder to feed my men.'

'Heard you brought plenty of captives back,' Gudrod said.

Sven nodded. 'Needed to find some way of making that raid worth the while.'

'And the town?' Halstein raised an eyebrow at Sven.

'Burnt to the ground.' Sven smiled when he saw the shocked faces of the men in the tent. There was never any point in destroying towns. You raided them, gave them some time to recover and then raided them again. Towns were resources where they could get more captives to sell and more gold and silver to plunder. So they had to be managed like farmers would manage their fields. But Sven was not here to be a farmer.

'By Odin, was that necessary?' one of the other men in the tent asked. A jarl from Norway with thick black hair and a long beard.

Sven shrugged. 'The gods want chaos, and that's what I'm giving them.'

'Aye, but that will anger the king of West Francia. The last thing we need is for him to bring his army down here.' Halstein shook his head.

Sven stared at Halstein as he finished his ale. He understood the man's concern. Halstein could not afford a pitched battle against the West Franks and he had found himself a comfortable place to camp. On a large island in the river that could only be reached by boat. It meant that they did not have to worry about attacks from the local people. 'You do not need to worry about the king of West Francia. He has other problems to worry about.'

'Other problems?' one of the jarls in the tent asked while

Halstein stared at Sven. But Sven was sure he already knew what he was talking about.

'The son of King Louis of East Francia is marching an army towards Aquitaine.'

'Why, in Thor's name, would he be doing that? Does King Louis want to start a war with King Charles?'

Sven shrugged. 'Not my concern. But I'm sure the last thing King Charles wants is for Aquitaine to go to his brother.'

'Well, King Charles has more to worry about than the son of King Louis when it comes to Aquitaine,' Halstein said, his smile suggesting he knew more than Sven. 'The nephew of King Charles, the man who claims to be the real king of Aquitaine, escaped from his prison and is raising an army. I doubt he would be happy about giving his kingdom to another of Emperor Louis's sons.'

Sven glanced at Rollo, who had followed him into the tent, his heart racing as he wondered what this news meant for him and Charles. King Louis wanted Sven to help his son gain the throne from King Charles. Would the fact that it might fall into the hands of this nephew be a problem, or would King Louis be happy that his brother no longer had control of Aquitaine? Somehow Sven doubted that and was about to rub the Mjöllnir around his neck as he thought about it when he remembered the small wooden cross he wore. Instead, he rested his hand on his chest. 'So you see? The gods have made sure King Charles has too many other problems to deal with than to worry about what we are doing. It means we can do what we want. What the gods want us to do to the men whose faith means to destroy ours. We can bring the bastard to his knees and make him bleed.' Sven wasn't sure which of the two Frankish kings he was talking about any more. But the truth was that he wanted both of them to suffer. King Louis for taking his son and now his grandson and King Charles for paying others to kill him and take his grandson. He felt the weight of Charle-magne's cross under his brynja, almost like it was burning him through the pouch it was in. But Sven ignored it. If he could, he would have killed the bastard that had made the cross himself.

'Why are you so eager to burn West Francia?' Gudrod asked. 'It almost feels like this is personal.'

'Aye,' another jarl said. 'I am also wondering what really brought Sven the Boar all the way here.'

Sven glanced at Rollo, thinking he might have gone too far, but then Halstein said, 'Have none of you heard?' He smiled at Sven, which made him frown as he wondered what the bastard was going to say. 'King Charles had paid Guttrom and his son to kill Sven and kidnap his grandson, or so they say anyway.'

'Was that how Guttrom could afford to raise an army to take the crown from his uncle?' someone asked.

'Aye, and he got Sven to join him, knowing how much Sven hated the old king Horik,' Rollo said.

'Why, if he was supposed to kill you?' Gudrod scowled at Sven.

'Because the bastard got greedy and hoped I would die in the battle so he could give Ribe to his son.'

'But Guttrom is dead and here Sven sits, drinking my ale.' Halstein smiled.

'Without his grandson,' another added, which caused some murmurs amongst the men in the tent.

Rollo took a step forward before Sven could say anything. 'Because Guttrom's son succeeded where his father had failed. He grabbed Sven's grandson while we fought against the old king. That is another reason we are here. We believe King Charles has the boy and we want to break him so that he has no choice but to give Sven his grandson back.'

Sven was glad about Rollo's quick thinking, because he did not know what to say to that. And he had to admit, it would make it easier for what he had to do next. 'So while you all sit here and lick your wounds after being beaten by a priest, I plan to burn this kingdom to the ground and get my grandson back.'

The smile fell from Halstein's face. 'Easy for you to say. You weren't there, Sven.'

'No, but Týr knows, I wouldn't be sitting here doing nothing either. I'd be out there, making the Franks wish they never resisted.'

'We've not been sitting here licking our wounds. We've been planning our revenge. Come next summer and the people of Orléans will wish they never fought back and that bastard priest will be crucified just like his god!' Halstein clenched his fists and Sven knew he had to choose his next words carefully. He needed Halstein and his men to do what he wanted. His small crew wasn't enough to draw King Charles's attention away from Aquitaine.

'Why wait until next summer? There is still time for more raiding before the winter snow comes.'

'Aye, and by waiting, you give the Franks time to prepare as well,' Rollo added.

Halstein raised an eyebrow at Sven while rubbing the spear pendant around his neck. Not all Danes wore Mjöllnirs. Some wore a spear, to symbolise their connection with the All-Father. The spear represented Gungnir, Odin's spear which he used in battle against the giants. Sven wondered if it brought Halstein more luck than the raven tattoo Sven had on his scalp. 'So what do you suggest we do, Sven the Boar?'

* * *

Roul walked towards the monastery at Soissons and took deep breaths to calm his anger. It had not been easy for him to escape King Charles's hall, but luckily, he knew the building and the city better than most. He was born and raised on the streets of Paris and knew of many places to hide, which came in handy after he fled the hall with King Charles's angry screams echoing behind him. The king he had loyally served for most of his life was calling for his head, and the thought of it made his stomach burn. As Roul had hidden from the king's warriors, he had sought a way to get his revenge against those who had ruined everything for him. Sven and Bero were going to die. He had already decided that, even if he didn't know how he was going to do it yet, but Roul knew he would never get close enough to the king to kill him. So he had come up with another way of getting back at the king who had discarded him like a broken horse. Even after everything he had done for King Charles and West Francia.

That was why Roul was approaching the monastery not far from Paris. Because tucked away in this holy building was the one man who could hurt King Charles more than anyone else. Prince Pepin of Aquitaine. Although Roul knew Pepin thought of himself as the king of Aquitaine. That was the reason he had been fighting King Charles for many years and was doing well until a few years ago, when he had trusted the wrong people and got himself captured and sent to this monastery. Pepin was King Charles's nephew, although they were close in age, and his father had been king of Aquitaine until he had rebelled against the Emperor Louis. As punishment, the emperor had taken the kingdom away from Pepin's father and had made King Charles her king. But Pepin and the nobles of Aquitaine had never accepted that and Roul knew that, even to this day, there were men who still supported Pepin. A few of them hid in the forest not far from the monastery, waiting for Roul to do what he had come to do. And that was to free Pepin so he could continue his fight against King Charles. Roul knew it would make King Charles look weak, and losing Aquitaine would be a tremendous blow to the king of West Francia, who already had more problems than he could deal with.

Roul hunched his back and affected the look of an exhausted messenger as he approached one monk in the church. 'Excuse me, father. But I have a message for the abbot from the king.'

The monk blinked at him in surprise. 'A message?'

Roul nodded and removed the letter with King Charles's seal from his pouch. King Charles had not written the letter, and neither had he put his seal on it. Roul had done both. He had forged a copy of King Charles's seal a long time ago, and it had been useful to him in the past. But never as useful as it was now. Roul almost smiled when he imagined the confusion on King Charles's face when he found out that he had ordered the release of Prince Pepin.

Roul followed the monk who led him to the abbot, an old man who looked annoyed at being disturbed, but Roul did not care. He bowed respectfully as he handed the letter to the abbot and then waited as the man opened it and scowled as he read the contents.

'Are you sure about this?' The abbot looked at him and Roul frowned.

'Sure about what, abbot?'

'The king really wants me to do this?'

Again, Roul frowned. 'Forgive me, abbot, but I don't know what you are talking about. I only deliver the messages. I know better than to read them.'

The abbot nodded and then looked at the monk. 'Give the messenger some food and ale and then go to Prince Pepin's room.'

'Prince Pepin's room?' the monk asked.

'Yes. It appears the king has pardoned our guest and that he is free to return to Aquitaine.'

14

'So what's so important about this place that we had to row upriver for days just to attack it?' Alvar asked as he stood with Sven and Rollo at the prow of their ship as they rowed upriver. Sven glanced over his shoulder, seeing that those nearby leaned forward so they, too, could hear the answer. This was the first time in many winters that Sven had seen his ship this full of warriors, but most were not his own. Ebbe had asked to sail with them and he had brought enough men with him to fill the rowing benches. Roughly forty men, not including the three of them at the prow and Ebbe by the tiller because he knew the river better than them. Although, Sven could have just followed Halstein, whose ship was just ahead of his. The river was wide enough so three warships could sail side by side, but there was no wind so the men had to row. That meant they travelled in a line, Halstein's ship at the front and more ships behind Sven. Ten ships in total and over five hundred warriors. Men and women from Denmark and Norway, their weapons sharp and their eyes fierce. Despite his reasons for being in West Francia, Sven felt the stirring of excitement in the pit of his stomach as his ship effortlessly travelled upriver. It reminded him of his youth and he realised that part of him still missed those days when he had set out to make his name.

'Angers, it's called,' Rollo answered while Sven reminisced about his youth. 'According to Halstein, the town sits between two major rivers, this one and another and is very important for trade in this area.'

Alvar nodded. 'So we attack this Angers and we hurt King Charles enough, so he has to come and deal with us.'

'That's the plan,' Sven said and glanced at the clouds in the sky. But not to check the weather. 'And if the gods are with us, we succeed and move on.'

'Move on?' Alvar raised an eyebrow at Sven.

'There's another town just like Angers further up the river,' Rollo said, unable to keep the smile from his face. 'We mean to attack that town as well. Cripple this area and send the people scurrying to their king for help.'

'But why not attack Orléans? Is that not the town that defeated Halstein?' Alvar asked and many of the men around them nodded in agreement.

'Because Orléans is further upriver and to get there, we need to row past these towns anyway, so we might as well attack them as well. More plunder and captives, that way,' Rollo said and then glanced at Sven. 'More problems for King Charles as well.'

Sven rubbed the small wooden cross around his neck and prayed that that would be enough to protect his grandson. It had taken a lot to convince Halstein and the other jarls of this raid. Many of them feared the retribution of King Charles, but that was exactly what Sven wanted. Although, he could not tell them that, so in the end he had to promise most of the plunder to the other jarls. His men had not been happy about that, but if these towns were as rich as Sven been told, then he was sure there would be more than enough for everyone. Enough even to please Fáfnir, the legendary dragon which guarded a hoard of gold in a cave somewhere. Sven only wished he knew how Charles was and whether Thora had found a way to rescue him yet. He also wondered where the son of King Louis was. Was the bastard already in Aquitaine, or was he still wasting time somewhere?

'That's why so many other jarls joined us?' Alvar said, looking over his shoulder at the ships behind them.

'Aye, and that is where the gods will learn the names of the warriors of Ribe!' Rollo punched his fist into the air and the warriors in his ship all roared their approval, even those who weren't from Ribe.

'And what happens when King Charles sends his army to stop us?' Alvar asked, but had the sense to lower his voice so no one else could hear them.

Again, Sven glanced at the clouds as he rubbed the raven tattoo on his scalp. 'Then we pray to the gods that we survive the battle and that it is enough to save my grandson.'

They all fell silent as Ebbe turned the ship and the men grunted as they rowed into the river Maine. Sven had learnt the names of the rivers and towns when he and Halstein had come up with the plan for the raid. It had taken them three days to get everything ready. Enough food and ale had to be gathered to last the men a few days, as there was no guarantee they could find food along the way. Weapons were cleaned and sharpened and armour repaired. Sven's own brynja gleamed in the sunlight and he was sure it was bright enough to blind Odin's remaining eye if the All-Father glanced his way. His sword had been sharpened, but he left his Dane axe back at the camp. Angers was a large and important town, which meant there would be warriors defending her gates and walls. And Sven did not have the strength of his youth to use the Dane axe and a shield at the same time, not like Rollo and Alvar could. So his sword would do the killing.

Before they had left the camp, Halstein had sacrificed ten captives to the gods so they would bless this raid and, as the captives' blood flowed down the river, Sven had made a silent prayer to Frigg, asking her to watch over his grandson. It seemed the gods had accepted the sacrifices as the weather had been good and they had seen no resistance along the river as they journeyed towards Angers. Even at night, when they camped on the river-banks, there were no attacks or accidents. It made Sven think of another sacrifice, the one his uncle, the godi who lived in the forest near Ribe, had made in his name. The old Christian priest he had slain in front of the hall in Ribe. Sven wondered if that sacrifice still had any power left in it, or if Odin had decided that the fact he had survived the attack on Ribe that night was payment enough.

Church bells rang as the town walls came into view, and Sven felt his heart racing in anticipation. He gripped the Mjöllnir around his neck and prayed that he would survive this. He was an old man, but he wanted to watch his grandson grow into a man.

'They know we're coming!' Ebbe shouted from the stern, the joy obvious in his voice.

'Warriors of Ribe! Prepare for battle!' Rollo punched his Dane axe into the air. 'Wake the gods with your voices! Feed Odin's ravens with your steel!' The men roared, but still they rowed. Sven shook his head at all the different things Rollo could think of saying before a battle. Most of it made no sense, but it got the warriors ready.

Sven scrutinised Angers and saw the fort sitting on top of a hill. High walls protected the town, but he still saw the church tower sticking out above them. His hand went to where he kept Charlemagne's cross and he wondered if the Christian god would bring him down using the cross, but then he shook the thought from his mind. The Christian god had no power over his gods, and

Sven was protected by Odin. He glanced at the fort again, which sat on one side of the river while the town was built on the other. That was his and Halstein's target, while the other jarls would take the fort. Sven had thought it was a waste of time and men because the fort would be too difficult to take, while the town had no fortifications and many churches, but many of the other jarls were young and wanted to prove themselves to the gods. Already Sven could see the towers as their bells rang. There was a bridge that crossed the river and Sven smiled at the townspeople flocking across the bridge towards safety. That suited the Danes, as it meant it would be harder for the warriors in the fort to come across the bridge and fight them. Although Sven doubted they would do that. The Danes outnumbered them, so most likely they would stay in the fort along with the townspeople.

Ahead of them, Halstein's ship veered towards the town and Sven saw Halstein signalling for Sven's ship to join him. Sven glanced over his shoulder and saw that Ebbe was turning the ship to follow Halstein. Sven freed his sword from its scabbard just before the ship hit the riverbank. His heart was beating hard and Sven could only pray it would not stop. He was at an age where he wasn't sure how long his heart could go on for, but the battle rage it sent coursing through him made him feel his youth again. It reminded him of the days when his beard was red and not grey, and his arms were strong.

'For Odin!' Sven roared and jumped over the side of the ship as soon as she stopped. Luckily for him, he did not have to drop far as he doubted his old knees could handle that, but he stayed on his feet and stormed the town with his two giant warriors on either side of him and the warriors of Ribe behind him. Sven wanted to laugh. He wanted to scream out his name so the gods would hear him. This was what Sven had enjoyed most in his youth. This was how he had made his name. A name that had sent shivers of fear down the spine of his enemies, whether they were Christian or Dane.

'For Odin! For Sven the Boar!' Rollo cried out beside him, his Dane axe ready to steal the life of any who dared to attack Sven. Halstein's men ran up one street and already Sven could hear screaming over the sounds of the church bells. Sven knew Halstein was going towards one of the churches, just like Sven was leading his men towards another.

'For God! Kill the heathens!' Sven heard and saw Frankish warriors streaming out of one of the streets. He realised he was smiling as the first man swung his axe at him and Sven lifted his shield to block the blow. But before Sven could stab his attacker, Rollo swung his axe and almost took the man's arm off. As the Frankish warrior fell to the ground, screaming and spraying blood everywhere, Sven stabbed him in the chest and stepped over his dead body. Another Frank stabbed at Sven with his sword, but Sven stepped to the side and, after deflecting his sword away, he sliced the man's leg open before Alvar killed him. The attack didn't last long as the rest of the Frankish warriors realised they could not stop the Danes, so they turned and fled.

'Run, you cowards! Run from Sven the Boar!' Sven beat the back of his shield with the hilt of his sword. 'Run from Sven the Boar!' he repeated, because he needed the message to be spread across the Frankish kingdoms. That Sven the Boar was in West Francia and that no town was safe from him.

'To the church!' Rollo ordered, and the men cheered as they ran towards the stone building up the road. The bells had fallen silent now and Sven guessed the priests had realised no one was coming to save them, so they had fled instead. But Sven did not join his men as they plundered the church. He did not need to see the chaos they caused in the house of the Christian god. Instead, he turned and studied the fort. Warriors stood on the wall. He could see their spears wavering as they watched the town they were supposed to be protecting burn.

Four of the ships had docked on that side of the river and Gudrod was leading his men as they captured those who could not make it into the fort. More people for the markets in the east, although Sven was sure many of the women would be used first by the Danes, and many would not make it to those markets. He shook his head in disgust and felt his hands tremble when he remembered he had once been like that. He had taken women for himself and had used them to fulfil his lust. But now he could not bear the thought of it, and he knew it had nothing to do with his age. It was all because of Charles. The very reason Sven had to ruin the lives of these people. All so he could protect the life of one boy.

Lost in his thoughts, Sven did not notice the two men as they snuck up behind him. And if one of them hadn't kicked a stone, Sven would not have lived to see his grandson again. But as soon as the stone clattered along the road, his instincts kicked in and Sven turned faster than the men had expected. He lifted his shield and blocked the spear of one of the men, before the other rushed at him with a rusty sword.

'Die, heathen!'

Sven gritted his teeth as he stepped back onto his weaker leg and felt it protest. He batted the rusted sword away and punched the man in the chest with the rim of his shield. As his attacker staggered back, his companion took advantage of Sven being distracted and stabbed at his exposed side with his spear. Sven sensed the attack and turned, but not fast enough as the point of the spear broke through a few links and snagged his tunic. He didn't waste time trying to figure out if the spear had cut him as he dropped his shield and grabbed the haft, keeping it in place as the bastard holding it tried to pull it free. Wide eyes stared at Sven and then glanced at something behind him. Sven turned and saw more Danes filling the streets, some kicking doors in and rushing inside houses. Screams filled the air and Sven could only shake his head as he saw the panic on the face of the Frank.

'You should have run when you saw us coming,' Sven said in Frankish, before he broke the handle of the spear and killed the Frank. He turned to the second Frank, who was on his knees and struggling to breathe. The man lifted his hand, as if begging Sven not to kill him, before Sven stabbed him through the neck. Sven sighed as he pulled the spear point out of his brynja, but was glad not to see any blood on it. A few links in his brynja were broken and Sven was sure his tunic was ripped, but that was nothing compared to the destruction being caused to the town. The energy he had felt before was gone now and again Sven felt his age. But even more, he felt his anger at King Louis for using his grandson against him like this.

But the warriors of Ribe cared little about how Sven felt. They ran into houses and took what they wanted, before setting the houses ablaze. All of them had been there when the Franks sent by King Louis burnt the hall in Ribe and endangered their families. And now the West Franks were paying the price for that.

'If this doesn't get King Charles's attention, then I'm not sure what will.' Rollo joined Sven. He glanced at the two men Sven had killed and raised an eyebrow, but said nothing about it as Sven shrugged. Sven noticed the bag in Rollo's hands and knew the man had found himself some plunder. But he could not blame Rollo, that was one of the reasons they were there.

'Aye, even the gods of Asgard would have taken notice of this. But we are not done yet. We need to move on. Let's go find Halstein while the men have their fun.'

Rollo nodded. 'What about the fort?'

Sven glanced at the fort across the river as the other jarls led their men to its gates. 'Let them die trying to take it. There is enough in this town to make everyone happy.'

'But not you.' Rollo raised an eyebrow at Sven.

Sven glanced at the pouch in Rollo's hand. 'I'm not here for plunder or to make my name.'

'Aye, Odin knows that, but the other jarls don't. They'll find it strange if you don't take your share of the plunder. And besides, you'll need it if you want to disappear with Charles after this.'

Sven rubbed his beard, regretting it straight away, as his fingers were covered in blood. *After this.* He had not really thought about what came after this. But more because a part of him was afraid that all of this would come to nothing. Or that Charles would decide to stay with his mother in East Francia instead. And that was something Sven could not think about. But Rollo was right. If he and Charles wanted to go somewhere, he would need gold and silver for them to survive. A growl escaped from his throat as he wondered why Odin insisted on dragging him back to this life. A life he had tried so hard to get away from because it had caused him nothing but misery.

'First, we get my grandson back, and then I worry about after.'

15

PARIS, WEST FRANCIA

'Sven the Boar! Sven the fucking Boar is in West Francia!' King Charles slammed his fist on the armrest of his throne. 'Why, in God's name, is Sven the Boar raiding my kingdom?' He glared at the old bishop as if he knew the answer, but the bishop could only shake his head. 'Argh! As if I don't have enough problems with the fucking Danes raiding my kingdom. Now Sven the Boar has joined them?'

Bero glanced around him, waiting for others to respond, while he wondered if this was the best time to deliver the other news he had. News that King Charles would not want to hear.

'Maybe he thinks that we have his grandson,' Ignomer suggested.

'Don't be a fool, Ignomer!' King Charles glared at the old warrior, who took a step back as if King Charles was going to strike him. 'My brother has the bastard boy! We've known that for many weeks, so I'm sure Sven the Boar does as well.'

Bero cleared his throat, drawing the king's ire, but the spymaster did not flinch. 'King Louis might be using the boy as leverage to get Sven to raid your kingdom, my lord king.' His informant in King Louis's hall had sent him a letter which had told him that that was exactly what was happening.

King Charles glared at his spymaster, his nostrils flared. 'Why?'

Bero shrugged, pretending not to know, before Ignomer responded. 'King Louis's son is marching towards Aquitaine, is he not?'

'You know he is! What is your point?' King Charles's face turned red as he stared at the old warrior.

'A distraction, my king. Sven the Boar draws our attention away from the prince so that he can just march into Aquitaine and claim the throne for his father while we chase after Sven the Boar,' Bero answered.

'So we don't chase after Sven the Boar and send an army to deal with the son of King Louis,' the old bishop said, smiling as if that solved everything.

King Charles turned his anger to the bishop, who shrunk even before the king spoke. 'We can't just ignore Sven the Boar! He is leaving a trail of fire and death in his wake. It's like Satan himself has come to punish me! Every day people fill my hall with their stories and tears, begging me to do something! He is making me look weak!' King Charles slammed his fist on the armrest again and winced at the pain.

'And not just in the level of evil, bishop,' Bero said, enjoying the fear he saw in the bishop's eyes. 'They're attacking places that would hurt us most. Churches are being looted, relics destroyed, and priests either killed or taken as slaves. Entire towns burnt to the ground. Angers and Tours, two of the most important towns in that region, sacked and looted. The tower in Angers will need to be rebuilt after they burnt it down and we are still waiting for a full report of what happened in Tours.'

'It's all unnecessary. Raiding our people is one thing, but this level of destruction, it feels personal. Like he is attacking me and not my kingdom.' King Charles leaned back in his throne and crossed his arms. 'What have I done to anger the man?'

You paid a man to kill him and kidnap his grandson, Bero thought, but didn't say. Kings did not like it when you pointed their mistakes out to them.

'Maybe it's a punishment from God for the fake' – the bishop's eyes darted around as if God Himself was in the hall – 'cross.' King Charles had made sure that news of the discovery of his grandfather's cross had been spread far and wide across his kingdom. The people of Paris, those old enough to remember the cross, were elated at this and many believed that while the cross was in Paris the Danes would stay away. Paris had been raided in the past, and many still remembered those dark days. Bero knew King Charles still had nightmares about it, and it still angered him he had paid Ragnar to leave Paris and his kingdom. He had heard the whispers that the raids were punishment because King Charles was too weak, unlike his brother, the king of East Francia. Some even claimed that East Francia never got raided because the Danes feared the wrath of King Louis, but Bero knew that wasn't true. East Francia got raided as much as the rest of the kingdoms. He knew that because King Charles had paid many Danish jarls to raid his brothers' kingdoms.

King Charles gripped the armrests of his chair and glared at the bishop. 'Are you saying God has sent Sven the Boar to my kingdom to punish me for making a cross?'

'I... I...'

'I think the dear bishop is merely suggesting that perhaps my king should make a donation to the church to ensure that God chases the evil that is Sven the Boar away,' Bero said, smiling as he enjoyed tormenting the old bishop. The man was a fool and the only reason he had got the position was because his father had paid for it many years ago.

'Make another donation! Have I not made enough?' King Charles glared at the bishop as if he had spoken those words. 'And what has that got me? Constant letters complaining about me keeping Pepin prisoner in one of the monasteries.'

The old bishop opened his mouth to say something, but then shut it again, which Bero thought was a wise move. But then, he knew it was time to deliver the other news to King Charles. If Bero had been a religious man, he would have prayed at that point.

Again, Bero cleared his throat and when King Charles looked at him, he pulled a letter out of his pocket. 'I'm afraid, my king, that I have news about Pepin, your nephew.'

'I know Pepin is my nephew! What news?' King Charles leaned forward in his chair.

Bero took a deep breath. 'Pepin has escaped from the monastery in Soissons, my lord king.'

King Charles's eyes bulged as his mouth dropped open and, for many heartbeats, he just sat like that staring at Bero. Ignomer and the old bishop glanced at him, neither certain if they should do something as even Bero began to wonder if King Charles was still alive. But then the king's mouth opened and closed a few times. Bero was glad that there were no warriors in the hall because he was sure that King Charles would order his death, especially after he heard the rest of the news.

'Escaped?' King Charles said after a while. 'Escaped? How?' He glared at the bishop as if it was his fault and Bero almost smiled as the old bishop paled.

Bero glanced at the letter in hand and then said, 'It seems that you, my king, had ordered his release.'

'What do you mean?' King Charles gaped as Bero handed him the letter he had been given by the priests from the monastery a few days before. He waited as King Charles opened the letter and read its contents. 'B... But I didn't write this,' King Charles said, his eyes twitching as he gaped at his seal on the bottom of the letter.

Bero knew the king hadn't written that letter. He knew that because he read all of King Charles's letters before they were sent off and the responses the king got. He also knew who had really written that letter and thought it was a pity that man had to be his enemy, because as much as he hated Roul, he had to admit the man was very good at what he did. The fact that after many weeks his best men still could not track him down only proved that. Bero knew he should have been concerned that Roul was still out there, most likely plotting to kill him, but he wasn't worried. He doubted Roul was foolish enough to stay in Paris, but he wished his men would find the bastard already. 'No, my king. I believe it was Roul who wrote the letter.'

'Roul?' Ignomer clenched his fists. 'What is that snake thinking?'

Bero wished he knew what Roul was thinking and what he had hoped to gain from helping Pepin escape. He must have known the chaos it would cause, but then perhaps that was it. Perhaps he wanted to make King Charles look weak, but still that made no sense to Bero. Roul had always been one of West Francia's most loyal servants, but he had made a mistake and in their world mistakes meant your death. Roul knew that as much as Bero did. 'Roul must have forged my king's seal to make the letter seem authentic to the priest at the monastery in Soissons.' Bero decided not to mention that he also had a copy of the king's seal. King Charles was not as decisive as his brothers, so Bero had learnt that it was sometimes best to act in the king's name and then inform him afterwards.

'Where is Pepin now?' King Charles crunched the letter in his fist as he glared at Bero.

'Pepin is most likely on his way to Aquitaine, but it has been hard to track him.' And that had annoyed Bero. That Roul had done this under his nose and now he couldn't find him or Pepin.

'So what do we do?' the bishop asked.

'Nothing,' Bero suggested and waited for the response he knew was coming.

'Nothing?' King Charles glared at him.

'Pepin wants what he believes is his crown. I doubt he would let the son of King Louis just march his men there and take the throne for his father. I suggest we leave Pepin for now. Let him fight the young Prince Louis and while his men are exhausted and recovering from that battle, my king can send his men and defeat Pepin again. Sven the Boar is the bigger concern right now.' Bero had thought long about it and this was the only real solution he could think of. Especially because he already had men in Aquitaine to convince the dukes there that it was better for them and their families to support King Charles than Pepin or King Louis.

King Charles leaned back in his chair and rubbed his chin. The smile on his face told Bero that he liked the plan. Just like Bero knew he would. King Charles hated fighting battles and, this way, it would be an easy victory for him. 'And what do we do about Sven the Boar?'

Bero played with the ring on his finger as he considered his next words. 'Nothing.' King Charles raise an eyebrow at him as the old bishop looked like he was about to faint. 'We send word to Duke Erispoë of Brittany and tell him to deal with Sven the Boar and the rest of the Danes along the Loire River.'

'Duke Erispoë?' King Charles scowled at Bero. 'Why Erispoë? If he defeats the Danes, then it'll make him look stronger than me.'

Bero had expected this question. King Charles hated looking weak, but he did nothing to change that image of himself. 'Duke

Erispoë recently swore an oath of fidelity to you, my king, and it's time we test to see how far his loyalty really goes. And besides, if he succeeds, we can say that my king has ordered him to deal with the Danes, and if he loses, then he will be the one who deals with the wrath of the Danes.'

'So we do nothing and let others solve our problems for us?' Ignomer's face went red. 'I don't like it.'

'You might not, but the last time we intervened in something, everything went wrong and, for all we know, Sven the Boar is really here because he has learnt that our king had paid for Guttrom to kill him and kidnap his grandson.'

'That was Roul's idea.' King Charles was quick to deflect the blame for that, which almost made Bero smile. It might have been Roul's idea, but King Charles had agreed to it, even after Bero had warned him not to.

'Exactly. That is why I suggest that this time, we do nothing and let God,' Bero glanced at the pale bishop, 'and Duke Erispoë solve our problems. When it is done, my king can claim that it is because we have the Cross of Charlemagne and that the Danes were defeated and both Pepin's and King Louis's claims to the throne of Aquitaine have been quashed.'

King Charles nodded. 'Yes, by God, I love it. We do nothing and I get all the glory. I mean, God gets all the glory,' King Charles corrected himself and the bishop crossed himself, but Bero knew neither man cared about that. The meeting didn't last long after that, and as soon as it ended, Bero rushed to leave the hall on the pretence that he had some important business to deal with. But really, he was going to the place he always went to gloat about how he played the king of West Francia again. His favourite brothel, the one with the whore that Roul believed worked for him. Bero had been enjoying going to her more than usual because every time he fucked her, all he could think about was how he had outsmarted that arrogant bastard.

It didn't take him long to reach the brothel, even though he knew he should have taken his time and made sure he wasn't being followed. But he paid men to do that for him, so that he didn't have to. He even had men inside the brothel, so there was no way for Roul to get to him. As he entered, the brothel owner made sure to look the other way. The man knew never to see Bero enter or leave, but he would always make sure that Bero's whore was waiting in his usual room.

Bero smiled when he entered the room and saw the whore on the bed, already naked and ready for him. He licked his lips as he anticipated telling her about how he had once again manipulated the king of West Francia. He knew she would never say a word to another. The last whore who did had a gruesome and public death, and this one was much smarter than her. That was why he had used her to trick Roul by giving him false information. Bero felt himself go hard as he thought about it and rushed to undress himself. He climbed onto the bed and crawled towards the whore, who opened her legs for him. But just before he was about to enter her, her eyes widened at something behind him. Bero was about to berate whoever had dared to enter his room and interrupt him when he felt the cold tip of a blade press against the skin of his neck.

'This is for my master,' Roul's voice whispered in his ears and, before Bero could even wonder how Roul had got past his guards, he felt the sharp pain as Roul sliced his neck open. The whore screamed as his blood soaked her and, in desperation, Bero clutched at his neck to stop the bleeding, but the cut had been too deep and soon he felt his limbs weakening and his vision blurring. And the last thing Bero heard before everything went black was the whore screaming and Roul's laughter, which would go with him to the flames of hell.

16

Hildegard watched her father's face darken as he heard the latest reports from West Francia. Those nearby took a step back as he clenched his fists, and a glance at Duke Liudolf showed Hildegard that even he was nervous. Duke Liudolf was here more than he was in Saxony, though she knew it was not to support her. The two of them had barely spoken since they had returned from Denmark. It seemed that Duke Liudolf had decided that being near her would only cause more problems for himself. And, as annoyed as Hildegard was about that, she could not blame the man. He had his children to think about, and she knew he was desperate for his sons to inherit his duchy when he died.

Hildegard fingered the large golden cross she wore around her neck as she felt her father's hall in Frankfurt go cold, as if the flames in the hearth fire were trying to get away themselves. But it wasn't just her father's anger that made the hall cold. They were approaching the end of September and the warmth of the summer sun was already a forgotten memory. Every day the weather looked the same, grey and wet, and the mood seemed to be reflected in Frankfurt. Or perhaps that was just how Hildegard felt, being kept prisoner in her father's capital and not being allowed to see her son. Hildegard wanted to spend time with Charles, to build a relationship with him so that he would prefer to stay in East Francia with her instead of leaving with Sven. But her father had refused to let her talk to her son and she dared not disobey him. Not because she feared what he might do to her, but because she feared what he might do to her son. The worst King Louis could do to her was send her off to the edge of his kingdom, something she doubted he would because it would raise too many eyebrows, but Charles... Hildegard shuddered at the thought. To ensure her obedience, her father had men around the monastery where Charles was kept, and Hildegard knew that if one of them reported she had been there, then Charles's life would be over. So she watched him from a distance and spoke with Father Leofdag instead. The young priest had been a surprisingly valuable ally whom she met every other day. He kept her informed of Charles's progress, although she was distressed to hear that he refused to read the Bible as she had instructed. At first, Hildegard feared that Charles had been corrupted by the heathens, but Thora had only laughed at that. She was another ally Hildegard had never expected to have, even though Gerold despised the warrior woman. Hildegard had found Thora new clothes and a place to stay, but worried about how she would be able to watch over Charles as she didn't speak their tongue. Thora had learnt a few words over the last few weeks, but it was not enough and they both knew she stood out. But Thora was resourceful and had found a way to keep hidden from the men watching Charles.

Gerold, though, concerned her, and Hildegard found herself not trusting the young man. He had been different since he had returned from Denmark, more distant and even more hateful of the Danes, especially Thora. The Danish woman had told her he was angry because she had beaten him and tied him up, but

Hildegard sensed there was more to it. But she didn't have the time or energy to deal with Gerold, so she often sent him away on pointless errands just to get away from his foul mood.

'Where is my son now?' King Louis's voice broke Hildegard from her thoughts and she saw the messenger take a step backwards as her father glared at him.

'My lord king, the last we heard, he was approaching Aquitaine.'

'He's been approaching Aquitaine for almost a year now!' King Louis slammed his fist on the armrest of his throne and Hildegard felt her heart racing as she fidgeted with the cross around her neck. 'And now we found out that Pepin has escaped!'

'Perhaps we should call the prince back, my king,' one of her father's advisers said while glancing at her for support, but there was nothing Hildegard could say to change her father's mind. Even if she agreed with the adviser. Her younger brother, also named Louis, had been reluctant to march to Aquitaine from the beginning and Hildegard knew because he felt their father was trying to get him out of the way. Her brother wanted to be king of East Francia, not Aquitaine, and so had taken his time marching to the kingdom in West Francia. He was also arrogant and believed he had the support of the Aquitaine nobles, but if the news about Pepin's escape was true, then God knew her brother was in for quite a shock.

'Call my son back!' King Louis looked like he was about to launch himself at the noble. 'I don't want to call him back. I want him to move faster and take Aquitaine before Pepin gets there! How did the bastard escape, anyway?' That was a question Hildegard had also pondered.

The messenger swallowed back his nervousness. 'We don't know, my king. The West Franks are keeping silent about it.'

Her father's eyes glanced her way, more out of habit than from actually wanting her opinion, Hildegard guessed. 'My brother set him free. That is the only explanation. He set him free so that my son cannot take Aquitaine. The bastard!'

More nervous glances were directed at Hildegard and she realised the men in the room wanted her to say something. They all understood why her father wanted Aquitaine. It was next to her uncle's kingdom and if her father decided to invade West Francia, which she knew he wanted to, then having an army in Aquitaine would mean not having to make a deal with her other uncle, King Lothair of Middle Francia. Lothair was the oldest of the three brothers and would have been the new emperor of Francia if it had not been for his younger brothers' greed. And Hildegard also knew that her father was just waiting to get his hands on Charlemagne's cross before he invaded his brothers' kingdoms. He believed the cross would give him the power to become the new emperor of a united Francia, but all it had done so far was tear her great-grandfather's empire apart.

Hildegard let go of her cross and stepped forward. 'I don't think King Charles released Pepin, Father.' Hildegard stood firm as her father glared at her. He might have been angry at her, but she was still one of his top advisers, and most in the hall would have found it strange if she had kept quiet. But that wasn't the only reason she said something. She had been thinking about this since they had heard the news of Pepin's escape from the monastery near Paris. And though she had to admit the timing of it felt strange, she still didn't believe her uncle had played a part in it.

'And what makes you say that, Abbess Hildegard?'

'King Charles spent many years fighting Pepin and his rebellion. Pepin had been a problem for him ever since Emperor Louis had made Charles the king of Aquitaine and he has no guarantee that Pepin would not cause him problems now.'

'Perhaps King Charles made a deal with Pepin,' one noble

suggested, smiling at her. The man had been trying to get closer to her father for many years, and Hildegard guessed he saw an opportunity now with the obvious tension between her and her father.

'What deal?' she asked him.

The man shrugged. 'Pepin can be king of Aquitaine, but must answer to King Charles.' There were a few murmurs as some agreed with the man and even King Louis raised an eyebrow at that idea, but Hildegard shook her head.

'Pepin would never agree and King Charles would know that. Pepin believes he is the rightful king of Aquitaine and would not want to answer to another because he knows it would make him look weak. And neither would King Charles free Pepin to stop my brother from taking Aquitaine for the same reason.' There was silence in the hall as many contemplated what Hildegard had said and her father's frown told her he agreed with her point, even if he didn't want to admit it.

'But then why doesn't King Charles send his own army to defend Aquitaine?' the man tried again.

'Most likely because he needs his men elsewhere,' Duke Liudolf said.

'Elsewhere?' King Louis asked him, but Hildegard was sure he already knew what Liudolf was going to say.

'There's been an increase in raids in the south of his kingdom, in the Loire Valley. King Charles is under pressure to deal with the Danes, otherwise the people might revolt against him.'

'So he freed Pepin to deal with Prince Louis, so he can fight the raiders,' the man said, grinning as if this proved his point. And even though Hildegard had to admit that almost made sense, she still could not see her uncle freeing a man he had spent many years fighting. But she knew her uncle better than the young noble trying to make a name for himself.

'My uncle, the king of West Francia, does not fight the raiders because he has no thirst for battle. If anything, he pays them to leave and there has been no word of any such arrangement.' She looked at her father, who glared back at her. 'But even if he did, I doubt those in charge of the raids would agree.' The smile dropped from the noble's face as others laughed at him.

'Do we know who is leading these raids?' King Louis asked, although he already knew the answer. But Hildegard knew her father did not want people to know that he had sent the devil to kill good Christian people just so he could hurt his brother.

'A Jarl Halstein is the overall leader of the raiders, but they say that Sven the Boar has joined him and, since then, the attacks have got worse.' Duke Liudolf glanced at Hildegard, but she ignored him as she watched her father struggle to hide his smile.

Hildegard had heard the same news the day before and had prayed long into the night for forgiveness for her part in this evil. What made it worse was the conflicted emotions she felt, because she knew that Charles's fate depended on the deaths of good people and the destruction of towns and churches.

'Has King Charles sent someone to deal with the raiders?' King Louis asked, almost leaning forward in his seat.

Duke Liudolf shook his head. 'As far as we can tell, he's not doing anything about the raids. He seems to believe...' Duke Liudolf hesitated and glanced at Hildegard. This time she did look because she knew what he was going to say and that her father would not like it.

'He seems to think what, Duke Liudolf?' King Louis asked, his brow already creasing in anger.

'He believes that the Cross of Charlemagne will protect his kingdom and will chase the raiders away.'

'The Cross of Charlemagne? My brother has the Cross of Charlemagne?' Angry eyes flashed her way and Hildegard knew that no matter what Sven or her brother achieved, her son was not safe in Frankfurt. She had not wanted to believe Sven when he had told her that the cross had been stolen by another Frank. And neither had she wanted to tell her father about that, because she feared what he might do. She had also hoped that she could come up with a plan to ensure her son's safety before news of the cross reached her father, but now she feared it was too late for that. 'My brother has the Cross of Charlemagne?' King Louis thundered the question at her, but many in the hall quailed under his anger. Even the timber post in the hall seemed to shake.

Hildegard's mind raced as she tried to come up with something to say, but no answer came to her.

'I thought the Cross of Charlemagne was just a myth?' someone said, a little too loudly, but Hildegard was glad because it took attention away from her.

'The Cross of Charlemagne is no myth, you dumb ox,' King Louis thundered at the man. 'That cross helped my grandfather defeat his enemies and build his empire! With that cross, I could be the new emperor of Francia and now my bastard brother has it! How does my brother have the Cross of Charlemagne?' The question was directed at her, but Hildegard could not think of an answer that would satisfy the king. All she could think of was the story the heathen priest had told her that day in what was surely the gates to hell. Of how her grandfather had used heathen magic to defeat the Saxons and how her family was cursed because the Norse gods were angry that Charlemagne had destroyed their sacred pillar and had built a church on sacred ground. Hildegard had not wanted to believe that story, but Bishop Bernard, God bless his soul, had told her it was all true. That the Cross of Charlemagne had got its power from the sliver of wood from the heathen pillar that Charlemagne had added to the cross. Hildegard looked at her father, but the only thing she could think of was that she needed to get Charles out of Frankfurt and the only way she could think of doing that was to ask Thora for help. But if Thora helped Charles escape, what would stop her from taking him to Sven?

Was Hildegard prepared to lose her son to the heathens in order to save his life?

17

———

Charles held his breath as he poked his head out of the door and saw nothing but an empty corridor. He glanced back at Father Leofdag, whose head was resting on his chest as he snored. For the last few weeks, the young priest had been looking ragged, with his eyes red- and blue-rimmed and his habit scruffy. Charles felt that something was bothering Father Leofdag, but every time he had asked, Father Leofdag had told him everything was fine. And then a few days ago, Father Leofdag had started falling asleep while he watched over Charles reading the Bible. Not that Charles had been doing much of that. He still struggled to concentrate as his own thoughts plagued him. And this time it was not just that his mother refused to see him, no matter what excuses Father Leofdag had made for her. It was also the knife he kept hidden under the mattress of his bed. The one given to him by Thora that day in the church a few weeks ago. The very sax-knife now tucked into his trousers. At night, when he was supposed to be sleeping, Charles would take the knife out from under his mattress and stare at it in the light from the moon that came in through the window. Not because he longed to use it, but because it meant that Thora, his guardian angel, was in Frankfurt.

Still holding his breath, Charles looked out of the door again, and when he saw nothing, he glanced over his shoulder and mouthed an apology to Father Leofdag. He was sure the young priest would get into trouble for this, but he was tired of being kept prisoner. His grandfather had told him he needed to learn to look after himself and not to rely on others, and Charles had decided that he was going to do just that. And besides, Thora was out there somewhere. All he had to do was find her and then they could leave Frankfurt. With a deep breath to calm his trembling hands, he placed one foot out of the room, almost closing his eyes as it touched the floor. When there were no shouts or lightning, Charles smiled and snuck out of the room. He had been planning this since the priests in this church had decided that Charles had been too idle and had given him daily chores, like cleaning the lavatory and working in the garden. At first, Charles had hated them, but then he realised it allowed him to leave his room for a few hours every day and, not only that, but it gave him a chance to see the monastery he was kept in. Like most monasteries, it was attached to the church with a door for the priests to use and a cloister surrounded by other buildings, but Charles did not know what many of them were for. The only buildings he could enter were the lavatory and the dining room. Even the main church was a place he was only allowed in on Sundays. Charles had soon realised there were many corridors and hiding places for him. And one thing Charles was very good at was sneaking around and hiding.

Slowly releasing the breath he had been holding, Charles ducked low and crept along the wall, his ears strained for any noise that would alert him to the presence of any priests. Although he knew none of them were inside the house. They were all outside, performing their own chores and seeing to the people of Frankfurt. But Charles's biggest concern was the warriors who were usually outside and around the church. He knew they were there to watch him, but while doing his chores, Charles had found a way to get past them without them noticing. And he was also sure that at this time of the day, they were most likely not watching out for him. Not only because it was the time he would have his lessons with Father Leofdag, but also because it was late in the day and they would be thinking about going to the taverns. Charles's father had been a warrior and although Charles had never wanted to be one, he had spent a lot of time around warriors and knew how they thought.

He came to the end of the corridor and stopped before peeking around the corner. Seeing nothing, he was about to move when he heard footsteps nearby. Glancing over his shoulder, he expected to find Father Leofdag standing there, and sighed with relief when the priest was not there. But when he looked around the corner again, he saw another priest walking towards him. His heart racing, Charles looked around for somewhere to hide, and not finding anywhere, he crouched low and pressed himself against the wall. Charles held his breath as the priest walked past without noticing him, but was shocked when he found himself gripping the hilt of his knife. He let go of the knife as if it was burning his hand, and wondered if he would have used it if the priest had discovered him. He realised he didn't know. Perhaps the priests had been right after all. Perhaps he had spent too much time amongst the heathens. Charles took deep breaths to calm his racing heart while he waited for the priest to disappear. After a short while, he glanced around the corner again and, when he didn't see the priest, snuck off in the direction the priest had come from.

It didn't take him long to get outside the dormitory and into the courtyard that he had swept clean that morning. As expected, the warrior who was supposed to be watching the door to the house was nowhere to be seen. But Charles still waited a few heartbeats just to make sure the man had not gone for a piss and when he was satisfied the warrior had left his post, he ran around the building to the rear where he had found a small hole in the wall which had been covered by a large plant. The hole was too small for most to get through and had most likely been forgotten about as the plants grew over it. For once Charles was glad of his lack of height because it meant he could squeeze through. Charles reached the hole without being spotted and, with one quick glance around him, crept through it. All he had to do now was figure out where Thora was and then he would go to her. Charles had spent many days trying to work out where she might be, or even if she was still in Frankfurt. He knew she hadn't been captured. Father Leofdag would have told him about that. And he doubted she would travel to Frankfurt just to give him the sax-knife and then leave again. Charles stopped and frowned before he crept out of the hole as he wondered how Thora had got to Frankfurt, something that had never occurred to him before. Thora didn't speak the Frankish tongue and, as far as Charles knew, had never been this far south of the kingdom before. He would ask her when he found her, Charles decided with a smile on his face. He also had an idea where he might find Thora. The market. Every market he had ever seen was filled with people from places Charles couldn't even imagine were real and there were many there that couldn't speak Frankish. So if there was one place where Thora would blend in, it was the market. Lost in his thoughts, Charles didn't think of checking to see if the way was clear and as soon as his head poked out, a hand gripped his shoulder.

Charles screamed, but another hand covered his mouth, this hand too strong for him to shake off no matter how hard he shook his head. He was lifted off the ground, his heart racing and eyes bulging as he was dragged away from the wall. Away from the safety of the monastery. He had been told many times that if people found out who he was, who his mother was, then his life was in danger. But he never really believed those words. In his panic, he didn't even think of grabbing the sax-knife he had in his trousers. Instead, he kicked out and struggled as hard as he could to free himself, but his attacker was just too strong for him.

'Charles, relax. It's me. It's Thora.' The familiar voice spoke in his ears and his heart skipped a beat when he looked up and saw her light-coloured hair and the scar over her left eye. Thora glanced around them and she put him down, but before he could say anything, she scolded him. 'What in Frigg's name are you doing?'

'I... I...' Charles was taken aback by her anger. He had thought she'd be happy to see him. 'I wanted to find you.' He lowered his head and looked at his feet, not wanting to see the anger in Thora's face. But then she laughed, which made him frown as he looked up at her.

'Aye, you are definitely your father's son. But Charles, that was very dangerous, what you did. The Norns only know what might have happened if it was someone else waiting for you there and not me.'

'I'm sor... you waited for me? How did you know I'd be there?' Charles stared at Thora, unable to understand how she always found him. It had been Thora who had found him when he had first gone to Hedeby to search for his grandfather, and then later again when he had run away from the smelly drunk she had taken him to. And Thora had found him in the church a few weeks ago. To him, it was only more proof that she was his guardian angel.

But if she was, then why was she still around? God was angry at Charles. He was sure of it, even if he didn't understand why.

Thora smiled as she ruffled his short hair. 'I've been watching that place for many weeks, Charles. I saw how you were scanning the yard as you did your chores and knew you were planning something.'

Charles frowned. 'How did you know I was planning something?'

'Because you have the same look on your face as Sven when he is planning something. And then I saw you sneak out of the house when you weren't supposed to and I just waited by the hole you had found.'

Charles surprised himself when he smiled, as Thora said he had done something that reminded her of his grandfather. 'Where is he? And why are you here and not with him?'

Thora sighed before she looked around. 'I don't know where your grandfather is. Only that he is in West Francia, raiding to keep you safe. And I am here to make sure that you stay safe.'

He sensed there was something else she wasn't telling him when she glanced at his grandfather's Mjöllnir around his neck. He usually kept it hidden under his tunic, worried that the priests might take it away from him, and it must have slipped out as he crept through the hole in the wall. 'Why are you really here?'

Again, Thora sighed, but this time with a smile on her face. 'You're becoming too smart.' She glanced around again. 'Your grandfather doesn't trust King Louis and neither do I, so we decided I would stay behind and try to find a way to rescue you and take you to him.'

Charles's heart raced at the idea of going to be with his grandfather again. But then he frowned when he thought of his mother. Even though he had not seen her since that day on the beach and that he believed she was angry at him, Charles still hoped that he could see her and talk to her. If they left now to go to his grandfather, then Charles might never get that chance.

'Charles. What's the matter?'

It was Charles's turn to glance around, although he wasn't really sure why he did it. 'If I leave now, I might never get to speak to my mother, but...' He took a deep breath. 'She doesn't want to speak to me, anyway.'

'Charles, that's not true. Your mother does want to speak to you.'

'No, she doesn't. She's angry at me for telling King Louis that my grandfather has Charlemagne's cross.'

Thora smiled. 'No, Charles. Your mother is not angry at you. She is desperate to see you and to talk to you. She has even asked her father to allow you to go to her church with her.'

Charles frowned. 'How do you know? And why hasn't she visited me then? Father Leofdag told me she isn't allowed to, but I don't believe him. She's the daughter of the king and an abbess. How can she not be allowed to?'

Thora put a hand on his shoulder as she tried to calm him. 'I know she's desperate to see you because I've spoken to her. Who do you think gave me this new dress?'

Charles looked at what Thora was wearing for the first time and saw that she was wearing a Frankish dress and that it looked new. 'You spoke to her? Then why can't I?'

Thora sighed. 'I won't lie to you, Charles, but the gods know the situation is very complicated and very dangerous for you now. That is why what you did today is very reckless and why I can't take you to your grandfather.' Charles raised an eyebrow as he tried to make sense of what Thora was saying to him. 'Your mother can't see you because her father has forbidden it and she fears what he might do to you if she disobeys him again. She might be his daughter, and she might be an important person in the kingdom, but she is still a woman and a mother. But she made sure that I have what I need so I can keep an eye on you.'

'You are working with my mother?' Charles scratched his head. 'But how did you get here?'

'After the meeting on the beach, I stayed behind and followed you here.'

'Alone?'

Thora shook her head. 'No, Gerold was with me.'

'Gerold!' Charles's eyes widened. That was the last name he had thought he would hear. 'Gerold is here?'

'I don't know where Gerold is, and that's what makes me nervous. Gerold works for your mother, but I don't trust him.'

'He works for my mother?' Charles felt like he needed to sit down, but there was nowhere for him to do that.

'Aye, she thought he might be useful, but like Loki, he's causing a lot of problems for her, so she sent him away on some task.'

Charles nodded, not sure how he felt about that news.

'What exactly are you planning on with that?'

Charles frowned and then realised his hand had gone to the hilt of the sax-knife. 'I...'

'Be very careful with that. Your grandfather wanted you to have it so you could protect yourself if you need to. But I pray to the gods that doesn't happen.'

Charles nodded as he let go of the sax-knife. 'So you're not going to take me to my grandfather?'

Thora shook her head. 'Frigg knows I hate to admit this, but right now, you are safer in that house. There is much happening and the curse of the cross still hangs over us.'

'The cross? Where is it?' Charles remembered the cross. He had been so occupied by the fact that his mother didn't visit him that he had forgotten about the cross she had given to his father.

'Your grandfather has it, but tell no one. They believe it was stolen from him in Ribe and we want to keep it that way. When the time is right, and if you still want to, I'll take you to your grandfather.'

Charles nodded. *If you still want to.* Thora's words rang in his head. 'I don't know. My grandfather lied to me, but...'

'Your grandfather cares for you, Charles. The only reason he is raiding West Francia now is because it is the only thing he can think of doing to keep you safe.'

Charles felt his irritation grow. This was not the first time Sven had gone off to fight people, because he believed it would keep Charles safe. 'He said that before he went to fight the king of Denmark.'

'Aye, he did.' Thora nodded. 'And he knows he was wrong. Believe me, Charles, there's not a day he doesn't regret doing that.'

Charles sighed. 'I know. He told me on the beach.'

'But this time, he has no other choice.'

'But if King Louis wants the cross, why didn't you just give it to him on the beach? He might have let me go then.'

Thora sighed. 'Because your grandfather wasn't sure that you'd want to go with him and he didn't trust King Louis.'

Charles remembered what King Louis had said the day Charles had told him about the cross. *You just made sure that your grandfather doesn't leave that beach alive.* 'I think King Louis would have killed him. He had a lot of men with him.'

'Aye, he did. That's why your grandfather decided not to say anything about the cross. He believes that as long as he does what he needs to to keep King Louis happy, then you'll be safe.'

'But innocent people are dying and their homes are destroyed because of it. Because of me.' Charles had never seen a raid before, but he had heard plenty of stories of the unspeakable things the Danes did to Christians and churches when they raided. The priests in Hügelburg had often told Charles about raids in the past, where entire towns were slaughtered and burnt. All in the name of their gods.

'No, Charles' – Thora put a hand on his shoulder again – 'not because of you. Never think that.'

'Then why?' Charles asked. 'Why does all this have to happen?' He felt the tears running down his cheeks as he thought of everyone who had died this summer because of him and the Cross of Charlemagne. Perhaps the heathen priest had been right. Perhaps that cross was cursed.

'I don't know, Charles. We can blame the gods for it all, but really, it has nothing to do with them. It happens because people are greedy and cruel.'

Charles wiped the tears away, glad that Thora didn't blame the gods like adults usually did. 'So what do we do?'

Thora smiled at him. 'You go back to the house and keep your head down. Don't worry, I'll always be here, waiting and watching.'

'And my mother?'

'If she can find a way to see you, I'm sure she will. But you be careful, Charles, and don't do anything this reckless again unless your life depends on it. Understand?'

Charles nodded.

'Good, now you get back before the warrior guarding the house returns.'

Charles nodded again and was about to turn to go back to the house when he thought of something. 'Maybe I can sneak out every night and you can carry on teaching me to fight?'

Thora shook her head. 'No, that would be too dangerous. We both need to keep our heads down. Listen to the priests and do your chores. Now go before I get angry.'

Charles returned her smile and rushed back to the hole in the wall. He felt better after talking to Thora, even though he wasn't sure what he had expected to happen when he had first snuck out.

But knowing that his mother was not angry at him and that she wanted to see him made him feel better. But it also confused him even more and, as Charles crept through the hole in the wall, he sensed that one day he would have to choose between his grandfather and his mother. And Charles hated that idea, because he didn't know whom he would choose to stay with.

18

EARLY SPRING, AD 855

Sven watched as Jorlaug raised the stick she was using as a sword, her muddy face an ugly grimace, and brought it down as if she meant to take Sigmund's head off with it. But Rollo's son saw the move and took a step back, before raising his own stick to block Jorlaug's. The small red-headed girl lacked the patience of an experienced warrior and kept beating down on Sigmund's stick until hers broke and when she realised what had happened, she screamed and ran away, her grimace replaced with a giant grin.

'I'll get you, you Christian!' Sigmund shouted, doing his best to imitate his father's deep voice.

'I'm not the Christian, you are!' Jorlaug screeched back as she ran away from the taller boy.

Sven sighed as his mind went to Charles, as it had often done over the long winter. After they had left Angers, its buildings burning and its streets littered with the dead, Sven's and Halstein's men had continued to Tours, another important town along the Loire River. Tours had met the same fate as Angers. After the defenders were beaten, the town was pillaged and the women raped, and those who had survived were taken to be sold as thralls.

Sven did not enjoy destroying those towns, but he needed to be ruthless and he needed King Charles to have nightmares about him. He had parted ways with Halstein after Tours, as Halstein wanted to return to their island base and Sven wanted to carry on raiding. He had not felt like they had done enough to force King Charles to send his army towards them instead of Aquitaine. Some of Halstein's men had wanted to stay with Sven and so Sven had two ships full of hungry warriors to plunder the lands and to send the Franks running ahead of them. They had raided for as long as they could before the weather turned and winter had forced them to return to Halstein's island base, both ships filled to the brim with plunder and captives. The warriors from Ribe, who had left their families behind to join him, were richer than they had ever been and spent most of the journey back singing songs of the gods and glory. But all Sven had felt was frustration. And the cold Frankish winter had done nothing more than make that frustration grow.

'She misses her aunt, so she pretends to be her when she and Sigmund play,' Ingvild, Thora's aunt, said. She had been sitting near Sven, and like him, had been watching the children play. For them, just like the young warriors from Ribe, this was an adventure, and they had made the most of it. Especially Jorlaug, who had convinced her mother to allow Rollo to train her to be a warrior. Rollo had got as restless as the children and had decided that training them would keep him and them busy and out of trouble. Some children of Halstein's warriors had joined as well, and soon you couldn't tell the children apart. Although, it had surprised Sven when Jorlaug and Sigmund had formed a close friendship, and he had been even more surprised when he overheard them talk about Charles one day.

'It was Thora's idea to stay in Francia and watch over Charles,' Sven responded, feeling like there was an accusation in Ingvild's words. He glanced at the blue sky, the sun sitting low as it was the early days of spring. At least the worst weather was behind them, and Sven knew soon he could go raiding again.

'Aye, so you've said many times before. I just pray to the gods that she still lives and will find her way back to us. With your grandson,' she added when Sven raised an eyebrow at her.

'Thora's the best warrior I know. She will return.' Sven felt confident about that, although he was less confident that Charles would be with her. It had been a long time since Sven and Charles talked on the beach and Sven knew that Hildegard had had plenty of time to build a relationship with Charles and convince him to stay with her in Francia.

'Jorlaug! Get your face cleaned and come eat!' Audhild, Jorlaug's mother, shouted before she handed Sven and Ingvild bowls of fish stew.

Sven grimaced, not because he didn't like fish stew, but because he felt like that was all they had eaten during winter. But the lands around the island had been plundered for more than people and gold. The livestock of nearby farms had been eaten long before Sven had arrived, and many of the wildlife was gone as well. And because it was only the beginning of spring, there weren't any fresh vegetables or fruit for them to eat either. But the river was bountiful, as if Njörd had made sure the Danes still had food to eat, and the wives of the warriors were very resourceful when it came to creating different fish meals. Sven, though, would give his right hand to Týr for some venison, slowly cooked over the hearth fire.

'That girl is worse than the boys.' Audhild sat down with them, but made sure not to look Sven's way. They had an awkward relationship because of her husband. The man had been a drunk who had resented Sven, even though Sven had paid for them to look after his grandson, and had decided to take it out on Charles. Sven had beaten the bastard bloody and not seen him until they found his body hidden in one of the empty houses in Ribe, his throat slit open. They still didn't know who had done that, and Sven often wondered if it had anything to do with the Frank who had tried to steal the Cross of Charlemagne.

Ingvild smiled as Jorlaug chased after another boy with a new stick, ignoring her mother's words. 'Aye, but she sends many of them running as if their lives depend on it. She's got a lot of fire in her veins.'

'That's why her hair is red,' Sven said, remembering something his mother had said about him once when he still had hair.

Audhild smiled before she glanced over her shoulder. 'Sven, some men arrived a short while ago. They looked like traders.'

Sven was about to spoon some of the fish stew into his mouth, but stopped as he raised his brows.

'They might have some news,' Ingvild said, to which Audhild nodded.

'Only one way to find out.' Sven put his bowl down and stood up, grimacing at his stiff back and aching joints. This winter had been the hardest on him yet and he wondered how many more he would survive with the way his body was going. Still, he had lost some of his rotund stomach and had built some more muscles, although they weren't as thick as they had been in his youth. But Sven felt like he was in the best shape he had been for a long time. If only his back and left leg would agree with him.

'You're getting too old for this, Sven,' Ingvild said, not for the first time.

'Aye.' Sven scanned the camp, looking for Rollo and finding him sitting with his wife by their tent. She was expecting again, which wasn't surprising. Just like in Denmark, the winter nights here were long and cold. 'Rollo! Come, the traders are back.' Rollo nodded before he kissed his wife on her forehead and rushed to catch up with Sven. Alvar, who had heard Sven, joined them as well as they made their way to Halstein's tent in the middle of the island camp.

'Think we'll learn anything new today?' Rollo asked as he fixed his hair.

Sven shrugged while willing his left leg to warm up, so his limp wasn't so obvious. It was the same every winter. The cold made the wound stiff, which made him limp even more. Because of that, he barely took part in the raids just before winter, instead he stood back and let Rollo take control. But he had made sure that they flew his banner and shouted his name. 'Bound to be some news one day. Only the Norns will know if today is that day.' Sven rubbed the new Mjöllnir he wore around his neck, next to the small cross Charles had given him. He had felt naked without Thor's hammer there to protect him and had taken a Mjöllnir pendant from one of Halstein's dead. It was a simple hammer made of bone and didn't have the intricate carvings of the one he had given to Charles, but Sven still felt safer with it around his neck.

'How's the wife?' Alvar asked Rollo as they walked through the camp.

Rollo smiled. 'She is doing well, although refuses to give birth to our boy in this camp.'

'You know it's a boy?' Alvar raised an eyebrow.

'Aye, what else would it be? Odin will bless me with another son.'

'Be wary of the gifts Odin gives you, Rollo,' Sven said while resisting the urge to rub the raven tattoo on his head. 'Old One-Eye always asks for something in return for his gifts and it's never something you want to give.' Rollo nodded, but Sven doubted he understood. Although, he didn't blame the younger warrior because he himself had not understood when he had been given the same warning by his uncle, Odinson, just before he tattooed the raven on Sven's shaved head. 'And your wife and child will be fine if we're still here by the time the baby is ready. Ingvild knows what she is doing.' When they had returned from the raids for winter, Sven had been surprised to find that old Ingvild had become the leader of the wives of the warriors. He guessed because she was older – Sven didn't know how old she was, but supposed she must have been a similar age to him – the others looked towards her for guidance. That she knew how to heal ailments and injuries had helped as well, and she even found herbs and roots in the lands near the camps to make potions, which she used to treat people with. Even some of Halstein's people came to her when they were ill or injured.

They entered Halstein's tent; the warriors guarding it knew Sven and his men well enough not to stop them, and Sven frowned at the large red-headed trader who was in the tent talking to Halstein and Gudrod, but it was the smaller man beside the trader who caught his attention. Something about him seemed familiar, but Sven could not place the man with his long hair and thick beard. He scowled as he searched his memory, but nothing came to him.

'Sven, are you all right?' Halstein asked and Sven shook his head to clear his mind.

Still staring at the Frank, who was blankly looking at him, Sven decided he had never seen the man before. Perhaps he just reminded Sven of someone, but still he couldn't get rid of the feeling that he knew him. 'Fine.' Sven studied the others in the tent. Apart from Halstein and Gudrod, there were some of the other jarls as well, including Jarl Egil, who had joined Sven after Halstein had returned to his camp. 'Any news?'

Gudrod frowned. 'By Odin, I still don't understand why you are so interested in what King Charles is doing.'

'Or not doing,' Jarl Egil said with a smile. 'We bleed his lands dry and nothing from the coward.'

Sven raised an eyebrow at Halstein, who nodded. 'King Charles is still in Paris and, according to our new friend here, hasn't even sent an army to deal with us. It seems you were right. He is too afraid.'

Sven nodded at that and although it was not what he wanted to hear, it was not surprising either. King Charles had a history of paying off Danish raiders to leave his lands instead of fighting them. But the bastard did not understand that that only encouraged them to come for more like the hound that keeps returning for scraps after you feed it once. 'Or he has something more important to deal with,' Sven said, and noticed how the companion of the trader's brows furrowed.

'Aquitaine?' Halstein asked and Sven nodded.

'Any news from there?' Rollo asked, making it sound like it was just a passing question and not important to them.

Halstein shrugged and asked the trader, who scratched his bearded chin.

'The son of King Louis is still making his way to the capital, although at the rate he is going, he won't reach it until the summer. If he even gets that far.'

'What do you mean?' Sven's heart pounded as he sensed news coming that he would not like.

The trader shrugged. 'It seems that Pepin escaped his captivity and raised an army to stop the young prince.'

Sven felt his heart skip and did all he could not to collapse, as his legs suddenly felt weak. If Pepin had raised an army, then it meant that King Louis's son no longer had the support he needed to claim Aquitaine for his father.

'We already know of Pepin's escape,' Rollo said as Alvar moved closer to Sven. 'And what is King Charles doing about this?'

'What does it matter?' Gudrod asked, and some of the other jarls nodded their agreement. 'It only means that King Charles is weak and is about to become weaker.'

Rollo shrugged. 'It matters because if King Charles believes us to be the bigger threat, then he might have made a deal with this Pepin, so he could send his army south instead.'

The trader responded, while the others all frowned. 'No, I was in Paris only a few weeks ago and there was nothing to indicate that King Charles was doing anything. Even the people in Paris are becoming restless at his refusal to deal with you lot or Pepin. And besides, why would he make a deal with Pepin? He spent many years fighting his nephew for control of Aquitaine.'

Rollo nodded and even Sven knew the trader spoke the truth. He took a deep breath to calm himself and then frowned when he spotted the trader's companion scrutinising him. Again, Sven felt there was something bothering him about the man, but he could not think of what. 'If King Charles loses Aquitaine, it will make him too weak to resist his brothers. But that only makes things better for us.' Everyone frowned at Sven as he struggled to calm his racing heart and not show his true emotions to the others. 'He'll need to stop Pepin from taking Aquitaine, but he can't do it while we rampage across his lands.'

'But he can't afford to send his army south, because he might need it to deal with his nephew,' Halstein said, smiling as he saw where Sven was going.

Sven nodded. 'So either he ignores us, which makes him look even weaker, or he pays us to leave, which makes us even richer.'

'And what of your grandson?' one of the jarls asked.

'Aye, you told us you are here to get your grandson back,' Gudrod said.

Sven shrugged, doing his best to appear calm even as his

hands trembled from the news he had just heard. 'You'll get your gold and I'll make sure I get my grandson back.'

Every fibre of Roul's body trembled as he stared at the man who had caused his downfall. The man he had travelled all the way to the Loire River to kill. But he had to be patient. He had to play his part and wait for the right moment before he could strike.

Roul had spent many months growing his hair and beard so that others wouldn't recognise him, even though he hated it. The long beard made his face itchy and the fact that he could not scratch it only made him more irritable, but so far it had worked. No one had recognised him when he had walked into the brothel in Paris before the winter. No one had even paid any attention to him, especially not the guard he had paid off, as he snuck into the room and slit Bero's throat open. Roul had to fight the smile as he remembered how that bitch of a whore had screamed as Bero's blood sprayed over her. She had to die, of course. The last thing he had needed was for her to warn others of his presence, and then after that had been done, he had just walked out. No one had even thought to look at the frail-looking man with his long hair and beard.

And now Roul stared at the last person who had to die and then his vengeance would be done. The man who had ruined his life by swapping the real Cross of Charlemagne for the fake one that Roul had taken to King Charles. The king he had been more faithful to than he had been to God. The same king who wanted him dead. And Sven would pay for that.

Roul glanced at the Danish trader as he spoke to the heathens. The man had to be paid a small fortune before he had agreed to bring Roul to this Danish camp, but Roul could think of no other way to get in. He had expected to find Sven in Denmark or East Francia, and was surprised to learn that Sven was raiding West Francia, especially because Roul knew that his grandson was in East Francia. But Roul did not care about any of that. All he cared about was slitting the heathen's throat and watching him choke on his blood. Now all Roul had to do was wait until nightfall, when the Danes would be too drunk to pay any attention to him. Then he would slip into Sven the Boar's tent and kill the bastard for what he had done to him. If God was with him, then he would find the real Cross of Charlemagne as well because Roul was convinced that Sven had it with him. And when he had the cross, Roul could take it to King Louis of East Francia. His life in West Francia was over, especially after he killed Bero, so perhaps with Charlemagne's cross, he could build a new life in East Francia. Perhaps even help King Louis become the new emperor of a united Francia and become his spymaster.

Roul smiled at the thought as he watched Sven's hands tremble at the news the trader had told him. He sent a silent prayer to God, thanking him for the fact that Sven would die knowing he had failed.

19

'What, in Odin's name, are we going to do now?' Rollo frowned as they made their way back to their tents.

Sven did not respond as he clenched his fists and tried to work out how what they had just been told would affect them. If Pepin had raised an army, then how would Prince Louis be able to claim Aquitaine? Did he still have the support of the Aquitaine nobles, or had they all offered their support to Pepin? He was the man they had all claimed as their king a long time ago, before King Charles had imprisoned him. Sven cursed Loki, feeling that the god of mischief and chaos had his fingers in this. And now what had already been a difficult situation only got worse.

Unable to hold his anger in much longer, Sven turned and kicked a stool he had just walked past, screaming his wrath into the cloudy sky. 'Fucking bastard!' The stool flew into one tent and the warrior inside stormed out, his face red with rage, and was about to berate them when he saw it was Sven, with Rollo and Alvar flanking him. He quickly paled when he saw the fury on Sven's face and even though he was not one of Sven's men, he turned and walked away. Those around who saw what had happened laughed, but they too stopped when Sven glared at them.

With nostrils flared, Sven stomped off towards his tent.

'So, who is the bastard?' Alvar asked Rollo and even Sven wished he knew. He could have been referring to Loki for interfering or to Pepin for escaping. Or perhaps it was at himself for not seeing this coming. But Sven had never understood the Frankish nobles and their ways. His life had always been lived with a sword and shield in his hands and his enemies' cries in his ears, while their blood soaked the ground. That was the life Sven had always understood, the only place he had ever really belonged. But since Charles had entered his life, even that wasn't really true any more, and Sven still remembered the fear he had felt the last time he had stood in a shield wall. Fear he had never felt before. He wasn't sure if it was because of his age, or because he had something more important to live for.

'Looks like the news wasn't good,' Ingvild said as they reached their tents and all Sven could do was grunt as he walked past her and into his tent. There he stood, his fists clenched and his eyes shut as he tried to think of what he needed to do. Taking a deep breath, he turned and left his tent again.

'How far are we from Aquitaine?'

Rollo raised an eyebrow at him and shrugged. 'Too far to really do anything, I'd say. And besides Sven, what can we do?'

Sven wanted to scream at Rollo for not helping him, but he knew the giant man was right. All he could do was hope that Prince Louis had the same steel in his blood as his father. Sven sighed before he sat down on his stool in front of his tent. Alvar brought him some ale, which he drank while everyone stared at him.

'So, what do we do?' Rollo asked again when Sven finished his ale.

Sven glanced at the sky while feeling the weight of Charlemagne's cross under his tunic. He was beginning to wonder if things were going against them because he was carrying the cross. Perhaps the Christian god was punishing him for carrying something so sacred to the Christians. They were in his domain, after all, and perhaps Sven's gods didn't have much power so far from Denmark. How else could he explain that nothing had worked out for them? Before winter had set in, Sven and his men had burnt the Frankish lands around them. Franks had been slaughtered or sold as thralls, churches pillaged and burnt, and yet there was no sign of the king of West Francia. And now they heard he was still in Paris and not planning on doing anything. Sven wondered what Charles would make of what he was doing, but he already knew the answer to that. His grandson would be disappointed and angry at him. Charles had never understood the lives they lived in the north or why they had to raid. He never understood that for Sven to survive, he had to kill those who wanted to kill him first. But Charles came from a different place than Sven, and Sven had to be honest. He didn't really understand his grandson either, especially his desire to become a Christian priest.

'Sven?' Rollo asked and Sven continued to look up at the sky. The sun was setting in the west and soon the day would be over.

Sven grimaced as he struggled to his feet. 'For now, we get some sleep. Tomorrow we prepare to go raiding again. And this time we make sure that we get King Charles's attention.'

Rollo nodded at Sven and went into his tent.

He struggled out of his brynja, which felt like it was too large for him now, another sign that he had lost weight on this raid, and placed it on his war chest. His hand went to the pouch with Charlemagne's cross inside his tunic, and Sven decided not to keep it in his chest. There was something that still bothered him about the trader who had brought them the news from Paris. The

trader was a Dane, but that still didn't mean that Sven trusted him
or the news he had brought. And then there was his companion.
Something about the smaller man made him nervous, but Sven
couldn't work out what it was. He dropped onto his bed, a bunch
of old furs piled on top of each other, and struggled to get his
boots off, wondering if he was seeing threats where there were
none. But with everything that had happened since Charles had
come into his life, it was hard not to. Even old friends had turned
out to be new enemies, and Sven didn't know whom he could trust
apart from Thora, Rollo and Alvar. Taking a deep breath to clear
his mind, Sven lay down and closed his eyes. Tomorrow would be
another day of not knowing where his grandson was or how he
was doing, and there was nothing more that Sven could do about
it than what he already was. And perhaps that was what really
upset him. The fact that he had no control and that the Norns
seemed intent on making him suffer more.

* * *

Sven's eyes snapped open, and he frowned as he scanned the
darkness in his tent. His hand went to the sax-knife he had near
his bed, his mind searching for what had woken him in the middle
of the night. An instinct for survival, honed by many winters of
sleeping out in the open, exposed to dangerous men, animals and
weather, had picked something up, and Sven had learnt to trust
that instinct. He lay still, not wanting whatever was in his room to
realise that he was awake as his hand gripped the hilt of his knife.
Sven knew someone was in his tent and he knew that whoever it
was was there to kill him. His heart raced with the familiar rhythm
it did when danger was nearby and Sven's eyes darted around the
tent, slowly adjusting to the darkness, but still he lay there, waiting
for his attacker to make the first move. He heard a footstep, so

quiet he would have missed it if it weren't for his heightened senses as adrenaline coursed through his veins, but still he waited. Whoever it was knew what they were doing. They must have done if they had got past the other tents and into his without waking any of his men. Sven wondered why they had not set guards outside his tent, and then remembered that Rollo had suggested it, but Sven had dismissed the idea. It would have made it seem like he was afraid. And in a camp filled with hundreds of warriors, Sven did not want to seem afraid. Image was everything and now he might die because of that.

Another footstep. Slow and careful, but coming towards him. Sven felt the sweat bead run down his head as he struggled to lie still. Patience had never been his strong point, but he knew he needed to wait. This was not like sleeping under the stars and needing to frighten away whatever was trying to kill him. No, this was different. Sven wanted to know who it was in his tent and who had sent that person. Another step, even quieter now and, then, there was a sudden change in the air. Sven rolled out of the way, ignoring the pain in his back at the sudden movement as his attacker's knife struck where his chest had been. He jumped to his feet and roared as he stabbed forward with his sax-knife, aiming where he saw the small silhouette of his assassin, but only finding air as the assassin twisted out of the way.

'Who are you? Who sent you?' Sven shouted as he stood in the middle of his tent, his eyes scanning the darkness for his attacker. Movement behind him made Sven turn, but he still felt the sharp pain in his shoulder blade. Ignoring the burning pain, Sven swung with his left hand and felt his fist connect. His attacker's grunt told him he had hurt the man, but when he brought his knife down again, he found only air again.

Sven panicked as he swung his knife around him, trying to keep his attacker at bay until help could arrive. 'Rollo! Alvar!' he roared into the darkness, hoping that one of his men would charge into his tent.

His assassin attacked again, perhaps feeling rushed by Sven's screams, but Sven caught the movement in the darkness and instinct helped him block his assassin's knife before it could pierce his chest and send him to Valhalla. For a moment, Sven wondered if he could reach Odin's hall of the slain if he died in Francia. But then he pushed the thought out of his mind as he swung his knife at his attacker. Sven could only make out a dark figure, but saw his assassin duck under his swing and jump towards him. His heart seemed to stop as Sven realised he could not turn in time to block the assassin's blade and that there was nothing he could do to stop the snake from killing him. The man was too fast and Sven too old. He had always believed that he would face his death with open eyes and a snarl on his lips, but Sven squeezed his eyes shut and thought of Charles as he waited to die. The knife cut through his tunic as if it wasn't there and Sven waited to feel the sharp sting as it cut his stomach open. But then the knife struck something hard. Sven felt it pressed against his stomach, and he sensed his attacker staring at him as he, too, wondered what had stopped the knife.

Sven reacted first, angry and ashamed of himself, grabbing his assassin with his free hand and headbutting him. He heard a crack and, ignoring the pain from the first blow, headbutted his attacker again. Sven did not let go of his attacker, even as his head swam, and felt his attacker's legs wobbling under him. His anger took over and Sven felt like he was still only twenty winters old.

'You sneak around in the darkness like a snake, trying to kill me?' Sven roared. 'You try to kill Sven the Boar in the middle of the night while he sleeps?' Before Sven could stop himself, he stabbed his attacker in the stomach. The man grunted as Sven's blade cut through his clothing and his stomach muscle, and Sven felt his blood wetting his hand as he held the knife there, twisting it to cause as much damage as he could. 'I am Sven the Boar! You cannot kill me! You bastard snake!' He lost himself to his rage and stabbed his attacker again and again until rough hands grabbed him and pulled him. 'You bastard! Who sent you? Who sent you? Tell me!' Sven roared as he was dragged out of his tent and under the night sky.

'Sven, stop!' Rollo's voice broke through the mist. Sven frowned as he stared at the giant warrior, and then he shuddered when he saw the full moon behind Rollo's head. 'In the tent. Someone attacked Sven,' Rollo said as he stared at Sven, his brows furrowed in concern, but Sven was not paying attention to Rollo or the others as they came out of their tents, alarmed by Sven's shouts. His eyes were fixed on the moon, and it felt like he was being judged by a power different from his gods. Sven's hand went to his stomach where the assassin had stabbed him and he felt the pouch under his tunic. Without thinking, Sven took the pouch out and then the cross. 'By Odin, Sven! What are you doing?' Rollo asked, but still Sven ignored him as he stared at the Cross of Charlemagne that had saved his life.

More voices could be heard as the alarm was raised around the camp and Rollo grabbed the cross from Sven's hands and tucked it into his tunic as a familiar voice could be heard. Sven glared at the giant warrior, but then realised what Rollo was doing as Halstein came towards them.

'What's going on?' young Jorlaug asked as she came out of the tent she shared with her mother and grandmother and wiped the sleep from her eyes.

'Get back in the tent,' her mother ordered her and then she turned to Sven. 'Sven, you're bleeding.'

Sven's hand went to his back as he remembered being stabbed, but he was still numb from the attack and knew it would be a while before he felt the pain of the stab wound.

'What is all the commotion about? By the gods, Sven! Did you wake everyone up because you had a nightmare?' The men laughed at Halstein's words, but then they all fell silent as Alvar dragged the dead assassin, his torso covered in stab wounds and blood, out of Sven's tent.

Sven saw who his attacker was and felt his anger taking hold of him again. The companion of the trader who had arrived earlier that day. Halstein saw the same and turned to Ebbe. 'Find the trader! Now! Sven, what happened?'

Sven stared at the dead man as Ingvild looked at his shoulder, but he had forgotten all about it as he realised why the man had bothered him. Under the beard and long hair, he saw the face of the Frank who had tried to steal the cross in Ribe. 'It's him,' Sven muttered, and knew that Loki was behind this.

'It's who?' Halstein asked as Gudrod appeared, frowning at the dead man.

Sven shook his head as he struggled to make sense of things.

'He was in Ribe,' Alvar said. 'He stole something important.'

Halstein glanced at Sven. 'And now he tries to kill you?' Halstein scratched his head and Sven knew he was wondering what he had not told him. But Sven did not care about that. Not at the moment. His hand went to the Mjöllnir around his neck and he was about to thank the gods for keeping him alive, but then a shiver ran down his spine at the thought that it was the Christian god that might have saved him. 'Sven, who is this man and why did he try to kill you?'

Sven glared at the corpse of his assassin. 'I don't know.' Which wasn't a lie. All he knew was that the man was in Ribe and that he had tried to steal the Cross of Charlemagne. In fact, he would have done if Thora hadn't swapped the cross out with another before. At first, Sven had thought the man worked with Hildegard, but when she had claimed not to have any knowledge of the man, they had assumed he worked for King Charles. But Sven could never prove it.

'The trader is gone,' the man who had been sent to fetch the Danish trader said as he returned. 'He left the camp just before sunset.'

Sven's anger took hold of him once more, and he turned to the surrounding men. 'Then find the bastard! Now!' No one argued, not even Halstein, who nodded to his men before turning his attention back to Sven. 'I think he was one of King Charles's men,' Sven said, feeling the sting from the stab wound as his battle rage wore off. Ingvild had removed his tunic and was busy cleaning the wound as Sven stood there. Out of the corner of his eye, he spotted Jorlaug sticking her head out of her tent, but ignored the young girl.

'So, instead of sending his army to deal with us, the king of West Francia sends an assassin?' Halstein raised an eyebrow. 'By Odin, the man really is a coward.'

'But we don't really know that he worked for King Charles,' Gudrod said. 'We only have Sven's guess and, besides, he came with a Danish trader.'

'Aye, a Danish trader you brought to the camp, Gudrod,' Halstein said, and Sven glared at the man, wondering if his words of reconciliation were really honest or just a ploy.

'The man came to me, told me he had some news that would be valuable.'

Sven flinched as Ingvild got back to cleaning the wound and tried to shake her off, but the old woman refused to move until she was done. He glanced at Gudrod, whose forehead was creased, not quite believing his response, but knowing there was nothing he could do about it. Not yet, anyway.

'Hold still, you grumpy bastard,' Ingvild berated him, and a few of the men smiled.

'Everyone back to your tents, there is nothing left here to see,' Halstein said, and as the men walked away, most of them murmuring to each other, Halstein turned back to Sven. 'Well, it looks like you got King Charles's attention after all, Sven. You should thank the All-Father that the bastard didn't succeed.'

Sven nodded as his hand went to where he would have been stabbed if it had not been for the Cross of Charlemagne, wondering which god he really needed to thank for his life.

20

Charles glanced around the courtyard and saw no one. The warrior watching over him had his back turned to him as he leaned his shoulder against the wall and was most likely thinking of the tavern he would later visit. The priests were busy performing duties of their own and even Father Leofdag was not there. Satisfied that no one could see him, Charles gripped the broom he had been using like a spear and practised the thrusts Thora had taught him the summer before, something he had been doing ever since he had snuck out and spoken to her before the winter. If Thora couldn't train him, then he would train himself.

The winter had been a difficult time for Charles. He knew his birthday was during the winter months, but he couldn't remember which month or day. He guessed he was ten years old now, but that didn't really matter. Charles's father would usually wake him up early on his birthday and take him to the church in Hügelburg, where the priests had prepared a large morning meal for him with some honey cake. Bishop Bernard had often been there as well, usually with a small gift for Charles. Charles had heard of the bishop's death, but no one would tell him how Bishop Bernard had died. Only that it happened while they tried to escape Ribe as it was invaded. Charles wasn't really sure how he felt about it. He had believed the man was responsible for his father's death, but then learnt that it was the opposite. That he had been looking after Charles and his father for his mother. Charles found he missed Bishop Bernard, though, and the stories he used to tell on his visits to Hügelburg. His father had also given Charles small gifts for his birthday, usually a small wooden animal he had carved himself or some new clothes if they had returned from a battle and he had extra money. He had never understood why his father always came back from battles with new weapons or armour and more coins in his pouch. But he knew now it was from looting the dead. Charles had believed that God would be against this, but he now understood that God cared little for what happened on earth. How else could Charles explain everything that had happened to him? If God had been as caring and as loving as the priests had always told him, then surely he would have intervened. But perhaps he had, and Charles had been too blind to see it. Thora was in Frankfurt, after all, and he was certain she was his guardian angel. And then there was Father Leofdag, who had refused to leave his side, all the way from Denmark. Charles frowned as the thought came to him, but then shook it out of his mind as he jabbed the broom handle forward like a spear. He had not spoken to Thora since that day, but would often see her in the church during services or standing outside the gate of the courtyard, smiling at him.

His room in the dormitory had been cold during the winter. Only the head priest could have a fire in his room to keep warm, and Charles was left shivering every night as he fell asleep. The nightmares had lessened, but he still got them. The raven tree, its trunk covered in blood, and the small monster eating something under its branches while the heathen priest danced around them, his laugh making Charles shiver even during the day when he thought about the dream. Father Leofdag had asked about it, as it usually left Charles angry and exhausted, but Charles would tell him he was thinking of his grandfather. Something which wasn't a lie. Throughout the winter, Charles had heard stories of his grandfather's raids in West Francia and the terrible things he was doing. The towns he had attacked and the churches he had destroyed. Priests killed and women raped, although Charles had refused to believe his grandfather had done those things. Father Leofdag had been less sceptical, though, claiming that Sven was heathen and had a reputation for doing things like that. It had only made Charles feel guilty because he knew he was the reason that his grandfather was attacking innocent Christians in West Francia.

That was when he had decided to practise the moves Thora had taught him. So that he would never again be in a position where others needed to do horrible things to protect him and to take his mind away from everything that was bothering him. To his surprise, he found the exercises calmed him and made it easier for him to sleep at night. But he still wondered how his grandfather was doing and if he still had the cross.

'What are you doing, boy?' A voice made Charles jump, and he dropped the broom, his cheeks red as his eyes darted around the courtyard, looking for a way out. But there was nowhere to go. Not even the hole in the wall, because he didn't want the priest to know about it.

'I... I...' Charles tried to think of an excuse which could save him, but nothing came to his mind. His eyes darted to where he had seen Thora before, but she was not there to help him.

'Well?' The priest crossed his arms, glaring at him as if he wanted Charles to cower, but Charles refused to. He had faced Danish warriors trying to kill him and had even stood up to the king of East Francia. And besides, he was the grandson of Sven the Boar. Charles refused to cower to anyone.

He puffed his chest out and returned the priest's glare. 'I was practising my spear thrusts.'

The priest gaped at him as he was taken aback by Charles's disrespect, but then he recovered his composure. 'Practising your spear thrusts,' the priest repeated as he glanced at the broom on the ground. 'Is that what you were supposed to be doing?'

'Yes,' Charles said, straightening his back. 'Because I'm going to be a warrior, like my father and my grandfather.' Charles wasn't sure if he really believed that. He still wasn't sure what he wanted to be, not any more, but he wanted to upset the priest.

The priest grabbed Charles by his ear, the old man catching Charles by surprise so he couldn't dodge out of the way. 'Boy, you have spent far too long amongst the heathens. It's time we reteach you how to respect your elders and God.'

Charles cried out as the priest dragged him past the laughing warrior and towards the church. He kicked at the priest's leg, hoping the man would let go of him and then he could run away and find Thora. But instead of letting go, the priest turned and slapped Charles across the face. Stunned, all Charles could do was gape as he was dragged into the church and towards the group of priests standing near the altar. Father Leofdag was there, shaking his head when he saw what was happening, but Charles knew that the young priest would not help him.

'What is the meaning of this, Father Rigobert?' the bishop asked, scowling at Charles.

Father Leofdag lowered his head after Father Rigobert explained what had happened and muttered, 'Oh, Charles.'

If Charles hadn't been so angry, he might have been ashamed of his behaviour, but at that moment Charles didn't care as he glared at the bishop, who was still scowling at him.

'Well then. I suppose the boy needs to be told how to behave properly.' He raised an eyebrow at Father Leofdag. 'Are you not responsible for the boy's education, father?'

Father Leofdag nodded as he looked at his feet. 'Forgive me, bishop. I am.'

'It seems you were too lax in your duties then, Father Leofdag. God teaches us to be firm and to punish the weak, does he not?' Father Leofdag nodded again, but stayed silent. 'Then perhaps I can think of a way to teach both of you how to perform your duties properly.'

Father Leofdag's eyes widened and Charles frowned as he wondered what was about to happen. His eyes followed the bishop as he went to the altar and took a cane from behind it before handing it to Father Leofdag. Charles's legs trembled when he realised what the bishop had in mind.

'I think five lashes should suffice, don't you, Father Rigobert?'

Father Rigobert huffed. 'I would recommend more, but your grace knows better.'

The bishop smiled. 'Father Leofdag. I believe it's time you do what you should have done a long time ago. You've been too soft on the boy and now he believes he can ignore his duties and strike one of our brethren. How long before he turns into the monster his grandfather is, who at this very moment is torturing and killing innocent Christians in the name of his false and vile gods?'

Father Leofdag stared at the cane in his hands, and then he looked at Charles. 'Forgive me, Charles.'

Before Charles could respond, two other priests grabbed his arms. He cried out as he struggled to free himself, wishing that Thora was there to help him.

'See, he even wears the symbol of the heathens in the house of God!' One of the priests pointed at Sven's Mjöllnir that Charles wore around his neck, which had slipped out while Charles had fought against the priests holding him.

'Not any more. May God save the boy's soul from the heathen magic,' the bishop said and plucked it from Charles's neck and threw it away.

'Amen,' the other priests said in unison as the bishop nodded to Father Leofdag.

'No—' Charles was about to protest when the first lash struck. He cried out as the pain bit deep into the pit of his stomach and, as much as he tried not to, he could not stop the tears as the second and third lash struck.

By the time Father Leofdag finished, Charles had to be held up by the two priests. The burning pain on his back had made his legs too weak to hold him as Charles choked on the snot and tears.

'Good. Perhaps that will teach him his place, the little heathen bastard,' the bishop said as the two priests let go of Charles, who collapsed and lay there crying. 'Father Leofdag, clean the boy and take him to his room. He'll not be fed for three days, and as for you, Father, I hope you will pray and beg God's forgiveness for your failures.'

'I will. Thank you for your guidance, bishop.' Charles was in too much pain to wonder why Father Leofdag was grovelling to the bishop. He thought of Bishop Bernard, who never would have had Charles lashed, and for the first time since he had been told of the bishop's death did he really miss the man who had always been kind to him.

Father Leofdag waited until the priests had all left before he knelt down and helped Charles up. 'God, please forgive me, Charles.'

Charles glared at the young priest as he wiped the snot and tears away with the back of his hand. 'Why did you do it?' The words came out strained as Charles struggled to catch his breath and flinched when Father Leofdag used his habit to clean his back.

The priest sighed. 'Because if I didn't, then Father Rigobert would have, and he is known for his cruelness. Even the priests here fear him. Charles, what were you thinking? You were supposed to be cleaning the courtyard, not killing your enemies. Whoever they may be.'

'I have many enemies.' Charles's face darkened, and he glared at the direction the priests had all left.

'Yes, forgive me, Charles. You certainly have. More than a boy your age should.' Father Leofdag picked up the Mjöllnir pendant that the bishop had thrown to the ground and handed it to Charles. 'You should be more careful, Charles.'

Charles took the Mjöllnir pendant from Father Leofdag and gripped it in his fist, wishing his grandfather was there to punish the priests for what they had done to him. He wanted to be angry at Father Leofdag for lashing him, but couldn't. Charles knew he should have been smarter. Thora had tried to teach him to slow down and to think before he acted. She had claimed that was what made her a good fighter, because she did not let emotions control her, unlike Charles's grandfather. But Charles had found that he was more like the old man that he had first wanted to be. 'I want to leave.'

Father Leofdag nodded. 'Yes, I'll help you to your room.'

Charles shook his head. 'No, I want to leave Frankfurt. I want to go to my grandfather. He would never let them hurt me.' Charles wondered if his mother would have stopped them, but wasn't sure because he didn't really know her.

'Charles,' Father Leofdag said, his voice soft. 'If only I could, but I don't know where he is or how to get to him.'

'Thora knows,' Charles said before he could stop himself.

'I'm sure she does,' Father Leofdag said as his hand went to his throat. Charles was in too much pain to wonder about that. 'But come, let's get you to your room and cleaned up.'

* * *

Thora clenched her fists as she hid in the church and saw Father Leofdag leading Charles out of the back door. She had been watching Charles train from a spot she had found which allowed her to see into the courtyard of the monastery, and had been impressed by his spear thrusts when he had been caught by the cruel-looking priest. Thora had wanted to intervene, especially when the priest grabbed Charles by his ear and dragged him to the church. But then Charles had lashed out and kicked the priest. Thora knew then that Charles was in trouble, but the last thing she could do was march into the church to help him. Thora would only interfere if she felt that Charles's life was in danger, and even though she was sure he would get a beating for what he had done, she knew Charles was still safe. The Christian priests could be cruel. She had seen that for herself in Hedeby, but they weren't killers. Especially not of children.

But seeing the marks on Charles's back, she wished she had stormed into the church. The boy had to learn, though, and pain was often the best teacher. In the future, Charles would be more careful and more composed, she was sure of it. But she would have to ask Father Leofdag what had happened, especially after the nervous glance he sent her way. Thora had run into the priest not long after her chat with Charles. He had wanted to report her. She could see it in his eyes, so she was forced to threaten him into silence. That had been easy enough. Her knife at his throat and a few words about how painful his death would be were enough to ensure Father Leofdag kept his mouth shut. She could have just told him that Charles's mother knew she was in Frankfurt, but Thora was concerned that that might cause only more problems.

Thora had spent the winter coming to the church every Sunday, only so that she could get a closer look at Charles. She made sure not to get too close, especially after spotting Gerold in the church on a few occasions, and at other times, she would come to her spot and watch Charles in the courtyard. She did her best to keep Hildegard informed, even though she knew that Father Leofdag did the same and Hildegard had kept her informed of what was happening in West Francia. Sven had been keeping his side of the deal he had made with King Louis, and even the Danish traders in Frankfurt would boast of what the old bastard was doing. Although Thora was sure they were exaggerating, especially when she heard one of them tell of how Sven defeated an entire town with two giants by his side. Thora knew who the giants were, but was sure there were more than just the three of them. She was glad though to hear that Sven still lived, but knew he would be miserable. Sven had never told her, but Thora could tell that he had lost the will to fight battles. The old man just wanted to spend whatever time the Norns gave him with his grandson, but the three sisters who controlled their fate had other ideas for Sven.

Thora was about to return to her room when something caught her attention. She hung back and watched as two warriors arrived and spoke to the one who was guarding Charles. Thora could not hear what they were saying, not that it would have made much difference, anyway. She had learnt some Frankish words over the winter so she could buy food for herself from the coins that Hildegard provided her, but she would still not understand what they were saying, unless they were talking about the prices of vegetables. And from the way the warrior glanced over his shoulder at Charles and Father Leofdag, she knew they weren't doing that. Thora also knew that no matter how bad Charles's day had been so far, it was only going to get worse. She wondered if she should find Hildegard and warn her, but knew she might not have enough time to do that. Her hand went to where she normally kept her sword, but it was not on her hip. She was forced to keep her sword hidden in her room and only carried a sax-knife with her, which was hidden under her dress. But she could not fight three warriors with a sax-knife.

Thora grabbed the Mjöllnir around her neck, hidden under her dress, and asked Frigg to watch over Charles while she rushed back to her room to get her sword.

21

Charles winced as he tried to sit on his chair and read the Bible, his back still burning. Father Leofdag had cleaned it when they got back to the room not that long ago, but Charles wondered how he would be able to sleep that night. Not that sleep would come to him anyway, he thought as his stomach growled and Father Leofdag glanced at him with a sympathetic smile on his face. Charles had not eaten since the morning and was forced to miss the evening meal as part of his punishment. He didn't understand how that was going to help him behave better, but guessed it was more because the bishop and the priests resented him for being here. As far as they were concerned, he was the grandson of Sven the Boar, the evil Dane who had tormented the lands when they were still young. None of them knew who his mother or his other grandfather was, and Charles doubted they would believe him anyway if he told them.

Charles looked at Father Leofdag, his eyes now closed in prayer and no doubt asking God for forgiveness for failing to teach Charles how to behave properly. Charles was supposed to be doing the same, but he couldn't. God might have been angry at him, but now Charles was angry at him and the priests in this horrible monastery. For a moment, he had wished his grandfather would storm the place and burn it to the ground, but then he felt guilty about those thoughts. Although, he refused to ask for forgiveness for them.

'You aren't praying, Charles,' Father Leofdag said, as he often did.

Charles looked out of the small window, seeing nothing but a darkening sky. 'I don't want to.'

Father Leofdag sighed. 'I understand, Charles. But you must ask for forgiveness for your sins.'

Charles jumped to his feet, knocking his chair over. 'What sins?' His hands balled into fists. 'What did I do wrong? What are my sins? I have done nothing and I'm being punished all the time! What are my sins?'

Father Leofdag's face softened and as he opened his mouth to respond, the door opened. Both Charles and the priest turned to look at the warrior standing there, his brows furrowed and his lips in a tight line. Just as Charles thought the warrior was going to tell him to be quiet, he spotted the knife in the warrior's hand, which he quickly hid behind his back, and the look of surprise on his face when he saw Father Leofdag in his room. Even in his young years, Charles sensed that something was wrong, but Father Leofdag did not seem to understand that.

'Forgive us for the noise. The boy is upset,' the priest said to the warrior, who stuttered before he could respond.

'Father, you are not supposed to be here.'

Father Leofdag glanced at the man's hand, which was still hidden behind his back, and Charles noticed how his hands trembled. 'I... I... stayed late this evening to ensure the boy did as he was told by the bishop. What are you doing here?' Father Leofdag got to his feet and stood between Charles and the warrior.

'I came to make sure the boy was in bed.'

Father Leofdag and the warrior stared at each other for what felt like a long time as Charles's heart raced before Father Leofdag said in a nervous voice, 'I'll make sure Charles gets to bed. You can go now.'

The warrior sighed and revealed the knife he had been hiding behind his back. 'God, forgive me.' And then he launched himself at Charles.

Father Leofdag screamed and pushed Charles out of the way. 'Run, Charles! Find Thora!'

The warrior grabbed the priest by his habit and almost lifted him off his feet. 'You shouldn't have been here, priest.'

Father Leofdag ignored the man and stared at Charles, his eyes filled with fear. 'Run!'

But Charles couldn't. He couldn't run because he knew if he did, then Father Leofdag would die and he did not want another person to haunt his dreams. And besides, Father Leofdag had stayed with him all the way from Denmark, even when he had been threatened by Ivor and King Louis. Charles could not abandon him. He searched the room, looking for something he could use to help the priest, when he remembered the sax-knife Thora had given him. As Father Leofdag struggled with the warrior, kicking him and scratching at his face, Charles rushed to his bed and grabbed the knife from under his mattress. He did not want to kill the warrior, but he did not want his friend to die because of him.

Charles pulled the knife from its scabbard, trying to remember everything Thora had taught him, but in the end he screamed to find his courage and rammed the knife into the warrior's leg, who was too focused on Father Leofdag to notice what Charles had been doing.

The warrior cried out as he let go of Father Leofdag and

turned his attention to Charles. Dark eyes glared at Charles, who was frozen with fear, when Father Leofdag grabbed him and pulled him out of the room. Outside the room, they ran into a second warrior, a man Charles had never seen before, when Father Leofdag pushed Charles away.

'Run, Charles! Get out and find Thora!' Father Leofdag threw himself at the warrior, who swatted him away, but it gave Charles enough time to dash past them and towards the front door of the dormitory. Charles thought about screaming for help, but then wondered if any of the priests would help him. So he dismissed the idea and ran as fast as he could. He knew he just needed to get to the hole in the wall, and once through there, he would be safe from the warriors. But as he ran, he prayed that Father Leofdag would survive.

* * *

Thora rushed back to her room to get her sword, ignoring the tavern owner and the other people in the tavern as they all gaped at her, and as she opened the door, she found Hildegard waiting there for her. Hildegard must have noticed the look on her face.

'Thora, what is the matter?'

'Something is wrong, I think Charles is in danger,' Thora responded as she went to where she had hidden her sword.

'Bastard!' Hildegard exclaimed, which surprised Thora as she had never heard Charles's mother talk like that.

'What?' She pulled the sword out of its hiding place. 'Hildegard, what happened? Why do they want to kill Charles?' Thora was convinced that was the order that had been passed on to the warrior outside the church. She had believed that Charles was safest where he was, but now she realised she was wrong. Sven's grandson was trapped inside a place she could not get into, and his life was in danger.

'My brother,' Hildegard started, and then went quiet.

'What about your brother? By the gods, Hildegard, I don't have time for this. What happened?'

Hildegard gripped the cross around her neck. 'My brother has failed to claim Aquitaine. Somehow, Pepin escaped and raised an army to oppose him. My brother decided that fighting a battle wasn't worth it and turned around. He is now on his way back to Frankfurt. My father is furious. He blames Sven. He thinks Sven hasn't done enough.'

Thora stared at Hildegard, her mouth open in shock. She did not know who this Pepin was, but Thora knew that Sven had done all he could. She had heard the stories from the traders and the reports that Hildegard had given her. But Sven could do nothing about the fact that King Charles refused to fight him. Word of his cowardice had spread throughout the northern kingdoms. That was the reason the jarls raided West Francia every summer. And now Charles was in danger because of it. 'Talk to your father, tell him to stop!' Thora knew it was pointless as she said it, but she couldn't stop herself. If Hildegard was here, then it must have meant she had already tried that.

'My father no longer listens to me. I sent Gerold to fetch Duke Liudolf. Perhaps he can talk to my father, get him to stop.'

Thora shook her head. 'It might be too late by then. You stay here, I'll get Charles.'

'How?' Hildegard's eyes went to the sword in Thora's hand. 'You can't go fighting my father's men in the streets of his city!'

'I'll do what I must to protect Charles. Even if it means fighting your father.' Thora turned and rushed out of the room before Hildegard could say anything and made her way back to the monastery. She prayed she was not too late as she hid the sword under her dress. Thora held on to the handle of the sword over her dress, so to others it would look like she was lifting her dress so that the hem would not get dirty. She would have preferred to wear trousers and armour for the fight she knew was coming, but that would have drawn too much attention to her, and at least with the dress, Thora could hide the sword.

When she reached the monastery, Thora was surprised to find that the warrior who was normally outside was gone and her heart raced as she wondered what that meant.

'Frigg, please tell me I'm not too late,' she muttered as she walked through the gate and into the courtyard. A few priests were walking around the cloister, and they frowned when they saw her enter. But just as one of them was about to say something, they heard a scream from inside one of the buildings around the courtyard. Thora pulled the sword from under her dress and rushed towards the building as the priests screamed and fled. She barged in through the door and saw a Frankish warrior standing over Father Leofdag. Without a thought, she lunged forward and stabbed the man through the back before either of them realised she was there. The warrior grunted and after she pulled her sword free, turned and frowned at her, before he dropped dead.

'Thora?' Father Leofdag asked, his face filled with confusion and covered in the blood of the warrior she had just killed.

'Where is Charles?' Thora asked as she rushed towards the open door of what she thought might have been Charles's room. But when she got there, all she saw was another warrior with a sax-knife in his leg. Thora recognised the handle of the knife just as the warrior spotted the bloody sword in her hand. Taking no chance, he freed his own sword and attacked. Thora took a step back and deflected the Frankish warrior's sword before kicking him in his injured leg. The warrior cried out, but stayed on his feet and swung his sword at Thora. The blade got caught in the door frame and Thora smiled as the warrior's eyes widened. Before he could pull his sword free, Thora sliced his arm open and then stabbed him through the neck as he staggered back.

The warrior tried to say something, but only a gargled noise escaped his open throat. Not that Thora would have understood what he wanted to say, although she had a good guess. The same thing most men called her before she killed them.

'Fuck,' she muttered as she looked at her dress. She had tried her best to get out of the way, but had still not managed to avoid the blood getting onto it. But that didn't really matter now, as she left the room and returned to Father Leofdag. 'Where is Charles?'

Father Leofdag just stared at the dead warrior, his eyes wide and his face pale.

'Leofdag! Where is Charles?' Thora grabbed him by his habit and shook him so that he looked at her. The priest blinked a few times and then finally spoke.

He pointed along the corridor. 'He ran that way. Why... why were they trying to kill him? He's just a boy.'

Thora shook her head, surprised that the priest was as naïve as Charles could be. 'They were trying to kill him because of who his mother is and because that bastard prince failed. And now Charles must pay the price.'

'N... no, but he's just a child.'

'Aye, and he'll never get a chance to grow old while we waste time. Now get up and grab a weapon! We have to find Charles before they do.'

'A... A weapon?' Father Leofdag's wide eyes went to the sword in her hand.

Church bells rang outside and Thora knew that soon more warriors would turn up, and if she was still here, then Charles would die. She cursed as she pulled the priest to his feet and dragged him out of the building. There was only one place where she could think of where Charles might have gone, because he didn't know where she was staying. And she had to get there quickly, but as she ran out of the dormitory, with Father Leofdag on her heels, she found a handful of warriors blocking their way.

One of them said something which made the others laugh and all Thora could do was growl.

'He said—'

'I don't need to know what he said,' Thora interrupted the priest. 'I need them to get out of the way so I can find Charles.' *Týr, guide my hand as I kill these bastards. Charles's life depends on it.* She prayed to the god of war, something she had not done for a very long time. The fingers on her left hand twitched, longing to grip on to the handle of a shield, but luckily for her, none of the four warriors facing her had any shields either. The only protection they had were the leather jerkins they wore and the weapons in their hands. She guessed they were not King Louis's best warriors. They would be by the king's side, protecting him from his enemies. These men were the ones who stood in the third row of a shield wall. The ones who prayed they would survive and make some coin from the battles. Not the warriors who stood in the front row so the gods would see them and they would make a name for themselves. But they still outnumbered her, and she had no shield or armour. Only her dress and her sword.

Before the warriors had stopped laughing, Thora attacked. Father Leofdag cried out in shock and all the first warrior could do was stare at her, his eyes wide as her sword opened his throat. Somewhere in the streets, a woman screamed as Thora turned and stabbed at another warrior. The man had the sense to jump back, but he had underestimated Thora's speed and didn't raise his sword to defend himself. Thora rushed at the man, stabbing him in the leg and, as he dropped to his knees, she chopped her sword into the back of his neck, killing him instantly.

The remaining two warriors glanced at each other, neither smiling any more as they just saw a woman kill their companions with the ease of a seasoned warrior. Which was what Thora was, but they couldn't see her as one because she was a woman – and Thora took advantage of that. Thora roared and launched herself at the two men. One of the warriors raised his axe to block her attack, while the other stabbed at her exposed side. Thora knew the attack was coming and turned and sliced the sword warrior across the chest. Her blade didn't cut through his leather jerkin, but it stunned both men and gave her time to step into the sword warrior and knee him in the groin. The man's eyes bulged as he dropped to his knees, but before Thora could kill him, the axe warrior swung his axe at her head. Father Leofdag cried out, which warned her of the attack, and Thora just managed to deflect the blow, but could do nothing as the warrior punched her in the gut. Thora grunted as the wind was knocked out of her, but had no time to recover as the axe warrior screamed something at her while lifting his axe to chop down on her head. Thora rolled out of the way and sliced the back of the warrior's leg open, but then she sensed the other warrior behind her and turned in time so his sword did not skewer her, but not fast enough to avoid the blade completely as it cut into her shoulder.

Thora gritted her teeth and, still struggling to catch her breath, stabbed at the sword warrior who had not turned from his attack and left his side exposed. Thora's sword found a gap in the man's jerkin and the warrior grunted as the sharp blade tore through his insides. Her heart then seemed to stop when the warrior turned and her sword slipped out of her bloody hand. Images of her husband flashed in her mind and, for a heartbeat, she believed she would die the same way he had done. But as she looked towards the axe warrior, she saw him limping away from the fight, his face pale and filled with fear when he glanced over his shoulder.

'Thora!' Father Leofdag screamed and Thora turned back to the sword warrior and saw him facing her, his face contorted in pain and hatred, but the man didn't have the strength to lift his sword. He just stood there and glared at her as his blood soaked his tunic and trousers, before he dropped to his knees, his sword falling from his hand. Thora took a deep breath and thanked Thor for protecting her. She struggled to her feet and walked to the dying warrior before gripping her sword, still in his side. She grunted as she pulled her sword free and stabbed him through the neck.

'Wh... why did you do that?' Father Leofdag asked, looking like he was about to vomit.

Thora cleaned her sword and checked her shoulder, ignoring the onlookers who gaped at her through the gate to the streets. The wound was not too bad, but it would hinder her if she had to fight again. 'To quicken his death.' The church bells were still ringing and Thora saw some priests running towards the king's hall. She growled and without waiting for the response from Father Leofdag, turned and ran to where she had taken Charles the last time they had spoken. The small side street near the tavern she was staying in. That was the only place she could think of where Charles might have gone, and she could only pray that fighting these Frankish bastards had not prevented her from saving Charles's life.

22

Charles hid behind the dormitory, his heart racing in his chest and guilt eating away at him. He had left Father Leofdag behind to die. He was sure of it, but he had no choice. That other warrior had come out of nowhere and there was nothing Charles could have done. He was not like his grandfather or his father, no matter how hard he had tried to be. He looked at his trembling hand, still red from the blood of the warrior he had stabbed as bile rose in his stomach. Charles still couldn't believe he had done that, but then he had spent most of last summer believing he had killed a man.

Church bells started ringing, which startled Charles and his heart raced as he knew he needed to get away. He had to find Thora because she was the only one who could help him. Perhaps they could even rush back and help Father Leofdag. He then heard men shouting and realised more warriors had arrived and didn't waste time trying to wonder why they wanted to kill him. Perhaps his grandfather had failed, but Charles couldn't believe that. Charles pushed himself away from the wall he was leaning on and ran for the hole in the wall he had escaped through in the autumn. He had made sure the hole was hidden from the priests and, when he could, he had even made it bigger so it was easier for him to escape.

As Charles reached the hole, the sounds of fighting reached his ears and, for a heartbeat, he wondered what was going on. But then he shook his head. He had to get out of there and he had to find Thora. As he cleared the plants that covered the hole, he wondered how he would find her. He knew she had a room nearby, but he didn't know where that room was. The only thing he could think of was to go to the place Thora had taken him after she had caught him last time. He remembered seeing a tavern nearby. Maybe she had a room there.

Charles stuck his head out on the other side to see if it was safe and was disappointed not to see Thora waiting there for him. He hadn't realised that he had expected her to be there, but then she had always known where to find him in the past. Taking a deep breath, he darted from the hole and made his way to where she and Charles had last spoken. Charles glanced over his shoulder to make sure he wasn't being followed, even though he knew he shouldn't, when he bumped into a woman, knocking her over and falling on top of her.

For a moment, Charles hoped he had bumped into Thora. That was how they had first met in Hedeby. He had run into her when he stormed out of the church. But then his heart stopped when the woman cried out and he realised it wasn't Thora's voice. The voice sounded familiar, though, and when Charles looked up, he gasped when he saw the shocked face of his mother.

'Charles? What, in God's name, are you doing here? Where is Thora?'

Charles just stared at his mother, his heart racing in his ears as he struggled to understand why she was there. He was even more confused by the cloak she wore that hid her habit. To anyone look-ing, she would appear to be just another woman, not the abbess

Hildegard. His mother looked around her before rolling Charles off her and getting to her feet. He almost flinched when he thought she was about to scold him, but then she pulled him to his feet.

'We have to get out of here. Follow me!'

His mother turned and dragged him the way she had come from. Charles resisted, afraid she was going to take him back to the church. 'No! Get off me! I can't go back!' Around them, people stopped and stared at the commotion, but Charles did not care about that. He just didn't want to go back to the church.

'Charles!' His mother hissed at him. 'We don't have time for this. Your life is in danger. We have to get you off the streets.'

Charles frowned, struggling to understand his mother's words. 'You know?'

'Yes, Charles. I know, and may God forgive me for not seeing this sooner, but we have to get you out of Frankfurt.'

Charles looked towards the church. 'But Father Leofdag! He needs our help.'

His mother barely stopped as she took him to the area where Thora had taken him before. 'I pray he doesn't get harmed, but there is nothing we can do for him other than that.'

Charles felt the tears in his eyes and knew he'd see the priest in his dreams that night if he managed to sleep. 'Where are you taking me?'

'To Thora's room. Now be quiet and hurry!'

'To Thora's room?' The words made him move faster, and soon they rushed into a tavern and up the stairs. His mother ignored the tavern owner as he asked her about the church bells and then swore at her when she didn't respond. On the top floor, his mother went to a room in the far corner and opened the door before pushing Charles inside. Charles just stood there as his mother closed the door behind them and studied the room, but he saw nothing that proved to him that this was where Thora had been staying. 'Where is she?' Charles asked and wondered if his mother had lied to him and if this was another trap.

His mother lowered the hood that was covering her head as she sat down on a chair and stared at him. 'She went to find you. She sensed something was wrong and went to rescue you.'

Charles frowned and then remembered the sounds of fighting he had heard. He had never even considered that that might have been Thora. Without a thought, Charles ran for the door, but then his mother's firm voice stopped him.

'Charles! Stay where you are!'

He turned around and glared at Hildegard. 'I must find Thora. She might need my help.'

'And how are you going to help her, Charles? You are just a boy,' his mother said, and Charles couldn't help getting angry at her words.

He clenched his fist and glared at her again. 'I'm not just a boy! I am the grandson of Sven the Boar!' Charles wanted Hildegard to react. He wanted her to get angry at him, but she just nodded.

'You're just like your father. He didn't like being told what to do either, but Charles, I beg you, stay here, wait for Thora. She will return soon.'

Stunned by his mother's reaction, Charles struggled to find the right words, so he just walked away from the door and sat on the bed. 'How do you know she'll be back? She might be outnumbered.' Charles thought of the fighting he had heard in the courtyard.

Hildegard's hand went to the golden cross she wore around her neck. It made Charles think of Charlemagne's cross, although his mother's wasn't as beautiful or as big. 'Because she has to, Charles.'

Charles raised his eyebrows at his mother. 'I thought you'd say something like God will make sure she does.'

His mother smiled. 'Thora is a heathen, Charles. Even I'm not sure if He will protect her regardless of whether she fights for one of His flock.'

Charles glanced away. 'I'm not part of His flock. Not any more.'

'Yes, I heard you lost your faith. Father Leofdag has been very distressed about it.'

Charles looked at his mother and felt the pain in his chest as he thought about Father Leofdag. 'I did not lose my faith. God left me.'

'Why would God do that?'

Charles shrugged. 'He is angry at me, but I don't know why. I tried to be a good Christian, even in Ribe, but it was hard to pray and sometimes I just forgot to.'

'God is not angry at you, Charles.' He heard the smile in his mother's voice, which only irritated him even more. He jumped to his feet.

'Then why does He allow all these things to happen? Why did He let my father die? And Alfhild and Oda? Why is He punishing me?'

His mother's hand went to her cross again as she seemed to think about what he had said. 'I don't know, Charles. I wish I did, but I don't know. Your father did not deserve what happened to him. He was a good man. But what happened to him was not God's fault, but my own. I'm the one who gave him the cross.'

Charles stared at his mother, feeling his anger disappear as the tears built up in her eyes. 'But why didn't God stop it from happening? The priests told me that God and His angels protect us and keep us safe. But they did nothing to stop my father from being killed.'

His mother wiped a tear from her eye and then looked at her

hands. 'I asked myself the same question many times when my father took you away from me, Charles. I often prayed and asked why He allowed my son to be sent away.' Charles was stunned by his mother's words because he had never thought about how she had felt. 'I believe God allows these things to happen to us because He wants us to become stronger than what we are. Only through pain and despair do we really learn about who we are and what we are capable of.'

Charles frowned. 'I don't understand. That is not what the priests in Hügelburg told me.'

His mother laughed. 'Most of those men had never faced any real hardship, so how would they know? Most priests I've dealt with know less about life than you do, Charles. But how could they? They never had to watch their children be taken away from them, or see their loved ones killed. Most of them bought their positions and used them to make themselves richer.'

Charles was shocked by the anger in his mother's voice as she spoke about the priests. 'Bishop Bernard wasn't like that.'

Hildegard shook her head. 'No, he was a good man. But he had his demons, and they caught up with him in Ribe.' Charles nodded, but did not want to ask about how Bishop Bernard had died. He didn't want that to be in his dreams as well. 'God did not abandon you, Charles. He has kept you safe even while you were in Denmark, and He has surrounded you with people who protect you and look after you. People like Father Leofdag and Thora, even your grandfather. But God is testing you. He is making sure that you are strong enough for what is coming.'

Again, Charles frowned. He was about to ask what she meant by that when the door to the room opened behind him. Charles turned, expecting to see Thora standing there, but then he gasped when he saw Gerold glaring at him.

'Gerold? What are you doing here?' Hildegard asked. 'I sent you to find Duke Liudolf. Is he coming?'

Gerold walked into the room and closed the door behind him. 'No, he is not coming because I didn't go to him. Instead, I called for more warriors and told them there is a heathen killing priests in the church.'

'Gerold? Why?' Charles's mother jumped to her feet and stepped towards Charles. But Charles was not paying any attention to her. All he could do was glare at the man he had once thought of as a friend.

'Because that bitch deserves to die!'

Charles screamed and launched himself at Gerold, who laughed as he grabbed Charles by his tunic and threw him to the floor. Charles cried out as the sores on his back stung and quickly rolled to his feet, just like Thora had taught him. 'She'll kill you.' He spat the words out.

'Gerold? Why would you do that?'

'Because of him!' Gerold jabbed a finger at Charles. 'And that bitch who humiliated me every chance she got!' He glared at Charles's mother. 'And because I'm done being your servant. Your slave to treat as you wish and to send away whenever you want to.'

'I took you out of prison. I gave you food and a purpose.'

'I had a purpose before this little bastard came into my life!' Gerold pulled a knife from his belt. 'And now I'm going to take him to King Louis and tell him how you betrayed him for this heathen bastard.'

'You will not touch my son. By God, I knew I should have let you rot in Ehresburg. You will never be the man your master was.'

'Bitch!' Gerold said, his face turning red. 'It doesn't matter what you think of me. Soon the king will know how much of a heathen lover you really are.' He took a step towards Charles when the door burst open for a second time in what felt like only a few heartbeats.

'Thora!' Charles exclaimed when he saw her standing in the doorway, her face contorted in pain and anger. Her dress was covered in blood and Charles saw the bloody sword in her hand. As well as the blood running down her left arm. But before he could say anything else, Gerold roared and rushed towards him. Charles did not know what happened next, as everything became a blur. His mother grabbed him and pulled him behind her as Thora stormed into the room, screaming his name. Then Gerold collided with Charles's mother and knocked both of them to the floor, but not before his mother pushed him out of the way. Hildegard cried out as Gerold turned to grab him, but Charles jumped out of the way and ran towards Thora, who stepped between him and Gerold, whose face was contorted in anger.

'I should have killed you in Ribe,' Thora said, pointing her sword at Gerold as Charles hid behind her.

Fear flashed in Gerold's eyes as he searched the room for another way out. But there was none. If Gerold wanted to leave, then he had to go through the door Charles and Thora were standing in front of. He lifted his knife, and Charles frowned at the fresh blood he saw on the blade. But before he could check himself to see if he had been cut, Gerold launched himself at Thora. 'You heathen cow!'

Thora stepped towards Gerold and drove her sword through his stomach. Gerold grunted as the sword burst out of his back, his eyes wide, before Thora headbutted him and she pulled her sword free. The man who had betrayed Charles, who had pretended to be his friend only to hold a knife at his throat the previous summer, staggered backwards. He dropped his knife as his hands went to the wound in his stomach, but his fingers could not stop the blood from soaking his tunic. Charles could only watch as Thora stepped towards Gerold.

'I always knew you were a snake. And it's time you die like one.' Before Gerold could respond, Thora swung her sword and Charles shut his eyes as it bit into Gerold's neck. He heard her swing her sword twice more before there was a thud on the floor and only then did he open his eyes and have to swallow back the bile in his stomach when he saw Gerold's head on the floor. As he stood there, his mind trying to make sense of what had just happened, a hand touched his shoulder. Charles screamed and turned, only to see Father Leofdag standing there, his face pale. Father Leofdag's eyes went to Gerold's head and before Charles could say anything, the priest turned and vomited outside the room. Charles had to cover his own mouth as the stench of Father Leofdag's vomit mixed with the smell of death, but before he could even think of emptying his own guts, he heard Thora's voice.

'Hildegard!'

Charles saw his mother on the floor, her hand covering a bloody patch on her dress. His eyes went to Gerold's knife, and he realised that the blood he had seen on the blade belonged to his mother. 'Mother!' He rushed towards her, all thoughts of vomiting forgotten.

'I'm fine,' his mother said, but her pale face made it hard for Charles to believe her words.

'Mother. No.' Charles felt the tears streaming down his cheeks as images of his father came to him. He did not want his mother to die just so that he could live, just like his father had.

'Leofdag! Get in here now!' Thora barked at the priest before she lifted her dress and pressed it against his mother's wound. 'Hold on, Hildegard. We'll get you out of here, get you to the church. The priests there will help you.'

Hildegard shook her head and looked at Charles. 'Don't worry about me. Just get my son out of here. Get him out of Frankfurt.' She hesitated as she stared at Charles, who had to swallow back the tears that were choking him. 'Get him out of Francia. Torkel was right to send him to his grandfather. He's not safe in Francia.'

Thora nodded, but Charles refused to listen to what his mother was saying. 'No, I don't want to lose you. I won't go.'

His mother placed her bloody hands on his cheeks and moved his face so he was staring into her eyes. 'Charles, you must go. I'll be fine. But you must leave before my father's men find you.'

'Leofdag! Get in here now!' Thora barked at Father Leofdag again, who was leaning against the door frame, his face green and his habit covered in puke. The young priest nodded and staggered into the room, his eyes fixed on Hildegard as if he was trying not to look at Gerold's decapitated body or his head. Once he reached them, he dropped to his knees and Thora replaced her hand on Hildegard's wound with his.

'Leofdag, you better make sure she lives. Do you hear me? If I hear she died, then not even your god will protect you from me.'

Father Leofdag nodded and then looked at Charles, the tears in his eyes only adding more to Charles's. 'I'll make sure she lives. I swear on my eternal soul, Charles.'

All Charles could do was nod. He did not notice Thora replacing her bloody dress with a new one as he looked at his mother again. Charles wanted to say something. He did not want to abandon his mother like he had abandoned his father. But Charles could not think of anything to say as his tears blinded him.

His mother took the cross from her neck and placed it in his hands. 'Charles, do not lose your faith. God is not punishing you.'

'Then why is He taking you away from me?' Charles struggled to understand why he was losing his mother so soon after he had found her. Especially before he got to know her.

'God is not taking you away from me, my son. He brought you back to me. He gave me the chance to see what a strong young man you've become.'

'I'm not strong. I'll never be strong.' Charles wiped the tears from his eyes so he could see his mother's face better.

'You are, my son. You are strong, just like your father was. Now, please. Go with Thora. Get out of my father's kingdom and live. I promise we'll see each other again.' His mother looked at Thora as the tears ran down her cheeks. 'Take care of my son, Thora.'

Thora gripped Charles's shoulders and pulled him to his feet, but Charles still held on to his mother's hands. 'I promise. I'll look after him as if he is my own.'

Charles saw his mother smile and then she looked at him again. 'Keep faith in God, Charles. That's what will make you strong.' She winced as she let go of him. 'May God be with you, both of you.'

'Come, Charles. We must leave before it's too late.'

Charles was too numb to fight Thora as she led him out of the room and out of the tavern. He heard people ask questions but could not hear the words they were saying or the shocked expressions on their faces when they saw the blood on his clothes and face. Thora rushed him out of the house and found a place for them to hide and, from there, they watched as more warriors rushed into the tavern. It didn't take long for them to come running out again, carrying his mother between them. Father Leofdag was with them as well, his face pale as he kept crossing himself, and Charles guessed he must have been praying for his mother's soul. He looked at the cross she had given him. It was smaller than Charlemagne's cross and was not decorated with gems and a large ruby. He gripped the cross and watched as the warriors took his mother to the church while some ran back towards the king's hall.

'Will she live?' Charles asked, his eyes still fixed on the church.

Thora put a hand on his shoulder. 'I don't know, Charles. Your mother's fate is in the hands of her god now.'

'Where do we go now?' Charles asked.

'I don't know, Charles. But we have to get you out of here and quickly.'

'Can we go to my grandfather?'

'The gods know I wish we could, Charles. But I don't know where he is or how to get to him.'

Charles nodded, still too numb to really understand what was going on. 'So what do we do?'

'We wait, Charles. We wait and the gods will show us the way.'

Again, Charles nodded and then looked at his mother's cross. *God, you better make sure my mother lives.*

23

SOMEWHERE ALONG THE LOIRE RIVER

Sven swung his Dane axe in a wide arc and felt the blow rattle up his arm as it struck its target. He let go of the haft and pulled his sax-knife from its scabbard before stepping forward and stabbing the Frankish warrior under the armpit. Sven growled at the Frank as his life left him and stepped back so the bastard wouldn't fall on him. He wiped his knife clean on the Frank's trousers and put it back in its scabbard before he pulled his axe out of the man's shield. He rolled his shoulder which had been cut by the assassin and was glad that it had healed well. He wanted to thank the gods for that, but knew it was because of Ingvild's skill and not the gods.

'Kill them all! Odin demands it!' he roared as he charged at his next opponent. The Frankish warrior, an old man with grey in his beard, dropped his spear and fled from Sven's anger. 'Coward! Come back and fight me!'

Close to him, Rollo stepped out of the way of a spear thrust and brought his Dane axe down, chopping his attacker's hands off before kicking the man to the ground and burying his axe in his skull. Alvar was dispatching his opponents with the same ease as Rollo and soon none of the Frankish warriors wanted to go near the three of them. Not that their opponents could be called warriors. Very few had armour, and those who did had either only helmets or old leather jerkins. Most of the Franks wore thick woollen tunics, but that was not enough to protect them from Sven's men.

'They're fleeing,' someone shouted, and Sven saw the few remaining Franks drop their weapons and run for the safety of the nearby hills. He sensed his men wanted to give chase and almost allowed them, but then decided against the idea. He needed his men to stay close.

'Hold!' he roared the order.

'Hold!' Rollo repeated, his deeper voice carrying further than Sven's.

Sven nodded at the giant warrior and then lowered his Dane axe so he could lean on it as he wiped the sweat from his eyes before surveying the area around him. The ground was littered with those who had tried to protect the small town from Sven's men, and already he thought he could hear the wolves salivating over the feast Sven had prepared for them. 'You know what to do,' he said to Alvar, who was checking the edge of his Dane axe.

Alvar nodded and ordered the warriors to search the houses, while Sven led a handful of men to the church in the centre of the town.

'By Odin, that was more resistance than I expected,' Rollo said as he fell in beside Sven.

Sven grunted as he glanced at the crisp blue sky, with not a cloud in sight and the sun shining brightly. It would have been a beautiful day if it had not been for the death he had brought to this small town further up the river Loire. He closed his eyes and pictured himself and Charles sitting outside and enjoying the weather as he told his grandson stories of the past, but then he pushed the thought from his mind as he opened his eyes and stared at the small stone church. 'Should have equipped their men better if they wanted them to stop us.'

'Or brought more men,' one warrior said. 'Feels like my sword didn't get enough of killing Franks today.' Some men laughed, but Sven kept his eyes on the church as they approached.

A few priests came out and formed a small wall in front of the church, all of them holding their crosses out towards the Danes as if that was going to stop them. Sven sighed and wondered why so many of the priests believed their crosses were weapons. Or perhaps they just believed that the Danes feared the wrath of their god, who so far had let them ravage the Frankish lands without even lifting a finger to stop them. But as Sven thought that, he remembered the snake that had slithered into his tent and had tried to kill him in his sleep. Even worse, Sven remembered that he only lived because of the Cross of Charlemagne. Sven gritted his teeth and struck one priest on the side of the head. The other priests cried out and ran before the man even dropped to the ground.

'Take everything of value and then burn it down,' Sven ordered as he walked into the church. Inside it was the same as every other Christian church he had been in, and Sven still wondered why the Christians were foolish enough to hoard all their treasure in these buildings and then not guard them properly. He walked to the altar at the back of the church and glared at the wooden carving of a man hanging on a cross. The son of their god. Their god who sacrificed his own son for the sins of his followers, but then seemed to save his life. Sven roared as the anger of that memory raged through him and lifted his Dane axe over his head before burying it into the wooden carving of the son of the Christian god.

Sven was angry and nothing he did seemed to calm that anger. He had left Halstein's camp soon after the attempt on his life, with six ships and over two hundred warriors with him as other jarls had joined him, and had spent the last few weeks burning and pillaging every town and church in sight. But nothing worked and with every church he burnt, he only seemed to get angrier. Sven didn't know why or what he expected. Perhaps he wanted their god to come down from wherever he hid so that Sven could confront him and ask him why he had saved his life. For it must have been the Christian god. Or perhaps Loki, who thought it would be funny for the Christian cross to stop the assassin's knife. That was what Rollo had suggested, but Sven couldn't believe that. If Loki had been involved, then Sven would have died that night. Sven pulled his axe out of the carving and wished he could speak to his uncle. The old godi would have the answers, even if Sven knew he most likely would not like them. He never liked what the godi had to say.

'We should leave soon, before the local lord sends real warriors,' Rollo said with an eyebrow raised at the chopped-up Jesus.

Sven glanced around him and wondered how long he had stood there. 'The priests?'

'Tied up and guarded by some carts we found. Along with everything the men could carry and the women who we managed to save from the men.' The town was more than half a day's march from their small camp near the river, so they had to steal some carts from the town to take the plunder back. But Sven was sure the townspeople would not care about that.

Sven nodded and glanced around the church one more time. 'Let's go. We'll head back to the ships and camp there for the night. Tomorrow we move on.'

Rollo nodded. 'You sure we should attempt to attack this Orléans? Halstein had more men than us and still failed.'

Sven shrugged as walked out of the church, before shielding his eyes from the sun. All around him, houses burnt as his men threw torches onto the thatch roofs, laughing and betting on who could burn the most houses. 'We are not Halstein. We are better. Orléans will burn and King Charles will learn what happens when he sends a snake to kill me instead of his warriors.'

'We still don't know that man was sent by King Charles.'

Sven glared at Rollo, but then sighed as his hand went to Charlemagne's cross in its pouch under his tunic. Rollo had given it back to him after Halstein and his men had left them after the attack. The trader had not been found, even though the men had searched throughout the night and the following day, but Sven was still convinced his assassin was sent by the king of the West Franks. He had to be, because the other option was something Sven did not want to think about. That the man had been sent by King Louis. And if that was the case, then it meant that Charles was already dead, and he had failed his son. If Sven hadn't been convinced that the assassin was the same man he had seen in Ribe, then he might have believed the second option more. Sven wished he had not given into his anger and killed the bastard, that way he might have found out who had sent the assassin, but like so many other times, he let the flames of his fury control him. Now he could only pray to the gods that he was right and that the assassin was a West Frank. Sven glanced at the sky, but saw no answer to his prayer and wondered if his gods were even in Francia.

'It doesn't matter who sent the man. We still have a job to do and, until Thora arrives with Charles or we die, we will keep on raiding and burning West Francia.'

Rollo nodded. 'Pray the Norns decide it's the first option, not the second.' He glanced at the Christian priests as they were being led to the carts waiting outside of the town. 'We should make a sacrifice to the gods before we attack this Orléans, even if it is just to give the men more courage. They'll fight harder if they believe the gods are with them.'

Sven grunted as he, too, glanced at the priests. Before he could stop himself, he pictured Charles walking amongst them, his hands tied and his head low as he was taken to be sold. His heart jumped and Sven had to grip Rollo before he fell to the ground.

'Sven?' Rollo looked around him, no doubt making sure that no one had seen this. 'Are you injured?'

Sven took a deep breath and shook his head. His body was fine, or as fine as a man his age could expect it to be. But his mind was troubled. Too many unknowns plagued it, and there was not enough ale to drown them out. 'We get the men back to the ships and then you do what you feel is needed.' Sven limped away, wondering who had sent that image. Was it the Christian god, pleading with him not to kill his people, or was Loki toying with Sven? He hawked and spat and went to grip the Mjöllnir around his neck, only to grab Charles's small wooden cross. Sven wanted to rip the thing off his neck, but it was all he had of Charles, so he just let go of it and limped to the carts waiting outside the town as his warriors enjoyed their victory.

That night, as the flames of their campfire danced away, Sven sat by his tent, brooding while the warriors of Ribe celebrated. Some of his men were playing instruments they had brought with them, while others sang songs made of old sagas. Some of the men, drunk on the wine and ale they had found in the town and the church, danced around the flames, much to the cheers of the others. Alvar was one of those men, his bare chest wet from the wine he spilled while he gulped it down. Despite his dark mood, Sven let his men enjoy themselves. They deserved it. He glanced at the moon as it shone through the clouds, wondering which god was watching over them as he felt the weight of Charlemagne's cross under his tunic, and decided he needed to get away from the revelry. Taking one last gulp of his ale, Sven struggled to his feet and walked to where they were keeping the captives. The men guarding them greeted Sven and thanked him for the jug of ale he had brought with him. He had wanted to drink it by himself, but then he saw how the four men longed to join their friends, so he gave it to them instead.

As the men enjoyed the ale, Sven stopped in front of the priests and watched as they cowered from him. They were different ages, some of them too young to grow beards, while others looked like they might have seen more winters than he had. One of those men glared at him as he gripped his cross. Sven was surprised the man still had it, but then he realised it was a wooden cross and of no value to his warriors.

'You still think your god will save you from me?' Sven asked in the Frankish tongue.

The old priest raised an eyebrow. 'God may not come to our aid in this life, but He promises us salvation in the next while you will burn in the flames of hell.'

Sven shrugged. 'Can't be worse than what I've already been through.' He had often wondered why the Christian hell was a place of punishment. For the Danes, Hel was the domain where those who died of age and disease went. There were no flames and no punishments. Instead, those who ended upon there feasted with Hel, the daughter of Loki and master of her domain. Few warriors wanted to go there, though, as there was no honour in ending up in the domain of Hel. But Sven had at times wondered if that was where he would end up. Perhaps Hel did not want him there, though.

'You mock us, but you wear the cross of Christ around your neck. I saw it when you attacked our church earlier today,' the priest said when Sven raised an eyebrow at him.

Sven pulled his grandson's cross out from under his brynja.

Some of the captives gasped when they saw it and a handful even begged him to let them go, but Sven ignored them. 'I wear a cross, but I do not worship your god.'

'Then why wear the cross?'

Sven sighed. 'It belongs to my grandson, who is a Christian. As was my son before he died.'

The old priest smiled. 'So the descendants of the mighty Sven the Boar chose to follow the true God. Is that why you attack us?'

Sven shook his head. 'No, that is not why we attacked you.' Sven frowned as he wondered why he was telling the priest this. Perhaps he just needed to talk to someone his age, someone who had lived long enough to suffer as he had done.

'It's doesn't matter, I suppose. This is God's will and we are His servants.'

'He probably killed his own son because he followed the true God instead of his false idols,' one of the other priests said, and Sven felt his irritation grow again.

Sven glared at the priest who had spoken. 'My son was killed by other Christians and not because of me. My grandson is being held captive by a Christian king so that I do his bidding.' He looked at the old priest again. 'You want to know why I attacked your town and your church? Because a Christian king is demanding I do it, otherwise he kills my grandson. Just like another Christian king ordered the death of my son.' He hawked and spat. 'You Christians believe you are better than us, but you are all thralls to your god. All of you, sitting here meekly and awaiting your fate.' Sven clenched his fists as he glared at the priests.

'I am sorry to hear of your son. My son was killed by a thief, so I understand your grief. But do not think we are slaves to our God and that we meekly await our deaths. We chose to believe in God because He gives us strength and hope, instead of the anger yours fill you with.'

'My anger keeps me alive,' Sven said, not wanting the priest's sympathy.

The old priest shrugged. 'If God decides that today is my day to die, then I welcome it. I can only pray that I will meet my son again in heaven.' The old priest looked Sven in the eyes. 'But you will never see your son in the afterlife, and for that, I pity you, Dane.'

Sven grabbed the old priest by his habit and pulled him closer. He glared at the man, but could not think of what to say to him, so he let go of the old priest and went back to the fire. Sven had spent many nights wondering where Torkel had gone when he had died. Was he now drinking ale with his ancestors in Valhalla or was he in the Christian heaven, doing whatever it was they did there? With a shudder, Sven realised he did not really want to know the answer to that. Because the truth might be something he could not accept.

24

Sven chewed on some dried fish, his attention on the old priest instead of the large town ahead of them. The conversation he had with priest still bothered him, but it only added to everything else wrong with his life at the moment.

'That's a large place,' Rollo said, shielding his eyes from the sun. 'Do we have enough men to take it?'

Sven swallowed the fish and looked at Orléans again. It had taken them a few days to reach the town that had humiliated Halstein the previous summer, and Sven was determined not to suffer the same fate. But Rollo's question was a valid one. The town was much larger than he had anticipated, even after everything Halstein and his jarls had told him about it. He glanced over his shoulder at his six ships, each filled with about forty warriors, and knew the only way he could capture Orléans was to take them by surprise. But that was not an option he had at the moment. Word had spread of his raiding this far along the Loire River and since they had left the town where they had captured the priests, they had found more than one village abandoned and nothing of value left behind. Animals that could not be taken with had been slaughtered and thrown into the river so that his warriors could not get fresh food. That did not concern Sven though, as they still had plenty of food from the last town they had attacked.

'Halstein couldn't take Orléans with more men than we have. Perhaps you've taken on more than you can chew, Sven,' Jarl Halfdan said. He was one of the younger jarls who had joined Sven, adding his ship with about thirty warriors to Sven's forces.

Sven shrugged, but he wasn't really listening. Neither was he thinking about how to take Orléans. All he could think about was his grandson as he bit off another piece of the dried fish. Sven could only pray that his grandson was still safe, and that Thora was keeping a close eye on him, but the attempt on his life a few weeks ago still plagued him and he could not help but wonder if that had anything to do with Charles.

'Sven, what do we do?' Rollo asked, and it took a few heartbeats for Sven to realise everyone was waiting for him to respond.

He shrugged as he swallowed the fish in his mouth. 'We get back to the ships and carry on upriver. Make them think we decided not to attack. If the gods are smiling on us, then they'll drop their guard and we can sneak back and attack them.' He looked at Jarl Halfdan. 'We don't need a lot of men. Just for them not to be expecting us.' This was something Sven had done in the past, and it had worked then. He could only pray that it would work again. The surrounding men all agreed, but before they could return to their ships, a horn sounded from behind them. For a heartbeat, Sven thought his ships were being attacked by the Franks, but as he shielded his eyes, he saw no Frankish army in sight, only a man on a horse racing towards them. Sven cursed the bastard that was blowing on his horn, even though the man was only doing what he was supposed to.

'What in the name of the gods is happening now?' Rollo asked, also seeing the horseman as the others around Sven glanced at him.

'I think he is one of us,' Jarl Halfdan said, and Sven frowned at him.

'One of us?' Alvar asked.

'Aye, a Dane.'

'Then what is the bastard doing out here? Is he one of our men?'

No one around Sven could answer him, and Sven felt his hands tremble at the thought that something was wrong. They had not sent out any scouts that morning and all the men had been ordered to stay with the ships. They were in enemy territory and needed to flee as soon as they could if they were attacked by a large force.

'We should find out who he is and what he wants.' Jarl Halfdan stated the obvious as they all rushed back to the ships. Sven winced as his limp made it hard for him to keep up with the younger men, but he was determined not to fall behind.

'What is going on?' Sven asked when they reached their ships and found the man lying on the ground as someone gave him some water to drink.

The man's face was covered in blood and dirt, as were his trousers and his leather jerkin. He looked like he had not slept for days, and even the horse looked like it was about to collapse. 'J... Jarl Sven.' Sven could hear Odin laugh in the man's voice. The All-Father loved chaos, and Sven knew that was what he was about to hear. 'The camp... it's under attack.'

'The camp! Under attack?' Rollo asked, his face suddenly pale and Sven understood why. His wife was there with his unborn child and son. Many of the men cried out in shock as they, too, had families on the island camp.

'Under attack? By who? Who is attacking the camp?' Sven's

mind raced. Had King Charles finally decided to send his army after so many summers of the Danes raiding his lands? And if so, why now? Because the assassination attempt had failed?

'Sigtrygg. He came with many ships and besieged the camp. Every time someone tries to get out, Sigtrygg's men kill them.'

'Who is Sigtrygg?' Alvar asked, and Sven could only shrug. He had never heard of the man, but guessed he had to be wealthy if he could afford enough men to surround the large island Halstein was using as a camp.

'He used to sail with Gudrod,' Halfdan said, and everyone looked at him. 'But last I heard, he was in Ireland.'

'With Gudrod?' Sven frowned as he wondered if Gudrod was behind this. He had always sensed that Gudrod did not like him, despite his words of friendship and forgotten pasts. 'Who sent you and how did you escape?' Sven asked the warrior, his eyes narrowed as he scrutinised him.

The man drank more water before he responded. 'Halstein sent us to ask for your aid. A group of us snuck out of the camp in the middle of the night, when the moon was covered by the clouds.'

'And you're the only one who reached us?' Rollo asked, glancing at Sven. But Sven noticed how Rollo's hands trembled and understood the fear he must have been feeling.

The warrior nodded. 'We found some horses, but some of Sigtrygg's men noticed us. I managed to lose them and followed the river until I saw signs of your attacks. That was how I found you.'

Sven glanced at the sky as he tried to make sense of what the messenger had said. A few birds zigzagged amongst the clouds, but there was nothing else to show him that the gods were paying attention to what was happening here.

'Sven, we have to go back,' Rollo said, as Sven knew he would.

Many of the warriors agreed, and even Halfdan nodded. Sven guessed the man also had family on the island. But something still bothered him as his hand went to Charlemagne's cross under his tunic and brynja.

Sven growled as he thought about how the gods were laughing at him. He did not trust the warrior who had found them against all the odds, but he knew he could not take the chance that the man was lying. Rollo had decided to follow him. He and many of the men had tied their fates with him and Sven could not ask them to risk their families just because he didn't trust the warrior in front of him. And then there was Thora's family as well. He had promised her he would protect them while she was in East Francia, keeping his grandson safe. Sven glanced over his shoulder at the large town which would have brought the king of West Francia to his knees if he had burnt it to the ground, and a growl escaped from his throat, as he knew that would never happen now.

'To the ships!' he roared and watched as the men jumped to their tasks of getting the ships ready. Sven glanced at Rollo and saw the worry on his friend's face. *We'll save your family*, Sven wanted to say, but he couldn't. The gods were cruel and often demanded a high price for their favour. And Sven could only wonder if this was what was happening. Odin had favoured them on this raid. They had got rich and had barely lost any warriors. Perhaps now the All-Father was demanding payment for that success.

Rollo and Halfdan repeated the orders as Sven turned his attention back to the town and thought he saw people on the walls watching them.

'We can always come back, take the town after we defeat this Sigtrygg.' Alvar rubbed the back of his neck.

Sven had considered that, but somehow didn't think it would happen. He had left a trail of destruction and fear behind him so that words of his attacks would reach this town. Fear was as powerful a weapon as a sharp sword, and Sven wanted the people of Orléans to be too terrified to defend their town when he attacked. But if he left now, then that opportunity was lost, which was another reason he was reluctant to leave now. 'The Norns will have already decided if we come back or not. All we can do is rush back to the camp and pray that we are not too late.' *Just like I was with Charles*, Sven thought and felt his own hands tremble from the memory of seeing Charles in Guttrom's tent during the battle at Jelling.

'The ships are ready,' Rollo said as he too glanced at Orléans.

Sven nodded and turned away from the town. He grimaced at the pain in his leg as he boarded his ship and took his position by the stern, even though he was not steering, Rollo was. Rollo called the order for the men to push the ship away from the banks of the river and turned it around as Sven still watched the town. The other ships followed and soon the men were all grunting as they pulled on the oars and raced to save their friends and families. Sven glanced at the man who had brought the message as he sat near the prow, barely keeping his eyes open. Then he glimpsed the old priest staring at him, and Sven felt the growl escaping from his lips. They had sacrificed three priests before they had left to attack Orléans, but Sven had made sure that the old man wasn't one of them. Sven had told himself it was because the gods wouldn't want old men to be sacrificed in their names. They wanted young blood, but he didn't really know why he decided that. The old man would not make them much gold in the thrall market, and that was if he even lived that long. Perhaps Sven just wanted to delay his reunion with his son in the afterlife.

'What do we do when we get there?' Alvar asked, distracting Sven from his thoughts.

'We kill every bastard that dared to threaten my family,' Rollo responded as his knuckles whitened around the steering oar.

Sven sighed, recognising the anger that he had once felt. The same anger that Rollo had shown before he had rushed off to Hedeby to find those responsible for the death of his mother. Sven would have thought that Rollo had learnt from that. He had been captured and beaten by Jarl Torgeir's men and had only lived because young Horik, the nephew of the dead king and the man who wanted to be the new king, had told Torgeir to release him. Sven had not thought of Jarl Torgeir since he had reached West Francia. The bastard hated Sven and Sven hated him because he knew Torgeir was behind the attack on Ribe that had resulted in the hall being burnt down and Hildegard escaping him. But Sven could not prove it because all those who knew of it were dead, which was another reason he had decided to not return to Denmark if he got his grandson back.

Sven had heard that young Horik had been proclaimed king of Denmark, and one of the first things he had done was to close the church in Hedeby and chase the Christian priests away. He glanced at the priests tied up by the mast of his ship, again picturing Charles amongst them, and wondered how he would have felt about that if he had still been the jarl of Ribe. Sven guessed he would have supported the move, but he knew that King Louis of East Francia would not be pleased. The only reason old Horik had lived as long as he had was because he had known it was better to keep the Frankish kings happy, something Sven had hated about the man, but he now understood why Horik had to do it. Sven could only pray for the sake of Denmark that the young king Horik would see the folly of that move before it was too late. He wondered though if it was the young Horik or if the move had been planned by his adviser, Jarl Hovi, a man Sven knew little about, but was told that he hated the Christians. Sven shrugged at his own thoughts. It didn't really matter, not any more. All that mattered to Sven now was getting his grandson back, and having to race back to the camp to stop an attack he wasn't even sure was really happening only angered him. 'Fetch that bastard.' Sven pointed at the messenger and a young warrior who wasn't rowing jumped to his feet. They had enough men for each rowing bench, but only half of them were rowing. The other half were resting so that they could take over when the others were tired. That way, they could row without stopping and reach the camp sooner. The warrior nodded and walked to the prow. Sven watched as he nudged the messenger awake and saw the confusion on the man's face before the young warrior led him to the stern.

'You want more information?' Rollo asked, and Sven nodded.

'We need to know how many men this Sigtrygg has and how they surrounded the camp. Tell me again what happened,' Sven said to the man when he stood in front of him.

The warrior nodded and told Sven how Sigtrygg's fleet had arrived one night, under the cover of darkness, and had surrounded the camp. Small skirmishes had been fought, but all of Halstein's men who had been outside of the camp walls had been killed.

'And Halstein did nothing while this happened?' Rollo asked.

The man shrugged. 'I don't know what Halstein could have done. Sigtrygg's force outnumbered us. And Gudrod had advised him not to fight. Said he would talk to Sigtrygg, get him to change his mind.'

'And did Gudrod talk to him?' Sven again wondered if Gudrod was behind this.

'Aye, but said Sigtrygg refused to listen. He had been paid to get rid of Halstein's camp, and that was what he was going to do.'

Sven rubbed his beard as he thought about that. 'Who paid Sigtrygg?' He wondered if it was King Charles. He had already used Guttrom to start a rebellion in Denmark, all so he could get to Charles and Charlemagne's cross.

The man shrugged for a second time. 'Gudrod says he wouldn't tell him.'

They all looked at each other as they digested this news and then Rollo asked, 'How many men does Sigtrygg have? How many ships?'

Again, the man could only shrug. 'Many more than Halstein. At least a hundred ships, I'd say, but it was hard to tell.'

Sven's eyes widened at that, and so did everyone who could hear what the man had said. He heard his men whisper the number along the ship and then someone shouted it across to the other ships. Sven had never seen so many ships together, and could only marvel at what that might look like on the open sea. But he guessed it meant that Sigtrygg had at least three thousand warriors. Sven closed his eyes and remembered the last time he had seen that many warriors together. It wasn't hard because it was the previous summer when Guttrom had fought his uncle for the crown of Denmark. Opening his eyes, he glanced at the clouds in the sky again as his hand went to the Mjöllnir around his neck. This time he found it and again wondered why Odin enjoyed fucking with him so much. 'Get some rest. You've done well.'

The messenger nodded and went back to the prow where he collapsed and fell asleep.

'What do we do, Sven? We have less than three hundred men with us. We can't fight a force that large.'

Sven nodded and saw the old Christian priest staring at him again. 'We pray, Alvar. We pray and perhaps sacrifice a few more of those bastards.'

'How many?' Rollo asked.

Sven still rubbed the Mjöllnir around his neck, missing the familiar touch of the one he had given Charles. 'As many as we need to make sure that Odin favours us.'

25

Thora rolled her shoulder and felt the muscle stretch. The cut to her shoulder had been deep, but it had healed well and she thanked Frigg that it had not been worse. But Thora wasted little time dwelling on that as she glanced at Charles, sitting by a tree and staring at the cross his mother had given him.

It had been a few weeks since they tried to kill Charles, and Sven's grandson had barely spoken since then. Thora knew he struggled to sleep. He had done even before in Ribe, before Ivor had kidnapped him, but now it was much worse than that. Almost every night he would wake up screaming, his face drenched in sweat and his eyes wild. He barely ate and, to Thora, Charles seemed gaunter than he had been before. She could almost hear her aunt's voice telling her to feed the boy more. Thora wished she knew how to help him and had prayed to Frigg every morning for guidance, but the mother of the gods remained silent, just like Charles did most days. Thora had never had children of her own, so did not know how to help Charles get through this, but she had promised his mother she would look after him.

After Hildegard was taken to the church, Thora and Charles

had stayed hidden until she felt it was safe enough for them to leave Frankfurt. It had been a tense time as warriors scoured the city, searching for those they believed were responsible for the bloodshed, and they had to wait until the following day before they could get out. And that they had only done because of an unlikely ally. Duke Liudolf.

It had been Father Leofdag who had found them. He must have seen where they went after they had left the tavern, or he was smarter than Thora had thought, because he had found them later that night. And the news he had brought with him had brought a smile to Charles's face, but only for a short while.

'Your mother lives, but she is very weak. Her life is in the hands of God now,' Father Leofdag had said as if that was good news. 'So you must pray for her every chance you get, Charles.'

'Praying is not going to help her. And besides, God doesn't listen to my prayers.' Charles had crossed his arms and walked away. Father Leofdag made to follow him, but then Thora stopped him.

'Give him some time. He needs to make sense of what has happened.'

Father Leofdag frowned. 'He should pray. That will help him.'

All Thora could do was shrug. 'He doesn't think so. But I'm glad that Hildegard will live.' She winced at the pain in her shoulder.

'You're injured.' Father Leofdag's eyes widened as if that was the first time he had seen her injury, but then she guessed he had been in that much shock while she fought the warriors that he most likely had not noticed the cut to her shoulder. The young priest had asked her to remove her top so he could treat her wound. At first Thora had been reluctant, but she knew she could not treat it herself, so she had done what he had asked. Thora had been surprised at how deft the young priest was at dealing with her wound and soon he had it cleaned and her shoulder bandaged. 'What will you do now?'

Thora had wondered the same thing. 'I don't know. I can't go to Sven because I don't know where he is or how to get there. For now, we just wait for things to calm down and then we leave Frankfurt. After that it is in the hands of the gods.'

Father Leofdag frowned. 'I doubt your gods will help you here, but I know someone who can. It was him who told me to come to you.'

'Priest, if you tell me your god, then I'll gut you here.'

Father Leofdag paled and shook his head. 'No, not God. Although, I'm sure He had a hand in this. But Duke Liudolf.'

Thora almost punched the priest when he mentioned the name of the man whose men had burnt the hall in Ribe and who had done nothing while Charles's father had been killed. But Thora knew she needed help to get out of East Francia. She still did not know the language, and she doubted Charles was in a state to help, so reluctantly, she agreed. In the end, Father Leofdag had been right and Duke Liudolf had helped them get out of Frankfurt and had even found them somewhere to stay near his own town.

It was a small hunter's cabin in the forest, which Thora preferred because it meant there was less chance that someone might spot them. Soon after the attack in Frankfurt, warriors had started asking about a Danish woman and a small child who had robbed the daughter of the king and had almost killed her. Gerold had been hailed as a hero who had died trying to protect his mistress, but Thora had not told Charles of this because she wasn't sure how he would handle that. Hildegard lived, and she had recovered from her wounds, although Thora had been told that she was still weak and had been sent back to her abbey. But this news had done little to cheer Charles up. He felt guilty for what had happened and, no matter what Thora said, nothing seemed to help. All she could do was watch him struggle every day, and she had never felt more useless in her life. Father Leofdag, who had left Frankfurt with them because he wasn't safe there either and now stayed in the church in Ehresburg, would bring them food every few days and even he was at a loss about what to do. He had tried to pray with Charles, but Charles had refused. All he did every day was sit by the tree and stare at the golden cross his mother had given him.

Thora sighed and knew she needed to find a way to break Charles from his thoughts. She got to her feet and rolled her shoulder again. Besides, she needed to train as well to get her shoulder stronger again. Thora walked to a nearby tree and scanned the branches until she found two which were perfect. She stretched up to break them off the tree and, after cleaning both of them, walked over to Charles and held one out for him.

Charles looked up from his mother's cross and frowned at her. 'What's that for?'

'We need to train, Charles. I need to get my strength back and you need to stop thinking about things you had no control over.'

'I could have stopped her being hurt. I should have.' Charles looked at the cross again. Thora had been avoiding this conversation with him, even though she knew it was needed. The boy was like his grandfather, always taking the blame for things only the gods controlled. Sven had spent too many winters wandering Denmark as a stinking drunk, blaming himself for everything that had happened and, since then, had blamed himself for Charles being taken. But they had all been fooled by Guttrom and his son, Ivor.

'How could you have stopped your mother from being hurt, Charles? She placed herself in front of you to protect you.'

Charles's hands trembled. 'I should have pushed her out of the way.'

Thora sighed and knelt down. 'And then what? Gerold kills you and then your mother.' Charles looked at her for a few moments, his eyes tearing up, and then looked at the cross again. Thora felt the knot in the back of her throat, but knew that Charles needed to hear what she had to say. 'Charles, there was nothing you could have done. Your mother did what she had to so that you can live your life free from the threat of her father.'

Tears streamed down Charles's face as a bird landed on the branch above them, its cheerful song at odds with how she knew Charles felt. But then nature did not care about the moods of people. Even that small bird understood how cruel life could be, so it sang its cheerful song whenever it could. 'But why does everyone have to die or get hurt to protect me? What's so special about me?'

Thora put a hand on Charles's cheek so that he would look at her. 'Everything, Charles. And besides, your mother still lives. And so do I and your grandfather.'

'But how do we know he lives? You've heard nothing about him for weeks.'

Thora smiled. 'Because I know your grandfather. And besides, I've told you before. Odin is not ready for Sven to be in Valhalla.'

'He might change his mind.'

Thora shrugged. 'He might, but I doubt Sven would go anyway. Not until he knows you are safe.'

Charles looked at the cross again. 'I want people to stop dying because of me. But I don't know how to do that.'

'Charles, that's not up to you. You can't control what other people choose to do. Now come.' She handed him the stick. 'Let's train and get our minds off our troubles.'

Charles took the stick, but did not get up. 'I don't know if I want to.'

'Charles, if you want people to stop dying because of you, then you need to learn to protect yourself.' She walked to the small clearing in front of the cabin and waited for Charles.

'My grandfather said the same thing.' Charles got up and walked towards her.

Thora smiled. 'Aye, the old bastard is rarely right about things, but if there is one thing he knows better than most, it's how to survive.'

Charles looked at the stick in his hand. 'How do I learn that?'

'You don't need to, Charles. You have his blood running through his veins and, besides, the gods know that you have already shown you know how to do that.' Charles frowned at her and, again, Thora smiled. 'Look at everything you have been through. And yet you still stand. You are stronger than you realise, Charles, but only you can't see that.'

Charles bit his lip as he thought about it. 'My mother says that believing in God will make me stronger.'

Thora nodded. 'Our faith in our gods often gives us strength when everything feels hopeless. That is why we often pray at our lowest moments. Not because we believe the gods will come down from Valhalla and rescue us, but because it gives us strength.'

'Even your gods? But I thought they were cruel.'

'Aye, they can be. But not all of them. Thor protects us from the giants and from Loki's mischief. Frigg, as well, can protect us from those who wish to harm us. Just like your god protects you and keeps you safe.'

'But it doesn't feel like He has.'

'Charles, we will never know why the gods do what they do, or why others have to die so that we can live. But never doubt that the gods don't protect us.'

'But how do I know He does when He doesn't answer my prayers?'

'Because otherwise Midgard would be a far darker place than it is.'

'Darker?'

'Aye, and colder. With ugly ice giants everywhere, trampling over lands and eating small boys who don't know the sharp end of a sword from the other end.'

'But I know that.' Charles frowned as he looked at the stick in his hand.

'Then show me.' Thora lunged forward before Charles even lifted his stick, but he saw her attack and jumped back.

'I wasn't ready yet!'

Thora laughed. 'The world doesn't wait for you to be ready, Charles.' She swung her stick at his head and Charles lifted his to block the blow, before jumping back again, the look of determination on his face making her smile. She wished Sven was there to see how strong his grandson had become, and prayed to Thor that the old bastard still lived. Because she doubted Charles could cope with losing another loved one.

26

'By the gods, would you look at that?'

'Aye, Odin knows, I've never seen anything like that.'

'Not even Thor himself could get through that.'

The men chirped behind Sven and he did his best to ignore them, but he couldn't. Because the same doubts rang in his mind as they studied the scene before them. Hundreds of ships blocking the river on either side of the island camp while the smoke from the campfires on the two islands on either side of Halstein's camp blocked out the late afternoon sun.

'Sven, what do we do?' Rollo asked, the fear for his family obvious in his voice.

I don't know, Sven thought, but didn't say. They had sailed for many days without stopping to get back to Halstein's camp as quickly as possible and now that they had arrived, Sven wished that the warrior who had brought them the message of the siege had been lying. Their ships had been left half a day's walk upriver, along with most of the warriors, as Sven did not want to alert Sigtrygg's men to their presence, while he, Rollo and Halfdan, with a handful of warriors, went for a closer look. Sven glanced at the sky, but saw nothing other than the smoke from the campfires and felt his hands tremble. For a few heartbeats, he considered going back to his ship and sailing away, but then he chased the thought away before it could take root. Thora's family were on the island and he had to protect them, just like Thora was protecting his grandson. Sven glanced at Rollo, his brow wrinkled, and doubted Rollo would let him leave, anyway. Not with his pregnant wife and son on the island, not to mention the families of some of the other men. Sven sighed and glanced at the sky again. No, he could not just leave and sail away. He had to find a way of breaking through Sigtrygg's camp and saving those from Ribe.

'I still don't understand why Sigtrygg's doing this,' Halfdan said, a grimace on his face as if he had eaten something foul.

'Because he's been paid to do it,' Rollo said as he gripped the haft of his Dane axe.

'Paid? By who?' Halfdan asked.

Rollo shrugged and all Sven could do was ask the question himself. They had tried to solve that mystery as the men rowed, but they were still no closer. The most obvious answer was King Charles, but Sven wasn't so sure. They had heard that King Charles was under pressure to deal with them, a sign that Sven's raids were having the desired effect, but Sven had hoped that King Charles would march his army here himself. It was possible that King Charles paid other Danes to deal with Sven, but that would only make him look even weaker. And then he'd have to deal with Sigtrygg's army if he succeeded.

'It doesn't matter who paid the bastard,' Sven said, the words almost coming out as a growl. 'What matters is that we break this siege and send the bastard back to where he came from.'

'And how do we do that?' Halfdan's eyes widened. 'It'll be like a small bird taking on an eagle.'

'I've seen small birds chase eagles away from their nests. It's possible,' one man said, and then looked at Sven for the answer to Halfdan's question.

Sven glanced at the sky again as he resisted the urge to rub the faded tattoo on his scalp or the Mjöllnir around his neck. Seeing an eagle would have been a good sign, he thought, but there was nothing but smoke and clouds. Sven didn't want to think about what that meant, so he turned and walked away, leaving the others waiting for an answer that wasn't coming.

'Sven, we need to do something. We can't just walk away,' Rollo said after using his long legs to catch up to him.

'We're not walking away,' Sven said, even though that idea still felt tempting.

'Then what do we do?'

Sven looked around him to make sure that he and Rollo were out of earshot. 'I don't know, Rollo. Odin knows I wish I knew, but I don't.'

Rollo nodded and then rubbed the Mjöllnir around his neck. 'We can't just attack them. They outnumber us by almost a hundred to one if those ships are anything to go by.' The giant warrior frowned as they walked back to the ships in silence while Halfdan and the others followed, their worried voices drifting over Sven as he longed for the days when all he had to think about was where to get ale from.

'What did you see?' Alvar asked when they reached the ships. Sven had left him behind to watch over the ships and the other warriors, not that the warriors of Ribe needed to be watched. Sven had learnt he could trust them, and Rollo's friend, Torgny, had shown that he was also a leader amongst the men. The only problem they had was when a few of Halfdan's men tried their luck with some of the shield maidens in Sven's crew, but they had quickly learnt to keep their hands and other parts to themselves.

Rollo explained what they had seen as Sven walked to his war chest and sat on it. One man brought him some ale, something they had very little of, and Sven nodded his thanks. He emptied the cup and before long his fingers were playing with the Mjöllnir around his neck as he tried to think of a plan. But that was not Sven's strength, and he knew it. As Rollo and some warriors tried to come up with a plan, Sven's attention was drawn to Halfdan, who was sitting with his own men. He wasn't sure why, but Sven suddenly felt like he could not trust the young jarl.

'Rollo, make sure we keep an eye on that bastard,' Sven said, interrupting the conversation happening around him.

'Halfdan?' Rollo raised an eyebrow. 'You think he is up to something?'

Sven shrugged. He did not know, but he had learnt to be more suspicious of people, especially those claiming to be friends, and there was something about the way Halfdan was glancing his way that made Sven nervous. 'Just keep an eye on him and his men.'

Rollo nodded and then smiled. 'I think I know how we can break Sigtrygg's siege, but it won't be fast or easy.'

Sven raised an eyebrow at Rollo. 'Tell me.'

Rollo waited until he had everyone's attention and then said, 'We wait.'

'We wait?' Alvar said and glanced at Sven, who wished he had more ale.

'Aye, we wait. Sigtrygg has about three thousand men with him, many more than Halstein has, assuming Halstein is still on the island, and many, many more than we have,' Rollo started explaining.

'Aye,' Alvar responded with furrowed brows. And from the looks on the faces of the surrounding men, he wasn't the only one who struggled to make sense of Rollo's plan. Not that Sven knew where he was going with this.

'Those men need to be fed, they need to be given ale. The gods know there is no way that Sigtrygg would have brought all those supplies with him. At best, he has enough food for a few weeks and he has already been here that long. His men will be running out of food and ale.'

'But he can just get more,' Torgny said. 'That's what Halstein does. Many of the farmers in the area supply Halstein with food and ale so that Halstein's army doesn't attack their farms.' Those around nodded as Sven listened.

'Aye,' Alvar said. 'And those farmers will just do the same with Sigtrygg. I doubt they care who they deal with, as long as their homes are protected.'

'That is why we need to attack those farms. Kill the farmers or chase them away. We stop them from supplying Sigtrygg and soon he runs out of food.' Sven understood now what Rollo was saying as he stared at the flames of the small fire one of the men had made.

'And how does that help us?' Alvar asked. 'Odin knows Sigtrygg is not just going to get on his ships and leave when he runs out of food.' More murmurs of agreement from the men around them. Sven didn't respond. The thought of attacking more people who were just trying to survive and fighting another large battle had left him exhausted.

Rollo took a deep breath and glanced at everyone around him until his eyes rested on Sven. 'When Sigtrygg runs out of food, then he will have no choice but to attack the camp. He will need to end the siege as quickly as possible before his men kill each other.'

The warriors gasped, and all of them stared at Rollo with wide eyes. 'Has Loki stolen your wits? My family is on that island!' one man said, his outburst causing many to look their way.

Rollo glared at the man. 'So is mine, but I see no other way.'

'But how is that going to help us?' Torgny asked, less outraged than the others.

'Because while Sigtrygg attempts to take the camp, we can attack them from behind. We don't need a large force to create confusion and fear amongst Sigtrygg's men,' Rollo said, his voice sounding like even he was doubting the plan now that he spoke it out loud.

'We don't have enough men. We will never get close enough to Sigtrygg to kill him,' Torgny said, and others agreed with him.

But Sven knew they had no other option. Granted, the plan was risky and, even if it succeeded, it might take many weeks to work. Sven wasn't sure if they had that time, though, but he trusted Rollo would have thought of that already. Sven's other concern was what to do with the captives they had tied up on the ships. They couldn't leave them sitting there, because they would need to be fed and kept alive. And the longer they sat there, the greater the risk that the women would be killed by the men who couldn't control themselves. But Sven did not want to let them go either, not only because of the loss of the gold they could bring at the markets, but the risk they posed. 'We don't need to kill Sigtrygg. And besides, do any of you know what he looks like?' Sven looked around him as everyone shook their heads. 'Neither do I. All we need is to give those inside a chance to attack Sigtrygg and then Halstein can kill him. Sigtrygg will be fighting on both sides and no army likes that.'

'We really have no other plan?' Torgny asked, and Rollo shook his head.

'None that I can think of.' They all sat around the small fire in silence, each man and woman frowning as they thought about what Rollo had said. Many of them looked like they were searching for better options, but they had none. Sven waited, stabbing at the fire with a stick, while his mind drifted to other places.

'Should we tell Halfdan?' Alvar asked, disrupting Sven from his thoughts.

Sven shook his head. 'Not yet. Not until I know I can trust him.'

'What do you think he is up to?' Torgny asked, and Sven shrugged.

'Only the Norns know.'

They all must have sensed that Sven wasn't going to explain and, after a while, went back to their own tents. The moon was up and the stars struggled to be seen through the clouds and Sven needed some rest before they implemented Rollo's plan. His hand went to Charlemagne's cross hidden in his tunic and again he wondered if the cross was really a curse on him. That was the only way he could explain the fact that everything seemed to be going against him at the moment. Or, again, it could just be Loki amusing himself.

A long while later, Sven heard the noise he was expecting. Men sneaking around and whispering to each other. Sven gripped the hilt of his sword as he tried to work out what Halfdan's men were doing, but he already knew. That was why he had extra warriors on board his ships, with strict orders not to sleep. Rollo and Alvar were nearby as well, their Dane axes ready. Sven waited, his ears straining as he listened to Halfdan's men sneak towards the ships. He had hoped that he was wrong, but then one of the other jarls had come to Sven and told him what Halfdan had planned.

Sven didn't have to wait long before he heard the first cry. A woman's scream which tore through the night and was soon joined by others as the rest of the captives cried out. Then came the unmistakable sound of metal striking wood, a weapon against a shield, and Sven knew it had begun. Gritting his teeth, he jumped to his feet, doing his best to ignore the pain in his back, and made his way towards the fighting. Rollo and Alvar were on either side of him, but if Sven believed that would stop Halfdan's men from attacking him, then he was wrong. They were halfway to the ships, where most of the fighting was, when a group of Half-dan's men formed a small shield wall.

'Get out of the way, worms,' Rollo said as he lifted his Dane axe. Sven couldn't see how they reacted in the dark, but knew they would ignore Rollo. Sven's warriors outnumbered Halfdan as the other jarls had sided with him, but Sven did not want to lose men because of Halfdan's treachery. Not when they had to rescue those trapped by Sigtrygg's siege.

'Halfdan! Where are you? You treacherous bastard!' Sven roared into the night. 'Halfdan!'

'I'm not risking my life to fight Sigtrygg!' Halfdan responded over the fighting on the ships. Sven scowled as he tried to see what was happening around him, but it was too dark. It brought back the memories of fighting in the streets of Ribe, not knowing who was friend or foe, and Sven shivered at the thought.

But he took a deep breath and shouted, 'Then leave! You don't need to steal my plunder and captives!' The small shield wall in front of them stood there, unwilling to move, even as more of Sven's warriors joined his own wall that Rollo was forming.

'Odin knows you don't need that plunder or the captives. Sigtrygg will make sure of it if you are dumb enough to attack him.'

'Odin only knows that you are a coward and a worm,' Rollo called out. 'What about your wife? She is still on the island!'

'I can get another one, especially with all the plunder I'll be leaving with.' His laugh echoed through the night and Sven had enough of trying to talk sense into the bastard.

He lifted his sword and roared, 'Kill them all!'

Rollo and Alvar reached Halfdan's small wall in a few giant strides and both swung their Dane axes in unison. Those of Half-dan's men who lifted their shields were soon dead or missing limbs and, before the rest of them could recover, Ribe's warriors, led by Sven, crashed through them.

He stabbed to the left and felt his sword strike something, but it was too dark to know if he had killed someone or just wounded them. Movement to the other side made Sven lift his shield, and his arm almost collapsed as a Dane axe struck it. His shoulder was not as strong as it used to be, and Sven was just glad that he kept the shield up before he stabbed his attacker in the leg. As the warrior cried out, Sven pulled his shield back and punched the man in the stomach with its rim. But he did not get to deal the killing blow as one of Ribe's warriors chopped at the back of the man's neck as he bent over. Sven scowled as he scanned the dark night, trying to see how the fight was going and where Halfdan was, but all he saw were shadows. He prayed the clouds would part so the moon could provide them some light, but the gods must have been too busy feasting to pay attention to him and so he had to move through the darkness towards his ships. Because he was sure that was where Halfdan was. Rollo and Alvar fell in on either side of him and, together, they killed any who came within reach.

Sven sliced the chest open of a warrior who rushed at him, his anger coursing through him at the thought that he had been betrayed again. For a heartbeat, Sven wondered what he had done wrong for everyone to turn against him. When he was younger, he had believed it was because people feared him, but now he wasn't so sure any more. A warrior came out of the dark and stabbed his spear at Rollo, who had to use the haft of his Dane axe to deflect the spear point. Before Rollo's attacker could pull his spear back, Sven stabbed him in the side. He twisted his sword before pulling it free and then he roared over the battle. 'Halfdan, you bastard! You better run before I get you! I swear by Odin I will rip your eyes out and shove them down your treacherous throat! You are afraid of Sigtrygg! Even the gods fear me! Halfdan!' He blocked the sword of another before Alvar crushed his skull with the flat of his Dane axe. Sven stepped over the dead man and stabbed at another who blocked with his shield, only for Rollo to cleave his chest open. 'Halfdan! I will cut your ears off and wear them around my neck! I will chop your hands and feet off and make you watch as I feed them to the hounds!' Sven beat his bloodied sword against his chest, ignoring the blood on the blade spraying over his face. 'Halfdan! You bastard! You better run!'

Rollo and Alvar killed more of Halfdan's men as they reached the first ship and hesitated as they glanced at each other. Sven did not know who controlled it or what had happened to the captives. They had gone quiet as the fighting continued, and all Sven could do was hope they weren't killed by Halfdan's men. More of Ribe's warriors joined them, and Sven frowned as he wondered where Halfdan had gone. He squinted into the darkness around him, but saw nothing other than his own warriors around them. Sven's frustration at not knowing took over, and before anyone could stop him, he roared and rushed onto the ship. He heard fighting in front of him, but it was still too dark to make out what was happening, so Sven stabbed at the first warrior he reached, praying he hadn't just killed his own warrior as he freed his sword and sliced it across the face of another who turned to face him. Soon, Rollo and Alvar were there as well, both giant warriors swinging their Dane axes and cleaving their way through the enemy in front of them.

The attack was too much for those on board and many jumped into the river to escape the onslaught of Ribe's warriors, who had followed Sven and his giants. A small group of warriors stood facing them still, but it was too dark to make out who they were.

'Torgny!' Rollo called out to his friend, whom Sven had put in charge of protecting this ship. 'Torgny!'

'Aye, I'm still here,' Torgny responded from the group and Sven sighed with relief. 'It's all clear.'

Sven glanced around him when he realised the fighting had stopped. He tensed, not yet believing it was over, and felt the others do the same. 'Get some torches lit,' he said to no one in particular. 'Halfdan!' he shouted the bastard's name, but there was no response. The sounds of fighting had stopped and were soon replaced by the cries of those injured and the frightened captives, many of whom prayed for their god to save them, but Sven doubted the Christian god was going to come down from his seat and get his clothes dirty to do that.

'Maybe he ran?' Alvar asked.

'Or he's dead,' another warrior said.

All Sven could do was shrug. 'We'll have to wait for daybreak to find out. Alvar, check on Jarl Baldur. See if the bastard is still alive. The rest of you, stay awake. The threat might not be over yet.' Sven heard some warriors complain, but he ignored them. They would be tired, and he was sure that many of them were reliving the attack on Ribe the previous summer. Just like he was. But just like that night, Sven still lived. All he could do now, though, was wait for the sun to rise and to pray that he would live through what was to come.

27

Sven watched as his men searched through the bodies of Halfdan's army, his body aching from exhaustion and his eyes barely able to stay open. But he refused to sleep. Not until they found Halfdan amongst the dead, or didn't. Although Sven would have preferred to find the bastard's corpse.

'What if we don't find him?' Alvar asked, echoing Sven's thoughts.

Sven glanced at the giant warrior standing beside him, his brynja still covered in the blood of the men he had killed. Not that Sven looked any better. 'Then we assume the worm has run to Sigtrygg and will tell the bastard about us.'

'Will it make any difference? They already outnumbered us before, but now? It doesn't feel like the gods want us to help those on the island.' Alvar rubbed the Mjöllnir around his neck.

Sven did the same and glanced at the sky. Alvar was right. It did feel like the gods had turned against them. Or him. Although Sven was never really sure that Odin was ever with him. That Halfdan had turned against him and had tried to steal his plunder was bad enough, but after the short battle they had found that many of the captives on Sven's ship had been killed during the fight, including the old priest, and those who hadn't died had fled. Sven wasn't sure who had freed them, but guessed it must have been Halfdan's men to create more confusion in the dark. At least their plunder had been saved, but losing Halfdan's men and those of Sven, who had died during the night, meant that Sven could not be happy about that. Sven's hand went to Charlemagne's cross hidden under his tunic, and he wondered if it was the Christian god who was responsible for this. Sven had always believed him to be weak, but after that night when the cross saved his life, Sven had wondered if the Christian god was stronger than he realised.

'We found him!' someone shouted. Sven turned back towards his ship and saw one of his men waving his arms in the air.

'At least we know he didn't run to Sigtrygg.' Sven winced as he limped towards the ship, Alvar by his side.

'Still don't understand why Halfdan betrayed us.'

Sven shrugged. 'He owed us no allegiance.'

'Aye, but still.'

Sven sighed and wondered if he would have done the same if he had been in Halfdan's shoes. 'He came to make himself and his men rich. And while things went well, he fought with us. But he knew we could never defeat Sigtrygg in battle and decided that it was no longer in his best interest to stay with us.'

'But he could have just left. Why try to steal our share of the plunder?'

Sven shrugged again. 'Because he probably didn't think we would need it for much longer.'

Alvar rubbed the back of his neck. He had stayed by Sven's side the entire night while Rollo was in charge of searching the dead for Halfdan. But it had been difficult under the thin moonlight, and they didn't want to risk torches on the ships, so they had waited until sunrise to see if Halfdan was amongst the dead. 'Perhaps you should have told him of Rollo's plan.'

Sven shook his head. 'Then he would have told Sigtrygg about it. What's done is done, Alvar. There's no point in trying to make sense of the Norns' weaving. They wanted this to happen, and so it did. All we can do now is move on and help our friends and families on the island.' Sven boarded the ship as Alvar opened his mouth to say something else, and walked to where Rollo was standing before looking at the corpse of Halfdan.

'Looks like he died leading the attack on the ship,' Rollo said. 'Most likely wanted to take the ship instead of just the plunder.'

Sven nodded as he thought the same. That was what he would have done, but he would have done it better and succeeded. Sven looked around him, seeing how tired the warriors of Ribe were. Most of them could barely stay on their feet and those with spears leaned on them, their eyes closed. 'Get rid of the dead and then rest.'

'What about Jarl Baldur?' Rollo asked. 'He risked much siding with us.'

'Aye, and thank the gods he did,' Torgny said, and Sven found himself agreeing with the man.

Sven glanced to where the other jarl was sitting with his men. Like Sven, he had lost more than a handful of warriors during the night, and many of them would have been men he knew well. 'Give him Halfdan's share of the plunder. He deserves that, at least. And then tell him he is free to leave if he wants to.'

Rollo nodded, not surprised by Sven's response, even if some of the other warriors were. 'I doubt he would leave us. His son is on the island, in Gudrod's care.'

Sven scowled as he scrutinised the young jarl. Memories of his son on the beach, surrounded by Frankish warriors while he sailed away, flooded his mind and Sven had to shake his head to chase them away. 'Do we have any ale?'

Rollo shook his head. 'All gone.'

Sven sighed. 'Clear the dead and get some rest. Tomorrow we begin with your plan.'

Rollo frowned and glanced around him. 'You sure it will work?'

Sven raised an eyebrow at the giant warrior, but he understood the young man's trepidation. Part of being a leader was making plans and sticking with them, even if you weren't sure yourself. The men looked to you to have an answer and few could deal with that burden. But Sven knew Rollo could. That was why he trusted him to lead when he couldn't. 'Only the Norns can tell you that, Rollo. But right now, we have no other choice. Have faith in yourself and the men, and the rest is up to the gods.'

'Then let's pray it works,' Alvar said, smiling at Rollo. Sven felt the same, but kept quiet. Rollo's plan was a good one and Sven knew it must have been hard for him to come up with that as his family was in the camp, but the only way they could break the siege was to attack Sigtrygg's army while they attacked the camp. And that was why it was risky, especially now without Halfdan's crew and those they had lost during the night. If their attack failed, then the camp would be overrun and their families would all be killed.

* * *

More than a week later, Sven watched as the warriors of Ribe burnt another farm to the ground. The livestock had been slaughtered and what meat Sven's small force didn't need was thrown into the river so that Sigtrygg's men couldn't get it. Sven was glad

that they were upriver from Sigtrygg's force, because it meant that
if the carcasses rotted it might poison the water so that Sigtrygg's
men couldn't drink it. The only risk of that was that those on the
island couldn't either. Summer had already started, though, and
Sven was impatient for Rollo's plan to work. It had been too many
weeks with no news from the rest of Francia and Sven had never
felt more blind. He needed to know how King Louis's son fared
and could only pray that the bastard had defeated Pepin and
claimed the throne of Aquitaine. At least that way, Charles would
still be safe.

'That's the fifth farm in almost as many days,' Jarl Baldur said,
almost sounding like he was enjoying the chaos of these attacks.
'Who knew there were so many? It'll take us another summer to
deal with them all.'

Sven glanced at the summer sun. 'We don't need to attack all of
them, just enough to force Sigtrygg's hand.' Somewhere a woman
screamed and Sven turned away from the farm. He had seen
enough death, but yet Odin insisted on forcing this life on him.

The last few days had been exhausting as they raced from one
farm to the next, attacking quickly and disappearing again.
Sigtrygg was aware of their presence and had sent small war
bands out to hunt for them, like wolves chasing foxes to keep
them away from their meals, which meant Rollo's plan was
having an effect. But so far the gods had been with them and they
had managed to stay ahead. But Sven knew it was only a matter
of time before Odin got bored and they ran into one of those
groups. And besides, Sven hated being the fox. He wanted to be
the wolf.

The sun was setting by the time they reached their new camp,
as they had to move camp on more than one occasion to avoid
Sigtrygg's hunting parties who were getting too close for comfort
and to make sure that none of the captives that had escaped or

were released brought Sigtrygg's warriors to them, and Sven frowned at Alvar's broad grin.

'Sven, it's happening.'

'What's happening?' Sven glanced at Alvar's mud-covered face. He had left a handful of warriors behind, led by Alvar, to keep an eye on Sigtrygg's camp because they needed to know when he decided to attack so they didn't miss their chance.

Alvar's grin broadened even more. 'They're making ladders. Lots of them. The attack will happen soon.' Everyone within earshot stopped what they were doing and stared at Alvar, as if they didn't believe what he had said.

'Are you sure?' Rollo asked and Alvar nodded.

'A large group of men went to the forest and spent the whole day chopping wood.'

'They could just be making their own camp to protect themselves.' Jarl Baldur raised an eyebrow and glanced at Sven as if he expected him to agree.

Alvar shook his head. 'Not with the wood they brought back. Trees that thin can only be used for making ladders.'

Sven frowned as he thought about it. Jarl Baldur made a good point, but he trusted Alvar and if he believed that Sigtrygg's men were preparing ladders, then that was what was happening. And besides, Sigtrygg would need ladders to attack Halstein's camp with its formidable walls and defensive ditch.

'We should attack the men sent to the forest to gather wood,' Jarl Baldur suggested. 'Give them something else to worry about.'

'No.' Rollo shook his head. 'That would slow them down. This has already taken too long.' The frown on his face told Sven that he was worried about his family in the camp, just like Sven worried about Charles and Thora in East Francia.

'Rollo is right.' Sven raised his hand to stop Jarl Baldur from arguing. 'What we should be doing is preparing for our own attack. If they're building ladders, it means that they're running out of food and must attack soon. And besides, we can't afford to lose more warriors in forest skirmishes. Let the men rest for a few days' – Sven looked at Alvar – 'and keep a close eye on Sigtrygg's camp. We need to be ready to attack when the moment is right.'

'But how do we attack?' Jarl Baldur asked, lowering his voice so many couldn't hear him. 'They still heavily outnumber us. It will be like a bee stinging a whale.'

Sven glanced at Halfdan's empty ship which they had dragged around with them since the bastard's betrayal, even though many had wanted to burn it, as a smile reached his lips. He had spent the last few days trying to work out how they could spread enough panic amongst Sigtrygg's men in order for Halstein to counterattack and Halfdan's ship was key to the plan. 'Let me worry about that, Baldur. You just make sure that your men are ready.'

Jarl Baldur scowled at Sven before he nodded and went to his tent.

'You have a plan?' Rollo asked when Baldur was gone.

'Aye,' Sven said. 'I have a plan, but don't ask me if it will work. That is in the hands of the gods.'

'A pity we don't have any more captives to sacrifice, just to make sure that Odin is on our side.'

Sven rubbed the faded tattoo on his scalp, agreeing with Rollo. But as much as they needed Odin's help, Sven feared what the price might be to get it. 'Odin will favour us. Even without sacrifices.'

'How can you be so sure?' Rollo asked and Sven didn't want to tell him he wasn't, as he remembered the sacrifice his uncle had made that night in Ribe.

'Because we are the bee who is about to sting a whale. Even if Odin doesn't appreciate the bravery of what we are doing, then Týr or Thor will.' Sven walked back to his tent before Rollo could say anything. He needed ale, but they had run out days ago and none of the farms they had raided seemed to have any. All he could do was lie down and hope sleep would take him, but without the ale to numb his mind, his dreams had been making it hard for him to sleep. Every time he closed his eyes, all he saw was Charles being taken away from him and Eydis, his dead wife, shaking her head at him before she turned and disappeared into the darkness.

Inside his tent, Sven glanced around to make sure he was alone before he pulled the pouch out of his tunic and took the cross hidden inside of it out. Sven rubbed the large ruby as he thought about his grandson and wondered where Charles was or how he was doing. He hoped Thora was still there as well, keeping a watchful eye on Charles. And then his mind went to the other news they kept hearing. That King Charles had found the long-lost Cross of Charlemagne. Sven frowned and wondered if it was possible for there to be two crosses. But if there were, then why had King Charles gone to all the effort of getting this one and Charles? Perhaps Rollo had been right and that the one the king of West Francia had was fake. A fake cross made to make the people believe that their god was on their side and that he would deal with the Danes ravaging their lands. Many of those Sven had raided over the last few weeks seemed to think that their god would smite them, but so far, the biggest threat they had faced was from other Danes. Although Sven was sure the Christians believed that their god was turning the Danes against each other.

Focusing his attention on the cross again, Sven wished he had somewhere to hide the damn thing. He felt nervous going into a large battle with it hidden in his tunic, even though it had saved his life before. Sven couldn't help but worry that the cross would curse him and cause his death, but there was nowhere to hide the large golden cross. He couldn't bury it, because he might forget where it was, and he didn't feel safe leaving it in his war chest, either. Sighing, Sven knew he had no choice but to carry the cross with him when they fought Sigtrygg. But just to feel safer, Sven rubbed the Mjöllnir around his neck and asked Thor to protect him from its curse. Then his fingers went to the small wooden cross Charles had given him and he asked Frigg to keep a watchful eye on his grandson and Thora.

28

Sven gripped the haft of his Dane axe, his heart racing faster than it had ever done before, and no matter how hard he tried to stay calm, he could not. His helmet was irritating him, the felt cap he wore under it making his freshly shaved scalp itch, and the metal feeling like it was squeezing his head. His brynja somehow felt heavier than it did when he had put it on that morning, and he kept checking to see if his sword was still in its scabbard and his shield was still strapped to his back. Unlike him, Rollo and Alvar seemed calm as they stood on either side of him by the prow of his ship, both dressed in their war gear, as were the rest of Ribe's warriors as they all waited, oars ready, for the signal. Jarl Baldur's ship was to his left, and Sven could see that the younger jarl was nervous as well. All of them were. What they were about to do was something that you only ever heard in the sagas of old and the warriors in those sagas were all dead. Some might have survived the battle, but Sven doubted that happened in real life. The story-tellers needed to keep the heroes of the sagas alive, otherwise no one would want to hear the stories they told. Sven wondered if a saga would be written about them if they succeeded and hoped it would, because he had never done anything this saga-worthy in his life. Or this dumb. He felt the weight of Charlemagne's cross hidden in his tunic where it had been since he had arrived in Francia and, again, he asked Thor to protect him from its curse, because Sven knew it was far too late to listen to his uncle's warning.

'Thor knows, I wish I felt your confidence,' Rollo said as he mistook Sven's smile. But Sven did not correct him. The men needed to think that he believed in what they were doing. He needed to think he believed. Otherwise, there was nothing to stop Sven from turning his ship around and sailing away. Sven was terrified, and there was not enough ale to numb that fear. But he realised he was not afraid of dying. Sven had lived a life longer than most, despite what he had been through. What Sven was afraid of was what would become of Charles if he did not survive this battle. It was a fear Sven had never really felt before, and it made him want to shit himself. He probably would have done if he had not emptied his bowels before they gathered for the attack. 'What if it doesn't work?' Rollo leaned closer and whispered to him. It was the same question Baldur had asked Rollo before, and Sven knew it would have been eating away at the giant warrior. 'What if Halstein doesn't understand what we are doing?'

Sven gripped his Dane axe even tighter so that Rollo wouldn't see his hand trembling. 'Then we die what some may call a glorious death and the gods laugh at us.' Sven glanced at Rollo's frown. 'It has to work, Rollo. We have no other choice.' He looked at Halfdan's ship ahead of them on the river, its deck filled with logs and kindling. Some men had killed a deer they had trapped and had prayed to Odin to guide the ship and kill their enemies. But the ship was not there to kill anyone. It was there to create chaos. And that was exactly what they needed. Sven had even prayed to Loki, the god of chaos, and asked for his aid, something no Dane did willingly. 'We just need to make sure that my flag flies high enough for those in the camp to see it. If Halstein sees it's us attacking Sigtrygg's rear, then he'll join us.' Sven's voice sounded more certain than he felt, but it seemed to calm Rollo, who turned his attention back to the front.

The day before, they had used smaller rivers and streams to get their ships around Sigtrygg's siege so that they were now downriver of the island. It had not been easy, but Sven felt it was the only way this plan would succeed. They needed to attack the main island and they could only do it from downriver. All they were waiting for now was the signal from the men Sven had sent to watch Sigtrygg's force. They had to launch their attack while Sigtrygg was attempting to take the walls of Halstein's camp. Otherwise, there would be enough warriors to repel them. But the waiting was worse than anything Sven had ever done before. There was too much time for his mind to wander and for his fear to take hold of him.

'There!' Alvar pointed to where one of the scouts Sven had sent ahead was hiding. The shield maiden was waving a flag in the air as they were concerned that a horn would alert Sigtrygg to their attack. Sven let go of the breath he had been holding as his bladder suddenly felt full. The time had come and, before giving the order, Sven glanced at the sky. *Odin, Thor. Make sure this works. Not for me, but for the families of my warriors and for Charles. After this, do with me as you please.*

'Light the ship!' he roared, and watched as those on Halfdan's ship started the fire before they hoisted the sail. Five warriors had volunteered to steer the burning ship towards where Sigtrygg's ships were docked. Three men and two women, young adults with their lives ahead of them, prepared to sacrifice themselves all for a place in Valhalla. Sven would have preferred some of the older warriors to do it, but they were too smart to volunteer for something like that. The wind picked up as Sven watched the flames take hold of the wood and the warriors move to their positions. Two went to the prow while the rest went to the stern. No one went near the oars because the ship would be pushed from behind by Sven's two ships. They had placed long logs between the ships and, at the right moment, those on Halfdan's ship would cut those logs loose before they jumped into the river.

'We have wind! The gods are with us!' Rollo lifted his Dane axe above his head and Sven could only hope that the wind didn't become too strong and kill the fire. But he pushed the thoughts out of his mind as he beat his chest to awaken his anger.

'Row, you bastards! Let's show Sigtrygg what the warriors of Ribe and Baldur can do!' Sven roared and felt his battle lust grip him as his ship sped up. The warriors of Ribe dipped their oars into the water and pulled as one, sending Sven's ship surging forwards. He saw Baldur give the order as well on his ship and soon their three ships were heading towards the island. Sven gripped his Dane axe as he stood by the prow, the island ahead of him growing larger by the moment. The wind was going strong and Rollo had given the signal for the warriors on the burning ship to open their sail more while the flames were still confined to the logs. But Sven knew that as soon as the sail was up, then the flames would spread there. The animal fat they used to waterproof and strengthen the sail would be too irresistible for the fire. Another signal was given and the two warriors at the back of the burning ship cut the ropes of the logs attached to Sven's ships, the warriors on those ships doing the same. This was one of the riskiest moments of the plan. If those logs fell the wrong way, then they could scupper Sven's ships and halt the attack before it even started. Sven gripped the Mjöllnir around his neck and saw Rollo do the same, but the gods were with them and the logs harmlessly floated between Sven's ships.

The warrior on the steering helm of the burning ship turned her and aimed the ship towards Sigtrygg's. Already horns were being blown on the island as some of Sigtrygg's warriors noticed the danger, but it was far too late for that now. Sven watched as a large warrior with a gold-rimmed helmet sent some warriors to the ships, although he wasn't sure what they were hoping to do, as those on the burning ship dived into the river, their part in this plan done. They would wait until the attack started before they joined the rear ranks. They all watched with bated breath as the burning ship, the sail alight now as well, struck the first of Sigtrygg's ships. The force of the blow caused the burning mast to fall forward, and it landed on another ship as the flames spread, their greed knowing no bounds. Even on his ship, Sven could hear the cries of dismay as those in the rear of Sigtrygg's army saw some of their ships on fire. Behind Sven, Ribe's warriors cheered as those on the beach tried to save their ships, but Sven could already see there were not enough of them to stop the flames. Not with the wind picking up and spreading the flames to the other ships. Sven prayed it would stay like that because they needed the chaos the burning ships would create for their attack to work.

'Brace!' Alvar roared and Sven turned his attention to his front and saw they were about to hit the beach on the island. He just had enough time to see ladders being lifted and placed against the wall of Halstein's camp and, as he watched, the defenders pushed one ladder off the wall. He searched the wall for any sign of Halstein and prayed that Halstein had seen his flag waving on top of the mast of his ships and knew what he needed to do before the ships hit the beach. Rollo gripped Sven's shoulder and held him upright, something Sven was grateful for because he did not have the strength in his legs to stay on his feet.

The deck of the ship trembled under Sven's feet as Rollo and Alvar jumped over the prow before the ship came to a stop. They landed on the beach, their shields in front of them as more warriors joined them and formed a shield wall, while Sven waited for the ship to stop before he jumped over the side. He grimaced at the jolting pain in his knees and was glad that his left leg held, although he was sure that if he survived this fight, then he would feel the pain from this for days to come. Gripping his Dane axe in both hands and not waiting for all the warriors to get off the ships or to see if Baldur was there, Sven roared, 'For Odin!'

Many of the warriors joined the call and soon they were storming towards the masses of Sigtrygg's army. Like a bee flying towards a whale. Sven led at the front, even though it was hard for him to keep up with the two giants on either side of him. He pushed the pain from his ageing body out of his mind and willed his battle lust to take place, but his fear kept it at bay. So Sven just gripped his Dane axe in his two hands and focused on the warriors ahead of him.

Those at the rear of Sigtrygg's army, who weren't trying to stop the flames from destroying their ships, had turned to face them, but they were slow to form their shield wall. Sven locked eyes with an old warrior, younger than him, but still older than the others around him. The man was well built and Sven had enough time to see the many battle scars before he ducked behind his shield. Sven didn't bother to raise his axe; instead he braced his shoulder and lived up to the animal he had got his byname from and barged into the shield of the old warrior. He grunted at the sharp pain in his shoulder and felt his fingers in his left hand go numb, but he tightened his grip on his axe as he barged the warrior to the ground and trampled over him, roaring as his battle lust slowly took hold of him. Rollo was beside him, his Dane axe in one hand and a shield in the other, as he kicked another warrior to the ground before he brought his axe down on the man's head. He lifted his shield to block an attack from another and Sven buried his Dane axe in the bastard's stomach, the weight of the Dane axe and Sven's strength enough to drive its edge through the warrior's leather jerkin. Alvar stepped forward and killed another who tried to stab at Sven as he struggled to free his axe, but the bastard who it was buried in had grabbed hold of the haft and was sneering at Sven even as his blood came out of his mouth and soaked his beard.

'Kill them! Kill them all!' someone shouted, but Sven didn't know if it was one of his men or Sigtrygg's. Not that he cared as he glared at the bastard who would not die and let go of his axe. Growling, Sven punched the man in the face and as his head snapped to the side, Sven kicked his legs out from under him, and finally managed to pull his axe out of the man's stomach.

'You ba—' the man started, but the word never came out as Sven stamped on his head. He looked around him to see what was happening, but couldn't see anything as he was shorter than most of the men. All he knew was what was happening around him, and it seemed that the warriors of Ribe, led by Rollo and Alvar, were holding firm. But Sven knew that would not last long and prayed that Halstein saw what he was trying to do. He glanced towards the camp walls and only saw a large warrior charging at him, his face an ugly grimace as he lifted his sword to kill him, but the man never got close as one of Sven's warriors sliced his leg open. The warrior dropped to his knees and Sven smiled as he swung his axe in a wide arc and took the bastard's head off. Sven roared as the man's blood sprayed over him and charged at another of Sigtrygg's men. He ducked under the warrior's spear and took his leg off with his axe, before he turned and chopped it into the back of another. His pains and limp were forgotten as he revelled in the chaos of the open battle. He swung his axe in wide arcs, feeling it bite into the bodies of Sigtrygg's warriors as they died around him. Rollo and Alvar stayed close, both resembling the giants mothers warned their children of as they killed any who came within reach of their axes.

Not far from him, the fire was spreading to more of Sigtrygg's ships as his warriors had to choose between fighting the flames or Sven's warriors. But Sven could not hear the fire as the flames destroyed ship after ship, not over the battle song being played out around him as warriors fought for their lives and prayed to the gods. Sven used the haft of his axe to deflect a sword and kicked his attacker on the knee. The man cried out, but his voice was drowned out by the battle, as his leg bent the wrong way and Sven smacked him on the side of his head with the flat of his axe. But before Sven could kill the man, he felt something strike him from behind. For a moment, he thought that his own warriors were attacking him, like they had done in Ribe, but when Sven turned, he saw one of Sigtrygg's men pull his sword back and Sven, had it not been for the shield on his back, might have died then. The thought killed his battle lust, just as Alvar killed the warrior who had stabbed him, and as Sven looked around him, he saw that Sigtrygg's numbers were starting to count. His men had abandoned trying to save the ships, which were still burning, and had joined the attack against Sven's small forces. Jarl Baldur lay dead on the ground, not far from where Sven was, his dead eyes staring at him accusingly. Even Alvar was struggling with the severe wound to his leg, but the giant warrior stood his ground and protected Sven as he had sworn to do. Sven glanced towards the camp, still unable to see what was happening, and wondered why Halstein was not attacking. Surely they had done enough to distract Sigtrygg's army.

Someone pushed into Sven as he tried to get a bearing on the fight and instinct made him duck just as a sword swung over his head. Sven saw his attacker pull his sword back, but could not bring his axe around to stop the next attack, so instead he dropped it and tackled the warrior to the ground. The man had not been expecting the move and did not have enough time to bring his shield down to stop Sven and, as Sven landed on top of the warrior, he pulled his sax-knife from its scabbard and stabbed his attacker in the neck. Rollo arrived and killed another as he stood over Sven, who struggled to get to his feet.

'What's taking the bastard so long?' Rollo roared over the battle din, echoing Sven's thoughts. 'We can't hold on much longer!'

Sven, back to his feet, pulled his helmet off his head as it had moved and was limiting his view. He rubbed a bloodied hand on the faded raven tattoo on his scalp and wondered if Odin had decided that this was his time. But Sven refused to go to Valhalla just yet. Not until he knew his grandson was safe. He pulled his sword from its scabbard and took the shield from his back.

'Shield wall! On me!' Sven screamed as loud as he could.

Rollo also dropped his Dane axe, took the smaller hand axe from his belt and stood next to Sven. Alvar fell in on the other side of him, his sword in his hand instead of his Dane axe. 'Shield wall!' Rollo echoed the order and slowly the warriors of Ribe came together to form a shield wall in the chaos that moments ago Sven had thrived in. But as shields locked together, Sven was feeling his age again, and knew he needed to get himself and his warriors out of there. At least that way they could fight another day.

'Kill them!' Sven heard someone shout just before Sigtrygg's warriors surged forward. Even with the safety of the shield wall, Sven knew they would not last long. Sigtrygg's army still outnumbered his, and Sven did not know how many warriors he had left after that initial attack. He had hoped that Halstein would attack immediately, but the bastard was either waiting for something or had decided not to attack at all. Sven swore that if he ever saw Halstein in Valhalla, then he would break his face for this.

'Back! Back to the ships!' Sven roared and felt Rollo look at him.

'Sven! No! My family!' Rollo protested as he lifted his shield to block a spear.

Sven had no time to respond, as he was forced to duck behind his shield. He felt the axe strike his shield and then lifted it so he could stab at his attacker, but all his sword found was a shield and then suddenly they were being pushed backwards by Sigtrygg's army. Sven strained as he tried to stand his ground, but his left leg gave way, and he dropped to his knees. Looking up, Sven saw the smile on the face of the warrior facing him, and his heart stopped as he saw the doors to Valhalla open in his mind.

29

Sven waited for the killing blow to come. Neither Rollo nor Alvar could save him as both giants were too busy fighting for their own lives and the warrior behind Sven was too slow to react. He didn't need to see what was happening around him to understand that. Sven had been in enough shield walls and always knew he would die in one. Even when he was wandering Denmark as a drunk, he knew he would die in a shield wall. And now the Norns had decided it was time for him to leave Midgard.

As the sword came towards him, Sven felt the weight of Charlemagne's cross and he knew he should have listened to his uncle when the godi had told him to throw the cross away. But Sven was never good at listening to others, and that was why he had failed. He could only hope that Thora would look after Charles and do what he had failed to do. He watched the sword, determined this time to face his death with courage, and then the blade stopped. Sven frowned as it wavered and then was pulled back. His heart pounding in his ears, Sven glanced around him and couldn't understand why Rollo was smiling. Strong hands grabbed him and pulled him to his feet, but Sven's legs refused to obey and Alvar had to hold him up for a few heartbeats until he understood what was happening.

'Sven! It's Halstein! The bastard is coming!' Alvar shook him until the words sunk in.

Sven blinked his confusion away, and then he finally heard it. Horns blowing from the camp and the warriors of Ribe cheering. 'Halstein is coming?'

'Aye, Sven. He's attacking Sigtrygg's flank. Look.' Rollo pointed somewhere, but Sven could not see over the heads of the surrounding warriors. Sven took a deep breath as he gripped his sword and glared at the warrior who had been about to kill him. Sigtrygg's army had stopped their attack as they too tried to make sense of what was happening, and Sven knew they had to act now. Even with Halstein's attack, Sigtrygg's army was still far larger than theirs and, once they snapped out of their confusion, they could still win this.

'Fight, you bastards of Ribe! Fight for the gods! Fight for your families trapped in the camp! Kill them all!' The words came out of Sven before he launched himself at the warrior who had almost killed him. The man barely raised his shield before Sven punched out with his and as the warrior staggered back, he stabbed the bastard in the chest, the force of his attack enough to drive his blade through the man's brynja.

'Attack!' Rollo roared and sliced his attacker's face open, and soon the army of Ribe crashed into the confused army of Sigtrygg. Sven's small shield wall surged forward and slammed into Sigtrygg's men before they had recovered from their shock. Moments ago, they had been about to wipe out Sven's army and now they were fighting a battle on two fronts while their ships burnt. Some of Sigtrygg's men, their panic gripping hold of them, tried to flee but were trapped by their own men. They wailed and cried out to the gods, some even killing those they had been fighting alongside. It was chaos and was what Sven wanted. Because Odin loved chaos.

Sven stabbed at his opponent, who raised his shield to block Rollo's axe, before twisting his blade and pulling it free. He ducked behind his shield and shoulder barged the warrior in front of him, his strength enough to drive the man back a few steps so that Sven could slice the leg open of the warrior beside him. The warrior cried out and dropped to his knees, before Rollo killed him in a spray of blood. Sven roared as he continued to hack and stab with his sword, its edge blunt from all the fighting. He lifted his shield to block the axe from his next opponent and stomped on the man's foot. He imagined he could hear the bones in the warrior's foot break, even over the sound of the battle raging around him, and as the warrior hobbled backwards, Sven punched out with his shield, trapping the man between him and the warrior behind him. The warrior's eyes widened, begging Sven not to kill him, but Sven was in no mood for mercy. Not after he had already faced his own death.

'Charles!' he screamed, spit flying from his mouth as he stabbed the man in the neck. Warm blood sprayed over his face, drenching the faded raven tattoo as he freed his sword, and Sven felt the gods were with them. Sven, who not that long ago had been gripped by the fear of having to stand in another shield wall, was laughing as his opponents backed away from him. 'I am Sven the Boar! Fight me, you bastards! Fight me so I can send you to Valhalla!'

A large warrior stepped forward and Sven grinned at him as he lifted his Dane axe above his head and brought it down on Sven's shield. Pain shot up his arm from his weakened shoulder, but Sven gritted his teeth and ignored it, even as his left leg buckled under him. Before the warrior could free his axe, Sven got his sword under his brynja, which came down to his knees, and stabbed up into the man's groin. The warrior screamed as he let go of his axe, the sudden extra weight almost pulling Sven's shield from his hands. But Sven could not hold that weight for long and let go of his shield as he pushed his sword deeper into the man. The warrior, his eyes almost bulging out of his skull, grabbed Sven around the neck and squeezed as he tried to kill Sven before he himself died. Sven tried to ignore the warrior's grip around his neck as he glared at the man and twisted the sword, but the large warrior still held on, even as his blood soaked Sven's hand. With his free hand, Sven struck the man's arms, trying to break his grip, but the warrior refused to let go.

'I'm taking you with me to Valhalla, you boar-fucking dwarf,' the warrior said in a strained voice, and Sven almost believed him as his vision began to swim, but he refused to die this way. His hand went to where his sax-knife was and he panicked when he realised the scabbard was empty. He tried to reach the large warrior's sax-knife, but it was just out of reach as his legs wobbled. All Sven could do was twist his sword, which he was struggling to keep hold of as the warrior's blood made the grip slippery. Sven thought he could feel the warrior's grip loosen, but it was not enough to let the air into his lungs. His legs felt too weak to hold him and Sven knew that if the bastard didn't bleed out soon, then he was going to die. He tightened the grip on the sword and tried to push it in deeper, but the sword had hit something hard and refused to move. As the battle around him started to blur, Sven realised the sword had struck bone, and there was nothing he could do other than twist the blade from side to side. But nothing seemed to help as the warrior continued to squeeze Sven's throat.

For the second time in that battle, Sven thought he could see the doors to Valhalla open for him, when he felt a fresh spray of blood over his face and the grip around his neck loosening. As Sven's vision focused on the warrior, he saw his confused eyes and the axe buried in his head. Rollo laughed as he pulled his axe free and grabbed Sven under the arm before he collapsed to the ground. Sven coughed as he sucked in the air before he glanced at Rollo.

'What took you so long?'

Rollo shrugged with a smile on his bloody face. 'I thought you had him.'

'Boy, when this is done, I'm going to beat you senseless.' Sven pulled his sword free and rubbed his neck, glad that Odin was not ready for him to die yet. But he hated that the one-eyed bastard kept taking him to where Sven believed he was about to die, only to drag him back again. It was as if Odin was toying with him, showing Sven who was really in control of his fate.

Rollo laughed as he punched his axe into the air. 'We're almost there! Keep fighting!' Sven frowned when he saw they were nearing the camp wall. He shook his head to chase the dizziness away and saw that Loki was not playing tricks on him. They were near the wall of Halstein's camp. Sven looked around him and saw his warriors pushing Sigtrygg's army back, while over their heads, the sky was grey with the thick smoke of burning ships. Already the sky was filled with carrion birds, waiting for the fighting to stop so they could feast on the dead. Sven wondered how many of those birds were really Valkyries, sent by Odin to collect those he deemed more worthy than others. His hand went to his neck and Sven considered if he would have been chosen by the Valkyries if it had not been for Rollo. But then perhaps one of the Valkyries had used her influence to get Rollo to save him. Everyone knew Valkyries protected warriors they were in love with, although Sven could not imagine how any Valkyrie could feel that way about him. No, perhaps Odin just didn't want Sven in Valhalla yet.

Sven shook his head and tightened the grip on his sword.

'Warriors of Ribe! Fight like you've never fought before! Show these bastards who they are dealing with! Odin is with us!'

Those nearby cheered and Sven watched as Alvar, bleeding heavily from his leg, blocked an attack with his shield and rammed his sword through his opponent's leather jerkin. He pressed his shield against the now dead warrior and used it to pull his sword free before he hacked at another of Sigtrygg's men. But then a spear streaked out between two of Sigtrygg's men and struck the giant in the chest. Alvar roared and used the rim of his shield to break the haft of the spear. He stabbed forward with his sword and then staggered back as another spear struck him. All Sven could do was watch as one of his giants dropped to the ground, a smile on his lips as the broken spear was still stuck in his chest.

'Alvar!' Sven screamed and threw himself at the remnants of Sigtrygg's shield wall. The warriors facing him lifted their shields, but Sven still crashed through them, with Rollo close behind him, as he hacked at anyone within reach. Sven stabbed to the left, feeling his sword strike something, but he did not waste time trying to work out what or who as he turned and swung the blade at another's face, almost slicing the man's jaw off. Sensing movement to his side, Sven turned and used his left forearm to block an axe aimed at his skull, but in his rage he did not feel the haft of the axe as it struck his arm. Sven stabbed his attacker in the stomach, but the point of his sword was too blunt to break through the warrior's brynja. The man smiled when he realised the same, but then Sven stepped into him and headbutted him in the chest. As the warrior staggered back, one of Ribe's warriors buried their axe in his face. Sven turned, looking for more bastards to kill, but his age was taking its toll and he could barely lift his sword arm to block another attack aimed at him.

'Sven! Get back!' Rollo screamed and pulled Sven behind him

before he could protest. Rollo killed the warrior who had almost killed Sven and then buried his shoulder in the back of his shield and shoulder barged into the warriors in front of him.

Sven staggered backwards, his breathing ragged and his lungs burning. His head still swam and he couldn't tell if it was from when he was almost choked to death or just because he was exhausted. He dropped his sword as he remembered Alvar and limped the few steps to where the young warrior lay. He was greeted by Alvar's glassy eyes and the smile on his lips. Sven followed his dead gaze to the sky and saw the birds circling above him. He patted Alvar on the chest.

'Go to Valhalla, my young friend. Go feast with your father and your ancestors. Soon we'll drink ale together in Odin's hall.' Sven couldn't tell how long he sat beside Alvar's body and was startled when a hand gripped his shoulder.

'He's dead?' Rollo asked, and Sven nodded.

'Aye, he's with his ancestors in Valhalla.'

'That's where he belongs.'

Again, Sven nodded and took a deep breath to stop the tears. So many young warriors killed while he still lived. So many lost when he should have died many more times. Sven knew that many believed he was blessed by the gods to survive for so long, but he knew the truth. He was cursed. Cursed to watch everyone die for his mistakes. That was the real reason Odin did not want him in Valhalla. Because the one-eyed bastard knew Sven would take his other eye if he ever reached the hall of the slain. Sven took another deep breath and wiped the tears from his eyes. 'It's over?' He looked at Rollo and saw the tear lines in the dirt on his face.

Rollo nodded. 'Aye, they broke and ran. Many jumped in the river to escape our blades. Word is that Sigtrygg surrendered himself to Halstein.'

'So the families are safe?'

Again, Rollo nodded. 'Not seen them yet, but it seems so. We should find Halstein.'

Sven looked at Alvar. 'Aye, we should. Make sure somebody watches over his body. And the rest of our warriors who died. They'll be buried with honour, not scavenged by the birds.'

'I'll see it done,' Rollo said, and gave the order to one of the nearby warriors before he helped Sven to his feet.

Sven winced at the pain in his knees for kneeling for so long. But that was soon forgotten as the other pains took hold. His left leg could barely hold his weight and Rollo had to give him a spear to lean on, as the many cuts he had got during the fight stung. His throat was raw from when he had been choked, and Sven struggled with the pain every time he coughed. He looked at the sky and was surprised to see that the sun had set.

'How long did we fight for?'

Rollo shrugged. 'Long, but not as long as the battle at Jelling.'

Sven's mind went back to the three-day battle they had fought against the old king Horik the previous summer as a shiver ran down his spine. He had hoped to never have to fight a battle like that again, but this came close. As they walked to where Halstein was, Sven scanned the battleground, picking out Ribe's dead and injured. Too many had been lost in that fight they should never have had to fight. So many who might have lived if Halstein had come out of his camp earlier. Young warriors who had wanted to make a name for themselves and now many would lie forgotten in Frankish ground. That was the life of a warrior, the one no skald ever sang about. Sven hawked and spat, angered at the pointlessness of it all.

'Sven the Boar! You live!' Halstein greeted him with open arms when they reached him.

'By the gods, Sven! What were you thinking charging at

Sigtrygg's army like that?' Gudrod asked, his eyebrows raised but still with a smile on his face.

'I don't care what he was thinking,' Halstein said. 'I'm just glad he did. That gave us the chance to break out and fight back.' He looked at Sven, the smile replaced by a serious face. 'Thank you, Sven. Without you and your warriors, we might never have been able to defeat Sigtrygg's army. I am in your debt.'

'So am I,' Gudrod said with a nod. 'You saved us and I dread to think of what that has cost you.'

Sven hawked and spat again. 'I did not risk my men for you, but for their families.' He turned his attention to Halstein. 'You could have come out sooner.'

Halstein glanced at Gudrod, who shrugged. 'We needed time to get the men ready, Sven. Just like Sigtrygg, we did not expect your attack.'

Sven wanted to be angry at Halstein, just like he wanted to be angry at the gods, but he did not have the energy any more, so he sighed. 'Aye.'

'My wife and son, where are they?' Rollo asked, breaking the tension. 'And the rest of the families?'

Halstein smiled. 'The families are safe, so are your wife and unborn child. We moved them away from the edge of the camp as soon as the siege started. Although, there is a small red-headed girl who insisted that she be allowed to fight.'

'She even took a knife from one of the men and charged at the wall.' Gudrod laughed. 'A relation of yours, Sven?'

Sven frowned as he wondered who they were talking about, and then he remembered. 'Jorlaug. No, she's no relation of mine, but her aunt is one of the finest warriors I've ever seen.'

'She takes after her aunt, then. Come, there's much we need to do. The wounded need to be seen to and the dead should be honoured.'

'Where's Sigtrygg?' Sven asked. 'And why did he attack you?' Sven looked at Gudrod.

Halstein shrugged. 'He fled. Saw the battle was turning in his favour and fled to his ship, which was saved from the flames. That's when his men broke. But he sent one of his men to us. It seems he wants to talk.'

'To talk?' Sven raised an eyebrow. 'Should kill the bastard, not talk.'

'Aye, but it might be interesting to hear what he has to say,' Halstein said, and all Sven could do was nod to that, before he turned to go back to his warriors. 'I have other news that might interest you, Sven,' Halstein said, and Sven felt his heart skip at the tone of Halstein's voice. 'The son of King Louis has given up on the throne of Aquitaine. They say he made it as far as a place called Limoges before he turned his army around and marched back to East Francia.'

30

'Are we going to see Aunt Thora and Charles soon?' Jorlaug's eyes were wide with excitement as she jumped around Sven. 'I want to show them my battle scar. Do you think Charles has any battle scars yet? One day I'll have as many as Aunt Thora. How many does she have?'

Sven glared at the young girl, his impatience and frustration making it hard for him to share her enthusiasm as Ingvild gave him a sympathetic smile. Thora's niece had been like this ever since she was told they'd be leaving the island camp and she seemed intent on sharing that excitement with him. And the battle scar she was so eager to show off was a grazed knee from when she had fallen over as she tried to attack Sigtrygg's men on the other side of the wall. In the end, all Sven could do was sigh. 'Aye, Jorlaug. If the gods are with us, then we'll see them soon.' But Sven did not feel optimistic about that. The news that the son of King Louis was returning to East Francia without the throne of Aquitaine was already many days old, and Sven did not know if King Louis knew about it. That was why he had to get to East

Francia as fast as the wind allowed. He was sure that King Louis would not care about what he had done here or that it was his own son's weakness that led to him not getting Aquitaine. Charles's life was now in danger, and Sven needed to get there to save him. But Odin knew he did not know how to do that.

'We'll be ready to leave soon,' Rollo said as he approached Sven. Sven nodded and watched as what was left of his army loaded the ships. Tents had been folded and packed away. War chests carried on board to be used as rowing benches and barrels with food and water were loaded, while the wives of some of the warriors said farewell to the new friends they had made. Even Rollo's son, Sigmund, looked unhappy to be leaving. 'He'd made new friends here,' Rollo said when he saw Sven looking at his son. 'It's hard for him to leave them.'

Sven nodded. 'He'll make new friends.' He gazed at the new earth mounds outside the camp. That was where the warriors of Ribe who had died were buried after the battle. More than a third of his force. And Alvar. A young man with so much promise. Sven felt the deaths of every one of them weighing on him. They had followed him for glory and gold, and now they were all dead.

'I'll miss him too,' Rollo said as he cuffed away a tear. 'Couldn't have asked for a better man to stand in the shield wall with.'

'Or to share ale with,' Torgny said from behind them. 'Halstein and Gudrod are coming, Sven. They must have finished their chat with Sigtrygg.'

Sven nodded and turned away from the earth mounds. Jorlaug was still skipping, unaware of the world around them as she fought battles in her imagination. Sven wished she wouldn't become a warrior like she wanted to. That way, she might keep her infectious smile. He then thought about Charles and his hand went to the small wooden cross around his neck. If Charles still lived, then perhaps it was better for the boy to become a Christian priest. Just somewhere far inland and away from rivers. But then he lowered his hand and found it resting on Charlemagne's cross and wondered if his grandson would ever really be safe as Halstein and Gudrod approached.

'Sven,' Halstein greeted him. 'Are you sure you want to leave now?'

'I need to leave,' Sven responded as he watched his men carry the war chests filled with their plunder. They had made enough for all of Sven's crew to live comfortably for the next few winters, even with the captives they had lost when Halfdan had turned against him. But Sven would rather have the warriors he had lost than gold to fill his pouch. 'What did Sigtrygg want?'

Halstein scratched his beard. 'He wants half our plunder, otherwise he refuses to leave and will attack again.'

Sven almost smiled at the bastard's audaciousness. 'Told you to kill him.'

'He still has more men than us,' Gudrod said.

'Aye, and the gods know we won't get lucky a second time,' Halstein added.

'So you agreed?' Sven asked, and shook his head when Halstein nodded.

'But at least we now know who is behind the attack.'

'King Charles?' Sven asked.

Gudrod shook his head. 'Duke Erispoë.'

'Who?'

'Duke Erispoë of Brittany. We've been raiding his lands as well, and he has made many threats against us.'

Sven frowned. He had never heard of this other duke. 'Is he an ally of King Charles?'

Gudrod shrugged. 'It's hard to say. They did battle each other in the past and then Erispoë defeated King Charles in some battle and they made peace. But Erispoë wants this region for himself and he and King Charles have clashed over it at times.'

'A bit like Loki and Thor. Friends one moment and then fighting each other the next.' Halstein laughed, but Sven could not share his humour.

'So King Charles could have told this Duke Erispoë to deal with us?'

Halstein nodded. 'Could have done, but Sigtrygg didn't know.'

'Are you sure you need to leave, Sven?' Gudrod scowled at him. 'Because Prince Louis failed to take Aquitaine? What does that have to do with you?'

Sven glared at Gudrod, still not convinced the man had nothing to do with Sigtrygg's siege, when Halstein put a hand on Gudrod's shoulder. 'Sven's business is his own. He swore no oath to either of us, so he is free to leave when he wants. The gods know that it's a pity to lose you, though. We could have accomplished much more with you fighting by our side, Sven.'

Sven nodded at Halstein. He wanted to tell them the real reason he had to leave but didn't think they needed to know. Sven had told his warriors that they could stay and join the other jarls if they wanted to, but all of them had agreed to return to East Francia. He had even gained new warriors, those who were loyal to Jarl Baldur, who had died in the fight. Sven had allowed them to join, but told them they needed to swear an oath to Rollo, not him. After Sven got Charles back, he planned to find somewhere away from Francia for them to settle and for Rollo to take over the army. Rollo had disagreed at first, but Sven had convinced him to do it. Rollo would be a great leader one day. Sven was convinced by that, and anyway, Sven was far too old for this life.

'May the gods be with you, Sven,' Gudrod said and then walked away, leaving Halstein behind.

'He's upset about you leaving. He believes that with you by our side, we can carve out a land where our people can live in peace.'

Sven grunted. 'Our people will never live in peace with the Christians.' His hand almost went to Charlemagne's cross, hidden in his tunic. Sven was desperate to get rid of the thing, but it was not his to throw away. That choice belonged to Charles. 'They hate us as much as they fear our gods.'

'Aye, I agree. But Gudrod believes it's possible.' Halstein glanced at Sven's ships. 'It looks like you'll be ready to leave soon. Farewell, Sven, I hope we never have to face each other in the shield wall. May Thor protect you and your men and Njörd fill your sail with strong winds.'

Sven gripped Halstein's forearm. 'Aye. And you, Halstein.'

Halstein smiled before he turned and walked away.

'I think he likes you,' Rollo said.

Again, Sven grunted. He had to admit that he liked Halstein as well. Even if he believed the man could have left the camp earlier during the battle. At least then Alvar might still have been alive. 'Aye, I have a feeling we'll be hearing many stories about Halstein. Might be a good idea for you to join him, Rollo.'

Rollo frowned. 'You think so?'

'Aye, the bastard reminds me of me when I was younger. He'll be a thorn in the side of the Frankish kings for a long time.'

'Maybe in the future, I will join him. Now, we get Charles and Thora back.'

If they still live. The thought came to Sven, and he shook his head to chase it away. 'Aye, let's get going.'

Rollo gave the order as Sven boarded his ship and made his way to the stern. The families were already on board, and were making themselves comfortable by laying down furs for the children and for Rollo's wife. A tent had been put up by the mast to protect them from the weather and bird shit, which blocked Sven's view of the prow, but he didn't really care. Jorlaug joined him by the stern, trying to look as serious as he did as he grabbed the tiller and waited while others boarded his two ships before they were pushed away from the wharves. 'Oars!' Rollo ordered, his voice carrying to the other ship as well and warriors rushed to get their oars and back to their war chests.

'Jorlaug, come here!' Audhild shouted at her daughter, but Sven raised his hand.

'She can stay here if she wants to. She's not in the way.'

Audhild frowned and then nodded while Jorlaug smiled at Sven, who smiled back. He sometimes wondered how she could be Audhild's daughter when she was so much like her aunt. But the girl looked like her mother. He remembered her great-grand-mother though, from when he was Jorlaug's age. She had been a fierce warrior that even his father had been wary of, so perhaps it was just in the girl's blood.

'How long will it take us to reach East Francia?' Jorlaug asked, shielding her eyes from the sun as she stared at where she believed East Francia was. Which was the other way.

Sven glanced at the sky, watching the birds soar on the wind for a few heartbeats, and then he shrugged. 'Many days, less if the wind is good.'

'We need to sacrifice a Christian to make sure Njörd gives us good wind,' she said with the confidence of a child who had never had to take a life just to please the gods. 'A pity we don't have any.'

'We should sacrifice you,' her grandmother said, smiling as she sat near the stern. 'That way, I might live to see more winters.' Jorlaug stuck her tongue out at Ingvild, who laughed.

Sven smiled and wondered if he could ever have a relationship like that with his grandson. He doubted it, though. The two of them were too different and could never agree on the same things. 'We'll give Njörd some gold when we reach the sea. Then he might give us good winds,' Sven said before he glanced at the other ship to make sure they were still there. Oars rose and dipped, the rhythmic noise helping to calm his frustration, but Sven still felt his hand tremble. He wished he did have someone to sacrifice to Odin, just to make sure that Charles and Thora were safe. The Norns were cruel, and Sven knew they had no qualms about ending the life of a child. They might even see it as necessary, and all he could do was pray that they had a better destiny in mind for his grandson.

* * *

Sven stood by the prow and glared at the beach where both his son and grandson had been taken from him. The clouded sky seemed to match his mood as all on board the ship knew to stay out of his way. That Sven had not had any ale for as long as they travelled from the Loire River didn't help his mood either. Only Jorlaug seemed not to notice as she stood beside Sven and Rollo. Sigmund was there as well, but unlike Thora's niece, he tried to match the mood of the adults with a scowl on his face.

'I can't see them. Are they not here yet?' Jorlaug asked, but Sven ignored her.

'How can they be there? They didn't know we were coming,' Sigmund said, and then looked to his father to see if he was right. Rollo ruffled his son's long hair as Sven continued to stare at the beach.

'What do you think?' Rollo asked him.

Sven glanced at the sky and wondered if their luck would hold. He had made sure to throw enough gold into the sea as they left the river so that both Njörd and Rán would favour them. It seemed to work as they had strong winds and calm waters, which meant the warriors could spend most of the journey recovering from their injuries. At night they had stayed on the ships, everyone having to find a spot to sleep on the deck, which wasn't easy, but they managed. The only ones who did not enjoy it were the children who got frustrated at not being able to run around, but they were kept busy after Rollo put them in charge of catching fish for their meals. Sven was glad for the salted meat and dried fish they had brought with them, otherwise they would not have had anything to eat. 'It seems quiet.' Sven's eyes went to the forest nearby, as they had done the time he had been here, but there was no sign of anyone watching them. And that worried Sven.

'Aye. Should we go somewhere else?'

Sven looked at Rollo. 'Is that what you would do?'

Rollo frowned as he thought about it. 'King Louis might know that we would return here as soon as we heard the news about his son. He could have an army waiting for us.'

Sven nodded. He glanced at the skies again, but the signs he saw were not from the gods. Birds flew carelessly amongst the grey clouds, which told him there was not an army waiting for them. But then it wasn't like he had never been wrong before. He rubbed the Mjöllnir around his neck and nodded again, glad that the tide was in. Otherwise, they'd have to wait. 'Give the order.'

Rollo turned and gave the order for the two ships to beach where they had the previous summer.

'I hope Charles lives,' Sigmund said, surprising Sven as he gripped the prow. He had thought that Rollo's son did not like Charles, but perhaps he had changed his mind.

'Aye, me too, lad.' Sven turned his attention back to the beach and beyond it, still trying to work out if they were heading into an ambush. In the distance, he thought he saw a person watching them from the dunes, but when he rubbed the seawater out of his eyes, the person was gone. Most likely a lookout to warn the nearby towns and farms of raiders. Sven remembered the arrogant

Frank who had tried to battle them the last time they were here and wondered if the bastard would try the same this time as he glanced behind him at his flag waving from the mast. Sven wanted the people of this area to know that it was him because he hoped they would send a message to King Louis that he had returned, but only after he had time to build his camp.

'Raise oars!' Rollo ordered as they neared the beach and Sven braced himself and saw the two children who had stayed with him do the same. Vibrations ran up his legs as the keel of his ship grated along the beach and Sven was grateful that he had stayed on his feet when the ship shuddered to a stop. Unlike Jorlaug, who had fallen over, much to the amusement of Sigmund. Sven smiled and shook his head as he waited for his warriors to jump off and form a small shield wall. They waited for a few heartbeats, everyone scanning the hills behind the beach, and when Sven felt certain no attack was coming, he gave the order to make camp. The children cheered as they jumped into the water, ignoring their mothers shouting at them, while the rest of his army got to preparing the defensive ditch for the camp. Rollo arranged for men to go to the forest for wood so they could build a wall for their camp while Sven scrutinised the area.

'You think we'll have to wait long?' Ingvild asked as she leaned on the side of the ship. She smiled as Jorlaug splashed some of the other children with water.

Sven shrugged. 'Depends on how eager the bastard is to see us.'

'Then you'll have to make sure that he is. I want to see my niece again, Sven. I don't have long left and she reminds me of my sister.'

Sven looked at the old woman who was younger than him and again wondered why he was forced to outlive everyone. 'Don't you worry, Ingvild. I'll make sure King Louis will want to see us.' He watched as Torgny led a group of warriors to the nearby town. It should have been Alvar, but Torgny seemed eager to take his place. Sven had told Rollo to send men to the town with a message for King Louis. He had also made sure that Torgny had enough men with him to emphasise the message. 'I'll promise you one thing, Ingvild. If King Louis has harmed either my grandson or your niece, then I'll burn every town and village in his kingdom.'

31

Charles wiped the sweat from his brow before he lifted the axe again and brought it down on the wood stump in front of him. Finally, on the third attempt, the block of wood on the stump split in two with a splintering sound which bounced off the surrounding trees. Charles would have been happy, but then he glanced at the pile of wood waiting to be chopped and groaned. He had lost track of how long they had been living in the forest near Ehresburg, but was sure it had been many weeks by now. And in that time, the only people Charles had seen were Thora and Father Leofdag when he brought them food they could not get in the forest and news about his mother. Her wounds had healed, which Charles was happy about, but he was upset when Father Leofdag told him that his mother was still very weak and could not travel. Thora and Father Leofdag would then talk together for a while, before he and Charles prayed together. It still was not easy for Charles, because he still didn't understand why God was letting all these things happen to him. But he wanted to make his mother proud and so he had tried his best to pray.

Most of his days had been the same, though. He and Thora

would wake up early and train before they ate breakfast and then Thora would find him things to do. He never knew that there were so many chores for him to do in the forest, but Thora always found something. Today, it was chopping wood, even though he was sure they had enough to last them many days still. Thora had told him it would help build muscle and make him strong, but he didn't believe her because it still took about three attempts to split a log.

Charles picked up another piece of wood and placed it on the stump, before looking at his palms, which were red from gripping the handle, but there were fewer blisters than there were the last time he had to chop wood. As he lifted the axe, Thora walked out of the cabin and called to him, her sword by her side as it had been since they had arrived here. Charles knew she was worried that someone might find them. Warriors roamed the roads and town, searching for him and Thora because they had been blamed for the attack on his mother. There had been a few times when they heard a noise and Thora would send him into the house, only for a deer or a fox to walk out of the trees.

'Charles, that's enough for now. Have some rest.'

Charles took a deep breath and lowered the axe, but before he dropped it, he pictured himself using it in battle. He knew many warriors used one-handed axes like this, but never really understood why. His father had used a sword, but Charles remembered he had had an axe as well. And then his grandfather had the large two-handed axe, just like Rollo and Alvar. 'Why do so many Danes like using axes as weapons?'

Thora walked towards him and took the axe. She looked it over before she swung it in slow arcs. 'Axes make good weapons. You can cut your opponent or hammer him, depending on how you use it. You can also use it to bring down an opponent's shield so someone else can kill him. And besides, they're much cheaper than swords and easier to get. So many warriors start with an axe until they are rich enough to buy a sword.'

'Did you use to use an axe?' Charles asked as Thora brought the axe down and buried its head into the stump. He knew it would not be easy for him to pull it out of there.

'When I was a young warrior, although I preferred to use a spear until I got my first sword.'

'How did you get it?'

Thora smiled at him, a smile he only saw when she mentioned her husband, who had died many years ago. 'My husband gave it to me as a wedding gift. I always hoped to one day pass it on to my children, but...' She shrugged and Charles felt bad for asking the question.

'Maybe you can give it to Jorlaug. She wants to be a warrior.'

Thora laughed. 'Aye, maybe I can.' Her face went serious as she looked west, and Charles wondered if she was thinking about her niece. He followed her gaze and thought of the last news they had heard from Father Leofdag.

'Do you think they are still under siege?'

Thora shrugged. 'Father Leofdag is due in a few days' time. Perhaps he can tell us then.'

Several weeks ago, Father Leofdag had told them about a Danish leader who had travelled from a place called Ireland and had attacked the camp where his grandfather was. Although, all they knew was that this new Danish leader had an enormous army and had laid siege to the camp. Charles had not understood what that had meant at the time, and Thora had to explain it to him after the priest had gone back. Father Leofdag had told them that the king of West Francia, his mother's uncle, had claimed that the heathens were fighting each other because of the Cross of Charlemagne which he had found. God was punishing the heathens by turning them against each other. Charles looked at

Thora. 'You still don't believe that the king of West Francia has the real cross?'

Thora shook her head. 'Sven has the cross, Charles. Not even Thor, with all of his might, could take that cross from him.'

'Then what cross has King Charles got?'

Thora shrugged. 'Only the gods know, Charles, but it's not the real cross.'

Charles frowned and was about to ask if it was possible that his grandfather was killed and that the real cross was given to the king of West Francia when they heard a noise in the trees behind them. Before Charles could react, Thora pulled him behind her, the axe already in her hand, although he never saw her pulling it out of the stump.

'It's only me,' Father Leofdag called out as he rushed into the small clearing, his hands in the air.

'Priest, what are you doing here?' Thora asked as she lowered the axe, but Charles saw her scanning the trees. He knew she didn't really trust Duke Liudolf, and Charles had to admit that he also didn't understand why the duke was hiding them from King Louis, like he had once done with Charles's father.

'I have urgent news that Duke Liudolf thought you should know,' Father Leofdag said, his face sweaty and red. Charles wondered if the priest was just hot from the summer's sun or if he had run all the way from Ehresburg, where he now stayed.

'What news?' Thora glanced at Charles.

'Please, water first,' Father Leofdag asked and Charles rushed to the barrel where they kept their water. The barrel was less than half full and he knew Thora would send him to the river soon to collect more. Although she always went with him and helped him carry the buckets back. Father Leofdag nodded his thanks to Charles when he handed him the cup with water, before he drank it all and wiped his mouth with the back of his hand.

'What news?' Thora asked again.

'It's Sven,' Father Leofdag started, and Charles's heart felt like it stopped when he thought the priest was about to tell them that his grandfather was dead. Charles had almost lost his mother, and even though she still lived after being stabbed by Gerold, he knew he would never see her again. 'He's here,' Father Leofdag continued, and Charles suddenly felt dizzy with shock when the words reached him. Even Thora frowned.

'What do you mean here?'

'H... he's in East Francia, on that beach. He demands to speak to King Louis. Something about a trade.'

'What trade?' Charles asked before Thora could.

Father Leofdag shrugged. 'I don't know. I wasn't there when the messenger arrived. But Duke Liudolf thought you should know, so he sent me to tell you.'

'Why?' Thora raised an eyebrow and even Charles had to admit he didn't understand it either.

Again, Father Leofdag shrugged. 'I don't know. King Louis is on his way to the beach, with a large army, and he wants Duke Liudolf to join him.'

Thora glanced at Charles, but he didn't understand the look in her eyes. 'How long before King Louis gets there?'

'A few days, less maybe. Why?' Father Leofdag also looked at Charles.

Charles frowned as they both stared at him. He heard the wind rustling in the leaves and what sounded like a raven calling out in the trees. Charles remembered the raven tree in the forest near Ribe and went cold. The tree still came to him in his dreams, and Charles was certain it would for the rest of his life. But as Charles thought about the tree, he realised why Thora and Father Leofdag were staring at him. Because now they knew where his grandfather was. 'I have to choose, don't I?'

Thora nodded as she lowered herself so their eyes were level. 'You do, Charles.' She glanced at the tree where Charles had heard the raven from before she looked at him again. 'Do we stay here, hiding away for the rest of our lives, or do we go to your grandfather and leave Francia?'

'We?' Charles raised an eyebrow.

Thora nodded. 'Aye, Charles. I made an oath to Sven that I would protect you, so if you choose to stay, then I stay.'

Charles's heart rose in his chest. 'But what about Jorlaug and the rest of your family?'

He saw the tears building up in her eyes as she thought about them. 'Sven will look after them. He'll make sure they have what they need. And besides, Jorlaug doesn't need me. She has her mother and grandmother.'

Charles chewed on his lip as he thought about her response. Thora was right. Jorlaug had her mother, unlike him. But was it right to expect her to stay in Francia because of him? And then he thought of something else and looked at Father Leofdag. 'Even if I stay here, will I ever get to see my mother again?'

Father Leofdag lowered his eyes and shook his head. 'I'm afraid not, Charles. King Louis has men everywhere looking for you and Thora. And your mother is too weak to leave Fraumünster.'

Charles nodded. His mother had almost died because of him and he knew that if he stayed in Francia, then Thora might die as well because of him. She already almost had, but God had kept her alive so she could protect him. He glanced at the small hunter's cabin they had been living in. It was dark and smelly inside, and cold during the nights because of the many holes in the walls. If he stayed in Francia, then this was where he would have to live, and Charles didn't want that. And besides, his grandfather was a good man. Charles saw that now. Everything he had done since last summer was to keep him safe and even though it hadn't worked out that way, Thora had told Charles how his grandfather cared for him. His hand went to his grandfather's Mjöllnir, which he still wore around his neck, next to the golden cross his mother had given him. And Charles had to admit, he missed his grandfather. He glanced at the sky, just like he had seen his grandfather do so many times. 'How long will it take to get to my grandfather?'

Thora also glanced at the sky. 'Many days and we'd have to be fast. We need to stay ahead of the king's group.'

Charles frowned. 'Do you know how to get there?'

Thora now frowned and then shook her head. 'Not really. And the journey will be dangerous. There are many who would not think twice about attacking a woman and a child travelling alone. And we'd have to avoid towns and farms, as well as those hunting for us.'

'But you don't have to travel alone,' Father Leofdag said, and both Charles and Thora looked at him. 'That was why Duke Liudolf sent me. He wants to help you get to Sven. He can hide you amongst his entourage.'

'Why?' Thora asked. 'Why is he willing to do this?'

'Because he understands Charles will not be safe in Francia and God made him see that this was the right thing to do.'

'But if King Louis finds out, then Duke Liudolf will be in danger himself.' Thora scowled at the priest, who could only shrug.

'I will pray that that doesn't happen, but you don't really have a choice. You don't know how to get there and, as you said, the roads won't be safe for either of you if you travel alone. And as you've said, you still have to avoid the warriors King Louis sent out to hunt for you.'

Thora sighed and rubbed the Mjöllnir around her neck. 'Aye.
We don't have a choice. When do we leave?'

'Are you coming with?' Charles asked Father Leofdag. The
priest had been his constant companion since he had been taken
by Ivor and had assumed that he would go with them as well.

But then Father Leofdag shook his head. 'I'm afraid not,
Charles. This is where our paths go their separate ways. I must
stay here where I can do God's work.'

'But you can do God's work where we are going, can't he?'
Charles asked Thora, who put a hand on his shoulder.

'We don't know where we will be going. And besides, I don't
think Father Leofdag would be safe living amongst Danes.'

'But grandfather will protect him.' Charles felt the lump in the
back of his throat. Father Leofdag had been his protector and
guide since the previous summer, and Charles did not want to lose
him. How would he know the path back to God if the priest was
not there to show him the way?

As if reading his mind, Father Leofdag knelt down and handed
Charles a Bible he had kept under his robe. 'You don't need me
any more, Charles. But there are people here who do. I will pray
for you every day and, besides, this might not be a farewell. God
willing we could meet each other again one day.'

Charles swallowed back his tears as he took the Bible from
Father Leofdag. He gripped the new leather cover that he would
have marvelled at if he had not been crying, but he kept his eyes
on Father Leofdag, seeing how the tears ran down his cheeks as
well.

Father Leofdag looked at Thora. 'Be ready to leave by sunrise
tomorrow. Duke Liudolf advises you to join the back of his
entourage.' He gave Thora the sack he had been carrying. 'There
are new clothes in there so you can change your appearance. That
way nobody should notice you.'

Thora nodded as she took the sack from Father Leofdag. 'Thank you, Father Leofdag. You kept Charles safe when we had all failed. Sven will always be in your debt, and so will I.'

Father Leofdag smiled. 'I don't need any of that. I did what God had asked of me. And besides, thanks to Charles, I discovered a strength I never knew I had.' He looked at Charles and put a hand on his head. 'May God be with you, son of Torkel and Hildegard. Keep praying every day and trust that God has something great planned for you.'

Charles nodded and wiped the tears from his eyes. He wanted to be strong, like his father had been. Like his mother was, so he straightened his back, but the words did not come out easy for him. 'M... May G... God be with you, Father Leofdag. We will meet again.'

'I will pray for it every day, Charles.' Father Leofdag smiled and, with a last nod to Thora, turned and left them in the clearing.

Thora put her arm around his shoulders. 'Come, Charles, there is much we need to do before we can leave.'

32

'Should we chase them away?' Torgny asked, staring at the few men they could see in the distance.

Sven followed his gaze and shook his head. The men were from the town not far from here, the one Torgny had gone to to deliver the message. Ever since that day, a group of men had watched them. But they kept their distance and would always send three men to follow the hunting parties Rollo would send out for wood and food. But so far they had not attacked, most likely because they remembered what had happened the last time. And Sven's army was larger now, despite the losses from the battle against Sigtrygg. But those warriors were growing frustrated. No one was allowed to go raiding or could venture far from the camp. Sven wanted his army nearby for when King Louis arrived, which he was sure would happen. He just didn't know when and that was what irritated him. Sven had never been a patient man, and now it was even worse because he did not know about whether Charles and Thora lived.

'We should gut them like pigs!' Jorlaug's outburst made the warriors laugh, and Sven could only shake his head at the young girl. She must have heard some of the men say that and had repeated it because she wanted to be a warrior like her aunt. The fact that Rollo had been training the children to keep himself busy had not helped. Sven glanced at the red-headed girl as she waved her wooden sword at the men in the distance.

'No, Jorlaug,' he said. 'We don't need to do that. They're just watching us.'

'Why?' Sigmund asked. Sven glanced at him and wondered why the children were always around him.

'Because they are afraid of us, so they watch us. If they think we are about to attack their town, then they'll run back and warn their people.'

'But why don't we attack their town?' Sigmund frowned.

'Because they have nothing worth taking. We attacked them last summer, and they didn't have much,' Torgny said, as Sven kept his eyes fixed on the Franks in the distance.

'And because we are not here to attack them. We are here to get Charles and Thora back. If we start attacking towns and farms in this area, then King Louis will kill them both, and probably all of us as well. So we wait and watch, like they do.' Sven looked up at the clouds and wondered if it would rain again. They had been beset by light rain over the last few days, which didn't help anyone's mood, but at least it had been warm and, when the rain stopped and the sun came out, they all dried out quickly. Worse, though, for Sven was that there was no ale or mead, so he prayed that the bastard king of this place would show up so he could make the trade for his grandson and Thora and go somewhere where the ale was plentiful.

They stood there for a while, the Franks watching them and them watching the Franks until the children got bored and ran off and many of the warriors went back to what they normally did in this situation. Which was nothing. Warriors were great at wasting time when they needed to, and because there was no ale, there were no drunken fights between them. Rollo also made sure he kept them busy by finding jobs for them to do or training the men. The new warriors had to be integrated, and many of them were still recovering from injuries and needed to get their strength back.

'Are you sure it will work?' Rollo asked when everyone was out of earshot. Ingvild was also there, scowling at him.

'We might be too late already,' the old woman said. 'Or they might not even be with him.'

Sven glanced at the sky again as he thought about the cross under his tunic. 'No, I'm not sure if this will work, and aye, we don't know if they still live or if they are with him, but what other choice do I have?' Sven was certain that he had reached East Francia before the son of King Louis did as travelling by sea was much faster than travelling by land, but he was also sure that a message would have been sent to King Louis to tell him of his son's actions, or lack of actions, and that King Louis would be furious. He would see it as a failure by Sven and that put his grandson in danger. The only chance Sven had now to save him was to give the cross back to King Louis. Perhaps he should have done that the previous summer so the cross could curse them and not him. 'Only the gods know what will happen now.'

'Aye, and they like toying with you,' Ingvild said. Sven clenched his fists, annoyed at her words, but he knew she was right. The gods enjoyed playing with him. Giving him hope before they crushed it in front of his eyes. And what he hated even more was that he still needed the gods to make sure that Charles would come back to him.

Sven pushed the thoughts from his mind. 'Make sure the ships are ready at all times, but that they don't look ready. We need to make sure that we can flee if things turn against us—'

'Which they most likely will,' Ingvild interrupted him, and Sven glared at her. 'What? The gods know they usually do when you are involved, Sven. Only Frigg knows why Thora stands by you, and this oaf as well.'

Rollo smiled, but then turned to Sven. 'Don't worry, it's all done as we discussed. How long do you think we'll have to wait?'

Sven shrugged. 'As long as King Louis makes us, but this time, I swear by Odin, I will not let him beat me again.' Sven turned and went back to his tent, wishing he had ale to drown his memories in.

It took three days for the king of East Francia to arrive and he came with a large army behind him. Sven's scouts had reported them the day before, which had given Sven plenty of time to make sure both of his ships were able to sail, but he still asked Rollo just to make sure.

'Aye, Sven. The ships are ready. Their warriors have all loaded their war chests and the women and children are on board as well. I even left a few men on each ship, only the ones too injured to fight,' Rollo said when Sven glanced at him. Sven nodded at that. 'But I really hope there's no fight. We don't have enough warriors to defeat King Louis.'

'Aye, Rollo. So do I, but like Ingvild said, the gods like to fuck with me. So this time I like to be prepared.'

* * *

'Charles, we're here,' Thora said, waking Charles up.

He sat up and wiped the sleep from his eyes as he looked around, frowning. 'At the beach?'

Thora shook her head. 'The town near the beach. Remember our plan?'

Charles scratched his head as he tried to remember what they had discussed the night Father Leofdag had told them the news. But Charles had been too upset to really pay attention to what had been said and couldn't remember. Even the last few days were a blur. He only remembered being woken up early the morning after and being handed a cloak and a sack of food. Charles had to wear a coif to hide his red hair, which he hated because it was too hot and made his head itch, and Thora had used dirt to darken her light-coloured hair. They also wore the new clothes Father Leofdag had brought them, but Charles's shoes felt uncomfortable because he had not worn any for a very long time. Thora had her sword wrapped up in a piece of cloth so others wouldn't realise what it was and he had frowned when he noticed the trousers under her dress.

They had left the hunter's cabin, which had been their home for a few weeks, and made their way to the road and waited. Just as Father Leofdag had told them, Duke Liudolf's column had marched past to meet the king on the way to the beach where his grandfather was and they had simply stepped out of the forest and joined the back of the column. Nobody had paid them any attention and soon Charles had understood why, as many other people had done the same as they had travelled north. Thora had spoken little while they travelled with Duke Liudolf, especially after they met the king's retinue, as she didn't want others to realise she was a Dane. They had also kept themselves away from the other camp followers, but when someone spoke to them, it was usually Charles who responded. On more than one occasion, he had to lie about his age, saying that he was younger than he really was, and saying that Thora was his mother and that she couldn't speak because of an accident, especially as some people seemed suspicious about them. Even in a dress, it was hard for Thora to hide that she was a warrior. It was in the way she moved and held herself, and Charles knew that some of the camp followers recognised it. He saw it in the way they glanced at Thora. Word of the attack on his mother was still everywhere and so was the fact that a Danish woman and a small boy were responsible for it, but so far, no one had asked them about it. Not that that had comforted Thora.

Just like the journey south the previous summer, King Louis stopped at various towns, but he did not stay as long this time as he had then, and Thora suggested it was because he didn't want Sven to stay in his kingdom for too long. But his force seemed to grow every time they left a new town, and Thora was worried that King Louis was planning on attacking his grandfather and killing him. Charles realised Thora was still staring at him.

'Do you remember our plan?' Thora said again.

He nodded. 'I do.'

Thora sighed. 'This is where we leave and make our own way to Sven. I remember the way from here and, if the gods are with us, then King Louis will stay here for a while before he goes to confront Sven. That should then give us time to get to your grandfather and warn him.'

'If God is with us,' Charles said.

'Aye, we might need his help as well,' Thora said as she glanced around her. Charles was on one of the carts which carried supplies for the many warriors, where he had been allowed to rest by its driver. The last few days had been a struggle for him and, as soon as he was on the cart, he had fallen asleep.

'So we leave now?' Charles asked, and Thora glanced around her and nodded.

'The sooner we get away, the better.' She looked at Charles. 'Remember, Charles, you need to do exactly as I say. Understood?'

Charles's heart raced as he thought about what she was saying, and he nodded before he jumped off the cart. He was about to grab the sack with what was left of their food, but then Thora stopped him.

'We won't need that any more. If all goes well, then by sunset, we'll be with your grandfather and sailing away from this land.'

And away from my mother and Father Leofdag, Charles thought, but did not say. He still struggled to accept that he would never see his mother again, regardless of whether he stayed in Francia or left.

Thora put a hand on his shoulder and led him away from the column as they approached the town. Charles's heart still raced as he expected someone to notice them and, from the way Thora kept glancing around her, he guessed she must have felt the same. But no one called out after them as the town grew smaller behind them. Then, Thora stopped.

'Bastard!' she hissed.

'What?' Charles looked around him, but didn't see anyone chasing them, so he didn't understand what had annoyed Thora so much.

'King Louis didn't stop.'

Charles looked back towards the town and saw that the king's column had carried on towards the beach. 'But you said he'd stop there, like he did in the other towns.'

'Aye, and it looks like I was wrong.'

Charles's hands trembled. 'What do we do now?'

He frowned when Thora removed her dress and threw it away before she adjusted the trousers she wore underneath. She also took her sword out of the bundle and tied the belt with the scabbard around her waist. 'Now, Charles. We throw caution to the wind and run like Hermod.'

'Hermod?'

'Aye. The fastest of the gods and Odin's messenger.'

Charles nodded and wondered how many more gods the

Danes had that he hadn't heard about when Thora grabbed his shoulder and pushed him forward.

'Run, Charles.'

Thora kept hold of his shoulder and was dragging him along faster than he could run, and more than once he would have fallen over if it had not been for Thora keeping him up. He struggled to breathe, just like he struggled to keep his feet under him, the wind lashing past his face, making his eyes water, but he was determined to make Thora proud and pushed himself as hard as he could to keep up with her.

'We're almost there, Charles. Keep going!' Thora shouted, but he struggled to hear her over the sounds of his own heavy breathing and his heart beating in his ears.

In the distance, he saw the sea and, as they reached the top of the hill, his heart leapt when he saw the camp on the beach. His grandfather was there, standing with a group of warriors, and even in the distance he could see Rollo towering over everyone. But then he got distracted as he wondered where Alvar was and his foot got caught in a plant. Charles cried out as he fell and pulled free from Thora's grip.

'Charles!' Thora stopped and pulled him to his feet, but she wasted no time to see if he had hurt himself. 'Shit,' she muttered, and Charles looked up and saw that King Louis had also reached the beach and, worse than that, he was pointing in their direction. A group of warriors broke free from the king's entourage and raced towards them as Thora dragged him behind her, desperate to get to his grandfather before the Frankish warriors got to them.

Over the wind on the beach, Charles thought he heard his father's voice, or it might have been his grandfather's, as he stared at King Louis's warriors, all of them brandishing their weapons, running towards them. 'Run, Charles!'

33

Sven gritted his teeth as King Louis and his army arrived on the dunes. As with the last time Sven had met King Louis, he was dressed in his finest war gear. His brynja blinked in the sun after it had been scrubbed clean from the blood and gore from the battle against Sigtrygg and his arms had three arm rings each. Sven wasn't wearing his helmet, though, because he still hoped to avoid a battle, but the churning in his guts told him that was not going to happen. He had his shield in his left hand and his sword, sharpened and cleaned, was still in its scabbard. He would leave the shield behind when he went to speak with King Louis, but first he wanted to see what the king of the Franks did.

Sven's warriors were standing behind him and Rollo, all of them ready for battle and with strict instructions only to attack when Rollo gave the order. As warriors do, they joked and mocked each other to hide their nerves as they watched King Louis's army form on the dunes, but many of them appeared confident after surviving the battle against Sigtrygg. It felt strange preparing for battle without Alvar standing on his left as he had got used to the giant warrior standing there. Torgny stood there now, and Sven knew the man was a capable warrior. He had survived all the battles so far, but if Sven was honest, he'd rather have Alvar there. Or Thora.

As they waited, Sven frowned as his ears picked up a noise in the distance, away from King Louis's army. At first he thought it was the wind or his imagination playing tricks on him when he heard Charles's name being shouted, but then he saw King Louis look to his left.

'Sven, look!' Rollo pointed to where King Louis was looking and when Sven turned his head, his heart stopped. He saw a woman with dark-coloured hair, and wearing trousers, pull a small boy to his feet and then both of them looked towards King Louis. Sven's heart thudded in his chest when he recognised the way the woman moved and, even with the hat on, he knew the boy was his grandson. He turned his attention back to King Louis and saw the group of warriors break free and run towards Thora and Charles.

Without thinking, Sven pulled his sword from its scabbard. 'Run, Charles!' Before Rollo could stop him, Sven took off, running as fast as his old legs could take him.

'Sven! Protect the camp and the ships!' Rollo roared and was soon running beside him, with some of the warriors following. Torgny caught up on Sven's left, the younger warriors doing their best to match his pace.

'Forget about me!' Sven screamed. 'Protect them!' He jabbed his sword towards Thora and Charles. Thora had hold of Charles's shoulder and was dragging the boy behind her, her sword ready in her right hand. And Sven knew she would need it, because the Frankish warriors were closer than his men and would surely catch them. 'Argh!' Sven cried out in anger as he pushed his legs to go faster. But he was old and so were they, and soon all the warriors that had followed him had run past as they raced to follow Rollo. That was when Sven heard a new noise, one that still haunted his dreams from his first encounter with King Louis many winters ago. As he ran, he turned and watched as King Louis's horse warriors charged those left in the camp: the warriors tasked with protecting the families and their belongings. About a third of his army held in line by Osborn, one of Sven's experienced men. But for Sven, his grandson was far more important, so he ignored that attack and carried on running towards Charles and Thora, who were about to be caught by the Frankish warriors. Besides, Sven had anticipated that King Louis would send his horse warriors to attack the camp and had prepared for it.

Sven struggled to breathe as the first of the Franks reached Thora and Charles before his men could, although Rollo and Torgny weren't far away. Thora turned, throwing Charles towards Rollo as she cut her sword across the chest of the first Frankish warriors and elbowed another in the face before he could protect himself. Rollo reached them a few heartbeats later and swung his Dane axe in a wide arc. Those who weren't killed jumped back to avoid Rollo's axe as the rest of Sven's warriors crashed into the Franks. Sven saw three of the Franks get around his men and run towards Charles, who had got back to his feet and was running towards him, his eyes wild with fear. Sven was only a few paces away and lowered his head as he ducked behind his shield. Just as Charles reached him, Sven barged into two of the warriors, knocking them both to the ground while he turned and stabbed the other in the side. His sword found a gap in the man's leather jerkin and sliced through his organs before Sven pulled his sword free and faced the other Franks charging at him.

'Stay behind me!' Sven ordered Charles as he braced for the attack. He lifted his shield to block an axe and turned to avoid being skewered by a spear, trusting that his brynja would deflect the spear point.

'The camp!' Charles screamed as Sven stabbed at another Frank, whose eyes widened when he glanced towards Sven's camp. Sven didn't need to turn to know what had happened. King Louis's cavalry had discovered the deep ditches his warriors had dug during the nights. There were no stakes in the ditches as they hadn't had enough time to make them, but they had filled them with water, which was sure to drown some warriors as their horses struggled. But Sven could not think about that as he opened the throat of the Frankish warrior who was gaping at the horse warriors as they fell into the ditches. At the same time, the warriors left behind in the camp rushed forward and killed those who were struggling to get out of the ditches.

Thora blocked another attack with a spear she had picked up from one of the dead Franks, before she cut her opponent's leg open and made her way to Sven's side. 'Sven! He has more men behind him. There are too many to fight!'

Sven nodded before swinging his sword at another Frank, who jumped back to avoid the blade before stabbing at Sven with his sword. Sven blocked the sword on his shield before Thora killed the man. 'Get Charles to the ships! They're ready to leave!'

'What about the camp?' Thora asked as the fighting continued.

'The camp is empty! Get Charles to the ships!' Sven ducked behind his shield as a spear came towards him. As soon as the spear struck, he rushed forward and knocked his opponent to the ground and stabbed him in the throat. He used the moment to get a sense of what was happening and his blood froze when he saw more Franks charging at him, with another group racing to get behind him. Sven growled as he realised King Louis had sent his entire army down to the beach. This was what he had wanted to avoid as the Franks attempted to surround him and his warriors. Sven knew the only chance they had now was to get back to the ships before the Franks could get behind him. 'Rollo!' Sven roared, not sure if the giant warrior heard him as he killed another two Franks with his Dane axe. 'Rollo! Shield wall! Back to the camp!' Sven roared, hoping his voice would get through to his warriors. He knew it had been foolish to rush towards Thora and Charles, but he could not have just stood there and hoped the gods were on his side and that they would reach them before the Franks caught up. But then, Odin most likely wanted this to happen. Sven was sure the one-eyed bastard wanted him to die on this beach.

'Shield wall!' Rollo roared and Sven realised the younger man had heard him. 'Shield wall on Sven!' Rollo made his way to Sven's right-hand side as he fought the Franks. Torgny made it to his left, and they locked shields as the rest of Sven's warriors slowly joined them. The Franks had realised what was happening and fought harder as they tried to stop the shield wall from forming. Sven watched as some of his warriors died trying to get to the safety of the shield wall, but there was nothing he could do. 'To the ships!' Rollo ordered when most of the warriors had joined the wall.

Sven blocked an attack, and Torgny killed the Frank. He then stabbed out with his sword and felt it strike something hard. He roared and screamed at the Franks as he blocked their attacks and tried to kill them, all the while the shield wall slowly moved back towards the safety of the camp. But Sven sensed they were going too slow and was worried about the other Franks that were rushing to get behind them. He could only pray that Thora and Charles made it to the ships. But Sven did not want to die on this beach. Not when he had another chance to be the grandfather he should have been from the beginning. The thought was like adding dried wood to the flames of his anger and Sven roared as he stabbed high with his sword, the blade breaking his opponent's teeth and cutting his tongue off before killing him. But then Loki played his next hand.

'Sven, behind you!' He heard Thora's voice and realised she was standing behind him. His heart almost stopped when he turned and saw what was left of King Louis's cavalry charging at his shield wall from behind.

'Horses!' he roared, and knew that his men would not be able to turn in time to face the cavalry charge, not when they were still fighting the Franks on the front. Rollo had also seen the danger and called for half the wall to turn, but Sven knew it was too late. He glanced at Thora and spotted Charles beside her, his eyes wide as his hand gripped her tunic. The boy had a knife in his hand, and Sven prayed he would not need to use it, because that meant that they would all be dead. He looked up and saw one of the horse warriors break free from the rest and lower his spear as he charged towards Charles and Thora. The battle seemed to stop for Sven and, without thinking, he broke free from the shield wall and turned to face the warrior on the horse, who was only a few paces away. Sven rushed forward so that Thora and Charles were behind him and braced just as the horse warrior struck. He felt the spear hit his shield, the force of the blow forcing him to step back and numbing his arm, before the horse collided with him and sent him flying. Sven heard nothing as he landed hard on his left side, the pain shooting up his left leg almost blinding him.

'Grandfather!' Charles's voice broke through the fog as someone grabbed Sven and dragged him back.

'Get to the ships! Run, you bastards!' Rollo roared as Sven was dragged along the ground, the movement sending fresh waves of pain through him.

Sven blinked the fog in his mind away and saw Rollo and Torgny dragging him behind them as they ran towards the ships. Thora was there with a shield and a spear as she and other warriors followed behind and kept the Franks back. Charles was running beside him, his eyes wet with tears as his hand gripped Sven's brynja like he was trying to help Rollo and Torgny.

'Charles,' Sven managed to get the word out and knew that if they wasted any more time trying to save him, then his grandson would never make it off the beach. He glanced at the broken sword in his hand and frowned until he saw the dead horse on the beach where he had been. He must have stabbed the horse as it struck him and broke the sword. Some warriors had stayed behind in a small shield wall, preventing most of the Franks from chasing after them. But Sven could not let them die for him. 'Stop!' he shouted and had to repeat it when Rollo and Torgny ignored him. 'Stop, I can fight.'

'Sven, don't be a fool!' Rollo responded. 'We're almost there.' Just as the words came out, Rollo and Torgny stopped. 'Shit.'

Sven knew what had happened before they even let go of him to get their shields in front of them. The Franks had surrounded them and now they were all going to die on that beach. He could hear the gods laughing in the sudden silence as his warriors realised the same. Odin had kept him alive through the many winters just so he could die on the beach where he had abandoned his only son. Sven looked at Charles, who reminded him so much of Torkel, even as Charles tried not to show the fear he must have been feeling, and felt his heart break. *Frigg, mother of the gods, wife of the All-Father. I beg you. Use your magic to protect my grandson. I offer myself, but please let Charles leave this beach alive.*

'We're surrounded,' one warrior said, but not in desperation. Just with a tone of resignation in her voice.

'Never thought I'd die on a beach in East Francia,' Torgny said, letting go of Sven so he could hold his shield and sword as he faced the Franks, who held back as if waiting for an order.

'Well, if the Norns decided that we have to die today, then that is what we do. But by Odin, we make sure that these bastard Franks never forget the warriors of Ribe!' Rollo's voice boomed and Sven was sure even those on the ships could hear them. The ships which were just out of reach because of Sven. He knew that if they hadn't wasted time dragging him behind them, then they might have made it and Charles would have been safe. Sven looked at his grandson and thought the boy seemed taller than the last time he had seen him. He also spotted the golden cross, smaller than the Cross of Charlemagne, hanging around Charles's neck, next to his Mjöllnir. Sven smiled, glad his grandson still had that.

'Father! No!' Sigmund's voice broke through Sven's thoughts as Rollo's son cried out.

Rollo looked towards the ships. 'Sigmund! You stay strong, my boy! You look after your mother. Remember me!'

Sigmund cried out again, and Sven pictured the boy having to be dragged back by his mother, Rollo's wife, who would give birth to their second child. A growl escaped Sven's throat as he remembered that Rollo's father had died on this beach so many winters ago. Unlike Rollo, he had never got to say his farewells, and Sven did not want another son of that bloodline to be raised without a father because of him.

Sven glanced around him, seeing the Franks closing in, but taking their time. They did not want to finish this quickly. They wanted Sven's men to suffer. Sven also imagined they had orders to keep him alive, because he was sure that King Louis wanted to make an example of him. 'No,' Sven said, shaking his head. He looked at his grandson and then Rollo. 'Help me up.'

'Sven?' Rollo frowned at him.

'By Odin, Rollo! Help me up. No one is dying on this cursed beach!'

'Grandfather?'

Sven looked at Charles as Rollo pulled him to his feet. He winced as he tried to stand, but as soon as he put weight on his left leg, hot pain shot into his hip and he almost collapsed. Sven gritted his teeth as Rollo held him up. *Odin, you bastard. Why now?* Sven thought, but knew that Odin was probably enjoying this. Sven tried to stand on his own again, but his left leg refused to hold his weight. He shook his head as he realised he might never walk on it again, and if he couldn't walk, then how was he going to protect his grandson? Sven looked at Charles. 'Don't worry, Charles. Everything will be fine.'

'How, Sven?' Thora asked. 'You can't even stand.'

Again, Sven glanced around him and wondered why the Franks hadn't attacked yet. They had surrounded his small force, and those in the camp wouldn't make much of a difference. Sven had hoped he could fight the Franks off so the others could make it to the ships, but Thora was right. He couldn't stand, which meant he couldn't fight. Sven looked up at the sky and spotted the two ravens circling above him. There were other birds as well, including crows, but it was the two ravens that caught his attention. And as Sven stared at them, his hand went to his stomach and he felt the cross hidden under his tunic. Sven sighed, as he knew what he needed to do. He glanced at Charles, who was staring at him with wide eyes. Sven guessed Charles would grow to be larger than him, so perhaps he wouldn't be picked on as much about his weight as Sven had been.

'Sven, what are you doing?' Rollo asked as Sven struggled to get the pouch out of his tunic, under his brynja, and then everyone around him gasped as he took the cross out of the pouch.

'Forgive me, Charles,' Sven said before he held the cross in the air. 'Louis! You bastard! I have the cross! I have your grandfather's cross.'

The surrounding Franks hesitated and more than a few

glanced back towards where King Louis sat on his horse. A horn sounded, and the Frankish warriors backed off as a horseman rode towards them. Sven recognised Duke Liudolf and wasn't surprised that King Louis had sent him.

It didn't take long for the duke of Saxony to reach them, and the Frankish warriors parted to let him approach, although a handful of warriors stayed near him. Torgny and Thora stepped closer to Sven, both of them with their weapons ready, while Rollo helped Sven stand. Charles stood on the other side of Sven, holding on to his arm and with his eyes on Duke Liudolf as he stopped a few paces away from them.

Duke Liudolf stared at the cross in Sven's hand. 'How do we know that is the real cross? King Charles of West Francia claims to have the cross.'

Sven hawked and spat. 'I don't know what cross that bastard found, but this is the cross that Charles brought with him when he came to me.'

Duke Liudolf raised an eyebrow, but Sven knew he wouldn't know whether or not this cross was real. Duke Liudolf had never seen the cross. Charles's mother had told him that no one had for almost a lifetime. 'And you had it this whole time. Even last summer when you were here?'

Sven nodded.

'Then why didn't you give it to my king? God knows things might have been different.'

Sven smiled and shook his head. 'If I had given this to your king, then he would have killed me and Charles. You and your god know that.'

Duke Liudolf's cheek twitched and Sven knew the man agreed with him, but didn't want to say anything. He looked at Charles. 'Forgive me, Charles. God knows I never wanted any of this for you.'

Sven glanced around him and sensed what was about to happen. King Louis would never let him leave this beach, just like he would never let Charles leave his kingdom. He felt Rollo tense as Sven leaned on him and guessed the giant warrior felt the same. But before anyone could do anything, a horn blew and warriors roared.

34

Charles grabbed hold of his grandfather's arm at the sudden noise of Danish warriors roaring behind them. Duke Liudolf's eyes widened as spears flew over their heads and landed amongst the Frankish warriors, but before he could do anything, Rollo let go of Charles's grandfather and punched the duke in the face and Thora shouted, 'Shield wall!'

'We're being attacked from behind!' a Frankish warrior screamed, his voice filled with panic.

Charles's head swam as he tried to make sense of the Frankish warriors crying out in dismay and the sounds of weapons clashing, but then his grandfather grabbed him and pulled him close. 'Stay near me, Charles, but when I say run, you bloody run, you hear me?'

Charles nodded, too afraid to argue even though he was tired of adults always telling him to run. One warrior, a large man Charles vaguely recognised, grabbed his grandfather and pulled him towards the ships, but Charles still didn't understand why. They were surrounded by Frankish warriors, but many of them were fighting an enemy Charles couldn't see, while others had

surrounded Duke Liudolf to protect him from the Danes. Charles
turned to where Thora was and saw her and Rollo fighting
Frankish warriors that were in front of them as more of the Danish
warriors joined them. Charles still knew little about battle, but
even he could see that Rollo and Thora had the upper hand as
they killed the Franks before they could recover from their shock.
Rollo chopped down with his large axe, the blade striking a
Frankish warrior on the shoulder and almost taking his arm off,
while Thora punched out with a shield she had picked up and
crushed another Frank's face before stabbing the man beside him.
The other warriors from Ribe rushed to their side and crashed
into the Franks, but then Charles realised his grandfather was
pulling him back towards the beach. Charles turned and saw that
the Franks behind them had all turned their backs to them and
were facing the water while a horn kept blowing from where King
Louis was.

'Grandfather!' Charles screamed, trying hard to be heard over
the battle. He wanted to know what was happening but his grandfather only told him to keep moving and so he did. He tightened
his grip on his grandfather's arm and did his best to help his
grandfather walk, but knew the other warrior was doing much
more than him.

'We're almost there! Keep fighting!' Rollo roared, but Charles
struggled to hear him as his ears rang from all the noise around
him. He had never known that battles were so noisy and it disorientated him so much that he almost fell over. But his grandfather
grabbed hold of him and pulled him to his feet, even while the
other man held on to his grandfather.

'Come on, Charles! Keep going!'

Charles nodded and doubted that his grandfather saw him.
Thora appeared on his other side, blocking the sword of a

Frankish warrior aimed at his grandfather or him, Charles wasn't really sure, before she stabbed the man in the stomach.

'Keep going! Show these bastard Franks who we are!' Thora cried out and sliced another man's throat open. Blood sprayed her and Charles, the hot, sticky liquid shocking Charles, and if it wasn't for his grandfather, he would have frozen. 'We're almost there, Charles, just keep going,' Thora said to him before she stabbed another Frank in the leg.

As Charles watched the surrounding battle, his feet touched water, and he cried out in shock. He had not realised they had gone that far and when he looked behind him he saw the beach littered with bodies, but he could not tell whether they were Franks or Danes as the battle raged on.

'Get to the ship!' Rollo roared at Charles's grandfather, before he turned to face the Franks. 'Shield wall! Protect Sven and Charles!' Many of the warriors rushed towards Rollo and locked their shields with his before the Franks could stop them.

Charles tripped and swallowed a mouthful of seawater before his grandfather could drag him out of the water, but at least most of the blood had been washed off his face.

'No time for a swim now,' Thora said and grabbed him by the shoulder just before his grandfather let go of him and turned to face the Franks. In one hand, he still held the Cross of Charlemagne, in the other a broken sword.

'Grandfather!' Charles cried out as Thora dragged him deeper into the water.

'Get him to the ship!' Sven shouted at Thora before he turned to Rollo. 'Rollo, get back!' Charles's grandfather then held the cross in the air. 'If you want this, you bastard, then call your men back!'

Nothing seemed to happen for what felt like a long time as Thora dragged Charles back, his feet not able to touch the bottom any more, but then another horn blew and the Franks stopped fighting, before they took a step back.

Rollo wasted no time. 'Keep formation! Back to the ships!'

Charles watched as the Danish warriors walked backwards while keeping their shield wall together and shouting insults at the Frankish warriors, before hands grabbed him and pulled him on to the ship.

'Aunt Thora!' Jorlaug shouted as Thora climbed out of the water, but Charles did not turn to see the girl run to Thora and wrap her arms around her. All Charles could do was stare at King Louis, his other grandfather, as he sat on his horse, too far away for Charles to see the look on his face.

Rollo shouted an order and half of the warriors turned and rushed back to the ships, while Rollo and the rest of them stayed, their shield wall intact as they faced the Franks who stood on the beach, looking uncertain. A few of the warriors got in the ship and pulled Sven out of the water. As soon as he was on board, Sven hopped to Charles's side and stood next to him and, like Charles, stared at King Louis.

They waited for the rest of the warriors to get on the ships, Rollo being the last one on board. Sigmund, who seemed taller than the last time Charles had seen him, ran to his father and hugged him before Rollo gave the order for the ships to leave. But he didn't really need to, as the warriors had already got the oars out and were rowing so the ships could get out of reach of any archers. An older warrior approached Sven who scowled at the man.

'Osborn!' Sven said to the warrior. 'You were supposed to protect the camp and the ships.'

The warrior shrugged. 'It looked like you were in a tight spot and the ships were safe after we dealt with the cavalry.'

Charles thought his grandfather was going to strike Osborn

but then Sven smiled. 'The gods know that I am in your debt, Osborn. If you hadn't attacked the rear of the Franks then my grandson would be dead.'

'I swore an oath to protect you, Sven. As did many of the warriors.'

Charles's heart raced when his grandfather glanced at him, his face serious. 'I don't care what happens to me as long as Charles is safe. So, I thank you again, Osborn. All of you,' Sven said to the warriors as they rowed. Sven turned to Charles and put his hand on Charles's shoulder, and when Charles looked at him, he smiled. 'Should we give him the cross?'

Charles glanced at the cross in his grandfather's hand. The most beautiful cross in the world, but as he stared at it, the words of the godi came to his mind. *No good will come from this cross.* Charles frowned when he realised the godi had been right. The cross had been nothing but a curse which had almost killed all the family he had. His hand went to the cross his mother had given to him, and then he nodded. 'But how are you going to give it to him?' Charles asked as the ships rowed away, leaving the Frankish warriors on the beach. In the distance, Charles saw King Louis rush down to the water while the other lords followed him. They raced past Duke Liudolf, who just stood where Rollo had punched him, and Charles hoped he wouldn't get into trouble for what had happened.

Sven smiled and threw the cross into the water. 'If that bastard really wants the cross so badly, then he can swim for it.'

Charles's heart stopped as he watched the cross turn in the bright sunlight, the large ruby glinting as it winked at him. As it fell towards the water, Charles saw his father in his mind, but not from the last time he had seen him, covered in blood and dying, but standing tall in his chain-mail vest and smiling at him. He tightened his grip on the cross his mother had given him and with a splash the Cross of Charlemagne that had caused the death of his father, and so many others, disappeared in the water. Charles realised he was smiling as the Danish warriors cheered.

'Sven! You bastard!' King Louis roared from the beach, his eyes wide and face red. He waded into the incoming tide and stopped when the water reached his waist before he grabbed a warrior who stood nearby and threw him into the water. 'Find that cross!' The Frankish warriors hesitated and King Louis grabbed another warrior and sent him after the first one. 'Find that cross or by God I'll hang you all! Sven, you bastard! I'll find you! Your life is over! You hear me, you heathen pig? You're dead! What are you waiting for?' King Louis turned on his warriors and nobles. 'Find that bloody cross!'

The warriors on his grandfather's ships laughed as the Franks stumbled in the water, many of them falling as the waves knocked them over, but Charles's grandfather hawked and spat as King Louis's tirade washed over him.

Sven grimaced as he lay down and stared at Charles, who realised how much older his grandfather looked. Thora came to them and knelt down as she took his grandfather's hand. Sven looked at her and smiled, suddenly appearing exhausted. 'Thank you, Thora. Thank you for keeping Charles safe.'

Thora smiled and nodded, and Charles noticed how many of the women and children had gathered around them. He spotted Jorlaug, who smiled at him, and Charles smiled back, surprised that he was glad to see the girl who had annoyed him so much when he was in Ribe.

'You have a new cross,' his grandfather said to him, and Charles looked at the large golden cross around his neck and nodded.

'My mother gave it to me, before she...' Charles realised he didn't want to say the words, but then his grandfather nodded.

'Keep it safe and remember her, Charles,' Charles heard him say as he stared at the cross and remembered the last time he had seen his mother.

'Where are we going, grandfather?' Charles asked, turning his attention back to his grandfather, his heart racing when he saw his eyes were closed. But then they fluttered open, and Charles smiled in relief.

'North, my boy. As far north as we can go and as far from Francia as possible.' His grandfather lifted his hand and placed it on Charles's cheek. 'And somewhere where you can be a priest, like you wanted.' Charles smiled, but did not tell his grandfather that he did not want to be a priest any more. 'Now, let me rest. I just need to... to sleep. I need to sleep.' His grandfather's eyes closed again and Charles felt fresh tears running down his cheeks. From behind him, he heard others cry as well, and looked at Thora.

'Will he live?'

Thora shrugged. 'He was hurt badly when the horse struck him, Charles. It's up to the Norns now whether Sven lives.'

Charles wiped the tears away and gripped the cross his mother had given him. 'I will pray for him.'

'Who will you pray to?' Thora stared at him as if she saw into his mind.

Charles looked at the cross again. 'I will pray to God. I will ask Him to help my grandfather survive and to make me as strong as him.'

Thora smiled. 'Good. Never forget who you are, Charles. That is what will make you strong.' Thora dug into the pouch she had been carrying and took out the Bible Father Leofdag had given him and handed it to Charles, who smiled when he saw it was still dry, although he was not sure how.

He ran his finger over the pages, feeling strangely comforted by them. Charles sat down next to his grandfather as Thora went to her family and Rollo to his. He saw that Rollo's wife was pregnant, and he hoped it wasn't going to be another tall boy who would pick on him, but then he saw Sigmund smiling at him and Charles smiled back, feeling like the days of Sigmund bullying him were long behind them and that the two of them might one day be friends. Charles closed his eyes and prayed.

Dear Father in Heaven. I pray to you for the first time in many months. Forgive me for my sins and for the sins of my grandfather. He is a good man, even though he believes in false idols. But I ask you to look over him and to help him recover. I do not want to lose him as I lost my father and mother. He is all the family I have left and I need him. Please God, make sure he lives and I will always be your servant. I will learn from the lessons that you have taught me and I will use them to make me strong. I will be the best of my parents and of my grandfather. I know I will never be a priest, but I will do my best to spread your word and light wherever I go.

Charles felt the sea breeze blow across his face and smiled.

Amen.

EPILOGUE

Sven grunted as he sat down on the large stone and stared out at the sea. He closed his eyes and took a deep breath of the sea air as the breeze cooled his scalp. Sven would never sail again. He was too old and his left leg had never healed properly after he had been struck by a horse on the beach in East Francia almost two winters ago. He glanced at the walking stick Rollo had made for him and smiled at the images of wild boars Charles and Sigmund had carved into it. The two boys had become good friends and, along with Jorlaug, were constantly causing mischief. Sven was glad about that, though. Charles needed friends. People who would stand by him and that he could trust. Sven only prayed that his friends wouldn't betray him like Sven's had.

Sven's fighting days were over, but he was at peace with that and what had happened. He had left the beach with most of his warriors, although there were still many who had lost their lives so that they could escape, and most importantly, he had his grandson back.

'When do you think he'll return?' Thora asked as she stood beside him. Sven looked at her and then smiled at Charles, who had joined them as well. The boy must have been about twelve winters old now and had grown since they had arrived on the group of islands to the east of Norway. The few locals that lived on the island called the islands Føroyar, which meant sheep islands, a name which was apt because Sven had never seen so many of the blasted animals in one place. Sigmund and Jorlaug arrived as well, all three children red-faced after their training session with Thora, who was asking about Rollo.

'I hope it's soon. He's been gone for a long time.' Sigmund scowled as he scanned the sea. Rollo had taken a ship full of warriors back to West Francia. He had wanted to join Gudrod and Halstein as they raided Duke Erispoë's lands as revenge for paying Sigtrygg to attack their island camp. Rollo had been gone all summer, but they heard stories about his raids from ships which stopped on the island to stock up on supplies. Thora had stayed behind, along with a handful of warriors, to protect the families and the small hall they had built on the northern side of the island. Rollo was their jarl, but everyone still called it Sven's hall.

'He'll be back soon,' Sven said and looked at Sigmund. 'Your father is one of the best warriors I have ever seen.'

'Mother says good warriors still die in battle.' Rollo's wife had been angry that Rollo wanted to raid, especially as their second child, a daughter, was born soon after they had arrived on the island.

'Odin is not ready for your father in Valhalla yet,' Thora said as she put an arm around Sigmund's shoulder.

'He doesn't have benches large enough for your father, Sigmund. So don't you worry. Your father will return before winter sets in.'

Sigmund smiled and then turned to go back to the small house he lived in with his mother and baby sister.

'I wish I was out there killing the Franks for what they did to us,' Jorlaug said, her fire not yet calmed by age or the strong winds on the island.

Charles and Thora shook their heads before Charles turned serious. 'Do you think they will ever find it?'

'The cross?' Sven scratched his beard. 'No, Njörd took the cursed thing down to the bottom of the seas and fed it to Jörmungandr. Or at least I hope so.'

'But how do you know they won't find it?'

Sven should have known that Charles would not be comforted by what he had said. The boy was still a Christian and didn't believe in their gods, but at least he had stopped trying to convince Sven to abandon them. 'Because the Frankish kings are still fighting each other and Denmark hasn't been invaded yet. The Cross of Charlemagne is gone, Charles. And I pray to the gods every day that it stays that way.'

The wind picked up as if the gods of Asgard responded to that, although Sven was sure Charles would believe that it was his god.

'Come, old man. If you sit here any longer, then the gods might decide to turn you into a stone as well,' Thora said as she turned to go back to the hall.

'Can your gods really do that?' Charles asked, and Sven smiled as the boy gripped the golden cross he wore around his neck.

'They might, Charles,' Sven said, and then rubbed his left leg. 'But I doubt they pay any attention to me now.'

Charles raised an eyebrow at him. 'But you said that Odin always asks for something in return.'

'Aye, that the one-eyed bastard does.' Sven looked at his left leg, which seemed thinner than his right. 'And he already has taken that something from me.'

'What did he take?'

Sven sighed and looked out to sea again. It was one of the rare days when the weather was nice and Sven liked to sit on the large rock and just stare out to sea. 'He took who I was away from me, Charles. I will never stand in a shield wall again or wet the ground with the blood of my enemies.'

Charles scratched his head and glanced at Thora, who smiled. 'Are you angry about it?'

Sven looked at his grandson and saw how much he looked like Torkel. But he also saw Hildegard in the boy's face. They had heard she had died from illness, and Sven hoped that was true. Charles had told Sven about what had happened in Frankfurt and how his mother had been left weak even after she had healed from her wound. Charles had cried for days when the news had reached them, but Sven had sensed that the boy had already known he would never see his mother again. But Charles had their strength, and Sven knew the boy would grow to be a better man than he was. Sven smiled as he took his walking stick and Charles helped him up, glad that he was given the chance to watch his grandson grow. 'No, Charles. I am not.'

HISTORICAL NOTE

Judging by the history books, Charles the Bald did not have a peaceful reign. West Francia was a popular raiding destination for the Danes and the Norse raiders, including famous leaders such as Ragnar and Björn Ironside, and he had to face repeated invasion attempts from his own brother, Louis the German. We can almost argue that Charles the Bald did not help himself by regularly paying the Vikings to leave, as he did when Ragnar, with his 120 ships, besieged Paris in 845, but considering what else was happening in his kingdom, it's hard to see that he had any other choice.

At the time when Ragnar, who some historians believe may have been the famous Ragnar Lothbrok, was besieging the capital of West Francia, King Charles was also fighting a battle against his nephew, Pepin, for control of Aquitaine. I talked about the conflict between Charles the Bald and Pepin II in *Thor's Revenge*, and mentioned how in 852, Pepin was finally captured and imprisoned in a monastery near Paris. But even after that, Aquitaine was still a thorn in the side of Charles the Bald. The people and nobles of Aquitaine refused to accept the authority of the man Charles the

Bald had made duke of Aquitaine and even went as far as requesting help from Louis the German. Louis the German sent his son, also named Louis, with an army to Aquitaine to claim the throne, but before the younger Louis could reach his destination, Pepin II escaped from his captivity (or might have been freed by Charles the Bald) and returned to Aquitaine. The nobles who had supported Prince Louis while Pepin was still imprisoned turned their backs on him in favour of the man they believed was the rightful king of Aquitaine. Prince Louis only made it as far as Limoges and, in 855, returned to East Francia. Unfortunately for Pepin, though, his success was short-lived. Having regained some of his lands and authority, Pepin continued his fight against Charles the Bald, but in 859, he was abandoned by his own people. Pepin would spend the next few years fighting Charles the Bald and, in 864, he joined the Vikings in the Loire Valley and attacked Toulouse. Unfortunately for Pepin, he was captured soon after the attack and was imprisoned in Senlis, where he died not long after.

Louis the German, though, did not give up on Aquitaine after his son's failure and in 858 invaded West Francia. Charles the Bald could not raise an army to defend his lands against his older brother and fled to Burgundy. As with Pepin II, though, Louis the German's victory was short-lived. Many of his warriors deserted his army, and others turned against him. On top of that, the bishops of Aquitaine remained loyal to Charles the Bald, which all meant that Louis had to return to East Francia and his quest for the crown of West Francia was over. In 860, both Louis the German and Charles the Bald made public vows of peace between their kingdoms.

Abbess Hildegard, the daughter of Louis the German and abbess of Fraumünster, was never attacked in Frankfurt and not much is known about her other than the legend of how Fraumünster was built. The church still stands in Zürich, although now it belongs to the Evangelical Reformed Church of the Canton of Zürich. Abbess Hildegard died in either 856 or 859 and her sister succeeded her as the abbess of Fraumünster.

The Vikings in the Loire Valley were another problem for King Charles and one that Sven tried to exploit in *Valhalla's Fury*. Viking raiders had been a problem for all three Frankish kings since their civil war, which left many areas undefended and just made them attractive targets for those from Denmark and Norway looking to enrich themselves. This was also not helped by the fact that the Frankish kings often used Vikings as mercenaries against their brothers' kingdoms.

The Vikings had settled in the Loire Valley in the 840s, most likely on the island of Île Bastille in the river Loire, and used this as a base from which they attacked important towns in the area. Gudrod Haraldsson, the son of Harald Klak, was one of these Vikings who took advantage of local politics to raid and plunder the Loire Valley. The Vikings didn't always have it their way, as Halstein, one of the leaders of this Viking force, discovered when he attacked Orléans in 854 and was defeated by a force led by the local bishop. However, Halstein would return to Orléans in 856 and sack the town as retribution for their resistance in 854. Under pressure to deal with the Vikings, Duke Erispoë of Brittany, who wanted control over Nantes, paid Sigtrygg, a Danish leader who had made a name for himself in Ireland and had in the past sailed with Gudrod Haraldsson, to attack Halstein's camp. King Charles the Bald might have been behind this plot, but unfortunately, we don't know if he was.

Sigtrygg brought between 105–120 ships with him and had command of roughly 3,500 warriors and laid siege to the island fortress of Halstein, and Gudrod (who only commanded about 1,500–2,000 warriors between them). Unfortunately for Sigtrygg, the island camp was well fortified and, when fighting started, he himself was injured and was forced to leave. Not without requesting and receiving half the plunder on the island. When the Vikings discovered that Duke Erispoë was behind the attack, they swore revenge against the duke of Brittany.

So, my dear readers, this is the end of the *Charlemagne's Cross* series and, unfortunately for Sven the Boar, the end of his fighting days. But the gods have rewarded him for the chaos he has brought and he gets to watch Charles grow into a man. What happens to Charles, I don't know yet, but I'm sure he has plenty of adventures ahead of him with his new family.

ACKNOWLEDGEMENTS

It pains me to say that this is the end of the *Charlemagne's Cross* series and I hope that you have all enjoyed reading about Sven and Charles as much as I have enjoyed writing about them. There are many people without whom this series would not have been possible. Some helped with editing and others had to put up with me as I dreamt of battles and distant times, and I would like to take this opportunity to thank them.

To my fantastic editor, Caroline, who not only helped make this series possible, but also helped to avoid plot holes and spotted the obvious things I had missed along the way. As always, to Ross and Susan for their amazing work of smoothing the rough edges and nicks out of my stories and making them shine.

To my wife, Anna, who was as supportive as ever, even while we were expecting our first child (a beautiful girl, if you are wondering). I could never do this without her love and support.

To M J Porter, Peter Gibbons, J C Duncan and the many other friends I have made along the way, for the many laughs and the words of wisdom.

And to my readers. None of my books would be written if it weren't for you and I thank you for your support and comments.

Happy reading and I wish you all the best.

Thank you.

ABOUT THE AUTHOR

Donovan Cook is the author of the well-received Ormstunga Saga series which combines fast-paced narrative with meticulously researched history of the Viking world, and is inspired by his interest in Norse Mythology. He was born in South Africa and currently lives in Lancashire, UK.

Sign up to Donovan Cook's mailing list here for news, competitions and updates on future books.

Visit Donovan's website: www.donovancook.net

Follow Donovan on social media:

 x.com/DonovanCook20
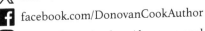 facebook.com/DonovanCookAuthor
bookbub.com/authors/donovan-cook

ALSO BY DONOVAN COOK

WARRIOR CHRONICLES

WELCOME TO THE CLAN ✕

THE HOME OF
BESTSELLING HISTORICAL
ADVENTURE FICTION!

WARNING:
MAY CONTAIN VIKINGS!

SIGN UP TO OUR
NEWSLETTER

BIT.LY/WARRIORCHRONICLES

Boldwood

Boldwood Books is an award-winning fiction publishing company seeking out the best stories from around the world.

Find out more at www.boldwoodbooks.com

Join our reader community for brilliant books, competitions and offers!

Follow us
@BoldwoodBooks
@TheBoldBookClub

Sign up to our weekly deals newsletter

https://bit.ly/BoldwoodBNewsletter

Printed in Great Britain
by Amazon